THE RIDERS AIMED
FOR THE BOAT....

The red beam grew in intensity and the tub-boat began to change. At its edges, it turned shadowy and indistinct; then it blossomed into the brilliant color of the beam, dropped to purple, then to the deep blackness of coal as if all the color it had were being drained from it. The boat crumbled into something lifeless, unearthly. It glowed with a darkness Ellman had never seen before nor ever wanted to see again. In a second it was over. There was only the barest smear of darkness seeping into the water to remind the watcher that anything had been there.

**THEY HAD COME FOR THE
LIFE OF TURLY!**

THE BLESSING PAPERS

William Barnwell

PUBLISHED BY POCKET BOOKS NEW YORK

Another *Original* publication of POCKET BOOKS

POCKET BOOKS, a Simon & Schuster division of
GULF & WESTERN CORPORATION
1230 Avenue of the Americas, New York, N.Y. 10020

ISBN: 0-671-83219-0

First Pocket Books printing May, 1980

10 9 8 7 6 5 4 3 2 1

POCKET and colophon are trademarks of Simon & Schuster.

Printed in the U.S.A.

FOR MY HAZEL-EYED
ALABAMA LADY

Man has no nature, what he has is . . . history.

—ORTEGA Y GASSET

Chronology of
The Blessing Papers

2018—United Council of York: studied human problems in the worlds of faith and fact.

2019—Council of Methe: announced merger of faith and fact in the Church of Spirit and Science.

2020—The Falling.
The Coming of the Papers to Thomas Blessing, Head of the CSS.
The Fires.

2075—Creation of the Universal Mythic Sequence Church.

2090—Creation of the Order of Zeno by John Vail.

2104—The Blessing Papers come to Vail. Split in the Order of Zeno.

2105—Vail hides the Blessing Papers.

2120—Turly of the Inniscloe Circle leaves for the South of Imram.

Prologue

The candle flames, frantic in their enclosed lantern spaces, swung at the waists of two men in orange robes and wriggled and jerked like frightened insects.

Carrying a large metal box between them, with the date 2020 etched on its side, the men moved down slowly and carefully through a narrow tunnel of rock. One of them paused, puffed quickly to take in the stale air, the smell of closeness, and bobbed his head to the other to proceed. Stooping to enter a smaller passageway, they hurried through, then put down their load for a moment to twist and arch their backs. The darkness huddled round them, made their bright orange robes look a dusky red in the candlelight.

John Vail raised a delicate blistered hand to his large forehead and brushed aside a wisp of coppery hair. In the half-light his clammy white face, strong lean jaw, hooded eyes large and full of violet-gray, were ghostlike. His mind ran to his task. There were many things to do, many details to remember before the job was done. The other man, much older, was looking at the

1

walls, his hands perched on his hips. Vail turned and squinted down the still, dusty tunnel ahead, his insect light now calm but attentive. Waiting.

A vivid red light clicked on around a bend in the tunnel. The two men lifted the box and quickened toward the light. They lurched around the bend and found beneath the downward red arc the entrance to an enormous room. From inside, in a different light—like day—came the sound of a rising wind, causing lonely dust to suck inward from behind the men, flapping the hems of their Order robes about their ankles, ruffling the green turtle and arrow emblems emblazoned on their chests. The floor of the room, clouded but unobscured by the dust, was covered with black and white squares. Directly across from the open door, studded on low patches of one of the huge, shiny metallic walls, were tiny rectangular ribbons of silver light, sparkling in rhythm.

As they watched at the entrance to the room, the men saw an opening appear at the base of the lights, a small dark square in the floor. A tripod pushed up from it offering a transparent platform. The two exchanged glances, then shuffled wearily to the platform and laid the heavy box on it gratefully. Both sighed as the box began to glow lightly, throb softly. A tiny bubble on its side turned from black pitch to a milky haze, which then bled quickly to pink. Vail touched it and his hand trembled; he was forced to rub it vigorously without wanting to, his eyes glazing to within himself, seeing something not in the room. He could feel its strange power where it lay, as if it were alive.

The lid of the box lifted without sound or apparent motion. The box seemed to the two men to have always been open. Vail reached into his orange robe and pulled out a sheaf of papers. One note at the top of the papers was written in a neat, exact hand, each letter of it com-

2

posed carefully as if to help the reader avoid any mis-understanding.

IF YOU ARE HERE AND CAN READ THIS, it began.

Vail looked up at Corvine and then down at the papers again. Leaning forward over the box Vail placed them reverently on the bottom, which was shiny like brass and surrounded on the sides with many glowing loops and whorls like the inside of a man, but solid. This done, Vail withdrew his hands, parallel and tense as if they still held the papers. After a moment of peering into the box, he tapped the bubble and the lid lowered itself with the same unseeing rapidity with which it had risen. Neither man could tell if the hum in the silence that followed came from the box or from within his own ears.

"The first sequence is set, Corvine," said Vail at last. "Would you do the second one?"

"Yes, yes," said the older man. He limped slowly to one end of the rows of studded light, pressed the tenth ribbon from the bottom row, counted up to the third ribbon on the next row and jabbed it twice.

But Vail had followed him. "Once! Only once on each of them," he bellowed, furious. Striding to the flashing strips, Vail stabbed a reject ribbon at the beginning of the row and repeated the sequence. The old man was cowering to the wall and trembling. Vail glanced at him and felt that his fear and forgetfulness were due less to knowledge of events than to age or fatigue. Vail softened. Corvine's untidy, fungus-gray beard was covered with a fine dust, his dark lips cracked and peeling. About his eyes, bloodshot and nervous, was a haunted look of long standing, a look that made him part of a bad dream.

3

"It is almost done now," said Vail softly. "The *right* sequences have to be followed."

Vail had the habit of flicking his wrists into the air at odd moments as if warding off flies. He flicked one now. Almost middle-aged, taller and leaner than Corvine, and beginning to bald on the top rear of his head, Vail rubbed his hands gently over his arms, over their swellings, over the rough surface of his fair skin. He reached out to his shrinking companion, who was now leaning with his back to the cool, impersonal wall, staring intently at the box.

"Corvine?"

"I have to know the time-period now," said the old man. High on his wrinkled forehead sweatbeads formed and fell down his craggy cheeks and onto his leathery neck with its thin, straining tendons.

The room was absolutely still. The two men stared at each other, the eyes of both lined with the wear of struggle and flight; the tiny furrows in their faces were drawn clear in the stark light like painted lines on tragic masks. The younger man shrugged and turned aside.

"Almost two more generations. Thirty-five years."

"No!" shouted Corvine. "No. I was very young, but I saw them. The Falling and the Fires. I saw what the box did, and I know this island does not need it ever again. You told me the problem of the Papers would be solved here. That's why I came, why I helped you."

Vail turned back to Corvine and raised one thick eyebrow when the old man had finished. "The time of hiding has to be long enough to ease our hurt today, but not so long as to lose entirely what we once had. The Fires will not hold us back always. You know that. The Order knows that." At the name of the Order of Zeno, Vail's wrist shot involuntarily into the still air. "There may be more loss when the Papers return to the surface, but even more if they do not."

"I don't believe that. There will be no loss at all if this monstrosity from nowhere is sealed here *forever*," answered Corvine, who had pushed himself up against the glossy wall. One hand was clinching and unclinching at his side; his eyes had grown bright with fever, the liquid in them throwing off tiny points of light. He stared at the box as one of his hands stole into a recess in the tattered orange robe. It stayed there and wiggled beneath the cloth, its fingers finding the tapered length of sharp iron that seemed to comfort them.

"If we seal it forever, there will be absolutely *no* record of what happened almost one hundred years ago on this island and in the world," said Vail, pointing to the year 2020 on the side of the box. "We have got to leave *something* for those who follow us. The box will be hidden for no more than thirty-five years. Then other steps will be taken for our children's sake. The box will help then, not hurt. This has been promised. The message of the box, Corvine, has to be trusted. We have no other choice. The Papers must first be lost, then found, or the future will not come."

"Why? Why?" sobbed Corvine. "The future should have its promise, yes, but our people must be allowed to reach that promise without any further knowledge of this thing, this power, this horror that destroyed everything man needed to be man." Corvine gestured hopelessly at the box. Tears moved on his cheeks.

Vail's face lost its expression, became blank. "There is no choice of time now. We still have much to do out there, you and I, and maybe more than we *can* do." There were no more flickings of Vail's wrists. Only calm.

Turning to the row of silver ribbons, Vail moved with

determination to the programming of the third and final sequence. He slid his fingers easily over the bright strips of light and as he did so he thought he heard a tiny pop. One more and it would be done. The cave and its secret would be protected for thirty-five years. Then no one could ever again use the box to deprive man of the truth about his position in his world. Vail was satisfied. Dreaming of the future, delving into the hope and fear of those years, thinking of his son and of his son's possible son, he reached for the last ribbon.

He did not make it.

Thin metal punctured his back and darkness rose in the room around him. Torn by the burning agony, Vail gave a choking cry as he slumped, unbelieving, to the floor, catching the edge of the box, falling forward over it, then rolling off to one side. Corvine moved back quickly as the blood of his victim spread out over the box and onto the black and white squares around it. He dropped his blade and hurried to the row of lights where he punched in a new series. Turning back to where Vail had been finishing the third sequence, Corvine froze.

Once glowing silver and rhythmically, the strips over Vail's body were now flickering a faint yellow, as if picturing miniature fires burning behind the dense console. Ignoring the color, Corvine limped to the wall and began to rearrange the strips. He felt joy and sorrow as the last length of light was touched. The box tilted and disappeared beneath one of the white squares. Corvine looked down at the still body of Vail and shook his head. He had been a good man, he thought. He had done much for the island. Corvine knew he had loved Vail and what he had stood for. But the thought ran insistently through Corvine's mind:

He had been a fool to think any man could ever again live with what was in that box!

As the giant door settled to the ground, there was a sigh like the sound of a thousand mourners. It startled Corvine, and he looked high up to see the overhead lights going out one by one. Soon he was cast into an almost absolute darkness. Only the thin yellow strips on the nearby panel remained, like the phantom lights seen behind eyes tightly squeezed. Since he knew the cave had been sealed with no exit, the old man backed to the wall, slid to the floor, and waited with his slack arms crossed over his raised knees. He did not fear death; he knew now he had been prepared for that possibility. Instead he was thankful that no one could ever find the cave or what lay buried within it.

The darkness was heavy and thick like ice. The only thing that moved was the light dust that fell gently to the vast, unseen solidity of the floor. The bodies of the two men were like shadows on shadow.

Chapter 1

Even as a young boy Smith had been attractive. His dark hair framed a finely sculptured face, a short rounded nose. It was a face that would later cause Circle women to look twice. But his black hair and chalk-pink features had made a striking contrast with Turly, whose odd white hair waved and flowed around a lean, naturally olive face. Turly also had unusually quick green eyes that seemed too alive to look at. But there had been an unusual bond between the two boys, a bond Smith had consciously felt ever since Turly and his grandfather Ellman had come down from Bellsloe asking questions about two people who might have come through the year before. No one could remember them and, out of weariness or despair, the old man had immediately petitioned for a place in the Circle at Inniscloe. As the vote was being cast, Smith had chased the unsmiling four-year-old Turly around the walls in great merriment. He had not been able to catch him.

The two outsiders had been accepted and had stayed, living alone most of the time on the shore of Inniscloe

Lake, hauling their catch as fishermen each day to the markets at the Circle. It had been at a Myth Time some years after they had settled in that the riders had come in dark green tunics marked with a large *H*. When Smith had learned what they wanted—information about a young man with white hair and a reddish mole over one eye—he did not wait, but slipped from the gate and headed west to Ellman's hut. Running all the way, arriving about noon, Smith saw Ellman first and warned him. The old man was clearly disturbed, but seemed to know what to do immediately.

"Smith, my boy, you did the right thing. Any later and it would have been too late to help Turly. And their identification was an *H?*"

"Yes. Branded on their horses and stitched on their tunics."

"Tell me, Smith, did any of the men seem older than the others, or in any way different from the others?"

"No. They were all the same, it seemed to me. There were five of them."

"Good, good," mumbled Ellman. "Hastings is not with them. We might be able to do it then."

"Hastings?" asked Smith.

Ellman ignored Smith and slipped into a little wooden hut made of horizontal gray planks. When he came out he carried an armful of Turly's work clothes. He untethered one of the goats near the hut and led it down to the shore of the lake. Turly was there finishing his small lunch of cheese and bread before taking off again on the water to fish. Both Smith and Ellman called to him.

"Turly!"

The young man looked up and saw Smith, who rarely came to the lake. He sprang to his feet and ran nimbly to him; his clear white hair, knotted by the air and

10

water, brushed across his eyes and momentarily blinded him.

"Do you cry to see me, Turly?" laughed Smith.

"Smith," said Ellman. "This is not a time to laugh." Reaching Turly, Ellman took him by the shoulder and looked into his eyes. "Turly, you know the cave north of here where you and Smith have played before."

"Yes, Grandfather," said Turly, who was puzzled now. It was not time to play if it was not time to laugh. It was fishing time, even if Smith had arrived unexpectedly. Ellman could not fish alone. It was too hard for just Ellman.

"I want you to go there with Smith and hide until I come for you. Do you understand? I want you to stay out of sight until I call for you."

There was a look on Ellman's face that Turly had seen only once before. It was a vague memory of the time his mother and father had left to go south, leaving him with his grandfather in Bellsloe. As the pair had walked out of the Circle there, and blended into the woods that bordered the Circle, Ellman had shaken his head, waved at his departing daughter and son-in-law, and held Turly's hand tightly. Even at the age of three, looking up into the old man's eyes, Turly could tell great sorrow and anxiety. A sense of dread. This was what Turly felt in Ellman now. He felt in himself a knot that shot fire up into his chest.

"Let me stay, Grandfather," he said. "I want to stay with you. I don't want to lose you, too." Turly could not understand, did not want to understand why they had to be separated.

He will go away and I will have no one.

Turly reached out his hand to Ellman and tried to touch the hurt, to feel the meaning of what was to happen. Ellman drew back and motioned to Smith.

11

"Take him to the cave now, Smith." Ellman was hard and decisive. Always had been. Turly could tell that he could do nothing else and so turned up the shore of the lake toward the tiny cave in the forest.

Ellman watched them till they were gone. Picking up the long thin knife used for cleaning fish and cutting rope, Ellman walked to the goat, lifted its head from behind, and cut its throat cleanly from ear to ear. The goat staggered and fell. Ellman wrapped a loose-fitting garment of Turly's around the goat, pushing the loose legs into the holes at top and bottom. He then dragged their smallest tub-shaped vessel up on the beach and put the goat in it. He arranged the goat bending over the fishing net as if it were in the act of pulling in the net. He lashed the dead animal to the bench seat and the oar locks. He stood back and checked his work.

It will do, he thought.

Taking the larger boat for himself, Ellman tied its lead rope onto the stern of the other one. He began to row vigorously to the middle of the lake about 180 meters out. Once there, Ellman anchored the smaller boat as well as he could, using a heavy net as a drag. Glancing up the hill to the east, he separated the two boats and began to row to the opposite shore. From there he could hide and watch what happened. If anything went wrong, he could circle the lake, get Turly, and try to escape further to the north. He would know soon. The riders would get the information they wanted one way or another and head for the lake at full speed. He was glad that Smith was a good runner, and that he had already worked out a plan in case something like this occurred.

The shore line was thick with underbrush. The earth was full and lush and Ellman had some difficulty pulling his boat up into the trees and out of sight. He lay at the

12

shore of the lake, waiting. At first all he saw or heard were the birds that were always there. Then through the thin haze at the top of the far hill, he thought he saw movement. There was a tiny bobbing of dark spots and then a shimmer of forms taking shape in a slow loping gait. Ellman blinked. The hazy blobs became five riders in dark green. He could not see the insignia at that distance, but he was certain that these were the men Smith had warned them of.

The birds had wheeled and disappeared. Other than the soft lapping of the water, there was no sound. Three of the riders split off and headed for the hut. The other two rode slowly down to the edge of the lake, stopped, and pointed out to the boat in the middle of the lake. The small figures seemed to be looking directly at Ellman and he involuntarily lowered his head. He knew they could not possibly see him, but he felt the fear and tension of facing the unknown. He looked up again and saw the two riders were talking together animately and gesturing out to the boat. The leathery vessel bobbed serenely alone in the water. Unconcerned.

Even though he had made the decoy, Ellman knew *he* could not see clearly what was in the boat, only the whiteness of the goat's head. He knew they couldn't see any more than that either. But he was afraid. What if they were not fooled? What if they could somehow manage to get out to the boat and check to see if it really held the person they were after? Ellman could not be sure what would happen.

The other riders, now on foot, ran up to the two on horseback. One got down and took something from his saddle. There was a flurry of activity. A tripod was set up supporting a long black needle. Ellman stared at it. A thin red beam of light stretched out from the point of the needle and moved almost languidly across the water to the boat. Where it touched the water steam rose and churned. When it touched the boat, something happened that Ellman would never forget.

The red beam grew in intensity and the tub-boat began to change. At its edges, it turned shadowy and indistinct; then it blossomed into the brilliant color of the beam, dropped to purple, then to the deep blackness of coal, as if all color were being drained from it. The boat crumbled into something lifeless, unearthly. It glowed with a darkness Ellman had never seen before, nor ever wanted to see again. In a second it was over. There was only the barest smear of darkness seeping into the water to remind the watcher that anything had been there.

The red beam pulled back into itself like the tongue of some malevolent beast. The riders dismantled the tripod and needle, packed them away, mounted, wheeled and were off to the south. They were gone.

Ellman released his breath. He had held it throughout most of the episode. Burying his face in his hands, Ellman knew he had been prepared for *something*. He had been warned of the possibility years before. But this! Lights that could kill. He could dimly remember when men fought with things other than knives. He had been a youth when he had seen strangers kill game from a great distance with weapons held in the hand. But even that was a novelty no one had wanted to learn, and the men had passed on through to the south. Had they returned, those who wished to kill without face-to-face encounter, without question or appeal? Ellman shuddered.

Looking once more to the southeast, Ellman raised himself on his elbows. Nothing. Running low then, he circled up to the north side of the lake. The branches of the trees and shrubs seemed more burdensome than usual and Ellman thought for a wild moment that they

knew of the riders and were with them. It was only fear.
It was like that sometimes in the depths of the forest, he
knew that. But now it was worse. Panic. Memory.

*A machine that sucks the life from living things. From
dead things. From all things. Riders who had come at
last for the life of Turly.*

If only Turly's father were there, thought Ellman. He
had warned Ellman of such things, but that had not
stopped the fear. He had been given clear instructions
about how to raise Turly, what to teach him, what not
to teach him. Ellman had tried to live up to that charge.
But he seemed to move in a mist in that regard. What was
the reason for all the care to be given Turly? Why had
his daughter gone south with her husband? Ellman had
wanted to be more sure about the need to go. His son-
in-law had been vague about that those many years ago.
He had simply said that it was for the best that Ellman
did not know about the trip, or what was to be done on
the trip, except that it was vitally important and that
their whole world depended on it. Ellman had gotten
nothing else from him.

It had been with sadness and reservation that Ellman
had accepted the couple's need to go. Only their injunc-
tion to protect his grandson and to keep him ignorant of
his real name until they returned had kept Ellman from
following his only child Deirdre. Even so, he had gone
as far south as Inniscloe after a year's wait to see if he
could learn anything about them. There had been nothing, no news. The trail had vanished not far from
Bellsloe. Old and growing older, Ellman had settled
down but had never given up hope that he would someday hear from them.

The cave where Smith and Turly were to wait was in
a beautiful spot. Small rivulets of water from higher
ground wound about the rise above the cave, ran down

through startlingly green moss, and dropped into pools barely large enough to dip one's hands in. Clear and cool. At evening, catching the dying rays of the full sun, they would become windows to another world. Any other time, thought Ellman, and he could lose himself to this beauty. But now there was terror and ugliness loose, and it must be dealt with. He hurried through the thinner underbrush, past huge trees covered with ivy and vines like clothed sentinels. He reached the small cave opening and called out. Nothing. His heart beating rapidly, Ellman crawled into the cave. He was unable to see or hear anything. The cave twisted to the left not far from the entrance; it was too constricted for his body to get through, but it was ideal for a young boy.

"Turly?" he whispered. No answer. Fear forced sweat onto his brow. The shadows of the cave and the cool, damp air weighed heavily on him and they suggested an isolation that was absolute. Ellman swallowed hard. Had he violated his trust? His plans, his hopes that one day Turly would find his father—what of them?

"You are not a good caver, Grandfather!" There was laughter outside the cave.

Ellman backed up rapidly, scratching his knees as he did so. He spilled out of the mouth of the cave into the warm air. Falling onto his back, Ellman looked up and saw Turly, his head framed in sunlight, his hands on his hips. Ellman could not see his face clearly because of the sun, but he could hear Turly's mischievous laughter.

"Turly!" he shouted. "You were to stay in this cave. Where in the Seven Steps have you been?" Ellman was mad, but he could not conceal that he was relieved to find the boy alive and well.

"Smith and I were worried about you, Grandfather. We decided to sneak back and see the riders."

"And did you?" asked Ellman, suddenly concerned.

16

The boy was hardly old enough to fish, much less learn of men who wanted to kill him with such deliberate casualness. What had Turly seen? Ellman stood up and moved around Turly before the boy could answer. His eyes out of the light, Ellman immediately saw that Turly's right arm was bleeding from the elbow to the wrist. It looked as if the right forearm had been flayed. Blood was smeared to the wrist and some fell to the ground slowly.

"What is this?" cried Ellman. "Circle! I told you to watch him, Smith." Ellman grabbed the arm and ran his fingers lightly up and down. Tearing small pieces of cloth from his tunic, he dipped them into water from the pools and washed the arm clean. He saw it was only a long spiral cut that was not dangerously deep. But it was enough to leave a good scar, Ellman could tell that.

"So what happened?" said Ellman.

Smith looked abashed. His face was red and he held his hands behind his back. "Ellman, you know I wanted to help. I came and warned you. But Turly said we could maybe help and that maybe you were wrong about the riders, that they might be able to tell him about his parents. He said anyway you would be glad of some help if they were bad. So we—he—circled back to the woods closest to the east shore to check on you. I followed. I tried to hold him, Ellman. I did."

Smith was flustered and ashamed, Ellman could see that. He, the older of the two boys, had been tricked by the younger boy into taking risks he would not have taken alone. Ellman understood that. He had seen that ability of Turly's several times himself. In looking for the best fishing spot, Turly had often tried to talk him into going places Ellman knew were not safe. He knew how the soft, imploring voice, soothing but intense, could lead Smith into giving in, into believing that

Turly was right and he was wrong. The piercing green eyes looking deep into you, making you squirm. It could be a dangerous trait in Turly, thought Ellman, or it could be his salvation. He wasn't sure which it would be.

"How did you hurt the arm?" Ellman wanted some explanation from Turly.

"We had not gone far, Grandfather. The hills are very rocky, and we tried to be as quiet as we could be. It was very hard. But I wanted to see the riders and protect you. We used the vines to climb up and look ahead. Before we got to the clearing near the hut, I climbed higher on one than I had intended. I became entangled and could not get loose by myself. I hung there, my feet off the ground. Smith was on a different path, I think." Here Turly glanced at Smith with lowered eyes, but with a hint of amusement. "I could not call out to him. If the riders were really bad . . ."

"You did not see them?" asked Ellman quickly.

"No. There was no time. I was dangling from the vine and twisting in the wind. Next to the tree was a thorn bush. As I tried to get free, a thorn caught me and tore as I pulled. I could not stop it. Then Smith came and pulled it out and let me down. We hurried back here since it was getting late and my arm was hurting. We thought you might be a rider and so held back until we saw you come out of the underbrush. We let you go into the cave to sneak up on you." Turly grinned and looked at Smith again, who was in better spirits when he saw Ellman wasn't going to be terribly angry.

"You were very lucky this time, Turly," said Ellman at last. "They were dangerous, the riders from the south. Men of Lord Hastings. I cannot say what they would have done to you if they had found you. You must never disobey me in this again. Do you understand?" Ellman's voice was low and ominous. Although he had gotten away with it this time, Turly could sense that there had in fact been great danger and he had been foolish to try something against Ellman's orders. He had almost pushed his grandfather too far. He knew he would remember his limits from then on. And he would remember the name of Hastings. But he also felt that his need to push would remain. It had driven him into doing some things he had regretted, things he had not mentioned to Ellman and never would. Turly did not know what was driving him, nor could he yet formulate the question of a drive at all. He did not know how to pose questions, but he could feel them.

The three returned to the fishing camp to find nothing greatly disturbed. Ellman reflected that the riders may have been after a particular person and that was all. They had done what they had come to do and so had left. Good, thought Ellman. Let them continue to think that is what happened. Satisfied, he entered the hut.

Turly went in with Ellman and noticed that his grandfather checked the old chest in the corner first, carefully. Turly had never been able to see inside that chest. Ellman could touch the shiny lock shaped like an eye and it would open; but no one else could touch it and make it do that. Turly had often wondered about the secrecy of the chest, but he had never tried to break into it to find what was there. He had wanted to, badly, but he was not *that* driven. He knew what Ellman would do.

Smith was given some lunch and then warned by Ellman. Nothing was to be said of what had happened there. Let it be forgotten unless the riders with the *H* returned. Smith nodded as he finished his last pieces of dry bread and cheese. He would say nothing and let the years cover it. Turly would learn to forget it, too. He would think of it sometimes when he would run his fingers lightly over his right arm and feel, tiny and thin like a swelling blood vessel, the scar running in a spiral from the outside of the elbow to the inside of the wrist. It would be a reminder of something unpleasant that had happened long before, although Turly would not always be able to say what.

Smith had walked back alone to the Circle community, his thoughts confused. Why had the riders wanted Turly? How had they known about him in the first place? Why had he, Smith, been so willing to place himself in danger to save the younger boy? Certainly they had known each other for some time, and had played together often, but what he had done meant that he had saved Turly's life and that he was now responsible for him in a way that had no appeal. It was one of the dogmas of the Circle.

Life is given and it is taken. If it is being taken, step aside or sign for it.

Not yet the merchant he was to become, and so more familiar with legal terms, Smith knew only that to save a life was to make one somehow responsible for that person thereafter. He and Turly were now bound together by stronger bonds than childhood friendship. He did not know what that was to mean.

Chapter 2

The fire was a dull orange. Turly, his sunken cheeks shadowed and made canyons by the flickering flames, felt its lure. Leaping and crackling, it drew him to it. He rubbed the small red mole just above the inner tip of his right eyebrow, dusted off his hands, and reached his slender, muscular arm out to the nearest flame of the supper fire, although he knew that it would burn him. A long thin scar spiraled his right forearm from elbow to wrist and seemed itself to burn purple as the light fell upon it. Turly's finger tips moved more quickly now. *What was it, deep within the flames?*

"Turly!"

"Yes, Grandfather?" Turly jerked back his shaking hand and looked warily across the small fire.

"Not again, Turly," said the old man.

Turly rubbed his hands together to still them and returned his attention to the stew bubbling in an old battered pot. He stirred the stew, yellow and thick, with a large iron spoon. The fire continued to burn, holding his deep green eyes, reflecting in them. His back was to the small wooden hut the two lived in. In front was the shore of Inniscloe Lake that fed them and gave them a way of living. Its varied smells, moving up to him and surrounding him, had long before taken Turly so completely that he was unaware of them.

As he sat and waited for the stew to cook, Turly felt himself a part of the gray, falling dusk. He was listless. His angular body hunched over the cooking pot, his eyes sad and far away. Regularly during the last few years Turly had felt that way. He did not know why. Ellman was always kind to him, and he loved Ellman and the lake and the life he had been living for many years. But Ellman was not his father or his mother. Turly did not know where *they* were, nor did he have any idea whether they were still alive.

Thinking of his parents often, Turly would fall into a revery of fantastic adventure. He would see his parents in great danger in the furthest part of the island, and he would rush to them and save them. They would recognize him at the last moment and greet him warmly and explain all to him. Then they would tell him that he was to be the new ruler of the island. It was wonderful, and Turly loved it. But he would always fall away and realize it was a dream. He would be depressed for days, lying about without saying a word, doing his work without joy. Every now and then, he would get a hint that Ellman knew more about his parents than he let on, and Turly would try very hard to press him. But Ellman would never admit anything of the sort. Ellman was his teacher, and his mother's father, but there were some things Ellman would not, could not, talk about.

Turly remembered the discovery of the month before. Ellman had forgotten to lock the old chest in its corner of the hut. Before Ellman had returned and slammed it shut, Turly had seen some things there that had moved

22

and disturbed him greatly. He had said nothing to Ellman, but held it in, mulled it over. It was one more puzzle in his life.

The fire seemed to tease and provoke. It had always seemed to offer an answer to his questions. It promised answers if it could take him, consume him. After consumption, there would be no need for questioning, no problems at all.

"We can eat now," said Turly, gingerly dishing the molon stew into two brown cups. He stood and handed one to Ellman, keeping one cradled carefully in his left hand. Ellman tasted it and then looked over at Turly. He could see the young man was in need of some diversion.

"Circle, boy!" shouted Ellman. "This stuff tastes like old persimmons. You'll never make good molon stew."

"Grandfather, the molon is hard to catch," sighed Turly, "and when I clean it, the muscles spasm and rupture before I can get the bad thing."

"I taught you better than that. This thing is supposed to be a delicacy." Glaring at Turly's deep green eyes while slipping off his shoulder belt, the old man caught the remaining molon where it had been lying in the fish net against the small curragh. He skillfully cut its throat and allowed the thin blood to spurt into the dust by the fire. Within thirty seconds its bright yellow skin was off, the six legs mere sticks.

"We don't need another molon, Grandfather," said Turly.

"Watch now, Turly." The old man was absorbed by his cleaning. He worked his right thumb and index finger into the lower end of the molon digestive tract. A distinct schlurp was heard.

"Good," said Ellman as he regarded the skinned molon.

23

Turly shrugged his broad shoulders and squatted again beside the flickering fire. He knew what came next.

With the speed of long experience, Ellman sank his teeth into the stump of the molon's neck and pushed the lower end up with his other hand. The molon swelled up to almost twice its original size. At the last possible moment Ellman, with a curved knife clutched in his left hand, reached out toward the white protuberance at the center of the molon's distended belly.

Turly turned aside, spat, and slowly scratched the tip of his long pointed nose.

"Turly, watch this," Ellman grunted between his teeth, his weather-worn face wrinkled and wet.

Turly turned back to him obediently. Right then he loved Ellman in the way one loves what one is used to, but the love was tinged with irritation.

Ellman's eyes bulged comically as he struggled to hold together the large lizard in a balloon shape with his one hand and his teeth as well as watch what he was doing with his knife hand eight centimeters from his nose. The point of the blade settled above the tension of the belly and went in quickly.

Turly ducked. Ocherous fumes fanned out in all directions from the belly of the molon, like a tiny volcano. The little cloud covered Ellman's head and drifted across the fire to Turly.

"Circle!" they both cried.

Ellman jumped up and down and started a violent dance, coughing and fanning his face. "Now that's the way to prepare the molon," sputtered Ellman, his eyes red and watery.

Turly had fallen back on the ground and lay there rubbing his eyes, trying not to smell anything for a while.

Ellman poured Turly's stew into a bush near the fire.

He diced the new molon and flung the bits into a clean pot. He filled the pot with water from the rain barrel and hung it on the spit over the fire. As he sat down he noticed that Turly at least had his mind on something else. That was good.

Overhead the moon was cold and silver. Far in the distance the night crickets chirped and a blackbird whistled. It was a clear spring evening.

"Grandfather, we have to talk," said Turly.

"I quite agree," said Ellman in a loud and overly pompous voice. "Your cooking has fallen as low as I can remember. If you don't improve soon, my grandson, I'll have to bring Colum back, and you know his ways. The Framer knows what would turn up in the pot, delightfully seasoned of course. I remember the time he . . ."

"Grandfather."

"I can't forget Colum. I wonder why he hasn't been around to drink with me lately."

"Grandfather, Colum has been dead for years."

"Dead? For years?" Ellman cleared his throat and his eyes seemed to flash for a moment. There seemed a touch of amusement in them as well, as if Ellman were playing with the idea of forgetfulness.

"For years," repeated Turly, who had never known what to make of Ellman's lapses of memory. It wasn't like him. There was a sense of hidden meaning in those lapses, a meaning Turly could not get at.

"When you found Colum in the Deep Wood, Grandfather, you brought him back here with you. Remember? He was the ugliest thing I'd ever seen. We'd have to go to Brit, I think, to find anything uglier."

"Don't be unkind, Turly," said Ellman sharply. "He was a good man and a good friend to you, as I recall."

Yes, thought Turly, he had been. Right after his

tenth birthday, he had seen Colum and Ellman come tramping into camp, talking together. Colum had stayed for many years, fishing and working with the two. It was on Turly's fifteenth birthday that he had found Colum's body in the woods, torn beyond recognition, rended by some kind of beast he had not known was in the North. As Ellman had buried what remained of Colum, Turly had been struck by how much he had come to like the little man.

Colum had taught Turly many things about the woods, about hunting and tracking, as Ellman had also done. But Colum's twinkly eyes would shift about in their sockets restlessly, his head perk up quickly whenever something of interest would present itself. Turly had liked that. Indeed, Colum's intensity had seemed to match Turly's own, though Colum could shift at any moment into humor and a light-hearted air about anything. Turly could not do *that*. Colum could attack any problem and seem to solve it with a brisk thoroughness unmarred by irritability, his sense of himself and what he had to do shining through all else. Turly reflected, there by that night's fire, that Colum had been even more of a friend to him than he had indicated to Ellman.

But Turly had learned about the nature of friendship only *after* Colum was gone. The loss had taught Turly a lesson, although it had not fully broken him of his tendency to recruit others into boyish schemes without regard for how they would be affected. He had almost always thought of his friends in the Circle as extensions of himself, tools to probe and explore with. They had never complained, had seemed to enjoy his plays. It was something Colum's example had tried to discourage. Turly felt some regret about this, and it made him resent the strange gnome. He felt that kind of resentment as he and Ellman talked about him. He wanted to change the subject, but Ellman went on as if reading his mind.

"A friend is a friend, Turly. You are what you are born with plus what happens to you. Colum was a part of what happened to both of us. I won't soon forget Colum and neither should you. He was odd in many ways, but worth the remembering." Ellman scratched the top of his head with one delicately gnarled finger.

Turly had sat up. This was his old grandfather, he thought. He was clear-headed and said things that made sense. It wouldn't last; Turly knew it just as Ellman knew it, but now would be the time to ask him about his parents again before the mist returned. He could also try to learn of the chest's contents. Perhaps something in the chest could answer his questions. Turly wanted to return to the oldest shadows and feel again their first sudden edge. There would be plenty of time later to meet Meriwether in the Old Clearing.

"What is in the chest, Grandfather?" asked Turly carefully.

Ellman seemed to fold into himself while shrugging his shoulders. His eyelids drooped. There was a long silence, punctuated by the breathing of the two.

"You saw the coins," said Ellman.

"Yes," allowed Turly, nodding his head.

"I thought so when I caught you. Did you also see the map?" Ellman seemed deeply affected, but also strangely resigned. The fire cast a long flickering shadow over Ellman, and a cool breeze blew up from the shore of the lake. The area immediately around the small hut rocked to and fro as if in a ship at sea, while the flames sprang up and whipped about in the slight wind.

"No," said Turly quickly. "I saw only the *coins* before you closed it." Turly was surprised and agitated. Something more: a *map*. He was eager and leaped to

27

his feet, ready to get to the bottom of this. A map! A map that must tell of his father's place. He almost jumped from foot to foot. He was like an intelligent rabbit, ready to bound wherever it sensed something of interest, no matter the possible danger. He had always been like that. He knew it frightened Ellman sometimes. No matter.

Ellman sighed and patted his knees with the palms of his hands. "I suppose it is time to tell you, or show you," he said. Standing up, he motioned Turly into the hut. They stepped gingerly into the stale dark of the room; it was small but comfortable, a square table in the middle, grass sleeping mats in opposite corners. Turly heard his grandfather fumble with the lock on the chest. Ellman pulled out the dark leather packet Turly had seen earlier in the chest and had partially opened. Ellman placed it on the table. He lit the hut lamp and the two gathered about the spreading light. The sparse decorations of the hut were thrown into shadowy relief. The driftwood, candles and nets. The ruggedly hewn lumber of the walls, aging in their straight gray lines, at various places sticking out splinters, showing light yellow grain beneath the surface.

Ellman showed Turly the coins. Then he slowly and tenderly unrolled a small map of Imram. The island sat like a great bird, or some fabulous beast, with its huge beak open in an eternal cry to the west, to the unimaginable realms beyond the water. Turly's eyes bore into the map to find its secret. He was familiar with most of the places marked on the upper half of the map. There was Bellsloe, where he had lived with his parents when he was very young. There was Inniscloe Lake where he now lived. He had heard rumors of some of the places to the south: The Lower Mountains. Straiten.

The outline of the island was of a deep blue to sug-

IMRAM

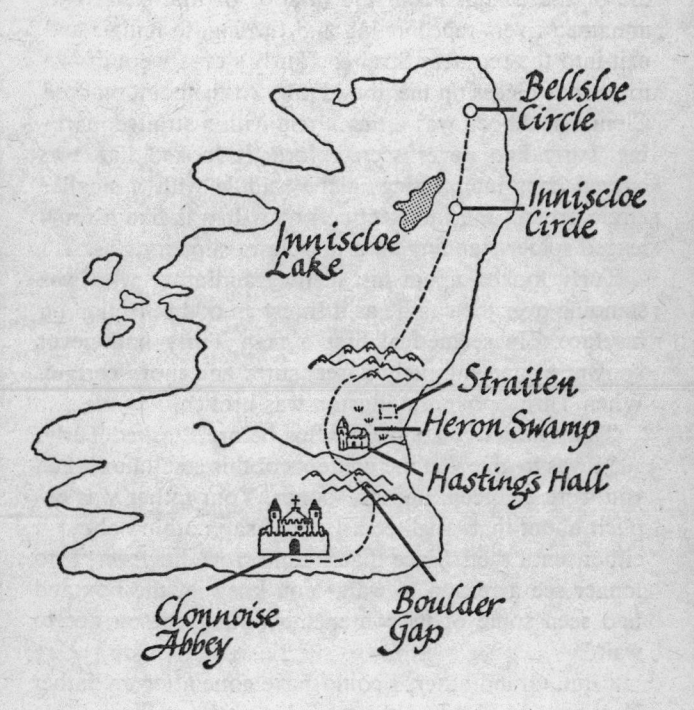

Bellsloe Circle

Inniscloe Circle

Inniscloe Lake

Straiten

Heron Swamp

Hastings Hall

Clonnoise Abbey

Boulder Gap

gest the sea that surrounded it. But Turly could see, in contrast with the musty brown of the map, a dotted red line stretching down from Bellsloe to the Lower Mountains, over them and across to Straiten, then across the southeast corner to Clonnoise Abbey in the lower middle of the island. From the interior of the island two unnamed rivers ran, looping and turning, to mingle and exit into the sea near Straiten. Turly's eyes were drawn to various places on the dotted line. At the point marked Clonnoise Abbey was a tiny circle with a strange marking Turly had never seen before. It looked like two curved lines intersecting in the middle with a smaller circle around the intersecting point. It was like a four-legged spider standing on a marble of slippery glass.

Turly looked up at his silent grandfather who was standing over the candle as it threw an odd reflection on his face. He seemed at first a man Turly had never known, a man infinitely wiser, surer and more certain. When Turly spoke the illusion was broken.

"Why didn't you show me this before?" asked Turly.

"I was to give you the contents of this small box when you were eighteen, and no sooner. Your father was explicit about that. Eighteen. I could say nothing about it either, until then. Since that is tomorrow, however, I no longer see a reason to wait. You knew of the box and had seen some of its contents. Another reason not to wait."

"But, Grandfather, I could have gone after my father long ago if I had had this map."

"No. Your father was quite clear about that, too. He told me that if he should not return from his trip within a year, I was to raise you as my own and keep from you all these things until you reached an age appropriate to action. Eighteen. You could have done nothing before now. I'm not sure there's anything to do *now*."

Ellman waved off Turly's excited protests and reached again into the leather box. "There is at least one thing left. I could never understand it, but your father must have." Ellman pushed aside the coins Turly had already seen, the coins with the face of the demon like the one on the Ritual Tapestry of the Mythic Sequence of the Circle. He then removed from the leather packet a thin piece of paper coated with a waxy material. This was the strangest thing of all:

Turly's Song

Upon A Knee
A Nothing Sings
And When It Does
It Gives Us Wings

"What does it mean?" exclaimed Turly.

"It is not for me to know," said Ellman calmly. "I wasn't told what it meant, if it means anything." The old man turned and started to leave the hut. He wanted Turly to look over his father's legacy by himself. But he stopped at the door and looked back. "I did feel your father was in great danger, and his mission urgent. He told me little of it, for my protection he said. He did say that if *you* were capable of knowing about all this when you were of age, then you would know. Somehow." Ellman left, letting the hut door slap shut.

It seemed clear to Turly that he was left with further mystery. Didn't he have enough already? The map seemed to point the way to his parents, but it did not say why they had gone, or whether they meant him to follow them. What was it they had been after? What of the coins and the nonsense rhyme? Were they riddles to be solved, pieces of a puzzle to be put together? Or were they only mementoes of the past, left by a father and mother he could only barely remember?

Turly mused upon the objects for some time, turning them over in his hands, trying to wrest their secret from them by sheer will-power. At last he sighed and carefully wrapped them up in a leather bag he carried around his neck for personal belongings. He would keep these things with him until he discovered their meaning, if it took him forever. Thinking this, he knew he would have to leave Inniscloe Lake soon, and perhaps Ellman as well. It was an exciting and disturbing thought. He loved this place, the days full of promise as the mist lifted off the lake early in the morning, the cry of the water birds as they moved clean and free into the bright air, the daily struggle with the nets and the hauling in of a varied catch, the cleaning and the preparing of their food and that of others. And the storytelling at night around the fire, when Ellman would pass on to Turly often fantastic tales of heroic struggles against unknown forces; there were rhyming lessons which had prepared Turly for being a better Framer, and reading lessons with stories printed by hand on old paper. Ellman had insisted on Turly's reading the stories; more than anything, he had insisted on that.

But Turly was stunned by the possibility of finding his *own* past, a past that belonged to him and not to a story. He wanted desperately to fill the blank spaces, the questions, the doubts. He was tired of hearing about the joys of others.

Others! *Circle,* thought Turly, what time is it? He was late for his meeting with Meriwether. He wasn't sure what time it was, but sun and supper were long gone. He had been completely absorbed in his new knowledge.

Securing the leather bag around his neck, Turly left the hut. Catching up a small jug of whiskey, an old specialty of Ellman's, Turly hurriedly shouted goodby to the old man and headed quickly eastward into the forest. The night sky was totally clear; the winds had stopped and Turly felt untroubled for the first time in many months. He would find his parents and learn the secret about them, hidden from him all these years. He would make a journey south and live with them below the Lower Mountains. The stars, blinking slowly overhead, were cold and serene. Looking up, Turly reflected that he had always loved the stars. He had often lain for hours by the lake at night, trying to see the people his grandfather sometimes talked about, the people who might be there. He thought he could imagine them now. And they were all like his parents, large and forceful, beyond care.

Part of an old tune came to Turly, its melody lilting and sweet:

> High above the scene is set:
> All remains and all is changed.
> What have I to do with this, O,
> Who live and love and die below?
> *Fol de rol de rolly O.*

Turly remembered the song from childhood. His father had sung it to him. His father had loved to sing. It was one of the few things about him that Turly did remember. Ellman had tried to keep the memories up, had sung to him songs and words he could not forget, but as a growing boy Turly had added other things to his mind. Like Meriwether.

A branch caught Turly in the face, stinging his cheek. In his rush to meet Meriwether he was being careless. Ellman had also taught him not to be careless. Survival meant care, attention to detail, constant awareness.

Everything had a meaning, Ellman often said, and to live and hunt well he had to learn that, just as he had had to learn the Basu skills of combat taught by the Circle teachers. Turly thought he could make it on his own as well as any man. But there were still doubts. He had been sheltered in many ways by the attentions of Ellman and the Circle elders. Sheltered from fears of the unknown, of strangers, of other parts of Imram. Turly was aware of the rumors of forces in the West beyond anyone's understanding. But Turly thought he was not as afraid of these things as some of his Circle friends, although he was still cautious of them. Turly ran a hand over his wet forehead. *Where was the Clearing?*

Turly thought he saw something move behind a tree in front of him; it was not Meriwether. He stopped and listened. Nothing. His thoughts were too excited tonight; he was seeing things where there was nothing. Running again lightly and confidently, he was soon in the middle of Old Clearing. On one side was a huge rock streaked with white standing out in the moonlight like a phantom guardian. On the other side was a thin stream sheltered by overhanging branches. Here was where the two usually met, halfway between the Circle and the lake. Where was she? Had she given up and gone home?

There came the sound of crackling wood behind him, and soft whispers. A gentle laugh and then nothing. Turly peered through the darkness, straining his eyes for a glimpse of the unseen. Silence now.

Turly thought he had missed Meriwether this time and so headed back to his camp. He was distracted by his thoughts of her, or he would never have overlooked the rope. Striding rapidly, Turly entered the narrow opening that marked the west trail to the lake. Just within the gloomier dark that separated the Clearing from the woods, he was temporarily blinded. His feet hit the rope, stretched ankle high, and he plunged forward to the ground.

Turly was on his face in the moist leaves of the forest, knees and elbows stinging from the impact. His short skinning knife was out almost before he hit dirt, and he glared wildly about for the enemy. Nerves alive. The smooth night air charged now with danger. Under the sharp awareness Turly could feel a cold liquid flowing down his leg. It was the whiskey. A loss, said a part of Turly buried far beneath the alertness.

A sharp laugh came like a slap on the face. "Turly, you were asleep! Even I can trick you!"

Meriwether! She could do this, thought Turly. She was good in the forest. She could be like the fox that could glide without sound through the bushes away from the dogs. She was good. Turly jumped to his feet and made for the laughter. He caught sight of light streaks of hair floating ghost-like from side to side as the girl raced from him into the woods. Turly chased her for about forty meters, grabbed her from behind, lifted her kicking and squealing into the air, flung her to the ground. She thrashed back and forth until he straddled her, pinning her arms, holding her wrists with both hands. Her face was in night shadows, but he could see distantly in his mind the beauty there. The gold hair, the light freckles, the slightly arched nose, the full bow lips, the moist blue eyes like early morning sky, the full body she had had ever since he had first taken her more than two years before.

"Turly, let me up," she laughed.

"Never. Not until you apologize," said Turly, furious that he had gotten into something unexpected and had been made a fool. He didn't like that, not even from Meriwether.

"But you weren't here, and I thought you had forgotten. Then I heard you. I was mad, Turly." Meriwether relaxed and tried to catch the expression on Turly's darkened face. It was not clear. She was frightened a little. Turly was unpredictable. Meriwether knew that if he thought he had been bested unfairly, he would be angry, too angry.

"Turly, I brought you something from Harve. He said to give it to you as a surprise. I did."

"What?" asked Turly, his anger fading now. He should not have been late. It was not Meriwether's fault.

"The rope I tripped you with. He had spent many weeks making it for you. It is for your birthday."

Turly stared down at Meriwether. "Harve wouldn't have tripped me like that," he said.

"I know," said Meriwether. "But I'm not Harve."

"Indeed. I could not do with Harve what I am about to do with you." The chase had excited Turly in more ways than one. He leaned his head down like a great bird of prey and took Meriwether by the throat, rubbing the skin of her neck to and fro with his teeth. Meriwether was pleased and made no sound as Turly rolled off and lay at her side. They faced each other in the night. Turly reached for the buttons on her tunic and fumbled with them. Undoing each one, he began to breathe quickly, forcing the sound through his mouth. Meriwether's breasts were free, and Turly rubbed the dark nipples lightly with the thumb of his hand. He moved his face to them and flicked his tongue over and around them, their uneven texture teasing him. Meriwether sighed, stretched out of her tunic, lay open to the stars and the moon. Reaching over to Turly she helped undo his thin rope belt. He slipped off his coarse-grained trousers and on his knees leaned toward Meriwether. He framed her face with his hands, rubbed his lips over her forehead and ears, letting his warm breath flow and spiral down onto them. Meriwether's hand found him. It moved back and forth in a gentle motion.

Turly's partially opened eyes, green and wide, looked up at the skies that seemed filled with light. The stars were infinitely cold, he thought, but this was warm and good. He had often felt this with Meriwether, but it was always new and fresh. It could not be fully remembered when separate from her. Sometimes Turly thought he loved her with a love that transcended the love for a single woman. She was all women. And more. He thought it must be the earth itself he loved, with its dark and emptying emotions, which could sweep him away into heights beyond caring, beyond fear and uncertainty, beyond even the concern for his heritage and his parents. He felt caught up in a great flow that held all things.

As Turly stroked her back and legs, Meriwether massaged Turly with her hands, her mouth. They played with each other in mounting excitement. Their bodies grew slick with sweat. Turly used his tongue on all parts of the girl he loved as she used hers to provoke him into a vast thoughtlessness. After a time Turly rolled over and awkwardly entered her. He lost track of the time flowing about him, making him one with Meriwether effortlessly until almost by instinct, in a final burst of speed and a mounting drive, he plunged with her into the rapid convulsions of pleasure. Behind his eyes Turly saw light merge with darkness, the twin sensations becoming one massive absorption into the world. Meriwether cried out with him, and it was like a cry of pain and betrayal.

They separated and Turly again felt the wet forest floor and the stinging in his elbows and knees. The two were silent for a while. Turly propped up on one elbow

37

and tried to read Meriwether's expression. There was spent emotion and the blankness of a face after long sleep, puffy and vague. It was good, thought Turly. He wanted to stay there and be with her always.

No. I want to take her to the south with me. Together we'll find what I am looking for and we will settle down and fish and raise children and grow old.

It was a pleasant thought, and Turly relaxed and enjoyed the whispering noises of the old forest, its smells clean and invigorating. He placed one hand under Meriwether's head and cradled it tenderly. After a time he remembered the events at the camp earlier in the evening.

"Meriwether," said Turly softly, "I want to tell you something odd about Grandfather and my birthday. It has to do, I think, with what I have always . . ."

"Later," said Meriwether. "Later." She loved Ellman and usually wanted to hear all about him. He had been like a grandfather to her, too, since the time her father drowned in the terrible storm the year Turly had arrived in Inniscloe. But now she was worried. She had to tell Turly something but did not know how to approach it. She wanted to tell him about her fears of growing up, of fulfilling Circle expectations. She wanted love and the passion that went with it, but she also wanted status in the Circle, the status of possessions and a great brown hut. She was strongly drawn to Turly, had been ever since she knew him, knew he could give her at least part of what she needed. His curly white hair, so strangely tinted with subtle coppery streaks that caught the sun, so beautiful to her, swept his broad shoulders and accented his olive skin, sunken cheeks, large forehead and piercing eyes. She had always taunted him about the small reddish mole, with tiny hair, perched like a rising sun above his right eyebrow. It would tickle her sometimes when they kissed. The deep natural color of his skin was heightened by his work in the sun at the lake, hauling in the huge fishing nets. The work at the lake had given his slim body a lithe suppleness and muscularity that was deceptive. And Meriwether knew Turly could beat almost everyone at the Circle in Basu fighting. He was now a man. A choice had to be made, a living choice.

But Turly was at times odd and unpredictable. He would be talking animately at one moment about something he had seen or done, and then his eyes would glaze, his large head bobbing slowly, drifting somewhere beyond recall. This disturbed Meriwether. At such times Turly seemed concerned only with himself and his problems. He did not seem to care about huts or possessions. He was not like the other members of the Circle, always quick to acquire things or to react correctly to the feelings of others.

There had been early rumors about Turly, that he was not really a true Circleman, that his father was from another part of the island and a man of some importance, and that he would one day cause great trouble for the Circle. But he was so likeable otherwise, during play with the Circle boys or at Myth Time, that no one had shunned him completely on such unsupported suspicions. He was simply a young boy taken both seriously and lightly. He was a part of Circle life but also, in a way barely discernible, on the outside of its normal affairs.

Meriwether worried about that, gave up the idea of telling Turly of her change of plans right then, and ran her hands over the upper part of his body, leaned over and kissed him. This time Turly quickly took Meriwether's mouth in his, rubbed lips together eagerly, mounted her and drove to the ordained end without pause, furiously, forcefully, the two leaping on the forest floor like beached fish, finishing together.

They dressed quietly and then held each other for a last time. Turly's pants had been soaked by the whiskey when his jug had broken in the fall. The trouser legs were uncomfortable and clung to his legs as if alive. But Meriwether was warm and Turly held her head close to his chest. She was more than a head shorter than he was.

"Let's meet tomorrow after the work is done," said Turly. "I have some things to show you, things Ellman gave me. Can you come?"

"I suppose," said Meriwether slowly. She was sorry she couldn't tell Turly her problem straight out, tell him to his face without fear. What would he do?

"Meriwether?"

"Yes, yes, I have some shelves to put up for my aunt, but it should go quickly. Smith and Harve have agreed to help." Meriwether felt momentary guilt. She met Turly often. She still liked him, still slept with him. And there was nothing, no code of Circle conduct, that forbade her to sleep with a friend. But she could no longer think of moving to Turly's fishing hut. That was over. Smith had laughed and called her selfish. She trembled slightly as she clung to Turly.

"It's late. We should go to our fires and sleep. You're cold now," said Turly.

"Goodby. I'll see you tomorrow," she said as she ran her fingers down his long, narrow cheek.

They parted, with Meriwether running to the east toward the hint of a false dawn in the still air, and Turly heading back to the lake in the deeper dark of the west. On the way he felt colder than the night, colder than he could account for. He had a sudden premonition of disaster. The trip he was planning? Meriwether? He did not know. He had odd dreams often, but not like this, not of a fear that had no object. He tried to shake the feeling as he reached the final path to his hut. All was peaceful as he stepped into the camp clearing. In the distance, sitting by the fire, his grandfather hunched over the dying embers.

Without greeting Ellman, Turly stepped into the hut and stopped cold. What had happened? Had grandfather drunk too much whiskey and gone mad? The inside of the hut was a mess. The old chest was smashed, papers were strewn at random around the floor, nets had been ripped off the wall, the wood floor had been ripped up in several places, the grass mats had been scattered. *Search! Grandfather!* Turly wheeled, burst into the dim light outside. His grandfather's back was still to him.

"Grandfather?"

Silence. The shadows that earlier had seemed happy and full of adventure and hope now flickered ominously like vengeful spirits. *My Circle!* thought Turly deep down where it mattered. *What has happened?* He reached Ellman in seconds and touched him gently on the shoulder. As if waiting for a command, the shoulder dipped slowly and fell to the ground. Turly screamed as he saw Ellman's face. It was pock-marked and torn almost beyond recognition. Like Colum's. Like Colum's, he thought through the numbness. Ellman's fingers were broken and lay like useless bean sprouts at the end of fallen stalks. Turly shuddered as he bent to Ellman. It seemed clear that someone or something had been here to find the things in the chest. Ellman had been alone. He would not have told anyone anything, Turly knew that. The tears ran down the boy's cheeks as he blamed himself for not being there. He might have been killed

41

as well, but at least Ellman would have had a chance. Demons in the almighty Circle, sobbed Turly over and over again, his head shaking back and forth in sorrow and anger.

The manner of Ellman's death was a bitter thing to Turly. Tortured and torn. It seemed another of the endless mysteries he was heir to. *Why?* He tried to pick up Ellman and noticed something else. There was no blood. Not anywhere. None on his clothes, none in his veins. Turly stared for a long time at the blue-white color of Ellman's face. This had been no ordinary struggle. A chill began at the base of his spine and crept upward to his scalp.

Turly sat and thought. It was almost dawn. He knew he could stay there no longer. Whatever had come for his grandfather, and what his grandfather had, might come back for him and what he now had. His fingers went immediately to the pouch around his neck. It was still there. How could anyone have known Ellman had those things, and why had they waited till now to come for them? These were questions Turly had no answer for. But he knew that now *he* would have to leave. He would bury Ellman, gather his few possessions, and go to the Circle.

It was after dawn. Turly tied his things into a bundle, tossed them over his back, stepped out of the hut. He could hear the birds in the growing light. Looking over at the fresh mound of dirt, Turly stooped to pick up one of the last of the burning sticks on the fire. He stepped back to the hut. After a moment's indecision, he set it afire. The old wood caught immediately. Turly raised his forearm over his face to protect it from the heat as flames licked upward. He walked to the edge of the forest and looked back to the hut in which he had lived for fourteen years. He felt deeply his loss. The hut going up in flames seemed to him a signal of the end of his youth. But the flames also drew his eyes inexorably as he stared into them. The flames seemed to speak to him: *There are no answers here.*

Turly turned and disappeared into the deep woods.

Chapter 3

The Circle village consisted primarily of weavers, craftsmen and merchants who catered to the needs of hunters and fishermen. Two hundred meters in diameter, a circle of tall, pointed logs bound tightly together served as the only fortification. A large gate, facing the east, was the only way in. About thirty-five round huts lined the inside wall of the compound. There was room for more. In the center of the enclosed area, the hub of the wheel, stalls were set up to allow for trade. At each corner of the small rectangular stalls, poles rose upward to support a horizontal covering for the goods on display. Under many of the stalls were hidden the barrels of Circle whiskey, always on hand.

The huts themselves were of various sizes, the largest being almost nine meters wide. But each hut had a white circular base, topped by a brown thatched roof. The effect was one of a line of giant mushrooms. Inside each mushroom was a single room, some more fully appointed than others, depending on the worth of the owner.

Inside Smith's hut was a carved brass chest. It implied modest wealth. In the center of the floor was a cooking area raised on a charred brick platform. On top of it was a pair of andirons holding old logs, its four arms curved up and outward at the top into the likeness of strange beasts with forked horns and faces staring with pitiless expressions. A spit stretched across the andirons from beast to beast. Shredded food from the night before still clung to the long black shaft. Looping around and above the fireplace, the inside walls were stained gray from years of smoke. The charcoal aroma blended with other domestic smells to create a sense of settled home life. A pile of black rugs and white pillows lay scattered in another corner. It was occupied.

Smith stretched and yawned. He scratched his thatch of dark hair and rubbed the small roll of fat around his middle. It would be a good day, he thought. The traders from Bellsloe and Hardin were bringing their furs and leather goods to Inniscloe to trade with other merchants from the east. Circlemen might never build towns like Straiten in the south, thought Smith, but there would at least be better money made from this larger kind of meeting. A single alliance of northern businesses would not be possible, he knew that. Petty bickering always spoiled any attempt at unions of any kind. But Smith chuckled as he reflected that the one sure way to sweeten the bait was to offer wealth. Wider trade would be the key to any future union, he was certain of that. And if a little force of arms could help things, well, so be it. The Circlemen were feared for their Basu skills of hand-to-hand combat, even if they were only meant to be defensive skills. A threat might do the trick. Anything to make the goods mingle.

Smith slipped on his loose-fitting trousers, tied them at the waist and ankles with leather thongs. Standing up, he wrestled into his best red tunic, collarless with an open neck, and wrapped a decorative leather chain around his neck. There were elaborate whorls knit into the hem of Smith's tunic; at the cuffs, which flared open at the elbows, were figures of prancing deer and hunters bending to aim arrows. Finally, he put on tough leather shoes, lace-ups with a slight reinforcement in the heel.

Meriwether would be happy to see him today, thought Smith. As he finished tying his shoes he mused that she would be able now to move to his hut. When he had told her of his possible new wealth, she had been ecstatic. But the thought stopped Smith. What of Turly?

He is my closest friend. Has Meriwether told him?

According to the laws of the Circle, a woman had the same rights as a man—before she married. She could pick and choose according to her own lights and was bound by no law *until she moved to a particular man's hut*. At that point she was bound for life. She retained her rights in property; but to insure harmony in the Circle, she could not sleep with another woman's hutmate. It was not done. The woman was bound to one hut. Before moving, a woman could sleep with every unattached man in the Circle, if she wished, and there would be no problem. But after choosing, all that stopped. Attachment Time was a solemn ritual attended by the current Framer, who assured the melting together of two Circlefolk into a single economic and social unit. The origin of offspring was thus clear and unquestioned. No man would raise another's child. One of the very few punishments in the Circle was for willful Detachment. If a woman strayed, she was taken to the swamp near the Deep Wood and released into its mists to wander without aid. Even if she survived, she would be separated from her friends and family forever.

Smith was glad that Meriwether had not yet chosen

Turly. Smith could not have given her up. He thought she felt the same way. He would have had to follow her into the mists. Well, that was no matter. Meriwether had not chosen Turly, and Smith hurt for Turly's ignorance of the reasons why she had not yet done so. Ellman had been so intent on training Turly for odd things, things no one at the Circle could understand, that little time had been left for him to build up the possessions Circle life required. Pots and bracelets, rugs and tapestries, all of which signified a man of property. Someone a woman could be proud to choose. Turly had none of that.

Smith knew Meriwether still saw Turly, still slept with him at times, but a "beast not chosen is not a beast that lasts," as Circle Dogma put it. Meriwether was like any other woman: proud of her freedom to choose. She wanted to make a good choice and show the Circle at large the wisdom of her decision. This had to include property, roots, things to hold on to. Didn't Turly know that?

Smith did not like the thought and pushed it from his mind. But he knew that, if it were necessary, he would stand up to Turly, fight him, even though he was responsible for Turly's life. Smith briefly remembered the time eight years before when he had helped to save Turly after the riders in green had ridden into camp. He had warned Ellman in time. Thinking of all that, years later, he still could not understand what it had all meant. The riders had never returned, and the whole incident had been reduced to a tale of childish adventure to be laughed about when recalled. Meriwether had come after that. The two things were like hard knots in Smith's mind.

Smith stepped out into the morning air and stretched his arms. The mist had risen and the sky was blue, touched with a brightness which promised another brilliant spring day. It was March 21, 2120, a day to remember. Smith looked around. Across the compound the other merchants were already setting up their tables. The front gates were open in anticipation of the north traders, the miners and smelters of Bellsloe. In return for their furs, raw iron and brass, they would be given supplies and finished utensils, sharp knives and traps for hunting, ornaments for their women. The fishermen would come too, but they would trade for different items. Both traders and fishermen were crude and even barbarous at times, but they worked to live, enjoy life and affirm themselves at Myth Time, as did the other members of the northern Circles, whether they stayed in a compound or not.

Smith walked over to Meriwether's hut, directly across the Circle from his. He knocked at the entrance several times. Meriwether's aunt stepped out and put a finger to her mouth. Her hair was standing out in gray shocks, her large nose an aging potato. Her gimlet eyes bore into Smith's chest, not looking at his face.

"Yes, Smith, she is here but asleep. I was not to know, but she came in late, very late, about three this morning. I believe she had seen Turly. Don't disturb her yet. She needs her sleep. If Myth Time is as demanding this season as last, she will need it."

Smith was not surprised. Meriwether could come and go without telling anyone. It was her right. He thanked the old woman and turned his attention to his stall. His assistant Harve was almost finished with the arrangement of pots and pans and trinkets. Smith waved at him from a distance. Harve was a giant of a man, well over two meters tall, a good hunter when he wanted to be. But he was childish in the head, a result some said of the time when he was very young and had wandered away from the Circle and had been captured by the Shee, a legendary people who lived in the mountains. They would occasionally come down to steal away a man or woman. If these unfortunates ever returned, they were found to be somehow different. Harve had been found, and he had not ever been the same. His speech was slow and his wit even slower. But he was basically gentle, and he had been accepted by the Circle as a man caught between two worlds and unable to live in either fully. Harve and Turly got along well together, telling stories and walking in the woods.

Smith did not believe in the old stories, but he found it good business not to scoff at the tales that circulated in outlying areas. Some folks were serious about their stories, while some came to the Circle simply to trade their winter-hunting furs. Better to be safe and treat all things with solemnity, Smith thought, chuckling. The Circle Sequence was the only route to truth beside business. Smith knew that.

"Harve! How are you this marvelous morning?" shouted Smith.

"Smith! I'm glad to see you," drawled Harve. There was a great rumbling deep within Harve's beard, a vast expanse that reached from his splayed nose to his huge stomach. The beard was a pure auburn, the finest of its kind Smith had ever seen. Harve's tunic, a gift from Smith, was of a deep maroon flecked with gold threads. Smith often thought that Harve's size was meant to make up for his lack of thought. Certainly he was well endowed everywhere else. The women would giggle about it to Meriwether who had passed on the facts to Smith. Meriwether swore she had never made the *cupla* with him, although she had no aversion to doing so. The occasion had never presented itself; and too, Harve was inordinately loyal to Turly. Harve would do nothing to make Turly angry. He would insist on going hunting when Turly was to go, and he was always there at Myth Time when it was Turly's turn to be Framer. Smith had always meant to ask Harve about that loyalty, which on several trading days had meant Smith had been short-handed. But he never had asked and now probably never would. He wondered how Harve would take Meriwether's choice of Smith over Turly. It would depend on how Turly took it, he supposed. Well, no matter. Harve was a good, simple man and an able-bodied assistant. A man Smith wanted on his side in any fight if at all possible.

"Are we ready for the day, Harve?" said Smith cordially.

"Yes, let them come," answered Harve while rolling a barrel of rainwater behind the stall. "If they do not buy today, they will be like the squirrels who chatter in the branches while the ground is full of ripe nuts for the taking. See this fur coat," said Harve, shoving a black wool jacket into Smith's hands. "It is soft, so soft I can run my fingers through it and think of water if it could be picked up and worn. It makes me think of something else, too, but I forget." Harve looked up into the sky and stared. His great eyes dreamed of things no man could know and remain altogether fit, or so Smith thought as he watched the huge child ponder.

The day was well underway by the time the stall was ready. Smith cleaned up in front of the stall, brushed the dirt level, then sat back on a stool behind the goods to be sold. He heard something odd over behind Meriwether's hut, but at first thought it was the old woman cleaning a rug. It was a distant grinding that came and went, a whirling deep and resonant. Smith glanced over at Harve who did not seem to hear it. Not alarmed, Smith surveyed the compound grounds. There was nothing unusual going on; some had stopped as had Smith to look up, but most were busily engaged in beginning the first day of Myth season trading. The sound stopped, and Smith thought no more about it. The heat and talk were rising, and he was gathered up in the tide of human activity that signaled a community at work and play. There was laughter, cursing, giggling, haranguing; the smell of cooking pots and the aromatic soaps of the washing tubs. Smith breathed deeply and was content. These were his people, and he loved everything about them.

The first man in green slipped between Harve's hut and Meriwether's. No one saw him as he quickly entered her hut and disappeared. At that point there was a swirl of action at the front gate. Several late-comers were running into the Circle shouting wordlessly and waving their hands in the air. They seemed like puppets in a show. Their exaggerated motions were comic and without meaning. Smith was interested but still not alarmed.

Then the gates were filled with men on horses. The dust rose in violent clouds to partially hide the rush inward. *Circle!* thought Smith as he jumped from the stool. *These were not traders of the north!*

As the riders swept further into the compound, swords drawn and flashing in the air, Smith felt fear rise in him. Dressed all in green, each rider had a large *H* stitched on his tunic. They were the old riders from the South, a group of the green riders Smith quickly recognized from years before. Dismayed, he could see the tiny spots of red appear wherever the riders' swords touched down in the milling crowd. It was chaos. The Circle was unprepared for an attack. Before Smith could move, one rider wheeled and headed right for him. The front legs of the horse rose and fell in a headlong gallop; the motion hypnotized Smith. He could only crouch and watch as the fierce charge bore down on him. At the last moment he awoke. Leaping wildly to one side, he rolled under the stall.

Where was Harve!

Smith looked out from beneath the wooden front and thought he saw something slip behind Meriwether's hut. *Meriwether!* He had to get to her. The screaming and confusing suddenness of the attack was still paralyzing many of the Circlemen. The riders, about ten in all, were scattering the crowd over the central area of the compound, killing at random when they could control their horses. Smith could see flashes of white teeth in hideous grins.

Smith reached his hut and grabbed from one wall the long blade given him by his father when he had been initiated into the Circle Sequence years before. He unsheathed its keen edge and raced back into the terror on the grounds. Dodging both runners and horsemen, Smith slanted to Meriwether's hut. With a feeling of great dread he burst into the small room. She was gone. Her aunt lay in a pool of blood, her dark eyes looking up at the roof in amusement. Smith could spare no time for grief. He turned and, watching cautiously, ran from the hut. Meriwether was nowhere to be seen. Smith was filled with one rushing, burning purpose as he headed for the front gate. He had to find Meriwether.

One green rider had fallen from his horse and lay sprawled in the Circle dust. Smith did not slow as he drove his blade angrily into the man's back. The man slumped into the dust again, not moving. There was no one else in the immediate area. The Circlemen who happened to be in their huts at the time of the attack had rallied the others and were making a defense against the far wall. In the Circle that morning, there had been fewer than thirty Circlemen in all, and twelve of them were now dead as far as Smith could tell. Out of ten riders, only one was dead. Smith could not tell at that point who would win this fight. He looked over to the center and saw the bodies lying like actors in a play, waiting until someone could tell them to get up. The red stains on them did not look real.

The gate was only a second away, and Smith could see Harve behind the far door fighting one of the riders. Why was Harve over there? Smith knew the rider had no chance. In fact, at that very moment, Harve seemed to step into the horse, and he decapitated the man on it with one blow. The rider continued on for several feet, then fell slowly from the saddle, toppling with comic abandon into a cooking fire. Harve looked over to Smith and opened his mouth. Smith could hear nothing because of the noise. The huge man's jaw opened and closed several times as he pointed violently at Smith. What did he want? Smith stepped into the gate opening.

Something hit Smith from behind, and he lurched forward with the force of the blow. His face was pressed violently into the dirt. For a moment he was stunned, incapable of thought. Then rousing his strength, Smith bucked and rolled to one side. Whatever was on top of him spilled to the ground, but was quickly back on him. Smith saw through a haze. It was a man in green, and he had his hands fixed firmly on Smith's throat, choking, squeezing. Smith looked up at a face contorted with hatred. Huge bushy eyebrows bristled over eyes penetrating and bright with blood-lust. The thick lips were curled and the teeth bared as the man continued to apply enormous strength to Smith's neck. Colored lights began to jerk in Smith's eyes. He could not break the hold on him, and his weapon had been lost in the initial jolt. Death was near. Smith could feel it, smell it. But if he died, what would become of Meriwether, and the Inniscloe Circle? But these thoughts, and all others, began to fade as life was choked slowly and inexorably from his body. Was this what it was like to die? thought Smith. There was no real feeling, some pain, no drama, only a last alternative.

Resigned to death, Smith caught a glimpse of white hair at the corner of his eye. The weight of the green rider was lifted from his chest. There was a cry of defeat and a burble of rage, coming it seemed from far away. Sitting up and rubbing his neck, Smith shook his head to clear it. Who was it squatting there? It was Turly, grinning, wiping his knife on his pants. The man in green was lying on his back spread-eagled with a red hole in his chest. Smith looked again at Turly, whose eyes were feverish with delight.

"We are even, I think, from long ago," said Turly.

"We are," said Smith slowly, coughing. "And happy about it."

At that moment the sound of horses at full gallop diverted their attention from the momentary victory. Bursting out of the gate, the remaining riders were yelling and cursing. Only five of them were left. Smith and Turly, not overly eager to battle men on horseback, but wanting to repay them as much as possible, had themselves in position. They had both pulled their short knives and were waiting to one side. As the horsemen plunged past, Turly and Smith tossed their knives at moving backs. Smith missed his man, but Turly was right on target. One of the five fell with the knife buried between his shoulder blades. At this the others reined in and turned. Smith knew he couldn't take on all of them and prepared to rush back into the Circle. But one of the riders cried out and pointed at Turly. He motioned to the others who also stopped and stared at him.

Turly returned the stare with clear olive-colored eyes. He did not know who the men were, what they wanted, or why they were interested in him, but he was not going to be made to run and hide as he had ten years before. No wound would stop him now. He would go to *them*. His childhood nightmare, Hastings, would be faced at last.

Turly had crouched and bunched his shoulder muscles, liking the feel of it. But the riders had shaken their surprise, turned, their horses like toys, tossing and jerking. They rode madly down the forest path and were gone. There remained only the sounds of the dying, screaming and moaning to be helped. Turly looked down at the man he had killed. He was satisfied. He had proved himself in real battle, not simply in Basu practice. He was a fighting man now; he knew he could not actively seek combat, could only be defensive. He was glad, however, that he could kill when necessary. His eyes burned with pride.

"Well, Smith," he said, "we've done well today. But why were they here?"

Smith wanted to ask Turly why *he* was there. He wasn't really expected until the next day, Myth Time. "I'm not sure," he said. "They killed a number of good people. Maybe it was a replenishing raid."

"Maybe," said Turly. "I know they've done it to Circles further north. But listen, Smith. Last night someone or something came to *our* camp. Grandfather is dead."

"Circle," gasped Smith. *Ellman dead*. He could not conceive of it. The old man had grown to be a respected fixture in the Circle, especially as a Framer. At many Myth Times he had proved to be quite potent. It had been his time the next night. He would be missed. Smith could say nothing, reached an arm out to Turly in silence. Turly clasped the arm and they turned to enter the Circle. Smith suddenly remembered. He pulled his arm from Turly and stepped back.

"What is it, Smith?" asked Turly.

"Turly, they have Meriwether."

Chapter 4

Turly was stunned. *Meriwether taken.* In the hands of such men as these many things could happen, unpleasant things. There were tales from other Circles of the north about missing women, women who had gone to work in the fields or to gather food in the forests, women who had left in the morning and had never come back. Sailors from the east sometimes foraged into those areas and into surrounding Circles. They could account for some of the missing women. Taken to serve as unwilling mates on the rugged coasts of the land across the waters that some had spoken of as desolate and chidden of the Circle. But the riders in green were something else. They were from the south and had rarely raided a Circle before; and when they did, it was almost never for anything except food. Why they had come that day and taken anything at all was a puzzle to Turly.

"Are you sure?" Turly asked Smith.

"She is gone," said Smith. "Her aunt lies in a pool of blood in her hut."

"Are there others missing, or just Meriwether?"

57

"I don't know," replied Smith, who bent wearily to pick up his knife. He wiped the blade on his trousers as he went back into the gate to check on the missing. Three women in all were gone. It seemed that Meriwether had not been singled out.

"That's good," said Turly. "That means they were only foragers who have no particular mission up here. They can easily be followed."

"Perhaps," allowed Smith. He was not certain. He was not a hunter and knew little of the forest skills Turly had long since acquired. It might be an easy thing for Turly to think about following the riders, but it was not easy for Smith. There had been something about them Smith had felt, feared. It was still fresh, the hands at his throat, the jerking lights in the darkening eyes.

He remembered the dark fury of the man who had almost killed him. There had seemed something maniacal about him, something more fierce than a man taken of blood-lust. He had seemed possessed. But Smith was not a man to let such things trouble him overmuch, and he let the thought slip from him as the general confusion of the Circle began to settle out into a regrouping of forces. The small community was licking its wounds and preparing to bury its dead. The dead riders were carried outside to the garbage pit and hurled bodily into hunks of old cabbage and dry bones the dogs no longer wanted. Later they would be burned. The Circle dead were cleaned and wrapped in linen. There were twelve dead in all. It had been a costly defense. But it was done, and that night during the Framing they would be given up.

Harve walked over to Turly. Laying a huge hand on the white-haired shoulders, the simple-minded giant rumbled his sorrow and regret to him. He had tried, he said, to get to Meriwether in time. He had seen one of the strangers on foot take her from her hut. During the confusion at the gate, he had made his way to the Circle entrance to head him off, but the man had disappeared. It had confused him. That's when Smith had appeared, and when he had cut off the head of one rider and tried to warn Smith of an attack from the rear but had failed. He was sorry, he said, that he had done none of those things well.

It was clear that Harve was deeply affected. Turly was moved and assured Harve that it had not been his fault; there was nothing anyone could have done to prevent what had happened. Harve was crying now, bent to the ground to vent his helpless fury at the loss. He is huge, thought Turly, but only a boy. Where Harve fit into the scheme of the One he wasn't sure, but there was a place. It was written.

The Circle was returning to normal. Throughout the long afternoon, preparations were made for the night meeting. From surrounding fishing camps like Turly's would come all members of the community to take part in the Mythic Sequence and the Pulling of the One. Long tables were set up in the main hall, one vast room, the biggest hut in the compound. Cooking fires burned most of the day and late into the evening. The only other preparation was the selection of pipes used with the beaca. There was one central ritual in the ceremony: the feeling of brevity and oneness. Beaca helped to achieve this sense of an absorption and separation that existed side by side. Caught in the smoke of the beaca weed, all would revolve about a single core and all mystery would resolve itself.

The ceremony itself took place four times a year, once in each season. Each ceremony was presided over by a single Framer who would direct the unity and invoke the One Myth. Since it had been Ellman's time this season, Turly was chosen to replace him for that evening. It was neither honor nor payment. All Circle-folk were involved in the Sequence and all would at some time be Framers and some would be repeaters. But there were no separate priests to form an elite; no one, or thing, to separate each member from his role in the Sequence.

Turly accepted the offer to Frame and knew that he could not set off after either his parents or Meriwether without first setting himself in the Sequence. A late-comer had reported riders heading south at a furious clip; he had not been able to tell if there were any women with them, but they were all in green. They had to be the raiding party. They were going south and so was Turly. It was convenient at least. He could combine two duties into one; there would be no split between his needs and those of the community. He could go with no ties to break, and none to hold him to the Inniscloe Lake, where Ellman had died.

Smith was as eager as Turly to take off after the riders. But for a different reason. He wanted to save Meriwether for himself and not for Turly. He could not bring himself to tell Turly the truth, although he knew that it would become harder and harder to do so once they set out. But any number of things could happen before they found her, he thought. They might make it no further than the Lower Mountains. Many tales had come up from the south, and none sounded good. Savage groups, mysterious beasts never seen before in the island, occurrences that defied explanation. Smith shuddered. He was not a coward, but he was not really a full fighter either. Circle men were trained to defend the Circle only. How long any of them would last was a question no one asked openly, but it was on everyone's lips. That would be a part of the future, and the future was a part of the Sequence. That feeling at least Smith shared with Turly.

Dusk came late in the spring season. The west had flared into a beauty of orange and watery blue and stretched onto a huge canvas that hung over the horizon from one end of Imram to the other. The first star signaled the beginning of the night ceremony: It was the miraculous star that led each member into the darkened corridor of the main hall. The night sounds were pervasive in the Circle. Turly, dressed in his ritual tunic with its circular collar, walked slowly to the meeting place. He heard the clicking of tiny legs, the whirr of filmy wings, almost felt the slant and speed of bats, and a fresh scent of warmth and deep peace came through the air into the Inniscloe Circle. The earlier sorrow and hurt at the loss of Ellman was now to be soothed and forgotten as hurt always must be forgotten,· thought Turly as he approached the hall. He looked up and the panorama of the skies stopped him briefly. Whatever was to befall him, this would remain. He remembered similar evenings sitting with Ellman in front of their hut. It was a sight that made up for much, he thought.

But as Turly watched, a small tatter of cloud raced over the moon and into the darker sky behind him, and he felt a foreboding he could not explain. If he was to complete his coming journey, Turly knew that he would face many dangers and must overcome much, and he might well be overwhelmed. He might not make it through to the end. But that did not matter. That was as it should be. He felt inflamed by the thought. Uncertainty was life and life was uncertainty. Only in the Sequence was there a chance for certainty. With this thought, Turly turned and ducked through the skins hanging at the entrance and entered the main hall of the Universal Mythic Sequence Church. He was ready again to search for answers in the Circle ritual.

The hall was dim with torches placed at several spots along the wall. Most of the Circle members wore white or black woolen garments—the color of their sheep. Their cloaks reached their knees. Turly could see the crowd of round collars bobbing and tilting in the half-light. Indistinct shadows played against the ceiling high overhead, its huge wooden beams suspended in gloomy space, the cords that bound the thatched roof to the beams snaking up into the darkness at the top. At the front of the hall where Turly was heading stood a large table covered with an elaborately woven yellow cloth. Across the front panel that faced the partially empty chairs was a scene that portrayed the journey of them all: A child was born; he grew to manhood; he struggled and he died; he rose and walked again. In between the stylized scenes were minute notations that had been handed down for longer than anyone present could remember. In the corner nearest the theme of death stood one symbol larger than the others. It was a demon with tiny horns holding its rotund sides in merriment and it seemed to be looking directly at whoever happened to be looking at it. It was a disquieting note that could not be readily explained in terms of the larger Sequence. Framers had inconclusively debated the point. But it had come down to the Circle members with the other Circle materials, and it would continue to be woven into ritual clothes and portrayed in Sequence art.

Facing the assembled members, Turly mused that tonight they would gather. Tomorrow they would select volunteers and head south. It was right. Ellman would have wanted it, and Turly needed it. Turly as Framer for that night knew the Sequence ritual and began it with solemnity.

We are here and many, for us, for the dead and the unborn.

There was silence in the hall as Turly began the Framing. He turned from the large table and moved lightly to the chest at the rear of the hall about three meters from the table. There he removed a large wooden bowl. Taking it carefully in two hands, he returned to the table and set the bowl on it. He then motioned the Bearers forward.

As Framer I must give you Oneness.

Turly stood with arms outstretched, encompassing them all, taking in his arms the mythic journey reaching from his right hand to his left on the Ritual Tapestry.

And I will do so.

He parceled out to each Bearer a portion of the contents of the bowl. In silence they carried their smaller bowls into different parts of the hall. As one Bearer passed the bowl of beaca down a row, another would pick it up at the end and carry it to the next row. Each member present removed a small white pipe from his tunic and stuffed into it the shredded mixture from the bowl. Fire was passed from hand to hand.

As Framer I must lead you through the Sequence.

There was again silence as Turly lifted up his head and closed his eyes. For a short period he remained that way and then began to chant the Circle credo in a singsong manner. The Circle members repeated each of the seven steps without self-conscious pause:

I believe in the birth of me and of the miraculous signs.

In the true memories of youth.

Turly's voice was slow and came down hard on "true." A distinct rhythm entered the Sequence as Turly went on with it, entered into it, drew the Circlefolk with him. The beaca was yet to work at its best, but it would come. It would come.

Turly raised his voice now and injected intensity into it. The perilous journey.

I see the desert and the inward terror.

The journey to come, the multiple struggles.

At each step Turly would stop and shift his position to indicate a new slot in the symbolic shift from beginning to end of the Mythic Sequence. Dim smoke began to fill the hall. Turly was drawing on his own pipe between steps. He continued.

I will know the death of me and the coming to despair.

The whisper. The words moving out into darkness, into a wordlessness that could not be reached, but trying. Then rising to hope.

But the rebirth of me from the fire of the Circle itself.

The final breathing and the going to the higher One.

The beaca smoke rose in tendrils from here and there in the group. It rose and melted together. It merged and became one level of overhanging cloud floating, trembling gently to and fro as the surface of a lake on a calm day shifts with the barest hint of liquid motion. The first Sequence step was over. Turly was now to choose one of the seven steps to explore in more detail. It would be now that the audience would be caught, if at all, and the skills of the Framer made apparent. Lesser Framers could always involve an audience on beaca. That was easy enough. But at the really good times heaven and earth could melt and flow together as one thing; the higher One and the lower One could merge. At such times there would be no distinction between yesterday, today and tomorrow, between what had happened and what was to come. It was all one. And into that reality they would all gladly step. Turly wanted such a Myth Time now. For himself, for Meriwether, and for Ellman.

Turly closed his eyes and saw behind them the forms flowing and coming together. He could see the earth form and the heavens settle into the solidity of life. The mist of nothingness receded and upon that marvelous shore stood a small figure. From deep within him flowed knowledge and faint understanding; it merged with the old tales, and Turly began to Frame the reality he saw. First hesitantly and then with increased confidence and speed until he had finished, he sang the tale of the man who had overcome great odds and had won at the end a great reward. And beneath it all, behind the words he enjoyed creating, he thought of Ellman:

There was a man who had no need for death.
A man who lived with animals.
With speed and love he ran and talked to them
Until he lost himself in woman
Who took him within herself
And he became human.

(ah)

He remembered his old friends:
The fish returned to the sea
The goat to the mountain
The fox to the woods
The birds to the air.
He was in a vast aloneness
And was afraid.
With the woman he began the world
And weariness entered in
And others came, sons with long days
And daughters who brought life.

(yes)

THE BLESSING PAPERS

Their strongest son set out to kill death
And his mother said: why do you wish
A restless heart like your father,
To make a journey
You may
Never understand,
To face
A door you cannot open?
The youth tossed in dreams.
Through many days and adventures he moved
His eyes open though all
His body was asleep, alone in some deep forest.
He repeated the things men had to learn.
(yes, yes)

But all his friends died,
Crumbling inward like tissue.
With nothing left behind and he felt
Hollow.
They would not have let him die
He thought
And went for death to demand his friends.
For days he struggled,
His burden on his back
That he could not throw off,
But with his strength he endured until death cried
   out
And gave him the sacred stalk of eternal life.
(ah)

And he left,
Sleeping at last by the sea.
But things he could not tell
Devoured the stalk
And left nothing behind.

In anguish the man knew he had lost
And fell upon the ground
To give himself to the earth.
In dreams he saw the Circle
Turning and turning in a widening whirl.
Caught up *he* whirled.
Beginning and end were one.
The fire and the earth
The soul and the body
All one in the Circle.
He rose and moved to the sea
To a boat scarred and torn
He sat in it and began to sail the old waters.

       (yes)

The boat glided on burning waters
Going westward toward the ball of fire and its
Red ending.

       (oh, yes)

It ended where the sea ended
Its great sound muted in thunder
And there dressed like the sun at morning
He entered the fire on the last beach.

       (no, no)

And the crying of birds rose through the air.
His face was full of youth
The circling of the birds his chorus
His ashes falling, falling light,
Deep into the earth and into the heart,
The colors of sunflowers and turquoise
And the bright red of gold.
But his heart rose out of the fire

       (yes, yes)

Into the sky that stretched to the infinite.
It ended with the star at morning and night
His body changed now to light
A star that burns forever in that sky.

(ah)

Turly's voice rose and fell in rhythmic certainty, the audience following him and venting hope or despair in clear tones rising at different times from different parts of the hut. Turly's delivery had been slow at first and punctuated with inhalations from his pipe. His eyes were now themselves glazed and bright. He had never felt such unity and certainty. The hope of rebirth came from the deepest sources within him and he let them flow out and up, giving full vent to them. It was his fabrication from beginning to end, a fabrication that he had loved in Ellman and in himself when he did it; but he believed in it fully. His eyes dimmed with tears. He would come to that beach himself and he would enter that fire and he would be consumed. That was as certain as it could ever be. Like the end of all things, the flames would die and his heart swoon up and into the sky to burn there forever. That was their end and that of their friends who lay now in the ground outside in silent communion with them. To this end he committed them.

Turly leaned heavily on the table. His fingers arched downward into the thick yellow cover, the weight of his body tensing them into roots dipping deep into the earth. He slowly raised his head, his reddish-white hair lightly brushing his shoulders. Speaking softly he began to recite the Beaca Hymn. It was the traditional ending of the Myth Time service.

THE BLESSING PAPERS

Beaca is an Imram weed
Grown for us and for our need.
It shows our lease
We are at peace.
Think on this and take beaca.

The smoothest pipe is foul within,
Shows us man and stained with sin.
He does require
To purge with fire.
Think on this and take beaca.

The darkest ashes left behind
Puts us all in deepest mind,
How we must run,
Return to One.
Think on this and take beaca.

At the end, the silence in the hall was broken only
by a few hushed sighs. Overhead, in the northwest
corner of the ceiling, a small figure listened attentively;
its eyes glittered strangely in the dim lights of the
torches. Blinking the eyes once, twice, it scurried backward on the thick wooden beam and disappeared into a
smoke hole in the roof. Outside the night was still and
close. The stars did not move, their cold light eternal
and unchanging. The small figure stepped quickly down
a slim ladder placed there for the purpose, looked about
at nothing, and slipped quietly away from the chapel. All
was as it was before.

Chapter 5

The plain stretched before them in a long sloping arc. Beyond were the Lower Mountains. O'Kelly wiped the sweat off his brow with one hand while reining in with the other. Looking back over his shoulder, he saw his men trailing by a good forty meters. By the gods, there were no more good men left in the entire island, he thought. If they were not paid regularly and on time they would be off to a more slothful master.

"Move up," he yelled. The others spurred their mounts and soon pulled beside him. There were seven in all, with three prisoners. O'Kelly rustled his green cape and sat forward on his saddle.

"There will be no more stops until we need supper. You will keep up or answer to Hastings himself. Do you understand?" O'Kelly was tall and dark. A mane of jet black hair fell over his forehead and almost into his eyes. Running from the right ear down to the tip of his chin was an ugly scar, a reminder of a brutal past in the regional wars of southwestern Imram. His men feared him. He had been a leader of one of the strongest of the many groups in the hilly area bounded by the Shack River on one side and the West Sea on two others. Until Hastings had come.

With a hand more ruthless than O'Kelly's, Hastings had broken the backs of each band one by one until they all had given allegiance to him. Now they worked and fought for him even though none could fathom the reason behind his actions. They would scour the kingdom for certain papers; seek out a name or a face and report back in minute detail what had occurred; kill some and let others live. O'Kelly had long since given up trying to understand his master's motives. But the money was good and loyal service to a man who stood above all others was good. O'Kelly understood loyalty and devotion. He had been with Hastings for almost twenty years. He was one of the few lieutenants who had survived the purges of eleven years before. His allegiance had been unquestioned. And now he could repay his master with the information he possessed.

Riding behind the three smallest scouts were the three prisoners. They were good spoils, thought O'Kelly. It had been a rougher fight than expected. Circles rarely put up resistance. There was a certain fatalism in their religion, he thought. They had an odd willingness to go with events and this seemed to cause a reluctance to alter what they perceived to be the inevitable. Unless, he mused, the inevitable might be to fight. Perhaps he had simply stumbled on a Circle that assumed defense was imperative at that moment. Perhaps. He looked over at the golden-haired girl now riding beside him. She was not beautiful, but attractive in her way. The eyes were too widely spaced for his taste and her mouth at the moment too bitter. But the body was athletic, he noticed. And that was in her favor. Her sleeping garment revealed little and he had not yet had the opportunity to check closer. Her legs straddled the horse's flanks tightly and were brown and comely. It was hard to pick and choose in the middle of a fight, but he knew when he had caught sight of her stealing back into the Circle earlier that morning that this one at least would have to be one of the girls taken. Since surprise was to be their element, he had noted the hut she entered and later had stolen to it, taking her first while his men had staged a frontal attack at the gates. The other women had been taken later.

Hastings' Colorstealer had signaled the beginning of the assault. There were few such items Hastings let his raiding parties use, but the stealer was one. It was good for long-range use, and for making holes in the ground. By aiming the wand at the ground at the base of a Circle, a hole could be carved deep enough to allow a man to gain entrance without being seen and to escape with the same ease. The stealer was relatively useless in hand-to-hand combat, and so was never used for that. But it was very light and easily packed with the other gear. O'Kelly was in charge of it; no one else was allowed to assemble it—under pain of death. And he had always been able to back that up. But he was worried about other things now. O'Kelly had that day lost more men than he had intended to for women. Duty in the North could be hazardous.

But this loss was nothing compared to the other discovery. *The boy with the white hair still lived!* Hastings would reward him greatly for such information. And

72

yet he might also punish him dearly for failure to capture him. O'Kelly would have to be careful in telling the story. Bryan and Fulk had seen the boy, yet had done nothing; O'Kelly himself had seen him as he had passed over the hill to join his men. Standing defiantly in front of the gates was the very figure he thought he had killed years ago. Hastings would be furious to learn of this, but also glad that the knowledge was theirs in time to do something about it. The Order knew nothing of it. They would have to proceed as quickly as possible to Straiten and Hastings Hall and it was a two-day trip. No one had followed them immediately. O'Kelly's rear scouts had assured him of that. With a good start, all should be well. And ahead of them now were the Lower Mountains, stretching as far as the eye could see.

By nightfall they were in the foothills, stopping for a brief rest and food. From there, thought O'Kelly, they would push on all night to the base camp at Altoola; there they could refresh and sleep knowing they were within Hastings' jurisdiction. But for now there was time for brief relaxation. The girl with the streaked golden hair seemed to be arguing with the others about something. Well, we'll see about her abilities later, he thought. He glanced at his men. They, too, were getting eager to enjoy the spoils of combat. But before he could speak, the girl stood up and moved toward him.

"You are the leader here?" she asked with a certain admirable arrogance.

"I am, yes." O'Kelly looked into her smokey blue eyes. He could tell nothing from them. She was more and more attractive, yes. There would be fun when there was time.

"We are going to the south?" Now she licked her lips. A sign of fear, O'Kelly knew. He had seen it a thousand times.

"Yes."

"Then I must tell you. I know the man you are after. The man with the white hair. I can help you get him."

Chapter 6

The morning was clear and crisp. Thin wisps of smoke spiraled from the huts into the dawn as Turly began to assemble his party. Besides Smith and Harve, Turly had picked Bulfin, Garrett, and Kelleher to travel with him. All were either /close friends or relatives of the recent dead, and all therefore had strong reasons for going. They were also all some of the few very good fighters who respected Turly enough to follow him.

Turly checked their gear. The standard defense was the short dirke, a two-headed axe that was an all-purpose battle weapon sheathed at the waist. There was also a good supply of the shorter blut blade that was carried in a hidden sheath at the waist inside the pants and covered by the loose Circle tunic. Covered on both edges with serrated teeth, the blut could be pulled quickly and used to kill at close range. It could rip flesh out of all proportion to its size and weight. It was good to have. And of course there was the longer sword, thin and pointed, used for frontal assault, carried in a long leather pouch on the horse.

Enough supplies were packed for several weeks. Turly did not know how long they would have to track the green riders, but there were limits to what they could carry with them. There was dried fish, and flat corn cakes, and flour and sugar. Otherwise they would have to live on the land. Not easy for fishermen and traders, mused Turly. Turly had also tucked away his and Ellman's accumulated savings in gold grims. He strapped the thin coins in the black belt under his tunic and pulled it tight.

All was prepared, and Turly gathered the small group together for a final warning before setting out. But as Turly looked out over the compound lying quietly in the morning light, he seemed to feel a sense of decay, see the giant mushroom huts fall gently into some unseen abyss, settle into their own doom. Then the feeling was gone. There was no reason to think that this small isolated trading village posed any threat to Hastings' men, or that they would be back. Turly was tired from the night before; perhaps he was still feeling the effects of last night's exhilaration. One always paid the price for Framing the Sequence, but it usually passed in a day's time. He jumped up and down, breathed quickly in and out, bent over to the ground and twisted at the waist. He felt better as the blood rose to his head and into his sunken cheeks, the bones arching up beneath the smooth olive skin. His white hair brushed his silver tunic and his eyes, almost animal-like now, quick and alive, darted from man to man.

It was time to go, and Turly walked to each man, bending toward each as if to force upon him his own will, his own eagerness and resolution. Each man in turn tried to hold Turly's eye, but each wondered what his fate would be in the hands of a man whom no one could fully understand. As Turly spoke to them, they felt the twin motives of flight *from* something and *to* something.

"We will be traveling to the south," said Turly. "You all know the legends and have heard the tales. They are there for us to find; but—now listen—there will be danger. I want you to know that. If you want to stay behind, *this* is the time to choose. *I* am going to find word of my parents, and I will also return Meriwether to her Circle. I cannot speak for the rest of you. You know what happened here in the Circle and what happened to Ellman at our hut at the lake. If you still wish to go, let us mount our horses and be off." Turly immediately turned and moved toward Bleak Meadow, his black mare. He leaped onto her back and felt the strength spread through his legs.

Some of the Circle members had been standing around listening to Turly apprehensively; others had peeked through their doors. They were afraid, thought Turly. They did not know what happened beyond their walls. And they did not care. Even though they were all willing participants in the perilous journey of the Sequence, they feared the unfamiliar and would not make the effort to understand anything that was new. That is what Ellman told me, thought Turly, and it is true.

Someday that would change; it would have to change. Turly patted Bleak Meadow's neck as he reflected on that. It was not good to fear the outside so much. There could be more strength in all the north Circles joining together, more widespread understanding. But union had been tried before. Turly remembered the stories of a man who had managed to merge ten Circles in 2085. Cracks had appeared almost immediately, as Ellman had said. Local squabbles had prevented any real trust from developing. There were other things as well: unreasoning fear of outsiders, fear of change, fear of open spaces. It was as if something did not want any kind of lasting alliance in Imram, and it would insinuate minor bickering and distrust into any attempt to do so.

This bothered Turly as it had bothered Ellman who had taught Turly to stay a bit removed from all things so all things could be changed without hurt, if need be. Union was a need, Turly thought as he made one last glance around Inniscloe Circle, but it did not seem to him to be a pressing issue as yet. He had other things on his mind that morning.

Taking the Chapelizod road, Turly and his men set off, waving until the last signs of the Circle were out of sight. In spite of his exuberant spirit, and the prospect of answers to many of his questions, Turly felt sadness. He knew it was part of the fear of newness, but he also knew he might never again see that place. The lush green of the meadows in spring and summer, the sound of birds calling at evening with the stars out and glowing. That could all be lost. Setting his eyes to the south, Turly searched the horizon for clues of his future, but there was only the blue haze of a summer day beginning to form, and wisps of lazy clouds drifting from east to west. It was peaceful. But Turly knew he would have to be at the peak of his alertness to have any chance of reaching the Clonnoise Abbey and dealing with whatever lay there for him. But he *had* to get there. His ears almost twitched in anticipation.

At noon Turly called a halt. The group had ridden for miles through desolate boglands without so much as a tree or a hill to break the monotony of it. The brown tufts of bog grass, and an occasional iron-black bush jutting up into the sky like a clutching hand, had been all they could see. The men and horses were past that now, into greener land and rolling hills, but they were tired.

As the animals were grazing, a meager meal was eaten in silence. Afterward Turly took one of the water bags and began to stride toward a small flat lake about a hundred yards from their temporary camp. He had told Smith to try to divert the men from repeating the tales of horror they had heard. There were many strange creatures in Imram, Circle knows, thought Turly. And all had come in recent history, as Ellman had told him, Ellman who could not explain them. The six-legged molon was the least of them, and the most edible, tasting like the dark meat of a chicken. No one knew any more about where it had come from than they knew about a chicken. The molon was an accepted part of island life.

But the other things were not. There were legends brought up from the south and from the west about fabulous things of the night, more fierce than the molon, deadlier than man. There might be truth in the tales, and Turly knew he and his men would have to be careful once they had crossed the Lower Mountains, the dividing line between north and south Imram. Turly skipped a rock across the surface of the small lake. If the legends were true, and the things existed, then something very strange was going on in Imram. Ellman had taught him to think that, and to search for answers to such questions. Who had brought such things to the island? For what purpose?

Turly set down his water bag after filling it, and he buried his face in the cool water gratefully, blowing air out through his mouth, sending bubbles scurrying up against his cheeks and closed eyes. He sat up and gazed across the water into the distance. The land was now mostly gray rock and coarse green grass. Blurred rolling hills in the near distance gave the impression of a fore-shortened landscape. Turly felt the mouse-gray sky could scrape the top of his head should he stand too tall. It never did, but he was beginning to feel a gnawing sense of oppression. Everything was closing in, pushing down.

Well, thought Turly, it was no more than he had expected. Ellman had often spoken of the reasons men did not want to travel south. The weather and the landscape were two of the reasons. At least in the north one knew what to expect. The rain, the mist, the skies that matched rock. The mere fact that this was near the south made it somehow different. Turly could not easily put it into words.

But it was this way that the green riders had come, taking Meriwether with them. Whatever waited for Turly, he would have to continue. Otherwise there would be a rootless life in the Circle, with no parents and no children. The Circlefolk would take him in, of course, but continuity of generations was very important to them and to Turly, too. He was a Framer and a good one. He felt deeply the birth and the journey of man in his world, his death and rebirth into something good. Who could deny this to any man? Children insured the flow and motion of the One in action and were necessary to that purpose.

The fact remained that no arc stretched before Turly and, until Meriwether was found, none would stretch after him. He had to find both arcs or be lost.

Turly returned to the refreshed men and they all mounted their horses. Turly rode Bleak Meadow well, though he was not a true horseman. None of the Circlemen were; horses were kept only for basic purposes, not for wide travel. Smith's horse was a rich brown, with light splotches of yellow-white at the shoulder and haunches. Smith, a good businessman, had not spared the expense in selecting the best horses available for the trip. He wanted Meriwether even more than Turly could know.

Smith rode behind Turly and noticed that, from the rear, Turly did not look especially impressive. But he knew from long experience that steel muscles hid beneath the supple limbs, and lightning-fast reactions in his hands and eyes. Smith had always looked up to Turly, even though he was several years older than Turly. Smith always shrugged when he thought of this. There was something about Turly that affected everyone he met. You had to like Turly and respect him, believing he could do whatever he said he could do, somehow *knowing* it. Smith could not put his finger on the reason for this, but he did not worry overmuch about it. That was just the way it was. It was the reason the others had agreed to come south with them, and that meant a better chance to find Meriwether, the girl both men wanted. But Turly, whose eyes could make you look somewhere else, did not know this and Smith did not relish the moment of truth. He would hold his tongue for now and wait for the right moment.

Turly rode easily on his mare. It was a good day after all, he thought. He sniffed the air and the sweet smells of spring seemed to rise to meet him and he thought he would live forever. He forgot the earlier sense of oppression as he scanned the newly rolling countryside.

The single man appeared first. Coming at a full gallop from behind a grove of trees to their right, he rode as if possessed. His long orange robe flew up furiously in the wind. He saw Turly's party and seemed to head right for it. As the man did so, Turly pulled up and raised his hand for the others to stop. Immediately he saw what had made the man ride hard. About fifteen well-armed men in red uniforms were right behind him and closing fast. In that instant Turly also saw two men behind them, driving an enclosed wagon painted a pitch black. It seemed to Turly to have collected all the darkness of the night, of the country itself.

There was no time to do anything. In the confusion of the moment, the swords of Turly's men were only halfway out of their scabbards. Flight, even had they wanted it, was impossible. They were surrounded by long lances aimed at them, wavering with the ready skill of soldiers used to fighting. The man in orange had been caught in the same net. He breathed heavily and glanced with some interest at Turly. Otherwise he did nothing and said nothing. But the leader of the soldiers in red pulled up by Turly.

"Why are you here, strangers? By your look you are from the north, Circle people no doubt. Didn't your Framers tell you to stay out of the south?" The leader of the soldiers was greatly amused. His voice was hoarse and he rode tall and proud. A red slouch hat fell casually over his brow. On it Turly saw a familiar insignia. The letter *H*.

"We mean no trouble. We only seek south for trade routes." He motioned with some truth to Smith. "We escort this man to conclude certain arrangements with the Goidels."

The man's eyes twinkled.

"Goidels? What do you want with the Goidels? They are a treacherous people. You will only get in trouble, I assure you. You have to watch them constantly or you'll find a knife in your back. No, you don't want to trade with the Goidels."

And how about you? Turly thought. Would you put a knife in my back?

"We are soldiers of Hastings, not thieves and murderers," said the other, as if he had read Turly's mind. "I am Captain Dodder. This man," he pointed to the rider they had been pursuing, "has violated the laws of the south, and he must be punished. He goes with us."

"And us," asked Turly, "what of us? We have a long way to go." His horse snorted and pawed the ground. Turly was restless. There was more here than he had thought at first. He had the feeling that he had walked right into a waiting trap. What had the man in orange to do with it? The Captain seemed open enough, but his men circled Turly's group and made no sign of lowering their lances.

"Perhaps we can ride together," suggested the Captain, a full grin on his face. "We are heading back now to Straiten. There are many dangers in going through the mountains these days. Some even we fear. The Farks, for example, have multiplied until they almost control the northern slopes." The Captain, for all his military bearing, shuddered involuntarily. Turly felt that at least on this point he was sincere. Whatever the Farks were, the Captain feared them and he supposed that he should fear them, too. But did the Captain know about the other riders' raid on the Circle? And did he know that Turly was after them? He did feel that the invitation to travel south with the Captain and his men was not something he could easily turn down.

"We await your pleasure, Captain."

"Good, good. Please place your weapons in this bag." One of his men held out a large burlap bag. "You won't need them, and not having them may save some trouble later at the border. I know you understand."

Turly hesitated. They were helpless with the weapons, but without them they could be slain without a fight. He glanced around at his men. Smith was livid. He was not used to commands like that. Bulfin and Garrett sat immobile, their faces ashen. Harve seemed not to have heard anything. He was off his horse squatting, looking at something on the ground. Kelleher was sitting rigid, his eyes glued to the Captain's face.

"Are we prisoners too, Captain?" Turly's tone was low and ominous. He could not find what he was after in someone else's custody. If he had to fight, this would be as good a place as any, although the circumstances could be better.

"By no means," swore the Red Captain. "By the gods, you are a brave one, though. I believe you would fight to the end given the opportunity." He looked Turly over with a new respect. "Perhaps you are a brave man, but are your men? Do you wish to see them killed for nothing? No, I think you will understand when I tell you, you have no choice but to come with us. There are dangers you are unaware of. At our destination you will be given back your weapons and you will be free to go."

Turly did not trust the man, but he did not seem the kind to slaughter unarmed men. Perhaps he knew nothing of the other riders. Reluctantly, Turly motioned to the others and they dropped their swords and axes into the bag.

"I believe you northerners like to carry a small blade there under the tunic?" said the Captain with a twinkle in his eye.

Turly shrugged and pulled the blut from its sheath. He dropped it and felt a sense of utter helplessness descend upon him. The Captain wheeled and the soldiers in red fell into two ranks, one ahead of Turly's group and the other behind. The hands of the man in orange had been bound with a rope that circled his horse's neck and he rode bent over, embracing his mount. He was silent, his face an enigmatic mask. Was he part of all this, or had they stumbled into something they had not the good fortune to avoid?

They rode for several hours. Turly did not know what was in the wagon. It bumped along with no suggestion of having passengers. From the east a strong wind began to blow. Rain soon started to fall in great gusts, sheets rushing at them across the plain. The soldiers pulled on coverings against the water and buried their heads deep within them. Turly and his men were soon soaked, their tunics clinging to their chests. It was now darker than he had ever remembered it getting at this time of day. He looked about in wonder and then growing fear. He could see nothing. After a time he could hear nothing and called out several times. Nothing. He spurred his horse on to catch up, but he was lost in rain and darkness. And then he caught sight of something. It was orange.

The man's hands were free now, and he motioned Turly to follow him. Turly hesitated; going from what to what? he thought. At least the orange man seemed to know what he was doing. Perhaps with him he would have a better chance to help his men. He followed the stringy horse and its silent rider into the dark.

After a few minutes, the man began to slow; the air was now less thick and the darkness seemed to be receding. Turly could see the sun shining through the mist like a silver disc and then it became clear. He squinted his eyes and looked over at the figure, who now assumed the air of one who was used to giving orders and claiming unquestioned authority. Turly then looked back over his shoulder where the man was pointing and gasped. In the distance he could see a black cloud with distinct outlines floating slowly over the ground like a cloud that had fallen to earth and could not rise up again. It rolled and tumbled. Muted thunder sounded and brief flashes of light reflected from within it. It was heading toward the mountains in the distance. The same mountains Turly had been headed for. The soldiers and his friends were nowhere in sight. Turly thought that, obviously, the cloud had hidden them.

"A good diversion, don't you think?" The man's voice was soft and low with a well-modulated tone.

Turly stared. He was amazed and intrigued.

"You did that?"

"Yes. And a good thing. They were taking you to Hastings, you know. A stroke of luck on their part to find you that easily. If I had not led them to you like that, I doubt if you would have had trouble from them before you got to the foothills of the Lower Mountains." He spoke casually and with utter confidence.

"You seem to know a lot about me," suggested Turly. He watched the man with more care. He had heard of the sorcerers of the south but had never met one. The man's head was shaven and the polished top gleamed dully in the early afternoon sun. His orange robe was pushed loosely up his arms and Turly could see they were as thin as his horse's ribs.

"And your name?" asked Turly.

The other looked at Turly for a long time without speaking. He was of indeterminate age. The sun had tanned him into wrinkles, and there were dark spots on his hands and neck. But his eyes were young. He looked away and shaded his forehead with his left hand. Squinting into the distance at the black cloud, which was almost out of sight, he pursed his lips.

"Call me Oliver," he said at last.

"And where do we go from here, Oliver?" Turly

was getting restless. He wanted to get to his friends as soon as possible. And besides, the company of a sorcerer was a chancy thing. How could he combat magic? Ellman had taught him a few things about illusion but nothing like what he had just seen. He was in over his head now, and he knew it. He would have to be very careful. It appeared that he had to do whatever Oliver suggested, for the moment, and watch for his chance. A chill passed over him. Would there be that chance? What would happen to Smith and the others? For the first time Turly regretted persuading them into coming with him. They were simple men who had come because he had appealed to their sense of honor. They had accepted because that was what their Circle demanded of them. But Turly had not really believed that it would come to this. Turly thought briefly that the others might be killed when the Captain learned that he and the orange man had escaped. Even if they lived, he did not know where they would be taken. These and other doubts assailed Turly as he caught one last glimpse of the dark rolling cloud.

"We can beat them to the entrance of the North Gate by an old path I know," said Oliver.

Turly was surprised. "Why should you help me now?" he asked. "You are free."

"I owe you something," said Oliver, "and in any case I'm heading in that direction. My home is over the mountains to the south. There are only a few ways over, and there are still many dangers to be faced. I can get you there, and you can help if there is trouble. Agreed?"

Turly agreed. Oliver reached under his cloak and gave him a knife, the design of which Turly had never seen before. It was twisted so that any stroke in the body would guarantee great injury. It was twice as long as his blut and better balanced. At the end of the handle was an engraving of an arrow and a turtle. Well, he was happy to have something in his hand again.

Oliver wheeled his horse in the direction of the mountains and rode off. Turly, sticking the knife in his belt, had no choice but to follow. They rode together without speaking. Oliver's orange robe flapped in the breeze, his head erect and facing forward. The ground over which they rode was soft and spongy from the rain, and their horses made little noise in passing over it. Turly sniffed the wind as if to learn what awaited them, but there was nothing.

After reaching the first foothills, Oliver veered from the road. Turly soon saw an outcropping of quartzite rock twisted into a strange formation, which looked like a pair of arms stretched wide to receive any who came. Oliver headed for it, leaving further behind the regular trail that wound on up and to the right.

They entered its arms. Over the entrance Turly thought he saw engravings that teased his memory. Where had he seen them before? They had been defaced and stood in half-relief. He thought he saw, before Oliver urged him into the narrow pass leading sharply downward into the hill, the remains of a circle and within it the intersecting curves, like a four-legged spider astride a slippery marble.

It was the sign on the map. The sign at Clonnoise, drawn on his father's map.

Chapter 7

Darkness closed over Turly, smothering him with a dank, thick air. The horses had not stopped in their headlong flight, and the sound of their hooves echoed off the walls. Turly instinctively ducked, thinking the dark held many dangers.

Oliver's horse seemed to know exactly where to go, and Bleak Meadow followed. Turly strained his eyes to see and after a time caught the dull orange smudge of Oliver's robe in front. They rode downward for about fifteen minutes and then began a long slow ascent that soon tired the horses. Breath came quickly now, the sweat on their flanks more pronounced. Turly had ridden the whole way bent slightly forward to avoid an invisible ceiling that never lowered. His head bobbed directly behind the mare's ears. He was still thinking about the half-erased symbol on the cave entrance. What did it mean? Was he to find out now? If so, his journey was going to be shorter than he thought, for his father's fate seemed inextricably bound with the mystery of the symbolic spider on the marble.

At first there was only the barest hint of light, and then a definite pinhole appeared at a great distance. Turly tried to imagine depth and time in the passage, but could not. He had lost all bearings and had to trust Oliver. He did have the impression of a vast courtyard across which they were racing to a tiny gate. It was kilometers from one side to the other, and the race seemed endless. Gradually the gate got bigger and bigger and Turly realized, with increasing awe, the true magnitude of the gate and of the dimensions involved. The gate became normal size, but they had not begun to reach it. It loomed larger and larger, its great iron bolts and wooden slats becoming unbelievably magnified. The handle on the door was at an immense height from the floor, and from any human hand that would reach for it. Turly was transfixed. He rode his mount loosely now, in a trance, his eyes glazed as they approached the monstrous door. Then he noticed, far down in one corner of the wood, an iron gate, a much smaller opening. Oliver slowed for the first time and headed for this door. Turly, still overcome by the gigantic size of the apparition, gratefully followed Oliver to it.

Oliver and Turly dismounted. Oliver reached into the folds of his robe and withdrew a key, which glowed with the color of the sun. He inserted it into a slot in the center of the door, which opened with a slow creak. Oliver stepped in and vanished. Turly followed.

Immediately Turly knew he had made a mistake.

"You are a difficult man to find, Turly, but it seems not a difficult one to catch." Oliver stood at the head of a semi-circle of caped, hooded figures, their hands tucked into their orange sleeves, their faces hidden by the cowls of their hoods. On each chest was an arrow and a turtle, stained green. In the background, at the far end of the square anteroom, burned a single candle, guttering now and blowing with the slight breeze coming from the open door.

"Take him," ordered Oliver. Some of the silent figures moved toward Turly's horse and others toward Turly himself. Turly knew that if he did nothing now, he would be lost. He turned back to the smaller door from which he had just stepped. There were other figures standing there. He wheeled back just in time to see, from the corner of his eye, the blur of a club descending upon his head. Before he blacked out he heard Oliver, his smooth voice without malice, laughing long and hard.

When Turly awoke he found himself in a well-lit room, totally white, with no windows; from where he was strapped down, he could see no apparent entrances. He could not see where the light was coming from. He strained his neck to look behind him but could not. His head hurt a good deal, he noticed. He blinked several times and tried to shake the dizziness from his mind. He knew he was caught, but by whom and for what purpose?

He heard the sound of feet behind him, and knew he would soon find out.

"You are a stubborn man," said a familiar voice.

Oliver stepped into his view. Turly instinctively went for his throat, with no success.

"It was not necessary to resist as you did. We have only a few questions to ask you and then you may leave. I must say, though, that it seems we must bind you as we have done in order to get your attention. A violent man is ruled by violence. I hope you understand and, by the way, if you continue to struggle as much as you have been you will eventually strangle yourself."

Turly felt this was true. A rope stretched from each

corner of the table, where he was securely bound, to a common loop at his chest where, by a series of ingenious gears and pulleys, another rope extended to a harness about his neck. The more Turly thrashed and pulled, the tighter grew the noose. It was already uncomfortably tight.

"Here, let me loosen that somewhat." Oliver bent over and did something to the harness. Turly craned his neck, circling it to and fro to return the circulation. He was grateful. Oliver seemed to be a man, after all, who was not a willing party to all this.

"Now, let's talk a minute, Turly. We won't have this opportunity for long. I have business elsewhere and must be off, and there are others who would like to have you."

Turly glanced quickly at Oliver. "Why am I trussed up like a pig for the slaughter?"

Oliver laughed—again that smooth well-controlled timbre that implied authority and order. He placed his hands on his lips and looked directly at Turly.

"What do you know of the Blessing Papers?"

"The what?" Turly could tell by the way Oliver said the words that the "Blessing Papers," whatever they were, were of immense importance. He had never heard the name.

"The Blessing Papers, Turly. The Blessing Papers."

"I don't know what you're talking about," Turly said with all sincerity. He wanted to tell Oliver what the monk wanted to know and then to rejoin his companions, if it were at all possible. This annoyance about papers of some kind was ridiculous. A misunderstanding.

Oliver picked up a taper from the table behind Turly and lit it. The small flame sprang up in a yellow oval. Watching the man closely, Turly also watched the tiny fire with fascination. Once again he wanted to reach out and caress it, to take it to himself and become one with it. Oliver saw the intense interest and laughed.

"No, I'll not touch you directly with this, my friend. I have better ways, as you'll see. This is merely to start the process of persuasion."

Oliver reached behind Turly and touched something. There was a hissing sound, and warmth began to seep up from the table on which he was strapped. The warmth became heat, and the heat became almost unbearable. Turly squirmed and the noose tightened. He stopped and the heat increased. He involuntarily jumped, his buttocks wet and burning. The noose tightened again. It was a fiendish cycle. If the table got any hotter, he could not simply lie there; he would have to try to escape. And if he did that, he would die just as surely as if he were hanging from the end of a rope.

"What about the Blessing Papers, Turly? Tell me now before it's too late. They mean nothing to you, Turly; they can do you no good. Give me the secret now. Where are they, Turly, and how do we get to them? Tell me, Turly." Oliver loomed over Turly now, his own forehead sweating in the heat. His eyes glittered with some secret passion.

"For the Circle's sake, I don't know what they are," screamed Turly, feeling his flesh begin to burn beneath him. "I don't know. I don't know!"

Oliver reached behind him again. The heat began to subside. Oliver picked up a cup from the shelf behind him and lifted Turly's head to let him drink. All pain from the burns soon vanished. Turly felt whole and well, as if none of this had happened. He felt grateful to Oliver again. He was a friend, although Turly could not understand his part in all this. He looked up into

Oliver's face and, before slipping into the cool peace of sleep, saw through blurred eyes a look of infinite pity.

Turly drifted in a great sea of color, the sea-blue of low tides and eddies capturing easily the clarity of summer skies. The light pink of early morning, the deep liquid green of grass after rain, the garish yellows of the sun seen through squinted eyelids, all merged and flowed from unimaginable heights to yawning chasms of cloudscapes below him, parting to reveal even deeper prospects ending far, far away. Tornado funnels of mauve swung by in whirling majesty; huge galaxies of pearl-white stars revolved with glacial slowness, drifting and tilting toward him. Turly watched impassively as the kaleidoscope burst over him, rocked him, then drew him into a needle's eye of final white that sucked him quicker and quicker into dissolution.

With a final swirl of motion, Turly settled lightly onto his feet touching the gray rocks around the shores of Inniscloe Lake.

Far in the distance Turly saw Ellman coming to him in slow motion, his steps exaggerated and comic. He was waving something at Turly. Turly began to run to Ellman. He ran in the same slow motion. But the closer they came together, the faster they ran until, just before they collided, motion was normal and the concern real.

"Turly, where the demon have you been? The green riders have been here, and I thought you were lost." Ellman was younger somehow, his eyes squinting with concern and alarm.

"I have been here all along, Grandfather," said Turly. He felt groggy and uncertain. A vague menace swept over him. "Are they here now? What do they want? We have to run, to get away." Ellman held him. He had never known Ellman to be so strong. He tried to reach for him and missed. He would have to save his grandfather; take him to the cave to the north, protect him at all cost. He would do anything for Ellman. Even tell him—what? What would he tell him? They had to go. Ellman held back, looking deep within Turly's eyes.

"Turly, I've lost something and you must get it back for me." Ellman was strangely calm given the danger. *They had to get away.*

"Turly?"

"Yes, Grandfather?"

"Do you still have the map?"

"Yes."

"And the other things, you still have those?"

"Yes." He reached for the bag at his neck. It was not there. Turly struggled to find it. Ellman held him by the arms. The map, the coins, the song, all gone. What had they all meant? A strange legacy from a father he knew little about. But they must be important. Ellman was speaking. Turly had to concentrate on what he was saying.

"Turly, there is something that we must find. It is very hard to get to and very dangerous to us all, you, me, Smith, Meriwether, the Circle. We have to find it and destroy it. Do you understand, Turly?" Ellman's eyes glittered strangely. He now held Turly in a grip that caused Turly to cry out.

"I don't know what you're talking about. I don't know. Why is it dangerous? Where is it? Why is my father singing?"

Something stirred deep within Turly. He tried to catch it, to bring it to the surface, but it was more slippery than the late images of a dream upon waking. It was just fading, just out of reach. It was gone. Ellman's face was closer now, closer.

"What is it, Turly, what is it?"

"Nothing, nothing." Turly thought that he had seen Ellman's eyes somewhere else, that they had belonged to someone else. Who? Turly began to drift again, to drop upwards into the whirling clouds of color. Ellman pulled him back.

"Turly, where are the Blessing Papers? Are you going after them? Answer me."

Suddenly Turly knew who it was and it wasn't his grandfather; his grandfather was dead. Ellman's face began to fade and change, but the eyes remained the same as they looked deeply into Turly's, as if they looked deeper than Turly could know. The colors pulled him back and back into darkness.

Through a half-fog, Turly could hear voices. At first they mumbled and slurred. Then he could make out words.

". . . obviously knows nothing. He really knows nothing. He is of no further use to us. When he is able, take him to the deep vault. When I have time, I will question him on other matters. For now let him rest. I have things to see to." It was Oliver.

"What of the symbols?" said another, unfamiliar voice.

"Take them to the First Office and catalogue them with the rest. The map shows us only what we already know. The song is meaningless nonsense. Probably just a sentimental leaving. But someday it may be useful. About the coins, I don't know. They are at least of no concern to us. Do you agree?"

"Yes," said the voice.

There was the sound of soft padding as the men left, and Turly was alone. He was immensely tired. His back was again stinging with the burns, and his joints ached from his pulling and twisting against the ropes.

His head was throbbing, and his throat was dry. He tried to lick his lips but could not. He lapsed back into thoughtlessness.

Turly was first aware of an unfamiliar smell. It permeated the air and left him faint and nauseated. He rolled over and felt straw ticking beneath him. He could see nothing. He was in blackness so total that he began to hallucinate, to see colors that weren't there. His head hurt and so did his body. Reaching one hand to feel his head, he brushed against something soft and filmy. Instinctively he pulled back and tried to stare into the velvet darkness. There was nothing. Of how long he had been there, he had no idea.

Time was suspended. Turly lay dreaming of his past. He began to recollect all that he had known of his father. The huge head, the balding top covered by wispy strands of reddish hair. Sitting on his lap, the deep bass of his voice crooning softly to him of fairy tales and nonsense rhymes that circled and returned to a single refrain.

Fol de rol de rolly o.

A line that meant at the same time hope, disdain, unconcern and the deepest despair. Why had his father loved it so? Of all the rhymes he must have known to be able to sing so well, why did this one, repeated over and over again, hold so much attraction for him?

Fol de rol de rolly o.

That's the way he felt right now. Full of unconcern and despair. He did not know when, or if, he would ever return to his quest. It seemed at a dead end. He was being held for some unknown reason, for Circle know how long, in some vast underground cavern. His friends did not know where he was.

Turly slept fitfully.

When he woke again, he was momentarily confused.

Then he remembered, and he noticed that his pains were lessened. Perhaps Oliver had given him something to heal the wounds as well as make him dream of Ellman.

He was now ravenously hungry. He could still see or hear nothing, and could only surmise that they meant him to be hungry. Perhaps they meant him to starve here, to wither away in the darkness. Turly groaned for the hundredth time.

This time there was an answer.

"Are you awake, then?"

"Who is it?"

"Sean. I've heard you, and I thought me heart would break with the hearing. And me destroyed with me own tears."

"Are you a prisoner, too?" asked Turly. He was glad to have a companion of any kind, even one that by the sound of his voice must have come from the worst part of the island.

"And me after telling you as much! I'd teach you manners, and there's a truth." The unseen voice sounded truculent.

"Where are you?" Turly asked softly.

"Here, I'm right here. Are you blind, then?" The voice also had a touch of merriment about it.

Turly strained his eyes and thought he caught the barest hint of something in one corner, or what he thought was a corner. There was a sound of rustling and clicking.

"What are you?" Turly had grown alarmed. He imagined himself being torn to pieces for his few bits of clothing.

"Well, I am Sean." This was followed by a long, low laugh. It ended with a coughing fit. Whoever or whatever it was, it was sick, thought Turly. Small wonder in this place. It was damp and cold. But that answered only part of the question. The man was a prisoner, too. Why?

As if reading his mind, Sean spoke aloud. "We're trapped down here until they choose to see us again."

"They?" asked Turly.

"Why, don't you know? You have the honor of being the guest of the Order of Zeno." Turly noticed that the other man had dropped his affected way of talking. Obviously, he was a man who had been many places.

"The Order of Zeno?" It sounded strange. It was something Turly knew nothing about, but the orange robes, the green turtle and arrow insignia must mean something.

"You noticed the turtles and the arrows, did you?" The voice was no closer, but seemed more intimate now. A conspiratorial note had crept in. Turly was cautious but had nothing to lose.

"I did. Is it a religious order here in the south?"

"It is. And I am not reluctant to tell you that I wish I were somewhere else. The Order of Zeno is notorious where I'm from, and that's a fact."

"What is it they profess, and what do they want?" Turly noticed the cell seemed to be growing clearer, as if light were seeping in at a very slow rate. He could see what seemed to be a door and bars. He could see no windows.

"No one really knows. But this I do know. They would as soon carve you into bits as look at you. I swear by the stars they're as mean a lot as I've run into, and I've run into lots."

The man's voice was bitter as he spoke. Turly could discern an outline squatting to his right. A long beard and rags were all he could tell for sure.

"They believe in the paradox of the arrow and the turtle," said Sean.

"Paradox?"

"Yes. If you shoot an arrow in the air, does it come down?"

"Of course." Turly was annoyed. They should not be playing games, but trying to escape.

"Well, but does the arrow on its flight occupy a place in space?"

"Certainly it does. What are you trying to say?"

"Wait a moment, now. You've asked a question of me, and I'm trying to answer to the best of my weak ability. Now, when a thing occupies a place, is it at rest?"

"Well, yes. It is motionless in that place."

"Exactly. So the arrow is at rest at each stage of its flight and therefore will never come down." There was a tone of triumph in Sean's voice. He chuckled aloud.

"But that's absurd. Anything that is thrown up will come down," sputtered Turly. "That's so much nonsense."

"Not in logic. Consider the turtle that the Order is so fond of. If you were to race a turtle, after giving it a decent start, would you win?"

"I should hope so," said Turly, who was more and more amused in spite of himself.

"But between you and the turtle are a series of points. Yes? And are these points divisible or indivisible?"

"Divisible, of course."

"Yes, indeed, lad, for they are *something,* they have magnitude. But is there a point where you must stop dividing, where you run out of points?"

"There must be . . ."

"Are any of the points within the line without magnitude?"

"No, if one has it, all do, I guess." Turly was feeling light-headed.

"Then all are divisible, and you will never reach a point where you cannot divide them. Thus the line is of infinite distance since its parts are infinite. You will never reach the turtle because that turtle, once ahead of you, will always be at a new point, however closer you are to it. You will have to cross an infinite distance to get to it, and that you cannot do." Sean seemed to grin across the darkness.

"And that, my good man, is the tale of the arrow and turtle, and that's the truth." The light was a little brighter and Turly's eyes keener. He could see a shaggy head shaking.

Turly could hold himself no longer. "But that means nothing. It means that motion is not real, and I can tell like the nose on my face that it is real."

"Tell that to the monks, my boy, not to me."

"But what do they hope to show with all that?" Turly was both amused and agitated. He knew the monks could do better than that. He remembered Oliver's cloud illusion. He told Sean about it, and Sean listened attentively.

"Yes, they are able somehow to create such illusion, although I did not know that Oliver was capable of *that* one. I shall be more careful; if, of course, I ever get out of here. I might also sing you the holy jingle that is the Inner Hymn of the Order of Zeno. It may tell you something else, although I don't know what. Here it goes."

In a high-pitched, chanting wail Sean began to sing the words:

The arrow that is shot will never land
The race that is run will never be done
The ship that leaves will never arrive
The box that is seen will never be known!

Turly was mystified. What the demon did that mean?
He shrugged. The logic of most Circle Orders he was
familiar with. But this Order's logic seemed to have only
mystery and absurdity as its basis.

His head was beginning to hurt again. Sean had
grown quiet, listening. Turly heard something as well.
It was the sound of running feet.

The steps died away, but Turly thought he could
hear low murmuring far down the corridor. He turned
to Sean. The light was even better now and Turly could
see that Sean was gone. There was now only a pile of
ragged clothes bunched up over a small crate near the
corner where he had been. But as Turly watched, Sean
reappeared from under the rags.

"You've got an escape route!" whispered Turly.

"Indeed I do. But there's no place to escape to, unfortunately. I was checking to see what the commotion
was. It seems that you're marked to go."

"Go? Where? Why should I?" Turly did not like the
implication.

"Never have I seen a man so imbued with his own
importance," said Sean. "You are going, of course, to
your death. Didn't Oliver say something about it when
last you met?"

"Nothing to me. He did say to another that I was no
longer of use to them."

"Well, that's it, then." Sean rubbed his beard. "We've
got to use my route whether there's an end to it or not."
He motioned to Turly. "Come over here if you can."

Turly lifted his sore but useable feet off the mat. He

stepped gingerly over the cold stones to the corner. In the dark of the cell his hair glowed lightly with a life of its own. He squinted at Sean who was less than a meter from him and whose body was half-in and half-out of the box on the floor. Turly could see that Sean's eyes were bright, devious and cunning, but he knew that in this situation he had no choice. Whether he stayed and was possibly executed by the Order of Zeno or went with Sean to an uncertain fate, there was really no choice whatever. It was not the first time Turly felt caught between two such horns. He moved with what grace he could muster beneath the box.

Sean had secreted a few small tapers in the tunnel. As they crawled further into the passage Turly noticed drafts of air moving across the flames from time to time. Sean explained that he had merely found a natural underground ventilating system unknown to or unused by the Order, and he also allowed that he deserved the title of Best Scout in the island for finding it. The system had been extensively explored by Sean, but no real exit out of the mountain caves had been discovered by him. There were numerous outlets which abrupted on sheer cliffs, but offered no way down, and outlets into various Order rooms. The two men were committed to the passages. There was no way back.

Sean paused. He whispered to Turly to keep quiet and reached back to grab him by the hair. He pulled Turly's head forward and directed his eyes to one tiny hole looking out on the corridor that led to the room they had just left. In the corridor, he could see the flickering lights of a procession of some kind.

Turly soon heard noises: the shuffling of many feet, the jangle of keys, the chuckle of those keys being turned in a lock, the creak of a door opening, cries of rage and alarm, robes swishing, feet running back the way they had come. The last flickers of the torches vanished.

Turly felt himself shiver. He and Sean had been discovered as missing. It would be only a matter of time before they were flushed out. He sat back in the narrow tunnel and breathed deeply; he felt afraid but also excited, even exhilarated. His fatigue dropped from him and the old joy of seeking answers came to him again. Fire seemed to lick at his heart. It felt good now. Sean stirred next to him.

"Well, and the fret is on me. We have made it this far, however. If they knew of the tunnel, we'd already be taken. Or maybe," he said, rubbing a chin hidden in the dark, "they know we have no way out." Sean started forward again, hurrying this time.

The two traveled in darkness for some time. Turly's hands and knees were getting shakier as they went along on all fours. He had not fully recovered from the interrogation by Oliver. The excitement and joy he had felt ebbed with the passage of time. But he was determined to escape and get word about the Order to Smith and the others. Someone—either Hastings or the Order of Zeno —was definitely behind the troubles in the north. Perhaps the Order controlled the green riders. No. If that were so, they would also control the red soldiers from whom Oliver had ferreted him away. The Order must owe allegiance to someone other than Hastings. To whom then? The question pained Turly's mind. The man Hastings was enough of a problem, now he had Oliver, too. This shook Turly. But he was now familiar somewhat with Oliver. That still left Hastings.

Hastings.

A man of enigma and power. A man remembered from youth. What was *his* purpose? He would have to wait his turn, grinned Turly, until he dealt with the Order of maniacs he had been tricked into visiting.

Sean looked back at Turly. They were crawling in single file through dank passages of solid rock. On each side there sprouted smaller passageways leading off into even darker parts of the mountain. Sean urged Turly not to get lost or separated from him as some of the passages had not been explored by him and contained certain unnamed dangers. Turly shuddered as the breeze from one such opening blew a sickening odor across his face. Turly crawled a little closer to Sean to avoid making a wrong turn. He had no desire to strike out on his own at this point. His shoulders were aching now, and the thin scar on his arm began to twinge. He felt it with each arm-step forward.

Sean yelled. Something hairy flung itself at Turly's head. Turly ducked, but not before tiny teeth could sink into his tunic at the shoulder. Turly swore and struck out blindly. His hands caught sleek fur and held on. The furry body twisted and jerked in his hand. Turly felt sick but knew that in such dark, confined quarters this thing was at an advantage. He had to hold on. His fingers inched forward to its throat. He squeezed. A shrill sound broke the air open. In his surprise Turly almost let go. He felt Sean groping for the thing in his hands and warned him back. There was a distinct crack, and the thing went limp. Turly dropped it in disgust.

The candle had gone out. Sean relit it, and the flickering light showed an enormous rat-like creature lying twisted on the floor of the passage. Sean spat. It was about the size of a small dog. He placed back into his belt a wicked-looking knife Turly did not know he had.

"I've seen rats," said Sean, "but not like this one. We've got to be on our guard now. These things must be fearless, not having seen man before. I've heard them, but have never seen them before now. A good thing. You were lucky to get a quick grip on it; it could have chewed us to ribbons."

"Sean, we've got to find a way out of here. Take me to one of the holes looking out over the mountains. Let's see if we can't crawl out and down."

"Fine lad, but I'm telling you, you can't do it." Sean started out again, this time more cautious of the side outlets.

They soon reached a point where good, fresh air blew directly on their faces. Turly could see blue light ahead and raced to it on all fours. He breathed deeply in great gulps. Looking out he could see that Sean was right. The mountains stretched into the distance, snow covering only the tallest peaks, jagged teeth in a huge jaw. Below them was a sheer drop to nothingness. He perched on the ledge, which pouted like a lip below the mouth of the opening; for several moments he enjoyed the view and forgot that his life was in great danger.

"Turly, we've got to keep going," said Sean. "There may be an unguarded way out through the regular quarters. We'll go down into the living complex and look for a chance to escape there."

Turly agreed. That would seem to be the best alternative. The mountain slopes were denied to them, so the lower levels offered the only exit. He thought of the huge door and shrugged. Maybe there were other such doors elsewhere. He would worry about that when he came to it.

Sean turned back the way they had come, but at one point slanted off and began to wind downhill, his pace a little faster. The darkness was relieved now by a number of small outlets pointing into what seemed to be habitable rooms of the Order. Sean and Turly could hear low conversations as they silently passed the air ducts.

Sean stopped at one of them, inched forward and looked carefully into a room dimly lit. He motioned with his hand to Turly, who crept to the opening and looked down. Within was a room lined with books, and there was only a single monk to guard them. They were in luck.

Chapter 8

Dermot sat with his angular, bony face buried like a hatchet in the pile of manuscripts open on the table before him. A special scholar-monk of the Order of Zeno, Dermot's concentration was intense. His studies had been going extremely well and he was pleased with himself. But a particular problem had to be solved, and proof for the solution found so that he could finish his important long article "Continuity and Disintegration: The Blessing Papers and the Council of Methe."

Publication of this article in the *Order Bulletin* would make him eligible for Inner Order status. For even though Dermot knew every paradox of the Order by heart, could recite all the creeds, sing all its hymns perfectly, the rules were clear. Inner Order membership required a significant contribution to the furthering of the mission of the Order: the finding of the Blessing Papers. It also required the publication of such a contribution.

Raising a long skinny arm to his ear, Dermot jiggled the wax there with his index finger. His ungainly feet, coated loosely with leather sandals, shuffled and scraped under the big table. Dermot drew back and looked steadily at all the material he had gathered. It had not been long ago that Dermot had thought he might have to spend his life buried in the Order caves to puzzle out just one aspect of the Council that had led to the hated Mythic Sequence Church. But the energy that kept him going at the Council problem now, and in a way that seemed to justify his whole life, was his discovery that the solution to one problem might well lead to the solution of the other.

Dermot felt he would soon be able to *prove* to Oliver what he had already suggested to him as a very real possibility. Oliver had been quite skeptical about an heir to the Blessing Papers and had sent Dermot back to the library for more work. But Dermot was feeling good about it and believed that it was just a matter of time before he had his proof. A little more scratching, digging and prodding of the materials he already had. That would do it, he knew it.

The scruffy monk returned to the old documents about the Council of Methe of 2019 when the merger of science and religion had first been announced. Council literature, the bibliography of which Dermot himself had compiled, was not extensive. He thumbed through one of the fragile pamphlets at random. It was a fragment of Marcel Cosmos' *The Mythic Topography*. Dermot's finger followed the words on the third page:

A principal enemy of the early science and religion movement was Christianity. About 2017 the movement followers provided a refutation of Christian dogma and put in its place a dogma based on mythic and scientific writ . . .

Dermot did not fully understand what "science," "religion" or "Christianity" meant. But he knew what the Order of Zeno was, and he turned rapidly to an earlier volume. It was a brief anthology of selections from the Edict of York, 2018. It contained passages detested by the Order, and Dermot gritted his teeth as he read it:

> . . . we were fortunately met in official power and were considering everything that pertained to the public welfare and security. We thought that, among other things which we saw would be good for the good of many, those regulations governing the merger of spirit and science ought certainly to be made first . . .

Dermot mused over this point as he had done many times. By allowing advocates of such a merger legitimacy in both civil and ecclesiastical law, the door was wide open for the successful union of what would later become Circle doctrine—although a much-changed doctrine. Dermot moaned. What idiots! Hadn't they known? Hadn't they guessed?

When the Falling and the Fires had come in 2020, the seeds of the detested Circles were already there in the Church of Spirit and Science. Dermot stopped momentarily to wonder again why the *dates* of these events were known by all, but few knew the particulars of them. He shrugged because there was no answer he knew of. It was a mystery to more than one man, Dermot knew that. He continued to leaf through pages as he mused on the Falling.

The merger of spirit and science seemed to have forced up something that should have been left hidden. What that was exactly, and why there had been such a total collapse of all authority and order in the nations of the world, was unclear.

Dermot toyed with those images for a while. The pieces coming apart and lying scattered about like a child's puzzle. What had cut the world into pieces? What had flung about the nations of the world? The questions swept Dermot into a revery in which he could not think of anything but the violence of destruction, images of disintegration. The images confused him. They rolled in his mind but did not stick anywhere.

The Order monk had to wrench himself away from the images exploding in his head. He turned back to the words in his research work and, as he did so, felt better. Even though there were only a few histories left, and these were fragmented, he did have them to work with. Partial stories of the time were wrapped in loss like a fog. The fragments he was looking at were of the groups of oral historians and poets who had traveled in the north before the Circles had truly hardened into close-mouthed tightness.

The xenophobic Circles—the hated Circles—grinned Dermot. The folk of the Circles were hardly more than throwbacks, ancient relics of a time that *should* have been forgotten, he thought. They were, by their very existence, holding everything back. Their absurd sense of cyclic motion in life and time was dominant in the north, and it kept influences from the south at a minimum. The Circle was a guardian of the north. Why that should be so was also a mystery to Dermot, but not an important one. If the Circle had such a strong hold up there, one that could prevent the Order of Zeno from coming in, Dermot had found that it could also be helpful in giving up some of the missing pieces of the puzzle of the past. Important pieces.

The Inner Order did not know this, chuckled Dermot.

He had given Oliver some of his knowledge, yes, but not all, not yet. The monk who looked like an abused puppet reflected that the Inner Order had tried for years to find a way around the Mythic Sequence, but with little success. He knew that they thought the answer to the Order's problem of extending the Order throughout the island lay in the Blessing Papers. The fabled Blessing Papers.

Dermot agreed. The Papers were supposed to contain the secret of the Falling and a way to achieve the power to restore a union. The Papers were supposed to explain all. Therefore they *might* be used to further the aims of the Order. These things Order novices would argue about late into the night. Some would say the Papers were good and should be used by the Order to save the island; others that they should be destroyed to prevent others from using them for any purpose. But in either case they had to be found. In this sense the Blessing Papers were a nightmare obsession, a dark dream of peace and dominance that had been the Order's burden and its hope after man's lapse into savagery.

But whether help or hindrance, whether damnation or salvation, the Papers were the rightful property of the Order, all the monks agreed on that. To this end the ranks of monks had bent their intellects and their labors. They would walk among men seeking out any clue; track down any man who might be of any help to them; check any cave or vault that might serve as a hiding place for the Papers. And, more important, scholar-monks like Dermot would study all records of the past in order to find the string that led through the tunnel.

Through his studies Dermot knew that the major political leader of the south, Lord Hastings of Straiten, was the only man who could presently threaten their mastery in this matter, rival their cunning. Some thought he knew even more about the past than the Order. Dermot dismissed that, but he knew that if Hastings should find the Papers first, and the Order was aware that he had been trying to do so for years, he could wreak havoc on the Order's plans. He might be able to wield unlimited power in forming an island union of his own, bending to himself the allegiance perhaps of more than the rival Imram factions. *Perhaps even of those beyond the island.* Beyond the vast waters. A union of the fallen world.

Dermot shook his shaggy head. His neck bobbed loosely like a toy as he denied to himself the existence of any power that was not the Order of Zeno. It would be incomprehensible. Only legend.

No, thought Dermot, the island was the only place, the Order the only power. The Blessing Papers had to be found by the Order, and its union of all things into Pure Being made at last. And he was the one to find the Papers, he knew it. He stretched in his bare wooden seat and yawned. He thought he could find the Papers now because he had stumbled onto something, after much study and research, that even Oliver had given *some* credence to. Hints had been found in one of the oldest remnants of the past he had.

It was a fragment of a letter. No opening, no closing. Only a few words. Dermot's fingers shook slightly as he held up the brown scrap. He read it silently: ". . . would result in a child to the North into whose hands the history would fall . . . could then recover the things we talked about earlier. Watch for him . . . with hair necessarily like milk, the sun or moon for . . . and those . . ."

Every waking hour for several months Dermot had secreted himself in the Order library, putting it together,

113

piecing and arranging the tiny bits of Imramian history that had survived the Falling and the Fires, the only good pieces available in the island as far as he knew. The possible connection of events was startling to contemplate. Running from the ill-fated Council of Methe to the rise of Hastings was a conspiracy of enormous proportions. And from that conspiracy, and its tangled branches, Dermot had seen the possibility and he held it dear. Leafing through his article manuscript, he found the lines where he had expressed it:

There is now living in Imram one person who knows the whereabouts of the Blessing Papers. A man with hair like the silver of the moon.

The knowledge which he had gleaned trembled on Dermot's lips as he pronounced the sentence aloud. It hung in the still, musty air of the library like an intruder. But it sounded good to Dermot and he repeated it. It was his truth; he had found it buried in the past. Even though absolute proof was lacking, and might always be if he didn't keep looking, Dermot was confident that soon he would have enough evidence to fully convince Oliver. He might even learn where the man could be located. The Order would have him then, the man who knew the secret they all were seeking, and it would be able to force him to reveal his solitary knowledge.

Dermot sighed and bent back to his work. He shuffled through some of the documents he had used, checking them for possible errors. While his studies had been thorough, he wanted to go over them all again, hoping this time for a word, a phrase, that would send him like an arrow to the target. There were several paragraphs to rewrite, some footnote citation to do, and the article would be that much closer to publication. It would startle the Order.

Dermot picked up the obscure Fulhaven text that

tried, unsuccessfully, to trace the aftermath of the Council of Methe, but it made only vague allusions to the Falling. Dermot knew that the history of the Falling, and of the Fires that followed, was hazy. Why shouldn't it be? he thought. Other than a general belief that the merger of spirit and science had done it, no one knew *exactly* what had caused a fall from heights which no one could see the peaks of. They knew only that it had happened. But if the key people involved in the Council meeting were named, then their descendents could be identified and located. That was what Dermot was after, and he leafed feverishly through page after page of the old book. The monk mopped his brow several times, shook the sweat from his hand, let it spatter on the library floor. Order of Zeno! he cursed.

Dermot stopped on the last page. The first three sentences were underlined in red. He had underlined them. The words were still enigmatic to him, as provocative as the first time he had read them. They spoke of the Falling as the "result of the wedding of two things, their union, the shock of their gathering. The shock continues." Dermot looked up at a crack in the library wall. He knew the shocks continued. A general fragmentation of all old unions had spread for decades after the first jolt, and men had in only a few generations lost almost all ties with the past. Few had passed on anything of value about the time before the shock, and students of that period—what students there were—had failed to research the situation as well as they might have done, thought Dermot angrily. He was infuriated at the skimpy records and personal diaries of the early period which gave only the merest hints about those involved in the "wedding of two things," and the terrible result of their union.

Dermot ruffled through his other notes and scratched

his itchy scalp. The past rose up again like a giant empty board, and he was frustrated anew. Then he seemed to hear around him the plangent voices of the dead, their serried rows moving in precise timing like the waves of the sea, washing upon him their warning and their cry: *We must not be denied our rest, our forgetfulness, the promise that was given. You must save us and our children. You must return to us all the world of our fathers, the world that was before Imram and the burning. The motionlessness of Pure Being.*

Dermot squirmed in pleasure as he thought of Pure Being. The Order would wait till the right moment and then return man to his rightful place in the world, his only place. Unity under one banner, the Order's banner, the banner of Oneness and necessary paradox. The Order would allow man to be man forever in a state in which there would be no need for a return, as Circle dogma wrongly thought, since there would be no leaving of it. There was powerful emotion in Dermot's breast, and the creeds of the Order, written by John Vail, sprang to his mind. Motion is an illusion. Sequence doesn't begin. Nothing can arrive over an infinite distance. A box that is seen will never be known. Man is man.

The scholar-monk thought the voices of the dead cried for all the things they had been denied for so long, their impotent frustration drawing the faces in Dermot's mind into grimaces of pain and rage. He had trembled, and trembled now, and turned away, dedicated, each time he heard them. He felt the awesome responsibility of his self-appointed task. He was to serve the dead. And to serve them meant that he had to find and use something that was legend, and to find the man who might come to deny the swarming dead their due. It was an urgent task he had. He *would* do it.

There, that should satisfy even the ravenous dead, thought Dermot. When the Papers were found, legend or not, the Order would restore the island and man would be able to begin his rise away from the Circles. There were certain heresies to be overcome, of course, even within the Order itself. But they were no longer troublesome obstacles, thanks to Oliver. Oh, the good day would come. Dermot grinned and shuffled his massive feet. That was a day to prepare for. A day to reach for—and he, Dermot, would share in its glory.

Dermot heard a thump behind him. He looked over his shoulder and almost fell out of his chair. As if conjured by his own thoughts, a man with silver-white hair stood with sturdy parted legs and glowered at Dermot through furious green eyes.

Chapter 9

Turly's knees, elbows and shoulder hurt. He was ready to kill the Order monk in front of him, but restrained himself for good reason. He and Sean had to get out of the cave of the Order of Zeno, and they could not do so alone. The monk had to remain alive and be made to lead them to the nearest exit; and from the look of him, it would be an easy task. The man was clearly a book-worm, a pedant, one who spent his whole life amidst the works of others, who lived in somebody else's book.

The idea was repugnant to Turly, and he instinctively bunched his shoulder muscles and felt the ripple under his tunic. He would as soon die as be accused of such an atrocious affront to nature.

Sean had leaped down behind Turly. Not captured by the piles of rotting books or the thoughts of men who rot with them, Sean had his blade at the ready. He coughed into one hand and moved cautiously around Turly toward the monk who was cringing against the large wooden table where he had been working. The monk was still staring at Turly with what seemed to be fear and wonder. Well, thought Sean, why not? He had himself been taken by Turly's physical appearance. The curly white hair, the striking green eyes that changed, he noticed, as Turly's mood changed from calm to anger. The supple olive body tanned by the sun and honed to perfection by labor and hunting skills. The intense face with the red mole over the right eye that seemed the only defect in an otherwise hypnotic visage, hinting at more than physical capabilities.

Dermot had shifted his stare from Turly to Sean. He now saw the look of hate that emanated from the smaller man with the knife, and he began to back away around the table. If he could get to the door, he thought, he could raise an alarm and the prize would be his.

Capturer of the man with the white hair!

It was enough to make Dermot dizzy with the prospects. Within his grasp was the man whom, by his studies, he had determined to be the *one* man who could find the Blessing Papers. As a result he was extremely dangerous to the Order, and if he did not give them the secret, must be either killed or locked away forever. Did Oliver know, he wondered, that within this very mountain cavern was a man fated to undo all their work? Dermot was preoccupied with two things: the danger presented by Sean and the capture of Turly.

Dermot was snapped back to reality by two other things.

The first was a leg of the huge table that had little regard for the size or ungainliness of the monk's feet. Turning rapidly and making a break for the door, the tall, skinny monk caught his left foot under the leg and went down in a mad flurry of flapping robes and flailing arms. His orange hood whipped up over his head and blinded him as he thrashed to and fro on the floor.

The second thing was the knife at his throat as he rolled over and peered up out of his hood. Not a third of a meter from his face was the smaller man who glared at him with what Dermot could only describe as hate. He felt this might be the end. He closed his eyes and prayed to Zeno, his forehead gleaming with moist fervor.

Sean wanted to plunge his blade into the monk's throat. He touched the sallow skin with the point of his knife and drew blood, a drop that hung on Dermot's neck like a tiny ruby.

"Sean, no!" It was Turly.

"But this ass could give us away," choked Sean.

"Maybe. That's a chance we'll have to take. He knows the way out, and we don't."

Sean saw the wisdom of this approach. He lowered the knife after assuring the monk that he was more than ready to reapply it if the need arose.

Turly walked up to the sloppily robed monk and grabbed him by the front folds. Looking deep into Dermot's eyes, Turly stood silent for several minutes. He was momentarily uncertain of his course. It struck him that he had thought he had been buried for good back in the Order cell. He had gotten out. He thought he had been trapped in the winding maze of natural ventilation shafts. He had gotten out. But he was still deep in the mountain caves of the Order of Zeno, a strange group whose complete motives he did not know. He felt the vast weight of rock arching over his head. Many times before he thought fate had touched him, had guided his every movement. For what purpose had he been saved all these years? He did not know, but part of his journey now included this scruffy monk and he must trust him.

"Monk, do you know Oliver of your Order?"

"I do, yes, yes, I do know Oliver, yes, yes." At the mention of the Head of the Order, Dermot was startled. Did Oliver after all know of the white-haired one? If so, his theory had been believed. He had been elevated to status of Researcher Extraordinaire by the Inner Council because of his discoveries of the documents of the Council of Methe and the notes of its aftermath, but he had been denied Inner Order status until such an insight about the white-haired man could be proved.

Dermot had thought that Oliver himself had dismissed his assertion that there was one who possessed the secret of the Blessing Papers. Evidently he had not.

Dermot's fury began to rise. He had been used and then betrayed by Oliver. Oliver had stolen his moment of glory. Well, he would confront Oliver later. Now he had to devise a way to capture this man and turn him to his own use.

Turly's grip had tightened on Dermot. He did not like the shifty look in the monk's eyes which spoke of oiliness and ingratiation. It spoke, too, of betrayal at the first opportunity. That could not be helped. Turly would have to force the monk to take them to the nearest exit and hope that they could get there and out with a minimum of trouble. There was no other way that Turly knew of. He no longer had his coins, map, or song, although he knew the latter two things by heart.

"Monk," asked Turly, "is there an opening to the outside other than through the Great Doors at the front?"

"Oh, yes, there is," stammered Dermot. The back way, he thought, they wanted the back way, the way that leads by the Gabble. "There is a back way that leads south, to Straiten."

"Then by all that's bloody, take us to it," said Turly. *Straiten*. He thought that was better than he could have hoped for. The red soldiers were heading for Straiten

121

and Hastings Hall. He did not know how long he had been here. But going over the mountains the soldiers could not have made such good time that he and Sean could not catch them. And if Sean was as good a scout and tracker as he had said he was, they should make good time on the downward slopes of the Lower Mountains.

"Sean, take the front. The monk will be in the middle. I'll follow up. And you, Monk, Sean still has his blade and I my hands. Either of us would be happy to kill you. Do you understand?"

"Oh, I do, I do. There will be no trouble if you don't hurt me. I'm only an humble scholar of the Order, sir. I mean no harm to anyone. Only tell me, sir, did you talk to Oliver?"

Turly looked at the monk and laughed.

"Do you see my tatters, Monk? The burns on my backside, would you like to see those? Yes, I've seen your Oliver and could I get my hands on him I would restrict his throat."

Dermot gulped. "He knows you're here, then?"

"Oh, he knows. And by now he knows I'm missing from the cell he provided me and from the death he had planned."

"Death? Oliver was going to sacrifice you to Zeno?"

"Is that what it's called?" said Turly. "Well, I'll not wait for it, no matter what it's called."

Dermot was numb. Oliver had known of the white-haired man and had ordered his death. Had he also called a Trial Council and not included Dermot? That couldn't be. Oliver knew Dermot's interest in the matter and would have sent for him. Unless Oliver did not want him to know. Perhaps Oliver was more jealous of his work than he knew. Dermot thought that he would have to be more careful with Oliver.

Turly pushed the monk toward Sean. Sean took him by the arm and propelled him to the library entrance. The door there was of polished wood, dark and seemingly ageless as it swung open on silent hinges. Sean looked right and left in the corridor. He could see no one. He slipped out and pulled Dermot with him. Turly took one last look around, saw nothing unusual, and pulled the door closed behind him.

The outer passage stretched long and dark in both directions. Sean looked back to the cringing monk and jerked his thumb up and down the hall. Which way? he asked silently.

Dermot pointed to the left. He would have to do their bidding in one respect, he mused. He must not run into his fellow monks until he was ready to. He would not have his glory snatched from him this time. He would take the two men to the Gabble and let it do its work. He would have a struggle, he knew, to stay Gabble from the white-haired one, but he would give the other to him and that should be sufficient. Then he, Dermot, would have the legend in his hands.

The three walked in silence. The monk padded along in a slouch, his shoulder dipping to the right with each step, his gangly legs and arms moving constantly. Turly could not help but chuckle as he watched the monk's progress. The man was comic, he thought; but he may well kill us, and we almost certainly will have to kill him. This was not what he had wanted years ago, sitting around the fire at evening with Ellman. One of his ambitions then was to continue fishing as a living. He had been good at it. He had wanted Meriwether to choose him and they would live there by the water. That life was a peaceful scene, but Turly remembered it now with a feeling of sorrow. The notion of peace was lost forever, he knew that. At least until Meriwether was found. Then for a moment he thought Meriwether had touched his mind. With the merest hint of motion, like the brush of butterfly wings, she hovered there with the promise of the complete fulfillment of all that he wished. He shook his head and wondered if it were memory only.

The three men came to a crossroads in the semi-darkness. One passage reached ahead into a deeper dark. The other wound to the left in a downward slope. Dermot motioned to the left, and they began to slant down in a gently winding path that was less worn by feet than the one they had been on. The walls were narrower here and the group walked closer together as if in response. Their pace slowed as well.

"Monk," said Sean, "if you are leading us into the hands of your people, I must tell you that you will never know that we were captured. You will be the first to fall." Sean was explicit as he slid the knife across his throat in pantomime.

"I assure you that this is the way to the back gate, sir," said Dermot. "We must change paths two more times and then you will be out. But, sirs, I must also tell you that there are many perils for which I cannot be responsible. I can only lead you to the gate, I cannot stop the Order itself."

"Do your job, Monk. That will be enough." But Sean was troubled and he showed his worry with brusqueness. He turned, glanced back at Turly, and wondered what was driving the man. He knew Turly must be important, or the Order would not have taken him. Sean knew *he* had been taken by the monks because he knew all the routes over and around the mountain ranges of Imram. He had spent his life hunting in the mountains. He had been hunting when the Order took him with an illusion of cold that had put him to sleep. And then this man with unusual hair had been put in his cell with him. Why? There were other cells as good, or bad, he thought. Something tugged at his mind.

He stopped. *It had been by design!*

"Turly!" whispered Sean urgently.

"Yes, Sean." Turly moved up next to Sean who had placed one hand on the monk. Turly noted the new look of concern on the smaller man's face. The large nose, rounded forehead and brown eyes, reddened somewhat now, were framed in straggly brown hair.

"They may have planned this. They may have put you in my cell knowing I had an escape route. All of this may be designed to catch you at the end, or to allow them to follow you to wherever they mean for you to go." Sean was nervous but not afraid.

"That may be," allowed Turly. "But Oliver could not know *where* we would come out of the shafts. And that gives us an edge over him. We've got to keep on now and be ready for any surprise." Turly was edgy. It had also occurred to him that the Order had wanted him to escape. It was odd that his cellmate had had an escape route planned and ready to work. He had suspected Sean, but had not said so for obvious reasons. This announcement by Sean might lessen the possibility that he was working for the Order, but it did not remove it. He would get to the opening to the outside and then decide what had to be done.

The corridors showed signs of general disuse. Dust lay on the floor, and they could see no footprints of any kind except theirs. Glancing behind, Turly could see their prints stretch into the dim distance, and he had an eerie feeling that the ghostly markings were following them in a never-ending chase, always leading up to their heels but never quite reaching them and never quite giving up. But there was no sign of Oliver or the

Order. Perhaps Sean had been wrong and there was no plan and no trap. Turly's scar was tingling, and it usually tingled when there was danger, immediate danger. But Turly could see or hear nothing but the puffing of the skinny monk who was tripping all over himself in front.

They were passing now into an area that broadened into an arched platform, solid rock to the right and slitted openings off and down to the left. From within the slits light began to filter out as if the sun were rising in a cold dawn. The group stopped. There were voices.

"Quick," said the monk. "Back this way." Dermot pulled Sean's sleeve and pointed back the way they had come. It would be the Vail Session, in honor of the Founder of the Order. Every four months a procession would wind down into the deepest bowels of the earth to light tapers at the shrine to Vail. Acolytes normally were involved but sometimes higher levels participated. It was not a High Ceremony because the body of Vail had never been found. Until that was done, the ceremony would be secret and for the edification of the lower levels only. Dermot did not want to be discovered yet and so urged his captors to pull back into the relative safety of the passage which the procession would not take.

Flickering torches soon came into view, and shadows bounced to and fro in response. A line of monks, ten in all, came into view through one of the larger slits, rising from the steps that had led upward from a lower entrance. The monks moved away and down the opposite route. The light faded into nothingness.

"Where now, Monk?" said Sean. He raised his blade menacingly.

"Down the steps," whispered Dermot. "We have not far to go, but we must be careful if we are not to be

126

surprised. This level has more traffic than the others above. We were in an unused section of the library system where only the most rare of books are kept. I am," he declared with a certain pride in his voice, "one of the few who have permission to use that area."

Turly snorted. He did not trust the monk, but he did seem to be taking care that they not be seen. That was in his favor. They had come this far without incident. Perhaps he would make it out after all. Well . . . but he would not look to the last sequence until the whole had been run.

"Lead on, Monk."

They went off to the left and down the steps and out the entrance from which the procession had just come. For another hour or so they followed the monk's directions. A final branch had been taken. Soon Turly could notice a change in their surroundings. It was colder, for one thing. The air was easier to breathe, with less of a musty odor. They must be close to the outside. The thought spurred Turly on. He brushed by the orange-clad monk and saw a thin point of light far in the distance. It had to be the way out.

Sean yelled as Turly began to trot toward the light. To Turly it seemed very far away, like a child's voice at the top of a hill, muffled and indistinct. No matter. If this was the way out, there would be plenty of time for resting and the working of plans. He felt he had wings as the darkness slipped from him and the open air pulled him on. He was in a dream of floating effortlessly down vast distances, after the goal he had wanted all his life. There were Meriwether and Ellman gathered to meet him, and two figures he could not make out. His father and mother. They were here, and they were waiting for him. There could be no mistake. His father's head bobbed benignly, and his thin red hair diffused the light like a halo. His mother was tall and beautiful and raised her arms to beckon him to her. He was there. He was home and nothing would ever be the same.

He was running now with the ease of a youth spent in pursuit of wild rabbits in the flat marshland around Inniscloe Lake. He breathed effortlessly. He knew Sean and the monk were behind him; he could hear their cries and their footsteps beating irregularly on the flat stone passage. *Let them catch up if they are with me,* thought Turly. *I am free again.*

He watched the tiny opening as it widened. It jerked only slightly as he ran.

His mother opened her arms wide to receive him.

Turly hesitated. His scar twitched, the butterfly wings brushed his mind again with more urgency. What was it about his mother? He was puzzled, and beads of perspiration burst out on his forehead. He slowed to a walk.

Someone tackled him around the ankles, and he went down heavily. He rolled over and over clutching at his feet. It was Sean. So Sean *was* with the Order. He was trying to prevent Turly's escape and to keep him from his mother.

Mother!

He caught sight of the opening. His mother was fading, as were his father and the others. Someone in orange was standing in front of the wavering image of his family and was gesturing back to the struggle on the floor.

Sean had released his hold on Turly and had gotten to his feet. He sprinted forward toward Dermot. But the images rapidly changed shape. Turly could see, instead of his mother and father, something bent and gnarled, gray, with heavy thighs and long arms with strange hands. It looked up at the advancing Sean.

Sean stopped, staring at it curiously. He smiled and

raised his arm in salute. He began to stride for the creature. Dermot stepped aside.

Turly cried out as Sean walked into the arms of the thing. One hand reached out to Sean and fitted itself onto his face. Another, thin and sharp, penetrated one arm. Turly could see blood trickling down Sean's wrist.

Face. Blood.

Turly knew now what had gotten Ellman. And he knew now why there had been no struggle.

The Order had killed Ellman with this thing.

Turly leaped to his feet. Sean had dropped his dagger near the thing. Turly picked it up and advanced cautiously into the opening. Whatever the thing was, it was occupied with Sean. Turly slipped to its rear and sought an opening through its skin, thick like the bark of a tree. Whoever Sean might be, he thought, he did not deserve this.

Turly found what he was looking for. The skin was thinner at the armpits. As the thing held Sean, its arms were raised and allowed access to the heart, or what Turly judged to be the heart. He plunged the blade in. There was no reaction. He pulled the knife and plunged it again. Nothing. He did it a third time. This time the creature howled and dropped Sean to the floor. Sean's face was covered lightly with tiny red points as if he had the young sickness. He was also pale, but breathing. The creature turned to Turly and gazed at him with sad red eyes. It then turned and seemed to point out of the cave.

Turly needed no encouragement. He pulled one of Sean's arms around his neck and staggered out into the cold sunlight. Behind him he could hear whimpering. The soft wings had left his mind. He placed Sean against a rock and stole back to the cave entrance. Inside he saw the Order monk smiling at the creature, transfixed by something he saw deep in its eyes; something he had wanted for a long time was about to be his.

Turly turned away with disgust. He and Sean had barely made it away with their lives. He wasn't going to risk his again for a man who had tried to feed them to that thing. *He* could pay instead.

Sean's eyes were open. He looked at Turly blankly as if he did not recognize him.

"Sean?" said Turly.

"Yes. And you, my friend, have you come out alive, then? For a while I thought you were gone. The monk said something about the wrong man, and I wondered who the right one for that thing was."

"Can you walk, Sean?"

"I saw my partner. He was standing there, grinning. He was waving his spear and pointing toward a rare beast I could not see. We had never captured a rare beast, but that time we would. I *knew* it."

Turly helped Sean to his feet and they moved down the rocky path that led away from the Order caves. They might be followed, and if so Turly wanted to be as far away as possible.

"Turly, did it get the monk?" asked Sean.

"I think so. I don't really care."

"What did he see?" Sean's arm was blue at the puncture point. Turly thought of his grandfather. What had Ellman seen? His daughter? His long-dead wife? Turly himself?

"God knows, Sean, but I don't; and I don't want to know. I think the monk had been leading us to the thing the whole time. But he was also leading us to the south entrance. There, you can see the other side of the Lower Mountains now. We'll stop for a while for rest and then we'll move on. That is, if you still want to travel with me."

"You saved my life," said Sean. "I will not forget that. Both the Order monks and Hastings' troops are now my enemies. My partner is dead and my tribe scattered. There is nothing holding me here that can't be picked up later. And besides," he glanced at Turly, "I want to see how all this turns out."

Turly estimated that it had been about two days since his capture by the Order. That would be several days' start that the red soldiers would have on him. Sean said that the best thing to do would be to find the soldiers' trail at the closest point to their entry into the hills and then follow it quickly into the plains above Straiten.

Turly agreed and they set out with only a knife and their instincts. Sean warned Turly not to be surprised by whatever they might see. The general rule in the south of Imram was, if it did not attack, ignore it. Turly shrugged. He wanted to find his old companions and resume his journey to find his parents and Meriwether.

Turly reflected that he had been through a lot in such a short time. There would probably be more, much more. But he would face that too. He did not know what he was getting into, but he didn't care—had never cared—for his own safety. The importance of the questions driving him was enough to still any fears he might have. He was sometimes scared and depressed, but over it all loomed the fated nature of the journey. He felt like an actor in one of the Framed realities of his Circle Church. He would not be denied. And he would not be captured again either, he vowed. He would rather die than be trussed up like a pig waiting for another's question. But what if that were precisely the nature of his fate? This troubled Turly. He would struggle and do what had to be done and let the rest fall as it may.

The pair made a line straight to the southwest. The day was uneventful save for an occasional movement seen out of the corner of Turly's eye. But whenever he turned to catch it, whatever it had been was gone. He thought his eyes were playing tricks on him. The rocks were sharper than he remembered, and they cut into his thin shoes, made as they were for plains life. Sean was better off. His mountain boots came to his knees and were bound to his legs by leather thongs that wound like large flat worms from instep to calf. The soles were padded with several thicknesses of a toughened hide. The boots were varicolored because different hides had been used. Turly could see patches of brown, gray, black, and a rusty ginger that may have been fox.

Sean was also more nimble than Turly in the hills. He was often far ahead of Turly and had had to wait for him on several occasions. When the rock path gave out and snow littered the ground, their progress was even slower. Turly pushed on, slapping his hands to his sides for warmth. Sean assured him that soon they would be in a nearby mountain village that he knew of, and they could bargain for better gear. Turly puffed out a cloud of viscous smoke and said nothing.

Sean was the first to notice the change in sounds. There was a slow trilling like a flute gone mad. All else was silent. Sean motioned to Turly to make for cover. He did. They waited for what seemed an eternity, the trilling in their ears.

The trilling grew no louder. Sean stepped out into the open and cupped his hands behind his ears and rotated his head in all directions. He shook his head and beckoned Turly on. The trilling was moving away to the south. Turly felt the hackles on his neck rise; he tried to hide his agitation by adjusting his tunic and reaching down to lace his shoes.

"What is it, Sean?"

"I've lived in these mountains all my life, but I've heard it only once before," said Sean.

"Then you know what it is?"

"No. I said I've *heard* it before. *Heard it.* Not seen it." Sean shifted uncomfortably from foot to foot. He seemed more cautious than usual.

"What was the occasion, Sean?" Turly thought it best to be direct with this new turn of events.

"I was fifteen at the time. I had been hunting with my father in one of the wilder regions of the mountains, to the west of us here. We were heading for an old hunting village after a successful trip. It was almost sundown, like now. We were about to make camp when we heard this loud trilling like the sound of giant crickets in the distance. Neither of us had ever heard anything like it. My father was disturbed and started out to find what it was. He told me to stay there and guard the furs. About an hour later he came back. He didn't tell me what it was, and I didn't ask. He was as sick a man as I've ever seen, vomiting, crying. The next day we carried our furs all the way to Straiten instead of to the nearer village."

Sean had leaned back on a large rock streaked with white chalk and some of it rubbed off on his sleeves. As he brushed it off and prepared to move again, Turly saw the look in the man's face. It was not only fear, but also fascination and curiosity.

"Whatever this thing is," said Turly, "it's heading south. And that's the direction we're heading."

"That is right, Turly," said Sean. "Let's give it some time to keep going. At least for now, huh? There is a

133

small village not far from here. We'll stay there for the night." Saying this, his spirits seemed to rise.

In another half hour they were in the middle of a number of squalid huts patched by irregular hides, bolstered by a number of rotten poles. In the center of each square hut a small hole let out smoke that circled wanly into the growing dusk. Snow flakes were coming down gently. The two men looked at each other with relief.

Chapter 10

Sean stepped into one of the larger huts. He emerged a few moments later with a round little man who was smoking a very black cigar. His nose was large and red and he smelled of whiskey. But his eyes sparkled with merriment, something Turly had seen too little of the last few weeks. Turly wondered if the man's cigar was of beaca.

"Ah, in the mountains you are welcome, young man!" said the fellow. He wrung Turly's hand with surprising vigor and clapped him on the back, although he had to reach up to do it. He then ushered both men into his hut.

What Turly saw amazed him. The outside of the hut was a disaster; the inside was immaculate and well appointed. Thick black furs covered every square inch of the floor. On the walls, which were windowless, were colorful drawings in blues and yellows depicting all the majesty of the hunter's art. From the poised hunter to the stricken prey, the tale wound around the interior of the room. There was a touch of the Mythic Sequence about it, thought Turly.

There was a long table in the center of the room, groaning with food and drink. Tankards of rich brown ale with creamy white heads spilling over the tops; bowls of luscious fruit, red apples and tawny pears touched with delicate drops of moisture; great slabs of succulent meat, crusted portions falling off the bone. There were a variety of things Turly thought never to see in this part of the country. Where had this remote village gotten these goods? He glanced at Sean and saw him grin from ear to ear. He seemed to know what Turly had been thinking.

Two women and five children sat around the table with the plump figure who had greeted them. They ate amidst a babble of conversation that did not cease when the two strangers came in. White smoke curled lazily through the center of the hut and was eventually sucked up through the roof. Turly noted that even more food was being prepared at the hearth and his mouth watered.

"You are tired and hungry. Forgive my chatter!" Their host snapped his fingers and two of the older children jumped up and scurried to a side cupboard where they got two plates, which they filled to capacity with everything on the table. Turly could not tell if the youngsters were male or female. But he did know what food was and he fell to with Sean. They were soon filled. Turly wiped the grease off his chin with one sleeve of his tunic as he accepted one of the host's long cigars.

Turly was languid and self-satisfied. The wine was good and so were the cigars. He rolled one in his fingers; it was round and soft and the wrapper was velvet to the touch. The salt-and-pepper ash grew slowly as he drew smoke. He raised his head and looked at the ceiling. He thought he saw strange faces in the fumes that gathered there, and familiar faces that smiled and dissolved into nothingness. As he had done many times, Turly remembered the old days before Ellman had died and he had lived as a simple fisherman: days of labor and rest. Of food gleaned from the lake and from the woods. Of working with his hands toward a clearly defined goal that could be seen and later fondled when finished. Something distinct. Something concrete.

And now his life was like smoke that wound upward and dissolved. Nothing was clear and distinct. He was after something he was not sure existed, in a part of the country he was not sure he could reach, with companions he was not sure he could trust. Not, he thought, a situation he would have chosen for himself. He frowned as he took another puff and watched the smoke curl away from his face.

The meal was over and the small talk had ended. The owner smiled and bowed to Sean and said something Turly could not hear. He pointed to the door and made signs as if giving directions. When he finished, two of the older children got up and went out. Sean placed his cigar on the large tray that had a dragon's head painted on the bottom. It had been a good cigar.

"It's time for bed, my friend," said Sean. He yawned, wheezed and stretched. Winking at Turly, he moved toward the door. "You have the second hut down. Be up early to help arrange for our provisions. Have a good sleep." He grinned as if making a joke.

"But wait a minute, Sean, why aren't we . . . ?" Turly was about to ask, why aren't we staying in the same hut? But then he thought he knew and so didn't ask. Sean had been pent up in the Lower Mountains longer than he had. These were his people. When such an opportunity arose, when such things were available, he felt Sean could not turn them down. Who could blame him? Turly laughed aloud, and the owner's wife turned and looked at him with a mirthful stare. Turly stood up and stretched out his arms sleepily, like the slow hands of a clock.

The hut assigned to Turly was small and wretched looking. He hoped the inside of the hut at least was as comfortable as the one he had just been in. The door was a heavy flap of hide that felt slightly greasy to the touch. There was no light inside and Turly, blinded, quickly stripped to the buff, ready for sleep. He crawled into the mound of furs lying in a heap in the center of the room. It was warm and comfortable there. Turly was satisfied. Tomorrow he and Sean would go and, within a matter of days, if their calculations were correct, they would find his old friends and deal with Hastings' soldiers. Turly had not yet figured out how to do that. Well, now he was sleepy and content. Things had worked out so far. He could feel dreams coming on like silent riders over a hill. He had only to let them come.

Something warm and soft moved beside him in the furs. Turly scrambled out and jumped upright.

"What the demon!" he shouted. He groped over to one wall and felt wildly for a flint and candle. He found them and struck furiously until a small flame flared up and threw ghostly shadows on the walls. Turly wheeled and saw, lying with dignity, one of the owner's daughters. He could not tell her age. She seemed young, but her breasts were large and tipped with small brown dots. She had to be of age, mused Turly. Her thighs were whiter than her face and shoulders. Turly could see a lovely curve, one calf pulled up against the other leg. The girl gazed directly into Turly's eyes without speaking or explaining. She was proud, thought Turly. But proud of what?

As if reading his thoughts, the girl stood up. She was heavier around the hips than normal, a little extra for the cold winters in the mountains. Her face was pretty, in a nondescript way, framed by black hair cut in a bowl shape, falling straight from the part in the middle of her head. She stood in front of Turly for a long moment, as he tried to read her thoughts. Her eyes probed him. Then he reached for her. He felt warmth spread throughout his belly. He was rubbing her now, his hands reaching around her. As he cradled her, she leaned her head onto Turly's chest.

Turly stared into one dark corner of the tiny hut. His breathing was labored. While he cupped both of her large buttocks in his hands, his fingers squeezed and pulled as if they were weighing melons. The wine and food had released in Turly the vast flow he had almost forgotten he had ever felt.

They fell where they had been standing. The girl's thick mouth played over Turly as he strained to use his eyes in the partial light. The immense flare of her hips excited Turly as he had not been excited in a long time. He had known many girls—that was Circle custom—but the extraordinary dimensions of this girl were doing something inexplicable to him. Vast shapes rose in his mind. It was as if the girl filled exactly a primal shape he had carried about in his memory, buried in his deep self. For a time Turly simply caressed her, kissing, rubbing his tongue over her immense breadth. The darkness and the half-light lulled him into a world where there was only flesh. He wanted to fondle her forever.

The girl had been silent but now began to moan softly. She lay on her back letting Turly do what he wished.

Turly spread her legs out to each side as far as they would go. She was spread-eagled on the furs. He ran his hands up and down the length of her thighs, leaned down and licked her legs from ankle to hip.

Flipping the girl onto her stomach, Turly placed himself between her legs. He reached down and caught her at the hips, gently pulled them up off the floor. The girl raised her knees and rested on them, her head cradled on her folded arms. Turly looked down at her elevated buttocks, and guided himself to her where they gleamed in curves and humps like an inverted heart. He entered the indentation where the two halves of the heart came together. Holding the halves in his hands, Turly began to work. He pushed himself forward then back, at first slowly and luxuriously and then more urgently. He bent and put the driving force of his body into her. Even in the chilly room he was sweating.

The girl was moaning louder and rolling her head on her hands. Turly could see this vaguely, hear it, as his own eyes rolled half-closed.

Turly gasped and held on to her with greater force, driving, holding back. He did not want it to end, but he did want the peak. He reached the peak. Turly slid over the edge of frenzy into the mindless slope of union, of loss. His hips shook with palsy as his face rose to the ceiling.

Turly rolled over and wiped himself on one of the smaller furs lying by the pallet. He blew air into the space overhead and wondered if the girl would leave. She had remained quiet all that time, whether with rebuke or acceptance or inability he did not know.

The girl flattened out on the furs, dark and soft, and said nothing. The candlelight played about her slick body. Turly thought she might be a mute. He shrugged and, lacking anything else, started to talk about his youth and his recent adventures. He was feeling good now, more relaxed, his ordeal fading from his memory. After a time he grew more weary than he had been.

Sleep was on him before he could ask the girl her name.

Chapter 11

Captain Dodder scanned the horizon. There was nothing that he could see except a tan veldt rolling into infinity. The sudden black cloud had vanished, and he found to his astonishment that two of his prisoners had escaped. And two of his most valuable prisoners at that. They would have to spend some time looking for them, he thought. *I will pay for this as it is.*

He wheeled his horse in the direction from which they had just come, his red cape snapping like a flag in the wind. His good-natured disposition turned sour. Taking count of his troops, he hoped for no further sorcery or they would most certainly desert him. He thought his men were cowards anyway. Why had they left their mothers to join fighting men? It was a wonder to him when Hastings had signed them on. But then Hastings had signed a good many men on lately, in an attempt to beef up his forces to twice their normal size. There was clearly something in the wind. But Hastings kept everything to himself, mused Dodder. That might tell against him one day.

The prisoners had lamented the loss of their white-haired leader. The large one alone had threatened all of the soldiers if they did not return him. The other four Circle men were sullen and unresponsive, obviously uncertain what to make of the new turn of events. Dodder had found it necessary to place them in the prison wagon. The wagon was windowless and padlocked but had sufficient ventilation through invisible outlets in the seams of the wagon. In the growing cold of the mountainous area, heat would be no problem to them. They were more valuable alive than dead: pressed into service, they would all be good additions to Hastings' army. Dodder would especially like to see the large one enrolled at the Academy. He would teach him about military discipline.

The rest of the day was spent in scouring the northern foothills of the Lower Mountains. They could find nothing. It was as if the mountain itself had opened up and swallowed the two men whole. Dodder was used to the wiles of the orange monks, for he had encountered the Order of Zeno before. But he did not know that such large-scale illusions were in their power.

It had been a stroke of luck to stumble on the man the way they had. The orange monk had appeared from nowhere and led them a merry chase through rough country. He had not seemed to be trying to escape, but to lead them somewhere. And then suddenly there they were. It was almost as if the monk knew where the Circle group was and had led the troops to them. But why? To handle those that he had no use for? It could be. If he could only get his hands on that wretched monk, he would squeeze out the truth. Captain Edmond Dodder then reflected on the nature of military life. To be trained to kill and ultimately to be disappointed if you did not. If one builds muscles, one eventually has to use them. It is the same with armies, he thought. A well-trained corps means a well-exercised policy of using it. Threats. Blackmail.

But Hastings was different. He used violence only selectively and at odd times. And he never threatened. He acted. His policy was rarely articulated but always carried out immediately. Hastings paid well and disciplined well. His training academy was the finest in the island, and Dodder was an Instructor there, except when Hastings had an important mission for him to perform, like then. Dodder missed the barracks and the rigid camaraderie of the Academy. He loved everything about the corps and did all that he could to instill that love of honor and courage in the recruits. Of course there were those occasional malcontents who could not make the mark and tried to slip away back to their homes. The Sniffers always got them. It was a just end for deserters.

Dodder rode his horse well. He rode proudly with a long tradition of horse-soldiers behind him. Soldiers willing to sell themselves to the highest bidder, but then ready to fight to the death for him. And of course Hastings had always been the highest bidder in the island. There was no denying Hastings. And Hastings seemed to understand and appreciate the military tradition that had given rise to men like Captain Dodder. He had never abused the men who stayed with him after they had proven their loyalty in the Academy. He gave orders and they were carried out. Period. Although Dodder had wondered at some of the orders, he had never openly questioned them. Hastings seemed to have a grand purpose in mind, but he had never revealed what it was except to say that one day all Imram would be covered with the sign of the *H*.

Well, he picked an odd way to unify this scraggly

island, thought Dodder. If it were up to him, and it wasn't, he would march on the northern tribes with a great force and take them one by one. They had never shown signs of unity or common purpose. They could easily be subdued. Instead Hastings sent his men out for a single man, or to search a particular ruin for some old parchment. It was all beyond Dodder, and he had resolved simply to do his sworn duty and leave the rest to Hastings.

At the end of the first day, the men made camp and huddled about the fires as the night sounds came upon them with strange and urgent suddenness. None of them wanted to be out of a barracks and in the open like that. It was too dangerous. They talked quietly as if afraid to draw the attention of something in the night. The prisoners were somewhat relieved because they were locked up in the wagon for the night. All slept fitfully.

The next day the group checked several villages for Turly and the monk. No one had seen them. The villagers were taciturn and inclined to fade into the hills at the first opportunity. Dodder found that to speak to them, he had first to send scouts ahead to corral them. Even then, only the very old or young were caught in this fashion. The village huts were old, their pilings and skin coverings rotting in the cold air at a very slow rate. Rot was an invisible fire, thought Dodder, that eats all things, and was eating him even as he rode his horse. The thought was nevertheless a pleasant one, for it allowed Dodder to deal with time and fate in his own terms. If he could joke about it, he could live with it. But he felt marked by something even as he rode at the head of forces feared by every tribe in the south. What was the feeling? he thought. He was caught up in something he could not understand. Even these mountain

vermin could slip by him and gaze from eyes that
seemed to know all. He rubbed his own eyes with a
great gloved fist and accepted, as he had always done,
the brief life of a soldier.

The search yielded nothing. Dodder spent another
day in the foothills hoping to get some word or hear
some clue to the whereabouts of the one from the
north. But there was nothing. And so, reluctantly,
Dodder headed south over the Lower Mountains to
Hastings Hall. He would have difficulty explaining the
whole situation, but some word and some prisoners
would be better than nothing. Perhaps Hastings' elite
Drummers could get something from them that he could
not; they could ask questions that Dodder did not know
existed. Hastings allowed the Drummers complete run
of the Hall and complete mastery of the Interrogation
Rooms. They inevitably got what they were after.

They had easily gotten exact information from the
raiding party that had come down from the north just
the week before. The Drummers were able to get information which even willing witnesses did not know
they possessed. They had determined that the men had
indeed seen the white-haired youth whom Hastings
thought had been killed eleven years before in an
abortive attempt to secure information about something
of great power. A raiding group had reported killing a
youth who fitted the description given by the posters.
But it was in the early days of Hastings' hegemony and
mistakes had been made that had not been repeated.
The orders had been to bring the boy in alive, if possible. The raiding force had misinterpreted the orders
and had been severely punished. Hastings had raged
for days and then settled into a black gloom that had
lasted for months. He had then directed his attentions

to the Order of Zeno and various other enterprises that Dodder could not comprehend.

When he had then heard that the white-haired boy still lived, Hastings had marshalled all available forces and sent them north to cover all possible contingencies. It had been the sheerest luck that he, Dodder, had found the boy first. They had also been issued orders to capture all Zeno members, and so they had naturally pursued the monk. They had caught and then lost both of the men. What Hastings would say now, Dodder did not know, but he was understandably reluctant to hurry south.

The ranks were getting tired and hungry. The foothills were treacherous at this point where the trail was increasingly rocky, allowing their mounts little room to find good footing. Red capes fluttered in the chill breezes that swept down from the heights ahead. There was a feeling of foreboding which even the prisoners in their own despair felt. They looked about them at the thorn bushes and the dry heather scattered amidst the rocky slopes reaching up and over them on either side like parentheses. Dodder rode in front, one column of twelve soldiers after him, the prisoners in the center of a last column of twelve. Behind came the prison wagon, its grim black box-like structure unrelieved by ornament or design. It rolled along as if in protest, the horses that pulled it straining in an unnatural manner.

Some said that the Drummers had cursed the prison wagons so that none could enter or leave without knowledge of the locks or of the carriage itself. In fact, no one had ever been able to escape from a wagon, but that had been attributed to the vigilance of the home guard. In each group there were only three who held the keys to the wagon: the Captain, the First Lieutenant, and the Key-Keeper, who always rode with the

Captain. The soldiers paid little attention to the prison wagon and were glad when the prisoners themselves were not in it. Most of the soldiers were mercenaries and as such were unconcerned with anything but their own pleasures. But they were also common men who knew fear and superstition and wished on no one the fate of the black wagon.

The passage upward had narrowed even more, and the party had to travel in single file. The late afternoon sun was hidden by the slopes on the right and dusk had come early. The horses were jittery and Dodder determined to rest them for the night at the first opportunity. He rode silently, occasionally rising on his mount to check the passage ahead.

The first man fell without a sound. The second screamed and kept screaming with a small arrow lodged in his throat. He clutched at it as he rolled over and over on the ground. The others immediately dismounted where they were and crouched behind their horses looking for the enemy.

They could see no one.

Dodder motioned the column to follow him to a rocky shelf just ahead. He hoped they could make it there. A suitable defense could be made, although Dodder would have preferred a better place. Three more men fell before they reached the rocks.

Because it looked as if they might need every man available, Dodder ordered the prisoners released and given weapons. They received them gratefully.

The night was now approaching rapidly. They had yet to see any bowmen. The column was arranged in a small semi-circle with overhanging rock protection. Five of the twenty-four soldiers were dead. Dodder held the remaining number close, facing outward.

Garrett was the first to see them. He thought his eyes

were playing tricks. Then Harve gestured with his huge hand to a stand of pine not forty meters from their position.

Small children darted suddenly from tree to tree. Each had a hump on its back and a scurrying slant like the motion of crabs.

"Farks," said Dodder.

"What?"

"Farks. A tribe of midgets. They are all deformed in one way or another. Most have those humps you see on their backs. But some have other, even less savory, traits. Pray that you do not find what those traits are."

Bulfin leaned over from behind one of the rocks and swore.

"I thought they were children," he said. "They look exactly like children, ten or eleven."

"Children do not hang you by your feet and flay you alive, my friend," responded Dodder. "Even the Drummers will be kinder to you."

Bulfin pulled back in with his back to the rock. He gulped several times and wiped sweat off his forehead. All in all, he would rather be in the Circle about to cook pig or roast corn. Anything but this. He gasped as a tiny arrow deflected off the cliff above him and fell into his lap.

"We're cut off," allowed Dodder. "Someone has got to get around to the other side of the Farks."

No one spoke.

Smith thought of the Sequence and closed his eyes to the circling Farks. He spoke aloud.

I believe in the birth of me and of the miraculous signs.

Kelleher, no coward, joined with him on the second phase of the Sequence:

In the true memories of youth.

I see the desert and the inward terror.

Harve grumbled aloud and recited in his huge voice the remaining litany of the Circle ritual that held all Circlemen and gave them strength.

The journey to come, the multiple struggles.

I will know the death of me and the coming to despair.

Smith looked up to see Dodder staring at him with a look of profound disgust. He was fingering his short sword as if trying to decide whether or not to run Smith and the others through, or throw them to the Farks.

The litany continued with Bulfin and Garrett making the full complement. In ringing tones of affirmation, the Sequence swelled from the horror of defeat to the affirmation of resurrection. Strength and hope seemed to well up in the small group of prisoners as they finished the last phases of the Circle:

But the rebirth of me from the fire of the Circle itself.

The final breathing and the going to the higher One.

Dodder saw the flush of renewed hope and effort return to the Northerners, and he wondered at the nature of the Sequence, which he had always heard denounced in jeers by the rough folk of the south. It did seem fatalistic but also, in the end, to hint of something else, something he did not have the time to fully understand. He shrugged and turned away. What is understanding? he thought. They were ready to fight again, which was all he was interested in at the moment. Maybe later he would ask Smith to explain the finer points of the Circle heresy. But now he had to round up men to take risks and get through a bad situation.

Four of his soldiers volunteered to create a diversion. Smith also volunteered. They were sent by Dodder to the right, down the way they had come. When they reached the open path, they would scale the rock at that point to the left and come up the other side, above the Farks.

If the Farks could ambush and kill, fine. If not, they would simply wear their prey down and finish off what was left. They trusted to their numbers and their superior knowledge of the hills. Farks by and large spurned strategy. They might well hear the smaller group approaching from the rear and turn to deal with it, but they would not suspect such a move in advance. It was too complex a maneuver. And that was what Dodder was counting on. Whatever else he was, Dodder was a good soldier and a good strategist. Normally he would not use a diversion like this at all. The enemy would laugh at him. But not the Farks. As long as they got their blood sooner or later, they were content to sit and wait.

It had been fifteen minutes now since they had sent a rain of cover arrows in the direction of the Farks, and the five had slipped down the path.

Nothing happened. The Farks would occasionally fire an arrow down into the hollow. It would chip dust down on the assembled party and fall harmlessly into the ground or onto the gathered cape of one of the Red soldiers.

Dodder was watching the pines behind the Farks closely. He had counted something like forty Farks hidden in the rocks above. They would flit from rock to rock, clutching their short but effective bows in tiny fists. Their ugly grimaces could be seen leering down on them like scavengers. The ground at that point rose at a steady gradient of forty-five degrees from path level to some sixteen meters above their heads. The climb would be hard, but it could be done. It would have to be done.

Suddenly Dodder saw a swirl of red from high on the

hill about six meters behind the highest Fark position. It was one of his men! By god, they weren't so bad after all. And the prisoner as well was proving himself a man. If they could follow his instructions to the letter, all would be well.

Dodder watched as his men crept closer to the rear of the Farks. He thought he saw the tiny glint of flint striking flint. Soon he could see wisps of smoke rising in wayward gusts from the fringe of grasses in front of the stand of pines. The Farks had not yet noticed. Dodder turned to the others and motioned them to be ready at his signal. He turned back and noticed motion behind the rocks above. One Fark came running out and up toward the pines. He fell with an arrow thrusting out through his back, pointing down toward Dodder. The other Farks were now aware of the fire above them. It was not large or raging, but enough so to thwart the escape of the short Farks. The flames were beginning to rise now, and it became clear that the Fark party was closed in by fire from behind and angry soldiers in front. They began to panic and run in all directions. Those few who ran to the fire and woods were burned or felled by arrows from the handful of diversionary troops above them. Those that stayed faced something else.

Dodder raised his hand. The remaining troops charged up the hill after the Farks, their feet stumbling on the loose rocks. An occasional Fark arrow would catch a man and send him rolling back down to the path, but that was an exception. Fire and arrows had undone the Farks and they were in retreat. A general slaughter followed. Small misshapen bodies littered the slope.

It was soon over. The Farks had either been killed or managed to escape around the edges of the fire trap.

They would not be back soon, Dodder knew. It would be a long time before they tried to ambush Hastings' soldiers, he reflected with pride.

The patrol reassembled, moved back to the path below and proceeded on to the designated camp two miles on the other side of the Lower Mountains. Three more soldiers had been killed, and Bulfin had been wounded in the arm with a Fark arrow. Dodder saw that Bulfin received as good treatment as his soldiers before pushing on, for he was getting to like these north heretics. Even the giant had done admirable work, cleaving the heads of the Farks. He had been like a bull in the rushes of a pond, stamping and wreaking havoc. Dodder was glad that he had not had to harm Harve earlier. It would have been a pity to lose such a man for nothing. A little loose in the head, however. He had been warned of that by Smith. Harmless unless his battle fever was up. The others had also acquitted themselves well. Not used to organized fighting, he noticed, but still quite teachable.

The prisoners licked their wounds and felt pride in the fact that they had been allowed to fight and that they had done well. But they did so for one reason only: to be able to live and find Turly. They did not know where he was any more than Captain Dodder did, and were as bewildered. Their only move at the moment was to stay alive and hope Turly was too. Perhaps he was even now heading south and would meet them in Straiten.

Severe weather set in and the patrol settled down to rest for the night. Rations were running short and Dodder was glad that Hastings Hall was not far away. The local villagers were very unfriendly to any group not their own. But the interval gave Dodder a chance to talk to Smith and the others, and he gained a new respect for their faith and their ability. Smith told him of his hopes for the North and the trade possibilities in unifying the island. Dodder agreed about the unification scheme but argued the method. He was for unification by force under a powerful warlord like Hastings, and then the rest would follow. That would be a time of great prosperity in which trade would flourish in all parts of the island because all roads would be open— not as they were now. In time, all parts of the island could be represented in a general congress based on the feudal hierarchy of the military corps that was so successful in the southwestern tribes.

There was friendly debate on this point. But under the surface both men could feel the electric charge of division. They both knew any sort of union would be extremely difficult to form and maintain. It was not the first time that Dodder seemed to feel an outside force compelling disunity. Something had struck lines of division across the face of Imram just as surely as if fences had been built. He would probably never know what force that was, and he did not at the moment care overmuch. He had one job now, and that was to get these men to Hastings. He regretted having to do so. But there was no choice. He had respect for Smith and the others, but he was a soldier. He would reluctantly turn over his prisoners for routine interrogation, which would leave them crippled at best and dead at worst if they did not cooperate. Dodder thought sadly that they would not cooperate.

Smith had also come to respect and even like Captain Dodder. He was at least honest and straight-forward in his dealings with them, even if he were taking them to an uncertain fate. Smith had changed somewhat in the last week. He was riding for the first time to the dreaded south. He had fought for his life and that of his friends. While climbing in unfamiliar ground behind the Farks, he had felt clearly the soft life of the Circle slip from him as he felt the fat around his middle lose its compactness and begin to melt away. He was an ordinary member of the Circle, but he felt compelled now by forces he could barely comprehend. Even so, for the first time in his life he thought he knew what it meant to understand something new and different and it did not make him cringe. Instead he could sense a flow of gentle fire surge through his veins, a feeling of growing power as he conquered first one obstacle and then another; he believed now that he *could* handle the present situation. He *would* meet Hastings and rescue Meriwether without trouble.

Meriwether.

Smith thought now that he could face Turly and tell him that Meriwether was no longer his. Smith slept well there in the cold mountains far from his Circle hut.

The next morning the bleak sun rose cold and unwilling, but the sky was clearing and they could move on. Breakfast had been finished and the signs of the camp obliterated. The prisoners were allowed to ride with the troops since they had earned the right, and pledged their word not to escape. It would be a hard ride to Straiten, but it could be made in a day.

On the first rise Dodder stretched and looked out across the morning hills. The mist settled in the uneven cracks and gave a false sense of uniformity. The mountain scene looked like a gray lake with small islands dotting the interior. There was no pink in the dawn and Dodder shuddered involuntarily. He realized that the horses had been shy for some time now, for they had pranced and whinnied, ready to be off. He was ready himself and a feeling of uneasiness had descended on the men as something odd was sensed.

At first it was far off to the east. Then it grew in intensity—rapidly—until the hills seemed to drown in it. Dodder grabbed for the reins of his silver stallion as he rose on two feet and pawed at the sound in the air. Like great cicadas in an insane orgy of dissonance, the raspy trilling grew closer.

Dodder had never heard anything like it. He ordered his men to form a circle with the black wagon in the center and regretfully ordered the prisoners back into the wagon. He was not going to lose them now, so close to Hastings Hall; and, until he knew the nature of the threat, he was not going to risk them again. Smith and Harve especially were reluctant to give up their arms and crawl into the dark interior of the wagon. They could feel the dank fever that lurked there and wanted nothing to do with it. But they had given their word to Dodder that, if necessary, they would willingly give up their swords and become prisoners again. Dodder had been decent to them, and they would not dishonor their growing friendship. Perhaps it might yet work in their favor before the trip was over.

Smith heard the bolt shot and the lock snapped shut on the outer door. The trilling was muted inside the wagon, but he could hear its incessant rasp and he could feel that even the prison wagon was a comforting refuge. The horses were now clearly out of hand outside. He could hear the shouts and curses as first one, then another made a break for the open ground on the downward trail. Dodder was hollering to his men to take up defensive positions around the wagon.

The trilling grew louder and reached a peak of intensity within minutes. Smith and the others held their ears in agony. They could hear nothing but the sound of unnatural wood being sawed by monstrous forces, and the rapid beating of their own hearts. Kelleher hunkered in one corner and whimpered. Bulfin's arm was in a white sling, but he removed it to cup his hands over his ears.

Smith thought he heard the sound of screaming, but he was not sure. When he strained to hear, there was nothing. He finally put his ear to the wagon wall but could hear only the trilling. He thought something was pushing against the wagon, a gentle susurration like a wind against a swing. But he could not be sure. The noise went on and on. After what seemed an eternity, the trilling began to drift off to the west and gradually there was only silence.

After a time, Smith began to beat on the walls and cry out to Dodder to release them. There was no answer. The men tried to break out of the wagon but they could not. The doors were too secure and they could do nothing but await with fear what would happen. The wait went on and on. Smith could not tell the time in the dark of the wagon, but he thought it was getting late in the day.

They heard something pull at the lock on the door.

Chapter 12

Turly had risen early and was eager to be off. Sean met him for breakfast and, after being prodded, explained the mountain custom of hospitality. Although not a widespread practice, the giving of daughters and wives to travelers was seen as a means of educating the women of the tribe into the range of sexual tastes and exercises, and allowing them to test ideas of their own. They would make better wives for it, they thought. Sean clapped Turly on the back and asked if he had contributed to the lore of the tribe. Turly thought of the night before and wondered at the stoic quiet of the young girl.

The tribal master furnished them with all the clothing and weapons they needed. He stood around beaming and clutching a cigar in his teeth. Sean's credit was good, and there was no question that the things would be paid for. Turly paid for his things with several of his gold grims. Both of them now wore the standard mountain gear for that time of year: fur parkas, pull-over vest fronts with multiple pockets for flint, knives and small game. There were rough wool leggings that tucked into heavy boots with thickened soles. Turly was happy for that. His feet had not yet recovered from the beating they had taken since leaving the Order cave. He gingerly felt his toes and recognized several blisters on them. Turly would need such outer wear until he reached the plain of Straiten. There he and Sean could trade what they had for other, less bulky garments. Sean also arranged for Turly to swap some of his grims for currency good in Straiten itself, and they were ready to set out. Turly had lost the bag around his neck but not his money belt.

Their mounts were not as good as before, but they were solid and reliable. They headed south toward the Main Runner Pass that led to the other side of the Lower Mountains.

As they went into the upper end of the pass, Sean and Turly noticed to the right an area scorched by fire. They wondered about that because fire in this part of the mountain was almost always man-made. An incline led up a short rocky slope. There they found the mutilated bodies of creatures Turly had never seen before.

"Turly, look," said Sean. "Farks."

Turly looked. In several of the small hunchbacks were arrows with which he was not familiar. The midgets were extremely ugly, or at least those who still had faces were. The mountain scavengers had done their work well.

"Whose arrows, Sean?"

"The soldiers of Hastings. The same ones you have been telling me about, no doubt. They have been through here and not long ago."

"Then that means they are within range and my friends are with them," shouted Turly.

"Don't get so eager, my friend," said Sean. "All this

means is that the troop itself came through this way. They may have left your friends for dead back on the upper plain."

"But can you now follow and catch them before they get to Straiten?"

"Can a molon squeal?" asked Sean.

The two set out at a faster pace. The trail was still fresh although days old. The mountain air kept things well-preserved, given the circumstances. But further on they ran into more recent snow. The trail became harder to follow, but Sean seemed to have no trouble. He was good, thought Turly. He had the instinct of a hound and the eye of an eagle. Turly looked up at the sky. No, he thought, an eagle could not follow a trail in this weather. He hunched forward in his parka and hugged his horse for warmth. He wished he were back at the Inniscloe Lake with a warm summer breeze blowing across his face.

The weather finally eased, and Sean then pushed Turly almost to the breaking point. They did not stop to cook food but ate the meat fragments that were packed in their vest pockets. Turly thought the ordeal would never end. The sky was still gray but quiet now without the incessant howl of the high winds. The sparse mountain vegetation offered the only color relief. A patch of brown here, yellow there; some red, but little green. A depressing landscape.

Sean had been riding in front and had just topped a ridge. He halted and motioned Turly to join him. Turly kicked his horse in the flanks and soon stood beside Sean, looking down on a scene of pure horror.

Turly leaned over his horse and retched. He slid off and squatted to the ground. His mouth was bitter with the taste of his last rations.

Sean was sitting quietly staring at the circle of men

below. "I think I now know what my father saw, and why he did not go into the village that day."

For long minutes they said nothing. And then, in silent agreement, they moved cautiously down the path to the black wagon and the motionless puddles that surrounded it. The bodies of about twenty men lay sprawled in various attitudes upon the ground like deflated balloons. None had the true solidity of a man. It seemed as if their bones had been removed, and they were left as hideous parodies of men, like putty or jelly shaped in a rough human form.

One of the shapes seemed to look at Turly in recognition. Turly thought it was the face of the Captain who had captured him in front of the Lower Mountains. If that were true, he may have found his friends and he looked anxiously about on the ground. He could tell little about the bodies except that they wore red garments. That left the black wagon. Turly walked over to it and saw the lock, then picked it up and turned it from side to side. He would need a key.

Sean saw the problem and looked about for the Key-Keeper. He thought he found him, reached down gingerly to the muddle of outraged humanity and extracted a ring of keys. The thing shook like rubber as he pulled the ring free. Sean was a tough mountain fighter, but this had turned even his stomach. What could have done this; taken a man's bones without opening him up? Not a drop of blood had been spilled. There were patches of dark blue here and there in the bodies where the blood had gathered. Sean turned away and handed the ring to Turly. Their eyes did not meet.

Turly tried first one then another of the keys. He finally rattled the lock off and pulled the bolt. He had heard nothing inside the wagon and was apprehensive. What if he found the same puddles of putrescence inside?

"Turly!" shouted five voices at once.

They came tumbling out of the wagon shaking hands and thumping Turly on the back. Turly laughed and swung at his old comrades, while big Harve nearly crushed the life from him. Turly noted Bulfin's arm and gave words of sympathy. It was a warm show of gratitude all around. And then the prisoners spotted what was left of Hastings' troopers.

"Ah, Sequence," breathed Smith. He looked over at Garrett and Kelleher. "So this is what we heard."

"What exactly did you hear?" It was Sean. Smith looked at him and then at Turly.

"It's all right," said Turly, "I'll tell you about how we met later. Tell him what you heard."

Smith told him. Sean sat with head averted but listening with great intensity, interrupting him every now and then to ask a question. When Smith was finished, Sean stood up and looked into the distance. He said nothing for a while.

"It was what my father and I heard many years ago. I do not know what it was and I am not sure that I want to find out. There are things loose in Imram that were not always here. Things that seem unearthly. How they got here or why, I do not know. I just do not know."

Smith had not yet recovered from the scene on the ground. He felt great regret over the loss of Captain Dodder. He had felt toward the end a growing sense of hope that Dodder would be able to secure Meriwether for him and allow them both to escape to the North. Perhaps that was wishful thinking. Dodder was after all loyal to his master as well. Would Smith have trusted a man who would be that easily stolen from another? But whatever the possibility, it was gone now. He glanced at the shriveled skin of Dodder and shuddered. Dodder's last act had been to protect his prisoners, and he had done so with his life. Whatever his status had been, Smith felt ashamed nevertheless that he had cowered safely in the wagon while those outside, captors though they had been, had died horribly.

Turly had sent Harve and Kelleher after the horses, if the horses could be found. He gathered what weapons he could without disturbing the soldiers, but all the main provisions were on the horses and for the additional five members to make it to Straiten, they needed the horses and what they carried. While waiting for the others to gather the horses, Turly spent the time telling Smith what had occurred after Oliver's black cloud had covered them.

Smith marveled at the Order of Zeno and wondered with Turly at the purposes for which they worked. He had heard of strange things in the south. Everyone had. But they were always safely removed to another part of the island, and they had never bothered the Circlefolk. At least that's what Smith had thought until he heard of the Gabble and what it had done to Ellman. It was clear that the journey south to find Meriwether was going to be more complicated than Smith thought. He would still have to wait to tell Turly about their relationship. They would first have to deal with Hastings and with the monks of the Order of Zeno. He wondered what else there would be before journey's end.

Smith felt a growing depression. He was only a tradesman, a friend to a man who had become more than Smith could become, a man who followed a trail destiny had set for him, a trail that Smith knew *he* could not follow. Smith felt cut off even from himself. He had left the north and a comfortable Circle where the round of daily life went on without interruption, where the greatest cause for alarm was an occasional raid that could be warded off by closing the gates against it. He could not close the gates on this. It was too complicated for him; it threatened to overwhelm him. He had thought earlier that he could master the situation. He could not. He would now have to rely on Turly and Turly's instincts.

There was no going back.

Turly looked over at his old friend Smith and thought he could tell what he was brooding upon. He had not meant Smith to be caught up in these troubles. But Smith had gladly left for the south. He knew Smith cared for Meriwether, had known it for some time. But Meriwether was Turly's; he was certain of that and had wondered why Smith was so eager to join the hunt for her. Perhaps he was truly in search of elusive trade routes to the south. Smith had been like that more and more. Concerned with making a material fortune, getting on. Turly wished him well. Once Smith had saved Turly's life in a moment of generous courage, but Turly had repaid that and now felt Smith to have long since diverged on a commercial path, which Turly scorned but recognized as necessary for the good of the community as a whole. Smith was still a good friend, but Turly now realized that whatever he had to do, ultimately he would have to do it without him.

Harve and Kelleher came back with three of the troop's horses. With Sean and Turly's horses, that would be enough to make it to the trading settlement of Straiten. Harve rode alone since he was much too large for his horse to accommodate another rider. As it was, his mount seemed to stagger under him. Garrett and Bulfin rode another, and Kelleher and Smith made up the third. Sean and Turly packed as much as they could on their own horses and secured them tightly.

Without a backward look, the small party left the ill-fated camp. They had not been able to bury the soldiers, for none could bring himself to touch them further. They were left on the ground like obscene jellyfish stranded on an alien beach.

The trip down the south side of the Lower Mountains was made quietly. Each man pondered the events of the past week and made his own peace with what might come.

They soon reached a more heavily traveled part of the greater Straiten road. Paths joined into roads and roads into broad avenues. The party of mountain folk was not paid much notice by the other travelers. There were large wagons filled with produce, corn and wheat, and bundles of cane for the furniture trade. Small caravans of itinerant tinkers moved into Straiten for amusement or quick money, while soldiers in green and red and yellow capes passed singly and in groups amidst the travelers without interest. They seemed preoccupied with something else and hurried on their way. Jugglers in bright costumes tried to drum up audiences by the side of the road. Some travelers stopped and dropped small coins into pots set in front of them; but these were few and far between. Times had not been good in Imram and money was tightly held. Beggars in rags scuttled in and out of the flow of traffic unashamedly flaunting their crippled arms or hugging their starving babies to their breasts. Few paid any attention to them, either.

There was some talk about the legendary ruins on the coast, to the east; ruins no one ever wanted to go to. Stories of death kept away anyone who might be curious. And most Circlemen were not overly curious to begin with. Whatever was there was best forgotten by time, as far as they were concerned.

Garrett came up by Turly and pointed eastward. "Did the Fires do what some say they did over there, Turly?"

"Ellman said so, Garrett, and he always spoke truth."

"We can't go there to see for ourselves?"

Turly glanced at Garrett who was rubbing his short blunt nose with a muddy hand. "It is not safe. The Fires linger in some way, and there is nothing to see but ashes anyway."

"Ellman said that too? Had he seen the ruins?" asked Garrett, whose faint brown hair lay in long strands over his forehead. Turly was irritated by the way the man seemed to be more inquisitive than he himself was.

"I think so, I don't know for sure," said Turly as he turned back to his own thoughts while they trudged quietly on toward Straiten.

Turly tried to formulate a course of action as they got closer to Straiten. He knew no one there but knew also from talking with Sean that anything could be bought there, even information of the kind he wanted. The trick was to find the right person to buy it from. Sean had once known political spies in the city but only well enough to know that they might not be trustworthy. They would have to get there, try to be inconspicuous, and see what happened.

Turly finally called a halt for camp. Pulling off the main thoroughfare, the band chose a small clearing with ample firewood. Smith agreed to watch first. After a supper of dried provisions, beef and salt-fish washed down with mountain ale, the members settled by the fire and watched the flames dance in various colors. Each saw there some memory he treasured, some sequence of events that would lead him inexorably to the finest moment of his life. Each stretched to that moment with every fiber of his being. For some there was sadness in assessing the distance from the dream; for others the prospect of a dream itself served to warm them and to flood their hearts with well-being.

They spoke little as they smoked the long cigars Turly had brought from the mountain camp. Turly rolled the tube lightly between his thumb and fingers. He watched the tiny glow at the tuck and mused on the nature of his journey. He had come a long way to find answers, but he had raised more questions than he had known possible. He looked over at the other faces ringing the fire and saw floating orbs that contained the faces of his friends. Occasionally a hand would place something in that face and then disappear back into the darkness.

Turly took the next watch. He strained his senses out into the gloom and thought he felt something velvet and indistinct that was not part of the darkness itself. It was something else, but he could not make it out. Something watching, watching. But why? Then it was gone. Looking at the stub of his cigar, Turly shook his head and regretted his last two or three puffs.

He never knew how to deny the last few inches of a cigar and yet they were always the very inches to be avoided. It could be mighty good at the time, he thought, but the haze that would come later could also be unpleasant. Now Turly stood silently leaning against an oak tree, huge and impassive in the night. Wind touched his face lightly and he could smell rain. That much at least seemed clear.

There were no stars overhead now; they were covered and hidden by clouds that scudded across the sky from west to east like messengers to some cloudy source. The moon was in crescent and was almost above the eastern horizon. Turly watched it until he was lost in its vague movement in and out of the cloudy cover. Covered and revealed and covered. Turly sighed and turned his eyes to the ground. He thought again that he would have preferred to remain behind in the Circle or out at Inniscloe Lake. The most profound doubts assailed him. Why should he journey with his friends to almost certain death in the south? What was it he was after that was not long gone? His parents? Meriwether? Hastings? Did he think he could prevail where better men had not? He had revered Ellman more than any other man and now Ellman was dead, slain by a creature Turly had not known existed. What else is out there, he wondered?

Bulfin touched him on the shoulder and Turly wheeled with his knife at the ready.

"It's me, Turly. Bulfin. Have you seen or heard anything?"

Turly shuddered. He knew he could have easily killed Bulfin. He sheathed his knife and stepped away from him.

"No, there was nothing. I was thinking of the buzzing back in the mountains when you touched me."

Bulfin snorted in appreciation. "That would make anyone touchy. Get some sleep. Kelleher will relieve me later." He turned to the ring of light he had left behind and watched Turly step into it, his white hair alive. Bulfin shook his head. He did not understand Turly. He never had. But lately Turly had become even more introspective than usual. He knew the reasons for Turly's coming to the south, but they did not seem so crucial as all that. It was something else he could not understand. Something that was changing the Turly he had known. Bulfin started his watch and, like Turly, viewed the ragged clouds passing from dark to dark.

Turly lay down by Harve. The huge man was rolling

on his mat in obvious agitation. Turly watched the great bulk shift from side to side. What was going on in his head? thought Turly. He seemed to be able to feel the dreams of Harve, the darkly green landscape around Inniscloe Lake, the gray boulders looming up in stark contrast. The two, the gray and the green, merging and flowing together. And behind it all the rich red that seemed to be anger. At what? The agitation came and went. Scenes of beauty were touched and marred by scenes of horror as if bones beneath the skin were suddenly visible. There seemed no rhyme nor reason to it. But the whole was painted lightly in Turly's head. He was caught up in the childish giant's imaginings, his hopes and fears. Turly shut it off and turned away. He needed sleep, would need it for the next day when they would reach Straiten.

Across the fire, Kelleher had been watching Turly. The shadows played strange tricks about the white hair and olive face of the lithe figure who had been leaning toward Harve, staring at him. A line changed here, a line there, and Turly would be a sixty-year-old man, and a harassed one. Kelleher thought Turly *could* be sixty years old, a man bent by care and responsibility. He chuckled to himself. Not Turly. Kelleher had never known anyone who liked to play as much as Turly. True, he had been concerned with Meriwether and the thing with his parents, but that was understandable. He remembered how the younger men in the Circle at home had looked up to Turly for direction in their frolic or adventure, whenever he had been there. No one could come up with ideas or schemes better than Turly's. No. Turly would never change. And Kelleher for one didn't want him to. He turned over in his maroon mat. He wanted to be like Turly in everything, in play and in battle skill. But he knew

169

he would have to prove himself to do so. He knew he could do it, given the opportunity. He would not let himself, or Turly, down. Kelleher tossed for a moment then drifted off to sleep.

Outside the ring of fire, and opposite Bulfin's watch, two eyes glittered in the reflection of the flames. They blinked several times. After a moment of silent observation, the eyes turned south and melted into the night.

Chapter 13

The gates of Straiten were impressive. Higher than any two men, they stood solid and impregnable. The dark brown of their wooden poles glowered in the morning sun as Turly and his men passed through the heavy doors. Their mounts were panting in the steamy heat. Rain had soaked them earlier and they were ready for a good breakfast and a dry room. But they knew this was Hastings' territory, and they would have to watch every step they made. Turly was watchful.

The streets were straight and regular as if laid out by design. Each street was numbered and there was a marker driven into the ground at each intersection. The east and west running streets were odd; north and south even. The first east-west street at the northern boundary was 75. The streets to the east and west were wider than the ones going north and south. Turly frowned and wondered what that meant. He let it pass as his group moved down 50 into the largest town of the south.

Houses and hostels crowded both sides of the streets

now, hovering. They were painted alternately salmon pink, holly green, and earth brown. They hung over the travelers like predators, still and brooding, full of a secret life of their own that would never be fully revealed to the casual visitor.

Smith arched in his saddle and glanced rapidly from left to right. He took in all the sights and sounds of Straiten for a reason. He wanted to make a name there as the first trader of the north Circles, the leading man, the spokesman. And this was the fabled trading center of the south. Certainly it did not look like the den of thieves he had heard of. The stories were greatly exaggerated. He could make much money here, he knew it. It was not bad, not bad at all. People were everywhere, moving. If trade could be had, it could be had here with a minimum of trouble. Smith savored the prospect. He could sit down with any one of the prosperous traders he saw scurrying to and fro in the crowd bent on their daily tasks of buying and selling, their faces preoccupied with urgent matters. He would present them with his plan for a north-south trade route, and they would see the wisdom of his thinking. It would all be so simple. When he returned to the Inniscloe Circle, and then to Bellsloe, he would immediately set up offices and conduct the business of the new era in history.

While Smith rode happily engrossed in his dreams of commerce, Turly watched every face for possible recognition. He had noticed with increasing frequency his ability to vaguely sense feelings, not read minds, but to feel *emotions,* a person's basic attitudes toward him specifically, and toward others indirectly. It had begun consciously in the cell with Sean and had grown through the encounter with the mountain folk and the recovery of his friends and on the road to Straiten and now here in Straiten itself.

Turly could see in the nut-brown face of one of the workers from the southeast, for example, a basic distrust of everyone he met; on those of a southwestern fisherman, the taunting look of challenge, of arrogance and pride. And from the Circlemen, his own companions, he could feel the measured sequence and a sense of strength derived from another. Himself. But Smith had thoughts that were painful for Turly to feel. There was in particular one that tore at him. A sense of betrayal. He could not quite make out what it meant.

But Turly could not feel Sean's thoughts. He thought it strange that Sean was the only one that could not be felt. But then this power, whatever it was, was new and perhaps Turly was not using it correctly.

But he could not worry about that now. It would take all their resources to make their way in Straiten without being spotted by the spies of Hastings. It would be far from easy to make contacts and buy information concerning either his father or the enigmatic Blessing Papers, two things which Turly was increasingly beginning to associate in his mind, why he was not sure.

The mounts were tired and Turly could see that arrangements would have to be made soon for feeding them and bedding them down. They had come deep into the heart of Straiten now, weaving through geometrical mazes that seemed to lead always inward; one group of houses and shops looked like another, but with a dissimilarity that Turly could not decipher. Noon was approaching and the heat increasing. The robes and furs appropriate for the higher elevation in the mountains would now have to be discarded. They would have to buy more conventional clothing. Sean agreed to do that while Smith would bargain with a tavern owner for the price of appropriate rooms. Turly saw to the horses while Harve and the others were trying to be as inconspicuous as possible.

Turly struck a bargain with a small brown man with a hunch on his back. He reminded Turly of the small Farks of the mountains whose torn bodies he had seen. But this man's thoughts were clear: to do his job and nothing else. There were no intrigues in this man's mind. Turly paid with the currency he and Sean had gotten in the mountain village. Certain now that the horses at any rate were safe, Turly walked back to Garrett and Kelleher and looked around for Harve and Bulfin.

"I told you all to stay together," he said.

"I know," said Garrett. "But have you ever tried to stop Harve when he sees something he wants? Turly, he doesn't understand the danger we're in. As far as he's concerned, we're taking a pleasure trip, like a visit to the beach at Lands End."

"Which way did he go?"

"This way, not ten minutes ago." Kelleher had removed his hood and was sweating profusely. They all were. He led the way toward a colorful bazaar at the long end of one of the narrow north-south avenues. As the group moved into the confusion of reds and blues and yellows, Turly thought he saw a touch of orange. He stepped up the pace but saw nothing thereafter. The smells of the town mingled. There were the smells of cabbage cooking with pork; the dank aroma of vegetables going bad; the distinct and unpleasant odor of excrement and urine that flowed together in the streets. Turly could see dead rats floating in the gutter and small dogs lying with their legs in the air, their bellies bloated. All was not well in Straiten, he thought. The Circle was at least cleaner than this;

there was more concern for the well-being of the meanest member of the group community. Who would leave rats and dogs to rot in the Circle?

Turly dismissed these thoughts as they abrupted into the small square at the end of the street. Harve was over in one corner arguing with a man wrapped in pink robes with gold rings on his fingers. He held a golden replica of a fish. Its eyes were red stones that glittered in the noon-day sun. Harve was looking at it closely and fingering the tiny scales carved with exquisite care. Turly glanced around quickly. No one seemed particularly interested in Harve, but he could feel beneath them all a possible sense of interest as if far in the night one recognized the minute call of an insect that would come closer and call, in response to another and then another in a rising chorus. Turly would have to move fast. He walked up to Harve.

Harve turned and pushed the fish at Turly.

"See, Turly," he rumbled. "Fish. Beautiful fish. I think Meriwether will like it when we find her. Yes?"

Turly cringed when Harve spoke Meriwether's name. It was the last thing he wanted brought up in this crowded square. He touched Harve on the sleeve and bent him down to whisper in his ear. The giant grinned and straightened back up. He handed the fish back to the merchant reluctantly. Turly could sense disappointment in the merchant but that was all. The merchant swished his robes and turned to another standing by his stall. Harve and Turly walked slowly back to the group waiting in the shadows near the street entrance.

"How did you do it, Turly?" whispered Bulfin who had rejoined his friends. "I tried to get him to come back, and he threatened to hang me from the nearest pole. He was in love with that fish."

"It was simple. Meriwether has already bought one for him and wishes to surprise *him* with it."

"But we don't know that!" said Bulfin with exasperation.

"Neither does Harve. And I would much rather deal with him about it later when we find Meriwether than now when all could be lost. Besides, he may well forget about the whole thing by tomorrow morning. He will have *some* toy, at any rate. I promise you that. I had to trick him to save his skin and ours."

The group moved cautiously to the prearranged meeting spot with Sean and Smith. Turly did not like the idea of leaving Smith to his own devices in Straiten, but he was a more than competent business man; and Turly was certain that at least in this matter, Smith could strike a good bargain for rooms.

The day was turning hotter than Turly had thought it would. It seemed unusual weather, even for summer. In Circle country the temperature would rarely get above a mild warmth. Here it seemed much higher. Perhaps the stay in the mountains had done more to him than he had thought. The others did not seem as affected as he was. Even so, they had to change their appearance. The mountain folk they were dressed as were something of a curiosity in Straiten. With their large fur parkas and solid leather boots, they drew amused if unconcerned glances from casual passers-by. They would have to adapt to Straiten if they wished to remain inconspicuous.

The party reassembled at the corner of 47 and 70 where a small, finely decorated fountain relieved the sharp outlines of the intersections. Sean had done a superb job of scouting the city and refreshing his memory, as if it were a mountain range or hunting ground in the wilds. He knew in one morning almost as much as any inhabitant. But this had alerted him to one danger. When they all met again, he expressed his fear.

"There is no place to run to in case we are recognized," said Sean, who was handing out clothing in various sizes. Harve had a large yellow tunic with green flowers on the shoulders and straight brown leg-hugging trousers that tucked into well-fitting town shoes with thin soles and an embossed pointed tip. He pulled up to his full height and beamed proudly. The others had roughly the same kind of garments. They had sizes that were not exactly right but would do. Harve, being over two meters tall, was easy to describe and fit, although more had to be paid for his clothes.

"What do you mean, no place to run to?" said Turly, already knowing the answer. "Are we going to have to run?"

"I mean," said Sean patiently, "that if we are discovered for whatever reason, we are trapped here in this well-laid square with nowhere to hide."

"Well, we'll have to see that we are not discovered," said Turly. "Now, Smith, what of our accommodations? Do we have any?"

"Yes, and I did quite well, if I do say so. If we're ready, I think we'll find food waiting for us." Smith adjusted the last of his new clothes, a red-and-yellow striped tunic with grey pants, and set out westward toward a part of town that seemed less well-kept than the center and the east of Straiten had been. The houses were squatter and broader, the paint peeling and chipping in the likeness of scabs. The party traveled now in a line strung out to suggest a casual and unrelated assortment of afternoon strollers.

Sean was dressed entirely in gray and walked like a

cat, his senses stretched to the limit, sniffing every wind and letting nothing escape him. Turly watched him as he strolled in the lead point. Sean was an enigmatic man. Met in suspicious circumstances, he had proven his loyalty and concern over and over. Perhaps because he had yet to have an opportunity or reason to do anything else, mused Turly. Smith and the others were in their way good men, weak and capricious perhaps, but Turly knew them, knew their limits. And they were at their limits now, he thought; in the mysterious south, in a large city unlike anything they had ever experienced before, in search of something so far elusive, and possessed by someone or something of great power.

The Green Fox Inn hunkered on the corner of 55 and 90. Its green front was uninviting. Some of its wooden boards were hanging loose, and the paint, like much in this quarter, showed many years of rain and sun. Over the simple door was the sign displaying the logo of the Inn. The eyes of a fox, green like autumn grass, seemed to follow them into the dim interior.

Smith stepped up to the low desk set in the wall to the right near the stairs. The clerk there wore a greasy apron, his hair falling down over his eyes in great clumps, his hands rubbing together on the apron. He smiled and bowed slightly as he saw Smith. He looked around at each of the men and his tiny pig eyes seemed to suggest hunger as he watched them. Turly could sense greed but for no apparent reason other than high food and lodging bills. He glanced at Smith.

"The room, my good fellow," said Smith. He was swaggering a little and Turly watched him closely. Smith was not used to the ways of the south, none of them were, except maybe Sean, and it was Sean who stepped forward.

"Tell me," he said to the clerk, "how much are you taking off the price of one room for seven men?"

The clerk turned pale and looked from Smith to Sean and back again. Here was something he had not expected.

"Four grims for the lot!" blurted Smith. "He said that's a lot less than the winter rate here. And I got him to cut it by having him add a meal in the morning!"

Sean stared at Smith. His eyes said much that Smith did not understand. Sean turned to the clerk and reached for his tunic pocket. The clerk knew what was there evidently, for he quickly looked to the register and began to beam.

"As it happens, my men, an old party just left and I can give you their room for half, for *two* grims." Looking at Sean, whose hand had not left his tunic pocket, the clerk added that since the men all looked like good customers who would drink much ale, he would throw in supper as well.

Smith backed away from the counter in confusion. He knew something significant had happened but could not, or would not, acknowledge the fact. Instead he turned to the others and grinned broadly. "An even better deal. We are lucky today."

Sean took the key to the room and headed up the stairs. The air was musty and close, and there was only a single light at the end of the hall. The group had the center room on the left of the corridor; its windows overlooked the street. Turly brought up the rear of the party. As he topped the stairs he glanced back at the clerk. There was a look of unadulterated hatred on the face of the man who minutes ago had fawned and bowed under the steady gaze of Sean. From that distance Turly could not sense his thoughts, but he could guess them.

Closing the battered green door behind him, Turly spoke first to Sean. The others listened intently.

"Sean, if we are to get answers, we'll have to get them quickly. The man below may use every opportunity to turn us in. It was a foolish thing to catch him like that."

"Perhaps. But he was going to charge us double the going rate. And we will need all we have, to get what we are after." Sean did not look at Smith.

"What's done is done," said Turly. He went to the window and looked out. It was almost noon. He could see heat rise in the streets and from the roofs of the houses. "We will have to use the rest of the day to learn what we can. There is no time for lunch. Sean, you and I will contact your friends, if they are still in Straiten, and see what they can get. Harve and Kelleher, you stay here and guard the room. I don't trust that thieving clerk. Smith, you and the others drift through the streets near here and gather what gossip you may hear. But for *Circle's* sake don't start anything. We will meet back here at dusk. Is that understood?"

All nodded. Smith, still smarting under his mistake, led his men down and out first. Sean and Turly waited a decent interval, then left the same way. Harve and Kelleher were left alone in the room. Harve sat impassively. Kelleher hunched forward on one of the beds and ground one hand into the other.

"Why couldn't I go with Turly?" he said. "I'm as good a fighter as any of them. Better than some." He thought of Smith and the clerk and laughed.

"You will do what Turly says," rumbled Harve. His voice had an ominous ring to it. Kelleher looked up and saw the big man looking directly at him. He knew that Harve would do whatever Turly asked of him. And he knew that it was dangerous to even question Turly's motives around Harve. He looked back at Harve blankly and said nothing.

Sean turned to the right outside the front door and then right at the corner. He headed south on 90 street. They walked about thirty minutes, Sean telling Turly of his friends there in Straiten. They were in the twilight region, between merchants and underworld activists, with some political intrigue which Sean knew little about. Sean explained that he had not been to Straiten recently, but often enough in the past to know the local customs and prices. He knew he had made an enemy of two people back in the Inn, the clerk and Smith, but it couldn't be helped. If the clerk had known he could take them on this matter, he might have tried something else. Turly could see the logic in that and said nothing further about it. There were other, more pressing matters at hand.

Toward the south part of town a subtle change took place. The streets were cleaner and more polished. The Inns took on an air of greater prosperity. The paint was newer on the crowded streets, the windows of the houses sparkled in the summer air. Turly noted the change and recognized that this part of town had either more pride or more money, or both. Even the pedestrians they passed had a distinct air of difference, but with no less menace it seemed to him.

Sean stopped near the corner of 5 and 90. To the west on 5 the streets stretched beyond his seeing. The same to the east. But straight ahead four blocks he could see an open marshy area where nothing stood. They were coming to the end of the southern part of the town. There were the same groupings of buildings up to street 1, but beyond that there was nothing but trees and water.

Sean walked briskly to one of the corner houses on 5 and 90. He knocked three times on the dusty black door. There was silence within. Sean rapped three more times and a curtain quivered on the second floor. There was the sound of feet descending a staircase. The front door opened slightly and a bloodshot eye looked out. It passed from Turly to Sean and back. It settled on Sean and blinked.

"Sean, you mountain goat!" The door flew open. A man the size of Sean leaned out and took him in by the tunic sleeve. Turly followed just before the door slammed shut. In the dim interior Turly could see a sparsely decorated sitting room with two chairs turned against the wall to the left of the door. The stairs on the right climbed up into further darkness. Turly thought he could sense others higher in the house. Maybe two or three.

Sean and the other man were embracing and pounding each other on the back. The other man had a long black mustache drooping from each upper lip down to the chin but not meeting in the middle above the lip. It gave him an odd look. His skin was equally dark and his eyes glowed in the room. He motioned to Turly with his head.

"What is it this time you're into, Sean? The last time you were running furs past the west border guards to sell to the Fallows for beaca weed." The man grinned from ear to ear. He seemed good-natured but had a reserve of hardness, Turly could feel that.

"It's something else this time, Harrow, something good but more dangerous for all that." He turned back to Turly. "This is a man who helped me escape the Order of Zeno and saved my life in the bargain. He needs your help."

182

Turly's hair brushed his shoulders briefly and his scar tingled lightly. Harrow was a friend, Turly could feel that, too. But he was not a man to be taken lightly. Turly would have to tread softly to get what he wanted.

"The Order of Zeno, eh? Any man who bests them is a friend of mine. But saving Sean too, well, that's a different matter. Why didn't you leave him to the mountain buzzards?" Harrow was roaring and slapping Sean about. He then stepped to Turly and took him by the hand. "You are welcome, my friend. Come, let's see what this is all about and what we can do for you."

Harrow pointed up the stairs. Turly went first and Sean followed with Harrow bringing up the rear. As he ascended the stairs, Turly could feel the tension rise in the house. He said nothing, but steeled himself for whatever would happen. A narrow hall took them to a large room with windows opening onto the street they had just left. The curtains kept most of the light out, but Turly could see three other men sitting in silence around the perimeter of the room. Sean entered and immediately went to them, pumped them on the arm and exchanged greetings. There was a muted welcome by these three.

"Now, Sean, tell us what's troubling you to bring you this far south again." Harrow folded his arms and cocked his head. Sean looked at Turly first, then told them selected portions of their adventures as he knew them. He then asked about a man who might have come that way some eighteen years before with a woman, heading even further south. Also he asked about rumors of something called the Blessing Papers that the Order of Zeno might be interested in. At this, one of the men sat up. He stared at Sean and then at Harrow. Harrow motioned at the man to be silent.

"What do you want to know about the Blessing Papers?" Harrow asked quietly.

Sean glanced at Turly. "I want to know whatever there is to know about them," said Turly. "We can pay well."

Harrow excused himself and conferred with the other men. Their faces were hid in the half-light, and Turly could sense their consternation. They muttered for some minutes with a heated exchange at one point. Harrow then returned to Sean.

"We may be able to do business. We will do what we can about the couple, but there is little to know about the Papers. Come back this evening about midnight. We may have something for you then."

Harrow turned to the door to indicate that this particular item was closed to discussion. He led the way downstairs where he got out three goblets and filled them with a rich red wine. Handing one each to Turly and Sean, he raised his in a toast.

"Here's to your venture, Sean, and," inclining his head slightly toward Turly, "to yours." He then downed the contents in one gulp.

"Harrow, we appreciate your efforts. How goes your own trade?" Sean had finished his own cup and placed it back on the side table.

Harrow talked for about five minutes with Sean and Turly on matters of no importance, some local intrigue of years before. He seemed impatient to be rid of them and said as much. If they expected to have some answers that night, they had to let him work. Both agreed and left. As they walked up 90 back to their room, they had the feeling they were being followed. It was now mid-afternoon and short shadows fell across their paths from left to right. Chimney pots and slanted roofs cast their odd geometrical patterns upon the dark pavement. Turly walked boldly in the center of the road while Sean inclined to the left side in the shadows, turning from time to time to glance back over his shoulder.

He was always on guard, thought Turly. There are things to fear perhaps, but can a man live in constant vigilance without it doing something to the man? Turly cut his eyes toward Sean, muffled in gray, as they strode in silence back to the Green Fox Inn.

Chapter 14

In summer the sun always set late. The sky overhead was a high, clean blue, the blue one remembers from childhood. Earlier in the day rains had washed it clean as if a large chalk board had been scrubbed. Here and there an occasional cloud hung still in its position.

In the shadows below, Turly and Sean stood on a corner and surveyed their hotel. Neither liked what they saw. There was unusual activity in the front street. A troupe of circus performers had parked their gear, wagons, animals and cages, and were milling about in disregard of complaints from other walkers. From the corner they could see the window of their room but not inside. Harve and Kelleher should be on duty within. Turly looked at Sean.

"What do you think?"

"I smell trap," said Sean.

"Do you think the clerk recognized us?"

"Either that or he simply turned us in for whatever he could get. Front clerks get their choice of a prisoner's belongings if they are taken in their hotel."

"Well, should we check this closer or get out while we can?" Turly was apprehensive for his friends, but if they had been taken, there was nothing he could do now. He had to get back to Harrow's place later that night.

"I think we ought to get out," suggested Sean.

Both agreed that if all were well, Harve and Kelleher and the others would be merely inconvenienced by their delay in returning. If something had gone wrong, it was best not to give themselves away or they would be no good to anyone. The two pulled back into the shadows and waited for a time to see if anything out of the ordinary would happen. The circus troupe was still roaming about in seeming disarray. Some were working on an axle that was broken, but Turly noticed that they were going about it in the slowest manner, taking time in removing the iron rim that circled the wheel. Anybody familiar with that kind of wagon knew that it was useless to do that. A new wheel would have to be found. Looking at the wagon itself, Turly was sure that a wheel could be found quickly if it were necessary. He felt menace, but in that mass he was not sure at whom it was directed.

Sean grabbed at Turly's sleeve. He pointed with a long finger, which had the rigidity of intense purpose, toward the rear of the wagon.

"Do you recognize anyone there?"

Turly looked closely and his breath stopped.

The thin, bald figure was disguised in the trappings of an acrobatic performer, high collar covering much of his face, but there was no mistaking the gait and the bearing.

"Oliver!" whispered Turly.

"Yes, Oliver. Now why do you suppose *he's* here?

What would the Order be interested in here in Straiten?"
Sean had answered himself.

"What shall we do now, Sean?" said Turly. "We've
got to avoid both Hastings and Oliver. Between now
and twelve tonight we've got to stay hidden. Have you
got any suggestions?"

"As a mattter of fact I do," said Sean. He moved
down 55 away from the hotel and Oliver. He strolled
casually and Turly followed. They walked without incident for several blocks toward the east. The shadows
were beginning to grow longer now, and the smell of
dusk was coming to them from ahead where the blue
was turning purple. Sean turned south at 70 and began
to pick up the pace. He turned to the left when he could
see the stake for 63 squatting in the corner of the road.
Sean slowed and looked around. No one seemed to be
paying any attention to them, and he headed east. Turly,
who had stopped trying to find safety anywhere in the
city and had adopted Sean's stance of caution at all
times, followed. If it had not been for Sean's keen
mountain instincts, he would have already been in
Oliver's circus wagon.

At 10 and 63, Sean stopped at a tavern with red paint
announcing the name on the front window: The Red
Rodent. Turly chuckled to himself. Sean must know the
worst places in town. But if it was also safe, he would
stay anywhere. Both stepped into the smokey interior
of the tavern where a blue flame hovered at the tip of
heavy candles placed in each corner of the single room.
There were tables scattered throughout and Sean took
one that allowed them to face the entrance. A slim figure in red carrying a cloth and a tray walked over to
them. She wore a skirt that came to the knees, a loose
tunic that revealed much, and sandals that lifted her

heels in an appealing way. Dark hair tumbled in waves to her shoulder blades.

"What do you need?" she said.

"Two flagons of ale and two bowls of pickled molon eggs. Follow that with two beaca tubes and your best whiskey neat." Sean was grinning from ear to ear. What he had ordered could be found only in the best taverns and even then only for a high price. Turly wiggled uncomfortably as he felt the indignation of the waitress radiate to them. She was beautiful in the dim light. If she were outside it might be a different story, thought Turly. What was Sean doing?

"Look, we don't have that." The girl started to walk away and then turned and looked closer at Sean. A look of surprise spread over her face.

"Sean! Is it you? It is you! Where have you been all these years?"

The woman stuffed her rag-cloth into the red sash that bound her trim waist and put the tray on the table. Reaching over to Sean, she placed her lips eagerly on his. Without removing them she wiggled down onto his lap. After a moment Sean broke off and laughed aloud.

"Aha! Derva, you've improved with the years. I can feel what it is you have, and it's better now than then," he said.

"Sean, it's good to see you again. But why didn't you come by *once* before you left? I waited the whole of one night for you." She cocked her head at Sean.

"I'm sorry, but I could not." His eyes were merry but cautious.

Derva got up and looked over at the bar. The owner was watching her carefully. He was a large thick man, and Turly thought even Harve would have trouble with him.

"Let me see how soon I can get off." She walked over

and whispered in the man's ear. He nodded and said something to her. She picked up two flagons of ale and walked back to them.

"Here. I've got an hour and I can go. I'll bring some mutton in a moment and then finish my work." She gazed at Sean and shook her head in amusement. Another customer called her and she was gone.

Turly leaned over to Sean after taking a long drink from the cool flagon. Sean was staring after Derva.

"Do you suppose she still likes you, Sean?" Turly could not easily forget the trouble they were in, but he could also appreciate the unexpected turn of events. He had an innocent tone in his voice.

"I believe the girl was telling me something indeed," said Sean. "Come then," he said, brightening up with the thought, "drink up. We'll have supper here and a few drinks, and Derva will give us shelter until we have to visit Harrow again."

Several people drifted in and out of the Red Rodent. None paid any attention to the two men sitting quietly in the corner and finishing up their third round of ale.

At nine Derva took off her apron and put it in a closet at the rear of the tavern. She checked out with the large man at the bar and came over to their table. She said something to Sean, and the two men got up and left money on the table, which Derva picked up and put in her pocket. The group walked out into the twilight. In the west was one brilliant star that seemed to brighten as they walked north up 10. Turly was wrong about Derva. She was just as beautiful outside as in. Dark brows arched in peaks over her soft gypsy eyes. Her lips were full and red.

Derva turned into a small staircase opening on 10 near 67 and climbed to the second floor. She opened a door painted in a new coat of yellow. Inside was a small room only dimly lit by the last rays of the sun coming down from a skylight in the roof. Derva motioned Sean and Turly to a beige sofa against the wall. A low table of highly polished wood squatted in front of the sofa; a bowl of nuts sat on the table at one end, and a slim vase with bright artificial flowers in it decorated the other end. There were watercolor prints hanging on the wall, with bright scenes from the street life of Straiten and the white and gray mountains to the north. On the floor was a square rug with unusual designs woven into it. Turly thought he saw the same flow of detail that characterized the Circle art of Bellsloe. Stylized lines wound about each other within a given border, always winding in motion, but always still. The eye could follow the pattern in and around until it gave up in fatigue.

Derva moved to a door in the far wall. She opened it gently and looked inside. She stood for a moment, then closed the door and returned to the sofa.

"So, Sean, tell me now why you've come back." She crossed her legs. Turly could see the full white thighs under the short skirt of her red costume. He thought of Meriwether. It had been a long time now since she had been taken by Hastings' men. He had no way of knowing if she was still alive, or even where she might be held. It was logical to assume she had been brought to Straiten, but there was no guarantee of it.

While Turly was worrying, Sean was warming to the situation. He was obviously happy to see Derva again. He leaned forward and looked closely at her. "You really want to know?" he said.

"First let me tell you how we got out of the trouble you got us in when you made the deal with Caren to bring illegal goat hides in for mountain ale," said Derva, who had an ironic look on her face.

191

"Well, now, I can explain all that," said Sean quickly. "I had word from the north that an even larger supply was available. I left early to make an arrangement that would have tripled our sale. After getting out of town I heard that Hastings had learned of the deal, and everybody had been warned but me. I decided that it would be best to stay for a while in the mountains. I kept putting off coming back. And now it's been, what, three years?"

Derva pursed her lips. "Well, you're right about one thing. We had been forewarned, but only because your partner had been taken early and then released."

"Cole made it through all right?"

"Yes, but he's never been the same since. I think you should see him, Sean."

"Well, now, if we can, but, uh, Turly here has urgent business of his own." He looked over at Turly and Turly could feel Sean's guilt and shame rise. At the same time he could feel the almost physical ache of Sean *not* to see Cole, whoever *he* was. There was something there, thought Turly. He still could not read Sean clearly. But he could tell that Sean was very much drawn to Derva. Who wouldn't be? She had the physical charm and the open quality of availability that caused men to gravitate to her with a hint of possible gratification.

Turly also felt that if she wished, Derva could back Sean into a corner with this, but she had chosen not to. She changed the subject.

"Have you become a full scout for the mountain tribes, then?" she said. "I remember you wanted to do that and settle somewhere in the Lower Mountains."

Sean glanced at Turly again and chose his words carefully. "At present I am with Turly here; he has something he has to do. He helped me at a critical point and now I am helping him. And that is where you come in."

Sean coughed slightly.

"Yes?"

"Tonight we are meeting Harrow; you remember Harrow. We have asked for certain information and he is trying to get it for us. If anybody can get it, Harrow can. But other people would like to get their hands on us for several reasons it's best not to go into, people like Lord Hastings and the Order of Zeno."

At this Derva sat up. She stared at Sean and Turly. A frown creased her face.

"What have you done this time? You're a good smuggler and lover, but what would make those two get after you at the same time?" She was genuinely disturbed. Sean told her what he thought he could of the incidents of the last weeks. Turly did not interrupt. Her expression went from concern to interest to concern again. When Sean got to the part about putting them up until later in the night, she sagged.

"Sean, you know I'd do anything for you whatever you've done. But you should have told me sooner. I'm not alone anymore. You couldn't have known, but it's not like the old days. I can't pick up and go if Hastings' men show up. And the Order! Do you know what they can do to you if they catch you and want something from you?"

Both Sean and Turly nodded.

"And Sean. Do you know about Harrow?"

"He's the best underground man in southeast Imram. Best drinker and smuggler I ever knew. He likes his pay, but so does every man."

"I don't mean that, Sean. I mean that lately word has it that Harrow and his men have gotten into politics. The Movement against Hastings. Harrow is more dangerous now than he ever was. In more ways than one, you should not be seen with him. Don't go tonight, Sean!"

Sean lowered his head and thought a moment. That could explain Harrow's behavior and that of his men. But why did they agree to try for the information? Harrow would not betray an old friend, and certainly not to his political enemies. There should be no trouble. He looked over at Turly whose olive green eyes were as alive but as inscrutable as ever. There was the slightest hint of dark pupils that ran in an oval. The white hair fell on both sides of his face, framing it in the last light of the sun with the luminous brilliance of a floating mirage.

"Whatever you decide, Sean," said Turly, without being asked.

"We will go." Sean went against his better judgment here, but somehow he felt it right to do so.

With that over, the three fell into conversation about the current fashions of Straiten and the gossip on the businesses in the west that supplied so many goods and services to Straiten but were so mysterious an operation. The avenues leading to the west coast were always crowded with wagons laden with raw goods, and wagons returned laden with fabrics, iron goods, and certain chemicals used in cooking and preparing foods. There had always been rumors of fabulous houses where strange devices could transform the hides into clothing quickly and easily without the labor of many men. And of strange wagons that did not need horses. But these and other stories were only rumors and they were told by the folk in the east for amusement and sometimes to scare their children: We will send you west if you do not do what we tell you.

Derva offered the two men some light wine that had a good bouquet and a lingering aftertaste that was not unpleasant. They talked for several hours. It was almost eleven, and Sean was beginning to talk only to Derva. Turly knew what had to be done.

"Sean?" he said. "I need some fresh air. If you don't mind, I'll step out onto the street and have a smoke. I'll tap on the door when it's time to go."

"Be careful down there, Turly," said Sean gratefully. "There could be spies of Hastings or the Order anywhere."

"I will," said Turly as he got up and stretched his arms. Taking a cigar from his tunic, he walked to the door and let himself out. His last view of the room was of Sean rubbing his hand up under Derva's long legs.

The street was quiet. A few men staggered through the middle of the streets and some fell into doors opposite the stair where Turly stood. But the time passed uneventfully until Turly reclimbed the stairs to get Sean.

Turly tapped lightly on the door. Derva let him in. Her hair was looser, and she held a robe about her, clasping it at the neck with one hand. Sean was holding something with his arms.

"Turly, will you look at this now?" Sean walked over to him. It was a three-year-old child that had, unmistakably, Sean's features. *"My* daughter, Turly. And I never knew I had one. I knew there was a good reason for coming to Straiten, I just didn't know what it was."

Turly reached a finger to the sleeping child's chin and traced down it the shape of Sean's chin. He looked up at Sean and grinned.

"I'm afraid you're right, Sean. It would be a blind fool who thought it wasn't yours." He glanced back at Derva who stood quietly by the door as the two men whispered together. She had an odd look on her face.

"Now what are you going to do with them, Sean?" asked Turly.

"Do? I haven't thought about that yet. Nothing, I suppose."

"Has she *chosen* yet, Sean?"

"No, of course not. Here in Straiten, the women don't choose. The men do. And it's not a stigma as you might think to have a child here and no single mate. It only means you see men with more money, that's all."

Turly blinked. He had known of customs other than those of the Circle, but such knowledge had not come home to him as it did now. Well, it was up to them, he thought. He turned away and looked up into the dark of the skylight.

"It's almost midnight Sean. We've got to go," he said.

Sean gave the child back to Derva. Derva then pushed open the inside door with her foot and placed the sleeping child back into its bed. She came back out and closed the door. Sean and Turly were plotting strategy.

"Derva, I'll be back here in a few hours if all goes well," said Sean. "And then we'll talk. If we're not back, forget you ever saw us."

At the door, Sean leaned over to Derva and said something to her. Turly did not hear. He had other things on his mind anyway. He was about to get information about several things that had preoccupied him since his eighteenth birthday: Meriwether, his parents and maybe even the Blessing Papers. He was eager to be off. He murmured goodby to Derva who looked at him as one looks at a possibly dangerous animal, and then he descended the stairs. He waited for Sean in the midnight stillness.

The two walked rapidly down 10 and then turned west on 5. As they approached Harrow's house at the block of 5 and 90, both men slowed and walked with increased caution. The streets here were still. Very still. Turly felt that it was a part of town that was not usually dangerous to enter at that time of night. But now it was. He strained himself to hear the night and to feel the ambiance of Harrow's house. As with Sean's feelings, he could get nothing.

Sean stopped opposite the house. There were sounds from the marsh not far away that drifted up the street like tendrils of fog. Some croaks seemed near; others were very far away and dim and were like sounds that Turly thought he had never heard before. Then there was an air of unreality about the street and house that Turly thought he recognized. Where had he felt all this before?

At the second floor window a light appeared, flashing three times. Sean poked Turly with his elbow and then motioned him across the street to the front door. That had been the signal. Sean moved to one side and indicated to Turly that he should give the three knocks.

He did so. Immediately the door creaked open. Turly could see nothing inside, but he stepped in and groped forward with his hands.

"This way, gentlemen," said a voice that Turly thought was Harrow's. Turly turned toward the voice. He could not make out the feeling that came from its owner.

"Come, this way, up the stairs. Follow my voice. We mustn't light a candle yet."

Turly stepped gently toward the stairs that he remembered from that afternoon. As he climbed up, he seemed to know that Sean was not behind him: Where was he? The door had not closed behind him on the street; was Sean delayed for some reason? But Turly continued to climb up, up toward the answer to something he had sought, had felt deeply about, for years, ever since he was a boy. He would not be denied now. He flexed his lithe muscles and moved through the darkness heavily and slowly as if he were underwater.

Turly stepped into the room on the second floor. The door was closed behind him as he walked a few steps into the room and stopped.

He could feel it now. And he knew where he had felt this sense of illusion before. Reality crept into his consciousness.

"Oliver," he whispered into the dark.

As a moist cloth covered his face, Turly heard once again sardonic laughter. He heard nothing thereafter as he sagged into someone's arms.

Chapter 15

Turly's eyes literally popped open. He was aware of his situation at the precise moment that he regained consciousness. The ceiling was the color of bone. He looked down at a dark red bed cover and then over at a middle-aged man who was sitting in a comfortable arm chair with his legs crossed, an air of amused meditation on his freckled, oval face. He sat with a large loose paunch nestled in his lap, but his arms and legs were solid and muscular. He had a fringe of red hair that circled his head and a thin red beard to match it. The top of his head was bald and his bulging, frog-like eyes were an intense blue. Turly could feel their magnetism, and he could feel as well an ability to empathize that matched his own. He wore a white frock coat with an emerald *H* embroidered on it. The man had to be Lord Hastings.

"You are alive and well, I see." The voice was deep and soothing. Turly wanted to trust the man.

"What was given me?" Turly rubbed the side of his head and remembered the last moments of consciousness.

"A harmless gas that gives sleep. You will recover quickly. It seemed better to me to bring you here"—he gestured with his right hand in a general sweep that could have included the world—"willingly asleep rather than unwillingly awake. It would have been most tedious for several reasons."

"You are Hastings," said Turly. It was a statement. Hastings raised his eyebrows slightly.

"Yes. And you are the 'man with the white hair' who has caused me a great deal of trouble. It seems that a prophecy precedes you."

"I know nothing of a prophecy." Turly remembered the laughter in Harrow's room as he went unconscious.

"Oliver!" said Turly. "It was Oliver who trapped me. Why have I been taken here?" Turly was suddenly bewildered. He thought Hastings and Oliver were enemies.

Hastings laughed a long, deep laugh. "Oliver and I have worked together on occasion for our mutual benefit," he said. "This is one of those occasions. Oliver has certain gifts that are useful to me, and I have certain resources that are sometimes useful to him. But all in due time. Now I have certain questions to ask you. I want this to be a pleasant meeting for both of us, young man. We can help one another if you will be agreeable. I have some information it seems you are interested in, and you have some I am interested in. An exchange perhaps?"

Turly looked at Hastings. As he sat in the chair, the large man exuded an air of immense energy. Turly felt that this man, of all others he had met, could be a most formidable opponent. He wasn't certain what Hastings wanted now or whether he would help him at all, but there was nothing else to do but to go along and hope that the answer would come.

"Perhaps we could exchange information," said Turly, "if we both have the information the other wants. But no doubt Oliver has already told you of our conversation on the hot bed in his cave."

"Yes. Regrettable. The Order's methods are much too crude it seems to me. I could of course duplicate them if necessary, but you have shown a remarkable resistance to such approaches. I would much rather arrange something more civilized, more urbane."

"What is it you wish to know?"

Hastings uncrossed his massive legs. He put one hand on each knee and leaned forward toward Turly. His eyes looked into Turly's. Almost puffing outward, they seemed to probe more deeply than Oliver's had. Turly felt their force and had to resist them.

"I want to know exactly where the Blessing Papers are and how to get to them."

Turly groaned. He knew nothing of any Blessing Papers and had told Oliver so. Why did they think he did know? What caused them to believe that he, of all the men in the island, had knowledge of something like that?

Hastings sat back. He put one hand on his chin and rubbed his beard. He gazed quietly at Turly for a moment and then began to speak.

"It is possible, I suppose, that you consciously have no knowledge of the Papers, as Oliver said. But it's far more likely that you have *unconscious* knowledge of them. We will have to force it out, raise it to the surface by various means. And make no mistake, Turly. We will get that knowledge. And when we are through, you will not be the same person."

Turly shivered. He knew somehow that Hastings was right. He would never leave here quite the same person. Something would die here, and that part began to scream silently in the dark regions of his mind. But there something else stirred, and Turly felt its strength. He did not know why, but a great peace settled on him long enough to answer Hastings calmly and deliberately.

"You may do what you have to do."

Hastings was mildly surprised. He cocked his head at Turly and pursed his lips.

"This will be far more interesting than I thought. I am sure now that I am on the right path. Let us then pursue it." Hastings put both hands on the arms of his chair and looked at the ceiling. Turly thought at that moment how easy it would be to spring from the bed and take Hastings by the throat. He could hang on long enough to do the job, he thought. He could then make an escape.

"Try it, my young friend," said Hastings in a soft voice.

Turly did. He could not get off the bed. Perhaps it was the result of the drug he had been given, but Turly could not muster the strength to act against Hastings.

"Now that we've discovered the futility of that, let's begin our search, shall we?" said Hastings. "First some background information to set the stage. You may or may not be familiar with some of this material. Some of it is based on the cunning work of the monk Dermot. You have met him, I believe. He had an accident of sorts, I hear, but it was not fatal, fortunately or unfortunately. Did you know about his accident?"

Turly shook his head yes, but he didn't care about Dermot.

"Well," said Hastings, "no matter. Where was I? Yes. It seems, young man, that the history of the last thirty years or so has come down to you. No, don't interrupt me quite yet." Hastings waved his hand around in the air a bit, settled back, and prepared to talk at some length.

A knock at the door stopped him. Hastings called out to enter, and a tall man with a gnarled left hand came in. He sneered at Turly and then bent to whisper something in Hastings' ear. Hastings frowned and sat up.

"It seems our conversation will have to wait a moment," he said. "However, I will be back and we will continue. In the meantime," said Hastings, standing and waving his arm into one corner, "you may get up and wander around if you can. There are some items in the cabinet over there you might be interested in." Hastings smiled. Turly did not think it was meant to be a comforting smile.

After Hastings and his man had left, Turly lay for a time staring at the ceiling. He still felt weak but believed his strength was coming back. He glanced over at the wooden cabinet. It was an old one, and it was well built. The legs were like claws, and the top curved up and out in glossy spirals. Turly's curiosity grew, and he sat up. Dizziness swept over him. He sat still until it passed and, standing up slowly, carefully, he began to hobble to the cabinet.

There were glass front doors. Turly rubbed them in wonder. He had not seen much glass before. Clear, beautiful. Locked. Turly tugged for a minute and toyed with the idea of tearing the doors off their hinges. No. Hastings wanted him to see the things in the cabinet. He would be able to see them then. Turly looked into the cabinet front, his eyes weaving and bobbing as if trying to see something in the distance. He squinted his eyes. There were several book-lined shelves, with a number of smaller objects lying in disarray on them.

There was something familiar there.

Coins.

Coins like those his father had left him, coins marked with the face of the Sequence demons. Something else caught his eye. It was a painting of a young man standing in front of an old building. The picture was not in color, but Turly could see an intricate design in the windows of the building. The young man was intense-looking with a large rounded forehead, and he wore a light-colored robe with an arrow and turtle on it, like Oliver's. An Order monk. The eyes were hooded, large and penetrating, looking straight out at Turly, into him. Turly could not tell the exact color of either the hair or eyes, but the hair was light, like the robe. The picture was in shaded tones of brown and white. Turly thought it a strange painting, but he did not dwell on it. He was too interested in what the man was doing. He was standing with both hands open in front of him. One was pointed down to the ground, the palm open; the other was pointed up into the air. Turly thought he knew the man, but he could not recall from where. He had an odd feeling about the picture. He could not explain it, and yet . . .

Turly stepped away from the cabinet. There were rapid footsteps in the hall outside the room. He staggered back to the bed and collapsed on it just as the door opened. A small gnome-like man entered, carrying a tray balanced carefully on the fingers of one hand. The man looked at Turly and nodded. He turned to close the door. The tray he was holding was of tarnished silver. On it was a small silver cup. The gnome offered it to Turly by pushing the tray in his direction. Turly refused.

"You will feel better after drinking this," said the gnome with a high, crackling voice. He offered it again to Turly. This time Turly shrugged and took it. He downed the liquid and wiped his mouth. A strong warmth spread through his body. The weakness and dizziness were gone.

"Thanks," said Turly. He did not know why he said it. He was sure that nothing that happened to him here would be in his best interest. But there was little else to do. Turly then took a sharp look at the little man.

"Do you know me, young man?" asked the gnome.

Turly shook his head. He thought he was sure he had never seen this man before. A large white beard covered his face. Hairy wrinkles in the dark weather-beaten skin rolled like a plowed field. He had a thin hooked nose that nestled between great bushy eyebrows, and small glittering eyes. Turly thought there was a touch of benign sadness in them.

"Do you not remember old Colum, Turly?" The voice was soft and restrained.

Turly's head snapped up.

Colum!

But Colum had been killed years before. Turly had seen the body.

The old gnome laughed merrily. "Years have indeed come upon me, but I am the same man who befriended you and Ellman years ago in the north. We share many memories, do we not? Sorry I was to have to play that last trick on you. That was not *me* killed, but a friend of mine who had gotten too close to the Order of Zeno. It was regrettable, but I took the opportunity, passed myself off as dead, and moved on. Down here," he said, pointing to the floor with one knobby finger.

"But, Colum," blurted Turly, "whom are you working for? Hastings? If so . . ."

"Well, yes and no. I am in Hastings' employ, but I do not work *for* Hastings. There is a distinction."

Turly thought about that for a while. "You sound as if we had been *watched* in the north," he said. He was getting confused about Colum's role in his past.

"You *were* watched," said Colum, "and not just by

me. By some of the other watchers I could do nothing about. But I could do something about Hastings and the new Order. You were supposed to have been killed years ago. And you were in a way," he said, pointing at Turly's arm and the scar on it. "I fostered that belief down here. But when you were recognized some weeks ago, the hunt was on again. I went up there as soon as I could and followed you all the way down. It was a merry chase at times, I might add."

"In the Order caves, too?" Turly was perturbed.

"Yes, for a time. Unfortunately I cannot interfere often, so there was some necessary discomfort on your part, I know."

"Interfere?" said Turly, his eyes quickly narrowing. "In what? Whom *do* you work for?"

"I work for . . . someone other than Hastings or the Order. But I cannot tell you who right now. You are still in great danger and we must hurry. Later, later."

"But . . ."

"The drink I gave you will help you ward off Hastings' influence. You will no doubt have already noted that he can be persuasive."

"Colum, what of my other friends?"

"All who came with you from the north have been taken by Hastings. But the long-haired scout from the mountains eluded him. No one seems to know how he escaped Oliver's illusion. But listen to me, Turly. Hastings will be back shortly. Go along with him for now. He will tell you strange things. Some of it will be true, some not so true. But it is time you began to remember the past. Hastings is right about that." Saying this, Colum did not stay to be questioned. He slipped out the door he had entered. His long beard blew to one side with the draft of the open door.

Turly sat stunned on the bed. His strength had returned, but he was now mystified by this new turn of events. *A man he thought had died long ago. A promise of new revelations. The suggestion that he knew more than he thought he knew about the Blessing Papers.* Turly could feel a stirring in his mind, but it was thin and indistinct and elusive like an object seen in a dense fog. Whatever was there would have to wait until it revealed itself.

Lord Hastings opened the door and came back in. He was entirely at ease again and rubbed his ham-like hands together in anticipation of talking at last with the man who was supposed to find the Blessing Papers. Turly had shown great resistance to Oliver and to the initial contact. But Hastings was confident. He had never known defeat.

"You are ready now to have our talk?" Hastings touched one side of his massive nose.

"I am ready," said Turly. Just as well now as later, he thought.

Hastings settled back into his chair. He touched his fingers together in a steeple and began to talk.

"The Blessing Papers exist. No question. But there is a long story that leads up to our present quandary about them. Be patient."

Turly felt good now, better, and he sat back to listen. Interested, but wary.

"Stretching from a time long ago, about the 1890's, a line of thought evolved and grew across the twentieth century, until by the turn of that century the marriage of two seemingly opposed systems of thought became feasible. Early in the twenty-first century, for various reasons, it was possible to merge religion and science, the two forces of faith and fact."

"Faith and fact?" asked Turly.

"Yes," replied Hastings. "The states of *wanting* to believe in something, and the having of a solid reason for doing so. There had long been a war between these two states of mind. There were early laborers for a merger called, if I remember rightly, theosophists. They advocated a 'religious science, and a scientific religion.' Their basic concept of a discernible order in the world and beyond, both mental and extramental, could, they thought, be backed up by hard evidence, the kind any court of law would accept. They wanted to make rational the most irrational of human beliefs: the 'real' existence of God and the soul."

"There is no God," said Turly. "There is only the One we will all return to through the final fire."

"I know, Turly, I know," said Hastings, waving his hands around again. "The Circle has left its mark on you. I accept that. But please do not interrupt when I mention things that might go against your Sequence. We will be here all night otherwise."

Turly nodded. He wondered where else the story would take him. He did not like the training that Ellman had given him called into question. Disturbed, he sat on the bed with his arms folded over his knees, his head held to one side.

"Small wonder," continued Hastings, "that when the dominant influence of science, fact, ran into its own particular dead-end, theosophy and its adherents were there to step into a sudden and horrible vacuum and offer what seemed like a way out."

"Dead-end? A way out?" asked Turly.

"Turly, please," said Hastings. "Let me move on. I hope to make all this clear to you soon enough. The Blessing Papers are the end result of certain events in the past. Let me tell you what I know of that past."

Turly shrugged.

"Good. Now, a little more than one hundred years

ago, several things conspired to lead to the wedding of old foes, faith and fact. One concerned a shroud, another knowledge about knowledge itself, and finally a vial of red dust."

Turly rubbed the side of his head as if it were in pain. He could not follow the conversation closely enough to argue, even if Hastings would let him. It was as if he were again a student at Ellman's feet, forced to pull in information and store it without offering any back. Trying to understand something with no basis yet for doing so. He raised his hand tentatively into the air, enough so to make Hastings chuckle but not stop.

"Let me start with the shroud first, Turly. Then we'll go to the other things." Here Hastings leaned forward in his chair, his huge paunch bunching up like a pillow.

"What is a shroud, Hastings?" said Turly.

"A death wrapping. A sheet in which the dead can be clothed and placed in the ground or in a cave, or burned."

"I see," said Turly. "And the red dust?"

"One moment, young man," laughed Hastings. "One moment. Let me tell you about the shroud, an amazing relic of the past, even if it was controversial. It was called the Holy Shroud of Turin. On that death wrapping was pictured the anatomically correct shape of a man. How did it get there? Whose image was it? Was it a real image? It had been around for many years and was considered to be an oddity, a trick, an amusement. But it was claimed to be the true image of a Holy man of the past, a man who had *literally* risen from his death, a suggestion that goes even beyond your Circle resurrection, I believe. The image proved that event, some said. Others said it was only a clever forgery, a painting done years *after* the man had lived and died."

Turly rustled on his bed like a dog eager to go outdoors. There were things mentioned here that he wanted to go into in a way Hastings did not seem to be going. But he held his tongue.

"It was a marvelous image, whatever the case. I have seen it. There was a shoulder-length of hair, mustache and beard, a surprisingly athletic body for a Holy man, bent feet, thumbs curled into the palms, wounds at various places. It was the very image of a man killed by being nailed to crossed sticks of wood."

The thought chilled Turly. Hastings' eyes were wide with excitement.

"It must have been a truly startling thing, Turly, for the people of the twentieth century to learn, through various skeptical ways, that a thing of such a faith-ridden history *was* real."

"Real? What does this mean?" asked Turly, sitting up.

"Yes, well," said Hastings. "The *image* on the shroud was proved to be real, genuine; that is, it was neither painted nor faked. And it was not the result of bodily stains either. It was an extraordinary image proved to be that of a man who had lived about the time the Holy man had lived. At that point, it was just the image of a man, but not necessarily *the* man. Who could know if it was of the Holy man? A lot of men had died the way he had died. It was not uncommon. A mystery still remained. If the image were real, whose image was it, and how was it caused? If the shroud was genuine, what did it all mean, as you have asked, Turly."

Turly nodded his head in anticipation. He was beginning to follow the argument.

"It was here that the theosophists stepped in and offered an intriguing possibility. The shroud, they said, had been left behind by the Holy man so that a skeptical age of fact, with its advanced knowledge, could validate what had been dismissed as either myth or false history. That was a brilliant stroke. It appealed to the minds of both camps. In fact the followers of theosophical thought increased tremendously. Scientists were among them. Scientists, Turly, the masters of fact."

"And the *dust,* Hastings?"

"Let's wait a moment for that. I think it's time to look at the dead-end of knowledge. You see, there was a good reason why the masters of fact were willing to even *consider* the meeting of the two fields of thought. It concerned the nature of reality."

"The Circle knows what reality is," said Turly. "I have Framed it myself."

"Indeed," replied Hastings. "Well, to the old science 'reality' was what it could measure, what it could know about, what it could record and verify, what it could *see.* But even before the shroud controversy, science had developed something of a problem in that seeing."

"What was the problem?" asked Turly. His eyes were about to glaze. So many names, so many new ideas.

"As I understand it," said Hastings, "in any field of knowledge there is an initial period of discovery that is swift and often astonishing. Much knowledge about reality was gained in that way throughout the age of science. But as the knowledge in any field grows, it is known that there will be an end to that knowledge, to the gaining of any further knowledge. Now, that fact was not grievously clear as long as knowledge was limited to the world around us. There was always *something* new to be seen, more or less. A new hill to pass beyond. Salvation. But in the twenty-first century all that yearning outward had changed. An end to *all* human knowledge about man's world, and the end of any further possibilities beyond his world, was seen."

"Why?" interrupted Turly. He thought this a lie.

"When the study of 'fact' went *beyond* our eyes, that's when the problem came in," said Hastings patiently.

"There is nothing beyond our eyes," said Turly.

"Oh, come now, young man," retorted Hastings. "Even your Mythic Sequence makes allowance for the 'inward terror' of the unknown and the 'multiple struggles' of the self with the world, does it not? That could well include something beyond our eyes. And for our ancestors the knowledge they gained, or rather *could not gain,* was enough of an inward terror to drive them into a different kind of pursuit, a pursuit of that which had always been called the 'occult', the hidden, the unseen."

"But, Hastings," said Turly, *"why* does the *seen* run out?"

"For example. There was one branch of knowledge that tried to find the tiniest parts of things. Imagine, Turly, the smallest thing that makes up a rock. Is it like an even smaller rock? How small is it, and what makes that up? Is there a solid base for a rock in its smallest part? You don't know? Well, your ancestors knew. And that was the trouble. They had an instrument which could allow them to see some of the smallest parts of the rock. But even that magical instrument had limits. It suggested that the smallest parts it could see were not the smallest parts that there were. There were rocks within rocks within rocks. The instrument could be stretched only so far. There was a point it could not see beyond. Everything could be known about that rock up to a certain point. After that . . . nothing. Only conjecture. No facts."

"Fact had to accept faith after that point?" asked Turly, suddenly feeling that it was making sense to him.

"Something like that, Turly," allowed Hastings. "The

same was true in the other direction. Have you ever wondered about that *other* distance, Turly? How far does the darkness of the skies go? There seems to be no limit, I understand. At least no discernible distance. The black night might loop and twist and do a number of things, but at last fact has to yield to faith again. Our fathers could not *see* the end of the skies either. Two different boxes, Turly. One *vast* and beyond seeing; the other *minute* and beyond seeing."

"You know a great deal, Hastings," said Turly wearily.

Hastings raised his right arm, the white coat sliding down, exposing a thick wrist. "I do, and gathered with difficulty. But no amount of knowing about the past will bring it back. It is *now* we must deal with. All the past can do is let us understand the now."

"Then continue," shrugged Turly.

"The episode of the shroud brought the old argument of faith and fact to a head. Science was, at its heart, ready for a new direction, anything which might offer a way out of either finally closed box. And faith, because of the shroud's authenticity, was ready to give up its beliefs to rational scrutiny. It was thought that the two old enemies might set a new direction in human affairs, come together in a field that might prove to be endless. As a result of the shroud and the closed boxes of knowledge, good men of all stripes met to debate the options open to them."

"What options *did* they have?" asked Turly, engrossed, caught.

"On the one hand man could continue in a closed garden, a paradise of sorts in which all that could be known *was* known and repetition of old patterns would be the norm of behavior. Men might even deliberately *forget* certain things so that they would have the thrill of discovering them all over again. Man would have everything *possible,* but it would be a final box, a crib of a forever youth. Rather depressing, I think you'll agree."

"Yes, I suppose," said Turly, rubbing his chin.

"On the other hand," continued Hastings, "man could more or less abandon his material conquest of nature, space—examples of which would seem to us on the *order* of magic—and focus all his energies and factual methods on the inner sphere, the mind, the spirit. This seemed to be the only alternative to a golden age that had turned sour."

"Turned sour," said Turly.

"Yes. The merger of hope and skeptical inquiry into a psychic search seemed to offer a way out of the closed garden. It might lead to answers about man's world closed to him in his merely *factual* search. But this exploration of man's spirit would be subject to factual searching. It was to be only a shift in realms for both disciplines. Faith would fling open the myriad doors of fantasy, and fact would test the fantasies with its logic. There was at first much controversy, of course. But all the world's governments—after strife, anger, the destruction from the despair born of boredom—were convinced of the gravity of the situation and so gave their approval to a United Council, set up to probe the possibility of an official merger."

"You mean they actually . . . ?"

"The United Council of York in 2018 was a resounding success, considering. Sound logic was advanced. Ground rules were set up. At the Council of Methe in 2019 the merger was announced. In 2020 the Church of Spirit and Science was established. Thereafter, using his tools and objective logic, man was to seek his fulfillment in the realm of the spirit. The irrational would be made rational for the good of all."

"That *sounds* for the good, Hastings," said Turly. "But I can tell from the sound of your voice that it didn't work. Come to think of it, I can look around me and see that it didn't work."

"You catch on quickly, Turly. Good," said Hastings. "And you are right. Something did go wrong. Something unforeseen, although no one should have been surprised, given the nature of the enterprise. It was conceived of hope and despair; but it had an offspring that was a major catastrophe as far as man was concerned. Now, this is what happened. But listen, Turly, believe what you have to believe. Records of that time are almost non-existent. I have a number of reports, and I have a good library, but most of the records are based on second- or third-hand information. It is all quite sketchy. It seems *deliberately* so."

"Then the truth might be something else," blurted Turly, irritated at this confession of possible ignorance.

"I told you to believe what you have to believe. It is all any of us can do. I, now, have to act as if *my* beliefs are true. You see?"

"I suppose," said Turly. "Tell me what happened after the merger to cause the catastrophe." He was excited now. There were answers coming to questions he had not known existed as questions.

"Not long after the Council of Methe had sanctioned the Church of Spirit and Science, and set up its official offices for business, the Vatican, center of the traditional church of the time, released something it had concealed for more than two thousand years."

"What?"

"It was a small vial of dust said to contain the preserved blood of the same Holy man whose alleged shroud we have just been discussing."

"Ah, the dust," said Turly.

"Yes, now the dust. The dust led to the pit. To the pit out of which we have yet to crawl, if we ever do."

"But you said the shroud was authentic," said Turly, bewildered.

"Remember, Turly, while the image itself was authentic, the antecedent of that image had not been established. It was time to find out for sure whose image that was, or so the Vatican leaders thought. The man in question had, after all, been a powerful influence in the Western world, especially here in Imram if what I have read is true. That man's physical structure would be reconstituted from the secret blood and then matched with the image on the shroud. If there was a match, the question of his authenticity would be answered and, given the miraculous nature of the image, the new Church of Spirit and Science would have an auspicious beginning. Fact would finally validate faith. And both sides wanted this to happen. That had been settled by the formation of the new church."

"How could the Holy man be resurrected?" asked Turly who lay back on the bed, his hands cradling his head. He did not know how much of this to believe. He remembered Colum's warning about how persuasive Hastings could be. But the tale was certainly interesting, like the Framing of reality back home.

"The scientists of that time—our great-great-grandfathers—were able to reconstruct almost anything for purposes of study. They had long since been able to reconstruct the bones of animals—I have a few here—but they could also do the same for the *flesh* as well as the bone at that time."

Turly's eyes flashed. "They could resurrect the flesh?"

"Oh, yes," said Hastings. "Men who had lived ages before could be completely restored *if* any part of them had remained behind."

Turly shook his head in disbelief.

Hastings smiled wanly and went on. "The *flesh* could be resurrected, Turly, but not the mental processes of the resurrected creature. Only a shell for study could be had. But it would be a shell of the thing as it really had been."

"What could do this?" asked Turly, amazed.

"Something that was called the Rising machine."

"The Holy man was raised by this?"

"Yes, he was. But then it began."

"What did?"

"The Falling."

"Why?"

"The make-up of the man, the simulated cavities, the very substance restored pointed to something that was not of this earth, but was not spiritual either."

"The man was not Holy?"

"He was not even a man," said Hastings softly.

"How could they raise a man who was not a man?"

"He was close enough."

"How close?"

"The Holy man—an exact match for the image on the shroud, by the way—was neither a god nor a man. He was not even a fabulous monster of some kind, but a thing only wrapped in human flesh and semblance like a doll."

"The Holy man was a toy?" whispered Turly.

"Something like that," said Hastings. "A very well-crafted device, evidently, and the thought of such a thing coming so early in human history affected our ancestors as much as it is affecting you. It suggested that something inhuman had meddled in man's past, had tampered with it in one way or another. It was a terrible blow to the world's collective mind."

"Circle!" responded Turly, his breath holding in his chest like ice in a river.

"Beyond that little is known. The Fires that followed ruined records and scattered peoples. It removed too much of the past, too much," said Hastings slowly. "But such a discovery had shocked the world at large. There must have been mass hysteria."

"Because of the Holy man who was a doll?" asked Turly quickly. "Why? The Circle did not believe in this man. The Circle would not have cared."

"The Circle came *after* the Falling, Turly, not before. The Circle has its beliefs, as our ghostly fathers had theirs. They believed theirs, Turly, just as you believe yours. They had the props pulled out from under their beliefs. Could *you* take that, Turly?"

Turly remembered how disturbed he had been earlier when Ellman's teachings had been questioned by Hastings. He tried to multiply that many times. He could not grasp the result of doing so and shook his head at Hastings' question.

"I thought not," said Hastings. "Now, imagine this. If the Holy man was a 'toy' as you say, then whoever or whatever had created it was no god. And the toy was certainly not the very god of a very god. What then of the promise that had been made to men that the Holy man would be with them always? Was their heaven to consist of such toys? The mansion of many rooms, was it only a giant craft shop?" Hastings laughed a deep, booming laugh.

Turly huddled within himself, thankful for the drink Colum had given him.

"If this were so, Turly, heaven would be no better than the old closed systems man had already turned his back on. This helped the Falling too. The belief in *spiritual* immortality, so universal and so primal, was called in doubt, and the towering structure of theology based on the principle of the incarnation of a perfect god toppled and crashed to the ground. A system of thought, of feeling and believing, that had withstood so many attacks, and even outright persecution, could not withstand this. Institutional churches withered and died as their memberships faded into doubt and despair. Science also suffered a decline, a serious decline, because of this truth. People turned from its factual betrayal of the spirit."

"Then the knowledge of the Holy man-machine caused the Falling," said Turly.

"Yes. But that was not all. In both the eastern and western parts of this world—of which this island is only a small part—each major society had, in hope of fulfilled pride and arrogance, resurrected its leaders of the past. Without exception the heroes of man's rise, material and spiritual, were found to have been man-machines."

"I don't really believe this, Hastings," said Turly.

Hastings stared at Turly for a moment and then laughed uproariously. He pounded the arm of his chair and rocked to and fro as his body shook. "Then look on it as only a story, Turly. Stories can do anything. You know that?"

"Circle Framing can do more than that," answered Turly.

"Maybe so," said Hastings, "but my own story waits, because we now arrive at the moment of the Blessing Papers. The history of this period, however scattered, is still a little clearer than the preceding time. We know that shortly after the Falling began in 2020, and just before the Fires, a mysterious box was delivered to Thomas Blessing, Head of the Church of Spirit and Science. Rumor had it that the box contained papers explaining the reason for the man-machines and offering a solution to the problem of human response to such things."

"The Blessing Papers were named after Blessing?"

"They came to him first," said Hastings. "You must also understand that Thomas Blessing was a key figure in world politics of the time. He had been named first Head of the newly created CSS. Much was therefore expected of him when word got out about the box; rumors were everywhere about the possible meaning of the Papers, and hope grew, hope for a restoration after the Falling."

"And . . . ?"

"Blessing did nothing with the Papers, Turly, *nothing*. Instead he took the box and dropped out of sight. He and the 'Blessing Papers' were gone. Hope was gone as well. Disunity and fragmentation in human affairs grew, proceeded to spread with increasing rapidity. And then the Fires came, which more or less ended the world and left man with this island as we now know it. But this island was not untainted.

"There were active forces of division at work in the world in the early days. The Blessing Papers were blamed, rightly or wrongly. Union of any kind was impossible because of these forces. Even here in Imram *now* there are certain things that cannot be done, things *I* can't seem to be able to do. Like organize the north and the south, or find the Papers themselves, or find clear answers to old questions. And that," he said, while jabbing one finger toward Turly, "is where *you* come in."

"But, Hastings, I don't know anything about any of

this. Only what you have just told me," said Turly, flabbergasted.

"Never mind for now," muttered Hastings. "It is sufficient to note that after all these years—almost four generations now—people at large have almost forgotten the past. There are new names for just about everything, since names are memories and there are few memories left. Call it racial shock. Call it interference. But men all over the world, those who survived the spasmic catastrophe of the Falling and the Fires, drew back into the old agricultural and hunter societies they had been in once long before. It came naturally, I suppose. Only a certain low level of technical skill and knowledge was necessary to carry on. The magnificent machines that had once rolled through Imram without sound, and flew through her skies—yes, flew, like silver needles—were no more. Lost. Hidden. Gone."

"But, Hastings," began Turly.

Hastings raised a finger. "I have *some* of those things here in Hastings Hall. I'll show them to you in a moment."

"And the Circles?" asked Turly, anticipating Hastings.

"In the latter part of the twenty-first century, years after the Falling, a few men in the north managed to get a foothold of sorts and developed the basis for the Universal Mythic Sequence Church. A new Council, convened at incredible cost to the participants, met in 2075 to aid the confused populace, who had only fragments, tatters of myth, legend, odd assortments of fact and fable to guide them in their daily lives. Now, as you know, the Mythic Sequence is a marvelous mixture of myth and belief. The Sequence offered much—eternal life—in terms of an emotional 'framed reality,' achieved in beaca visions and a yearning for the One, itself a symbol of a finite infinity. In fact the Circle ritual was a little bit of both of the old systems. It offered an acceptable blend of faith and fact. Acceptable *if* you need blind trust in a One, and *if* the 'facts' you discover in visions are not closely tested."

"That's not so, Hastings, and you know it," cried Turly. "The framed reality of the Circle is meant to tell us what we know to be true in the heart. It gives us words that can lift us above the reality we can't stand for long."

"Yes," said Hastings drily. "But some were suspicious of it."

"But why?"

Hastings raised his voice to silence Turly's. "The Sequence spread as rapidly in the North as disunity had. As a result, some thought the Sequence to be just another step in the maneuvers of those who had first interfered in human history."

"The Sequence?"

"The Sequence. These men felt the Circle concept put man back in the same closed box science had found itself in. And just as depressing a box. A seven-step cycle that allowed only a few variations on it."

Turly did not interrupt Hastings on that. He knew it to be true. But he also knew that the variations were what gave life to the Sequence, gave life to the Circle believers. He would hold his thoughts for a while.

"Turly, are you listening?" asked Hastings sharply.

"I am."

"Turly, certain men wanted man to live as a questioner, not as a resigned acceptor, nor an inane repeater. Whatever the revelations about his past, they thought, man must be a wanderer. Countering the closed box problem, they saw that man must at least have the *feeling* of a world of open possibility. It was necessary to surmount the fact that he didn't have one. Man could live fully in a closed system only by not being in one. A paradox, no?"

"I suppose," said Turly. "But I see no difference in that and the Sequence insistence that a man must go on in hope of arriving finally on the other side of fire."

"There is a difference, Turly. It is the difference between the Circles in the north and the Order of Zeno in the south."

"You're talking about the Order beliefs now?"

"In 2090 the Order of Zeno was established by John Vail and a few others to give man a reason to go on living and growing as if the world were still open to him. 'Man In Less Is More' and 'Nothing Ends That Begins' were among their paradoxical slogans set up in the face of paradox itself: Man cannot live in a closed system; but he is in a closed system. By the way, Turly, *I* was one of the founders of the Order of Zeno, and a good friend of Vail's."

Turly stared at Hastings. The man was an enigma. A co-founder of the Order of Zeno and yet a strong non-Order leader in the south. What was he up to? Turly was confused again.

"That was almost thirty years ago," said Hastings, staring back at Turly, forcing his thoughts into the younger man. "Fifteen years after the founding of the Order, early in the twenty-second century, the Blessing Papers reappeared. Vail got his hands on them somehow. He kept them hidden, but held a special meeting of the Order hierarchy. The Order split between those who wished to destroy the Papers and those who wished to let them continue doing whatever it was they were doing. It was a hopeless split. I knew it, Vail knew it. Because of this, I should have seen what would happen. John Vail took the Papers and, just as Blessing had done, dropped utterly into darkness. No one knew where he had gone or what he meant to do."

"And so the Order has been looking for him ever since," said Turly, understanding what the mission of the Order was.

"I'll come to that in a moment," said Hastings, crossing his legs and rearranging himself in the large chair. "First something about the box. No one was sure what the message of the Papers was, but we all were told by Vail that, whatever it was, it had to be believed."

"*Had* to be believed?"

"Yes. Apparently that was one of the functions of the box the Papers were in. To force belief in the Papers. Now, that was a powerful thing to have in one's possession. This was, I'm sure, another reason why John hid the box. You see, the idea of having a way to force belief corrupted some into wanting the box for reasons other than the Order's stated intent of helping man remain man. For earthly or political purposes, for example."

"You," said Turly, pointing a finger at the bulging eyes.

"I was one of those," admitted Hastings. "At the time I no longer cared for the spiritual aspects of the drama. I was interested only in the political reunion of this island. I thought if I had the power of what came to be called the Blessing Box and Papers, then I could make this island great again, restore it to the past and to the future. And then the rest might follow, the discovery of what had happened and how to prevent it from happening again. Because of this I broke with the Order long ago."

Turly rubbed his eyes. He felt very tired now. Had John Vail gone through many discussions like this? He looked at Hastings quizzically, thoughtfully. Hastings misread him.

"Does Oliver know my intentions? He guesses at them, I suppose. But he wants the Blessing Papers as well, and for a different reason. He wants to destroy the whole thing. He is a survivor of that part of the Order which had wanted to lose the Papers entirely, get along without them and all their implications. Oliver believes the Papers must be utterly destroyed if man is to have a chance to survive, at least on the Order's terms."

"The Order's terms don't sound bad," said Turly.

"Turly, Oliver is Head of the *new* Order of Zeno, not the old, of which John Vail was Head. The old Order wanted to preserve human sanity in the face of a devastating reality—impossible man-machines of the past, a closed-system universe, possible outside interference in human history. The new Order wants to preserve man *for* the Order. It is determined to keep from him the knowledge of the Papers and to return him to something like the system that prevailed before the Council of Methe. A system with religious paradoxes to be sure, and with faith in them, but without science of any kind."

"I see," said Turly.

"And the new Order has become dangerous in a way the old one never was. It is full of fanatics. You met Dermot? John Vail was at least a good man. He wished merely to retain man's collective sanity in the face of possible insanity. That is a noble aim, don't you agree? But his original aim was perverted. The Order no longer wants to help the larger community of man, as I do."

Turly was again confused. Who was doing what, and why?

"John Vail dropped out of sight completely in 2105.

225

His Master of Rituals, Reed Corvine, went with him. The Order fell into confusion; Oliver stepped into the vacuum. No one knew where Vail had taken the Papers, and an intensive search turned up nothing. Since then, there have been several large-scale searches for the Papers. There have been no clues except one."

Turly stirred.

"There were good rumors to the effect that Vail had left a son in the north who had knowledge of the Papers. I sent for that son. All my men were in the north. They found him, but the fools killed him. They said they had misunderstood the orders. When the report came in, I thought never to find the Papers. I did not stop trying, however. To the north, south, east and west I sent spies to ferret out what they could. On several occasions I thought I was close, but nothing ever came of it. Oliver and I teamed up from time to time to test each other's knowledge about the Papers."

Turly stirred again. What was it he sensed in Hastings' words?

"Recently we both got word that Vail's son *still* lived. We both sent men north. Oliver got him first. But now *I* have him. And I will not make the same mistake I made before. This time I *will discover* the whereabouts of the Blessing Papers. Do you understand me, *Turly Vail?*"

Turly lay stunned on the bed. He stared at the man sitting in front of him. The full ruddy face was flushed with the mounting excitement of telling his story. Turly felt sure Hastings would do whatever he had to do to fulfill that last pledge. And he knew way down that the other thing was true. He was surprised as he admitted it to himself.

John Vail, founder of the Order of Zeno and last owner of the fabled Blessing Papers, *was his father!*

226

John Vail was the man who had left Turly as a three-year-old to hurry to the south on a mission which had reached out years later and had caught him in it.

Or maybe I have always been caught in it, thought Turly, dizzy again as new thoughts mingled with the fragments of old ones. A great Framer that was a machine; a great civilization that had collapsed for a mysterious reason; and a father whose old friend now sat in front of him in feverish anticipation of getting his hands at last on a legendary box about which so little was known, especially its location.

Turly frowned and shook his head. He felt something touch his mind again and again. It was as if he were seeing something from the corner of his eyes, swiftly cutting them, and finding nothing there.

Chapter 16

Hastings raised his eyebrows and tilted his chin toward Turly. His deep blue eyes, like pieces of an afternoon sky, regarded the young man for some moments with a steady growth of tension. The air in the room was like the moments before a summer storm breaks, the wind blowing the hair, charging it.

"Your father was a friend of mine," said Hastings. "A good friend. We parted ways on the best use of the Blessing Papers. I felt that political use of the Papers would be to our—to man's—advantage. John saw it another way. An honest difference of opinion. As it happened, John won. He took the Papers to somewhere, somewhere on this island, and buried them and himself as well. No one ever saw John Vail again."

"What of my mother?" asked Turly hesitantly. There was a certain cold tenderness in Turly's eyes that had not been there before. Hastings noticed it but said nothing.

"No one knows about your mother, Turly. She

dropped out of sight when John first got the Papers. She might be alive. She might be with John."

Turly considered that for a moment before speaking. "And the others? The interferers? Who were they?"

"Also a problem. They were never seen. The Box was given to Blessing and its contents revealed to him, that's all we know. It is a guess that there *were* others. But as I suggested, who else could have wreaked havoc on a whole civilization?" Hasting brushed the hair around his ears as if to get it out of his way.

"Enemies of the Council of Methe perhaps? A ruse to keep men from working together?" said Turly.

Hastings shook his head. "No. I think you need some instruction in pre-Circle times to understand what man stood to lose. Come with me, if you can stand."

Turly could, but he acted as if it were extremely difficult to do so for Hastings' benefit. Hasting took one arm and helped Turly through the door and out into the hall. Turly could feel Hastings' mind pulling at him, forcing him up and down to the left. He could resist it, but did not. The two shuffled down long dim corridors; they entered a room lit by softly glowing lights, and Hastings left him for a moment. Turly looked about at shapes hidden in shadow. There were wagons with strange wheels; cabinets of instruments he had never seen before and whose function he could only guess; and hanging from the ceiling was something, something . . .

More lights came on. Turly drew in his breath and held it. The room was incredibly large. Overhead great arcs burned with a slightly bluish tint. The room was lit as if by the sun. There were no candles. Glass cases were lined up in rows stretching away from him almost a hundred meters to the end of the building, which was almost a hundred meters wide.

"Are you impressed, my blasé young friend?" Hastings had returned and waved his hand toward the full immensity of the museum. "Let me show you my treasures, all preserved and gathered at great cost to me over many years."

Hastings walked to a wagon with dark fat wheels. The air was still and smelled faintly of metal. All was clean and well polished. Hastings pulled something at one side of the wagon. The wagon cracked open and Turly jumped back. Hastings laughed and pointed into the wagon; Turly reluctantly stepped in. There was a unique aroma inside the wagon that he could not describe. The seats were plump and soft. A single stick protruded out of the floor of the wagon, and was thick with a number of buttons and markings. Hastings sat beside Turly and touched something. The interior glowed softly with light. In front of him, Turly could see tiny dials and charts with slender needles inside them. They were blue and green and orange.

Hastings placed his feet solidly on the floor. There was a hum and they were moving. Turly gripped the sides of his seat, jerked his head around to Hastings and stared hard at the man who controlled half of Imram.

"It's only a vehicle, Turly, something you ride in. See?" Hastings tilted the stick to the left and the wagon moved to the left. He moved it back to the right and the wagon moved to the right. They were gliding down one corridor in between rows of glass cases. The light from the roof shed soft light into the cases and there was no reflection in them.

Hastings stopped at one of the cases about halfway down the row. He cracked open the wagon and got out. Turly followed on his side, bouncing on the seat in his haste to get out. Hastings chuckled.

"You will be especially interested in this, I think, Turly." Hastings pointed into the case. There were a number of tiny boxes with pictures in them. Pictures that changed. Turly looked closer. There was Smith and Bulfin and Harve. All of them were in the tiny boxes. And Meriwether. *By the Circle, there was Meriwether,* thought Turly, who had almost forgotten why he was there. She was impassive. None of them could see Turly, or showed that they could. They were in what seemed to be rooms like his own. A thought struck him.

"Can you see me in a box when I am in my room?"

"Indeed so, my friend." Hastings laughed again. He was enjoying all this immensely. Turly leaned over and watched the pictures for several minutes in silence. The small cubes sparkled in their cases. The likenesses of his old friends were lifelike.. He thought he could reach down and touch them. No wonder men feared Hastings, he thought. With things like this, why shouldn't he rule *all* of Imram?

"All of these things, you understand, are merely curiosities. I have no way to replace them should they no longer work. Some of my men are able to repair some things, but parts are impossible to get. So far these things have worked nicely. Come now, I have something else to show you." Hastings did not get back into the wagon, but walked through the rows of cases toward a far corner. Turly seemed lost in the huge room as he glanced first one way, then another. There was no way he could possibly see all these things even in a week, he thought. And he did not have a week. He shrugged and followed Hastings. He would see what there was to see.

Hastings stopped in front of a much smaller case. Turly stepped to the front and looked down. He immediately gripped the sides of the case and his heart sank. There were his coins, the map, and the song of his father that Turly had thought never to see again. *Hastings had the map.*

"Yes, indeed," boomed Hastings. "Oliver was reluctant to give them up, but I pointed out to him that they were useless to anyone who did not know what to do with them. Do you know what to do with them, Turly?" Hastings was watching him closely. Turly knew he had to answer. But this time he could answer truthfully.

"No, I don't know how to use them. But they are mine. My father left them to me for my eighteenth birthday. They mean something to me in sentimental terms only."

"Indeed, indeed. Tell me, Turly, if they mean nothing, why did you head south toward the place marked on the map? Why should you want to go there? If you lie, I will know it, Turly." Hastings scratched his scraggly red beard. There was an ironic tone in his voice.

Turly knew Hastings would have known a lie, even if Colum had not helped him. But Hastings said he had been watched on the little box. Colum must know about these little pictures. Did Colum do something to them, or was he with Hastings after all?

"I'm going to Clonnoise Abbey to find my *father*. I did not know about him when I left the Circle; I know only a little about him now. That's his picture in my room, in the bookcase. You know that. I don't care for the *Papers*. You can have those if you can find them. I want only to learn what I can of my parents. If what you say is true, I may yet find my mother."

Hastings gazed at Turly for some time. He played with the fringe of his beard with his right hand while the left hand cradled the elbow of his right arm. Finally he nodded.

"It would be extremely difficult for you to lie to me. Yet you might. Let us return to your room now. You need rest." Hastings turned on his heel and marched toward the entrance. Turly followed him while rotating his head to see what he could. Overhead, suspended by invisible wires, reaching almost half the length of the museum, a long silver machine pointed inexorably north. Perhaps it was an illusion, Turly thought, but it seemed in flight up there like a bird, its wings folded to swoop down upon some prey with the speed and agility only birds of prey have. It was beautiful hanging there. And his ancestors had made it. Turly reflected upon the kind of men they must have been. Giants, to have created all this. And yet their heirs lived with knives and horses. What could have happened? Perhaps Hastings was right to try to unify the island and restore such glory. Perhaps Hastings was not the demon he had been portrayed as being. He was rigid and purposeful, it was true. But if all this were at stake, wouldn't Turly do the same? It was a difficult thought.

And in a flash Turly knew that this was what Hastings *wanted* him to think. He had tampered with Turly's head again. He had wanted Turly to feel sympathy for him, to begin to like Hastings like a father. Turly would have to be careful.

The two returned by a different route down long, polished corridors, relieved at intervals by glowing murals that depicted the fight of mounted men with the strange figures whose heads appeared on the coins given Turly by his father. He thought he saw on one of the human figures the face of his father. Or was it of Hastings? Matted grays reached up into the blue sky, where stylized puffs of white cloud were frozen forever in a June afternoon. The drama below was equally frozen; the wounded died and were dying, some with

233

odd spears in their necks, others with a blaze of brilliant color surrounding them. It was at once beautiful and cruel. The faces of the demons were ugly, but they were not portrayed as being ignorant or subordinate to some superior demon who was not present. They had the glint of intelligence and even pity in their eyes, as if they did not want to kill. But they did kill.

Turly wanted to ask Hastings about the mural and the coins, but Hastings strode on ahead of Turly, engrossed with his own thoughts. Turly wondered if he could escape by himself. It seemed a bleak prospect if Hastings had eyes in every room. Perhaps he even had extended ears. But that couldn't be. Hastings would know what Colum had told him and change his approach. Or would he? How arrogant and sure was he? thought Turly. To what lengths would he go to get what he wanted?

Around the next turn in the corridor, Hastings stood with his hand on the door of Turly's cell. He pointed into it with the palm of one hand, a relaxed smile easing the intensity of his broad face. As Turly entered the room, Hastings asked him again if he knew where the Blessing Papers were.

Turly said no; Hastings left without a word, closing the door behind him.

Chapter 17

The next morning Turly was fed toast and water and taken by two guards to a small room fitted with tables and instruments which stirred Turly's memory.

It was very much like Oliver's torture room, thought Turly, but much more elaborate. Hastings was not there, nor was Colum. But Turly knew he could stand whatever they wished to do to him. He had had a vision of his father's scheme, sanity and purpose, and now nothing could change that. He would follow his father's steps to the hiding place of the Blessing Papers and use them to restore man to his rightful place in the world. *Whatever* that was. Turly knew the truth would be revealed when the Papers were found. The prospect of physical torture was little enough beside the plan that had been growing in Turly's mind.

The guards strapped Turly into a massive chair in one corner, with a view of the whole room. Heavy bands bound him rigidly to the arms and legs of the chair. His head could move only inches in either direction. The lights had been dimmed and Turly left alone.

Turly waited for what he thought was hours. Time seemed to stretch into an endless tedium. This made Turly restless and gloomy. He had things to do, places to go to, he thought. He could not waste time here with Hastings, playing games. He struggled with the straps but could do nothing with them. Not even muscles trained in heavy toil could break straps designed for the strength of the insane, or those driven insane.

The man with white hair bunched his eyebrows and felt the tiny mole ride up and down on the right one. He breathed deeply and held his breath. As his lungs gradually cleared, his mind started to go blank. He blinked his eyes and straightened his back. Something had tried to take him then. Something strong and with feline quickness had struck at his mind and been repulsed. Beads of sweat oozed onto Turly's brow. He felt faint like the time he had almost broken his wrist on the vine years before, when he had scarred his arm for life. The pain had almost made him faint and had drained the blood from his face. He felt like that now.

The lights brightened. Turly heard a faint tapping that grew in volume as it approached the door of the room. The tapping was soon a distinct drumming that rattled and reverberated in the halls. Then all sounds stopped. The door opened slowly and a large fat man with gray hair stepped into the foyer. He glanced at Turly and bowed imperceptibly. His eyes were kindly and looked about the room and at the instruments with something like love. He wore a white work suit and white shoes flattened with his great weight. His hair was parted in the middle, brushed down over his ears and bound in a bun at the back. At his throat was a red scarf with a small green *H* showing clearly at one corner. After one look around, the big man turned back to the door and motioned with his hand. Two other

236

men, bulging with their own stores of fat, entered carrying a third man between them.

It was young Kelleher.

Kelleher cast wild eyes at Turly. His mouth was taped and his hands bound behind him. The two fat men carried him to the table in the far corner. He was in a cold sweat, Turly could see that. He was also probably out of his mind with fear. Young Kelleher had never left the Circle before Turly had urged him to do so. Turly knew one reason why Kelleher had come. To prove himself as a man. But this was not proving anything. Why did Hastings want to use Kelleher, who knew nothing? Turly tried to say something to Kelleher but could not. He struggled once again against his own straps.

The first fat man directed the others. Kelleher was freed from his bonds and strapped onto the table. His gag was not removed and tiny wires were connected to his wrists and ankles. One of the men put tiny dabs of grease on each temple and placed wires there. After Kelleher had been wired, one man turned to a machine that had stood impassively against the wall. It now hummed and blinked with rows of lights. Several of the knobs were adjusted as the machine seemed to take on a life of its own. Turly had the feeling that the fat men were only servants whose job it was to serve this great wall of knobs and dials.

The job was finished. Kelleher was stretched upon the table with arms and legs flung wide in a wild parody of someone falling through space.

The first fat man then turned to Turly. He carried in his hand a bundle of wires leading from the machine, through Kelleher, and then dangling in his grip. He smiled kindly at Turly.

"You will pardon the inconvenience," he said. "There

will be a moment of discomfort as I attach these to you. If you like, I could gag you as well? No? Very well."

The man bent forward heavily and quickly inserted the tiny wires under the skin at several points. He was right, there was some discomfort, like the bite of fleas that stung and itched all out of proportion to the size of the insect. Turly did not wince. But he did grit his teeth. What were they doing?

"There. Now. Let me introduce myself. I am Head Drummer Boz. These are my first assistants, Bo and Ba. We are here to question you on some delicate points raised by my Lord Hastings. It seems that you are un-cooperative in spite of his great regard for you. The son of an old friend, I understand. He said not to kill you. Well, we won't. In fact, we won't *touch* you, except of course for the wires," he chuckled, "but that can't be helped. Now your young companion—Kelleher I believe is his name?—is a different story."

"Let him go," hissed Turly, "he knows nothing. He is only a boy."

"A boy indeed! Like yourself? And one who has killed at least two of Hastings' badly needed soldiers? Did you know that? No, I suppose not. He was not easy to take at the Hotel. In fact the big man was easier. The young one here did not want to give up at all, even in the face of overwhelming odds. He fought like a madman. But here he is after all. You say he knows nothing? We know that. Why do we then treat him as if he does?"

Turly was puzzled and enraged. He wanted to get at the oily fat face. Boz rubbed his hammy hands together in anticipation as if he were about to sit down to a huge meal.

"The answer is simple. The boy is only a conductor. Do you understand? He will feel great pain soon, incredible pain, pain that you will not believe. Yes, you will know. You see these wires that lead from his table to you? They are conductor cables. What he feels, *you* will feel. But it will be only an echo. Do you understand now?"

Turly did. In one awful moment he understood the diabolical power of the Drummers. They knew that he could withstand almost anything they could do to him *directly*. But if he were aware of the pain that others were experiencing because of him, then it could be quite different. Young Kelleher could not be expected to know what was in store for him. He didn't know the questions that he would be asked, would not know the answers to them. His pain would not be associated with what he did at all. The pain would depend on *Turly's* answers. And Turly could not answer. He knew some, but not all, of the puzzle of the Blessing Papers. And for the love of Imram, he must not give anything up. He knew that as a certainty. He could not give Hastings what he wanted.

"I see you do understand," said Boz. "And you feel that you can somehow overcome the problem. Let me tell you, young master, that you cannot. I have seen good men come into this room—better men than you even, stronger in the mind—and they have left broken and spent, empty as an old fruit sucked dry. I know, I know, you think you will beat that. But what of your friend? Will he be able to take it? Let's see."

Boz turned to the machine. He reached out one hand and did something with a small knob. Kelleher humped on the table first, then an instant later Turly tried to leap out of his chair. He could not. But there had been little pain. Was this supposed to make him cry out, to break him?

As if in reply, Boz remarked that that was only an

initial contact exercise to bring the two together. "I see that there is a momentary delay," he said. He turned the knob a bit further and tapped a dial with the index finger of one hand. He pushed another button. This time Turly thought the top of his head was coming off. He screamed and the sound was matched by another in the room, but muted.

"Oh, I'm truly sorry," said Boz. He walked over to Kelleher and removed the gag. "Now we should be able to hear you."

He turned to Turly. "I want to remind you that all this is totally unnecessary. My assistants and I receive no pleasure from this. We merely do a job, and do it well. We are paid handsomely and are held in some esteem in Hastings' hierarchy. You haven't heard of us? The Drummers? Well, no mind. This is what we do. If at any time you wish to say anything, anything at all about what the Master wants to hear, you have only to say so. Otherwise, otherwise I'm afraid we must continue."

Boz had spoken soothingly, and what he said he clearly meant, thought Turly. But he still had the feeling that Boz *did* enjoy what he was doing. And Kelleher. Kelleher could not take this. If what was just given was any indication, thought Turly, he would crack soon. But he had nothing *under* the crack; it was Turly they were trying to crack, and they were using Kelleher as a means to do that. Pain alone would not be enough. But to feel the pain of another at the same moment. That was clever.

Turly could feel Kelleher's fear. It radiated in the space between them. His eyes flickered past Turly's head and found a spot near the ceiling. The muscles in his jaw bunched; he was obviously determined to say or do nothing.

"Kelleher?" said Turly. "Kelleher, I'm sorry."

Turly felt the grinding begin in his lower rear teeth. The sound grew in intensity and was almost as bad as the pain that made him jerk his head back and away from it. He thought his teeth were being bored by huge grinders. He would have no teeth left if this continued. But there was nothing in his mouth. It was in his *head*, thought Turly. It was all in his head. He concentrated on that thought. The pain did not ease, but his ability to withstand it was increased. Kelleher's was not.

"Boz," shouted Turly, "Boz, stop it. Stop it."

The pain ceased at once. Boz walked over to Turly. He swung from side to side as he walked, his great bulk swaying with him. He stood before Turly with his ponderous arms held out to his sides like obscene sausages.

"Yes, Master Turly," he wheezed. "I believe the question now is, where are the Blessing Papers?"

Turly stared up at him. He could not answer the question. He knew it, and Boz saw it in his defiant eyes. Without looking back, Boz flicked one hand at the wrist. Bo pushed another knob. He felt pressure on the inner part of his leg, in his groin, and he passed out. The pain was still excruciating when he woke. He glanced over at Kelleher who lay white and inert. The two assistants had draped ice bags over his neck and forehead.

It is in my head, thought Turly. *There is no actual damage. It is all in my head.*

It was all in Kelleher's head as well. But Kelleher didn't know that, or he was unable to deal with it in those terms. He believed he was being torn. He felt his manhood had been ripped from him.

Turly could feel that. Kelleher's eyes were closed tight in fear and frustration. But over all was the pain.

Turly knew no one could withstand pain or wish any

more of it. Only the stopping of pain. If Kelleher could have given the Drummers what they wanted, at that moment he would have done so. But he knew nothing. Turly closed his own eyes and wept in despair. The lights behind his clenched eyes danced and swarmed in strange momentary shapes. Great bursts of color were thrown in profusion, arranged themselves in a hasty pattern, and then dissolved to make way for another one. Turly tried to lose himself in the color.

The pain stopped. Turly looked up. Boz was still in front of him, had been for the few minutes that the shock had occurred. He smiled wanly at Turly.

"Are you ready to tell us what we must know, or shall we go on? You have felt only the beginning of a programmed sequence," he added. "From here we go into a detailed destruction of the body. It will not be a real destruction of course, but to the mind it will seem real. It will lose piece by piece the parts it has been used to since birth and upon which it has depended every moment since. Kelleher's mind will believe the body is dying. And it *will* die if we continue to let it think so. Are you willing for that to happen?"

So they are making *me* responsible, thought Turly. He admired their technique while loathing them at the same time. He knew too, deep down, that he could not save Kelleher. Voices in his ear spoke to him of salvation. Of some last-minute trick that would save them both. But Turly knew that was the mind playing its own trick. It wanted only to save itself.

But Turly wanted to save the Blessing Papers. Whatever that meant, and whatever they might be, they could not belong to either Hastings or the Order of Zeno. Turly felt that with a physical force that seemed to nullify any force they could bring against him. Kelleher would have to die if he must, but the secret of the Papers could not be lost.

After that, Turly could not look at Kelleher. Boz sighed and turned away.

Turly screamed with Kelleher until screaming became a living thing that twisted and rose and fell of itself. External. And dying into the final darkness with the hoped-for release a lover finds in his mate. The embrace of it, and the dying of the living scream in a great pitch of sound.

Turly was reborn.

Boz lifted Turly's chin and pried open one eye with a beefy thumb. He did something to Turly's arm. Turly sagged.

He heard his name. Turly. It was a familiar name and a familiar voice.

"Turly. Turly, what are they doing to you?" Turly could hear the voice far off, feel it. It floated to him from a dream. He reached for it and held it. He knew that voice, had sought it for many days now.

Meriwether!

It was Meriwether. Turly looked up quickly, his eyes unable to focus. Boz wiped his forehead again with a cool, damp cloth and stepped back. Turly could then see Meriwether at the door, held by the two Drummer assistants. His head jerked clumsily toward the other table. Kelleher was not on it. His head swiveled back to the door where Meriwether was struggling feebly. She was dressed in white, as were the Drummers. Her hands were bound in front of her.

Turly realized in one awful awareness that Meriwether was next. She would go through what Kelleher had gone through; and he would have to feel all her pain, too—know her agony as his.

Turly cried out in fear and rage and helplessness.

"Hastings! Hastings!" There was no reply. Bo and Ba lifted Meriwether onto the table and began to attach the appropriate wires to her head and body. Turly shut his eyes and tried to be very far away. It did not work; it was no good. Boz spoke in the near distance.

"Turly? The Blessing Papers?"

How could they do this, thought Turly wildly. Was anything that important? Even the Papers that could change a world, *had* changed a world? Was he doing the right thing? Maybe Hastings was, after all, a man who would use the Papers to reach a goal similar to his own. Maybe. Maybe.

But not likely. He had seen the quick glint in Hastings' eye, the steely control, the sense of power. Hastings had manipulated Turly's mind, or had tried to. Hastings was torturing him even now. Had killed Kelleher. Could such a man rule Imram with anything approaching understanding, or love? Love. Love, caring, was something Turly had had little to do with. He knew that now, had felt it in the ebbing of Kelleher's life. He had cared for Kelleher at the end, but it was a caring that had come too late for the younger man.

There was still the question of the Papers. How long could he hold out? It might cost too much, thought Turly sadly. Too much.

Turly closed his eyes and leaned his head back as far as it could go. His mind held still, like the ripples of the sea on a beach, the memories of what had just happened.

Meriwether cried out to him. She was staring excitedly at Turly, but he had the sudden feeling that she was playing with him as if they were back in the Old Clearing where they had always met, and it was a good summer's night.

"For the Circle's sake, Turly," said Meriwether.

"What does he want? Give it to him, Turly. Please!" The wires hooked to Meriwether led across the floor to Turly.

"Meriwether, I . . ." It seemed absurd to Turly to ask her if she were all right. If they had treated her well. He wanted to ask her how they had known that she would be the one person he would care about. Of all the captured members of the Circle at Inniscloe, how had they known which one was his? The thought lingered with a nagging pull at his consciousness.

The thought vanished as the first wave of pain broke over him. Turly felt Meriwether's anguish as her flesh was pushed and pulled with savage force. He had not known how tender she was or how vulnerable to hurt. He felt her womanhood threatened, just as Kelleher's manhood had been threatened and finally taken from him. Turly could feel her agony and something else as well, a growing sense of betrayal. Of what, by what? Turly's own lips wanted to curl and cry out.

"Hastings!" cried Meriwether. "Lord Hastings?" The words coming out quick and loud with an edge to them, a question unbelieved.

Boz stepped to the table quickly and put a gag in Meriwether's mouth. Meriwether stared up at him, her eyes bulging in wild surprise. She struggled then with fury. It did no good. Boz looked down at her with great pity, it seemed, and then turned back to Turly.

"The program for women is different, Master Turly," he said. "Instead of simply breaking the body, and making the mind believe that is what is happening, as we did with your friend Kelleher, we use the exhaustion of repeated assault to destroy her. Meriwether here will in effect be *used* again and again in a most brutal fashion until she can take no more. While she has the sensation of being violated repeatedly—*in her mind*—other parts of her will feel as if they are being bitten and torn. Oh, it might be bearable initially. It will not be that way for long. You do understand, don't you, that we are doing this only because we have to? We have had women here before, of course. They did not last long. A feeling of intense shame finally overcomes them. That seems to work even better than pain. This feeling is helped and intensified by the machines we use. The women invariably wilt like fragile flowers, no matter how tough they are when they come in, no matter how experienced they are. If they have beauty of mind or body when they come, they do not have it when we are through. Pity. Look at her there, Master Turly." He pointed to her. "She is lovely all over, isn't she?"

If Turly had been able to move at that moment, Boz would not have lived past the last syllable. Turly writhed within. He felt a growing sense of fear and terror in Meriwether that he had not sensed in her when she had come in. Why? Had she not believed that this would happen? Had she been told *in advance* that nothing would happen to her? Did she *know* she was being used to make Turly talk?

My Fathers! thought Turly. That would explain her outrage. Had she collaborated with Hastings? Was she a part of all this? Turly sagged. He could not know for sure. How could he know? Meriwether had always been the woman he wanted to live with. Why this?

Turly stared at Meriwether as the thoughts ran through his mind. As if in response, Meriwether turned her face away from him and did not look at him again.

"Well, young man?" said Boz.

Turly said nothing now, thinking hard. Boz showed his first trace of anger. He waddled quickly to the console and punched two buttons.

Turly jumped involuntarily. Something was pushing

246

and scratching at him. He shook off a feeling at his neck. His eyes widened, shocked. Invisible hands flurried over him, touching and probing. In disgust Turly tried to elude them. He could not. There was rapid movement now. There was hurt. He could feel a pulling and tearing that he had never known possible before.

There is nothing there, he thought, *nothing there at all.*

A warmth permeated his body, a warmth that was full but short-lived as the probing went on and on. The rising sense of shame Turly was not prepared for, could not prepare for, and could not take. It grew in intensity as the torture continued. Turly knew on his skin the slime of many tongues.

It was the shame that finally broke Turly.

He could take no more of the violation, real or imagined, of the most private of Meriwether's physical and mental parts.

"Boz," said Turly wearily, almost whispering.

Immediately the sensations stopped. Boz said something that sounded again very far away. He walked over to Turly and laid his immense hand on his forehead.

"Yes, Master Turly. Are you ready?"

Turly looked up and swore to himself that, whatever happened, he would one day quite coldly and deliberately kill Boz. But his eyes were unfocused and wandered about the room. The console was dark now, the dials lying still and quiet. The moaning from Meriwether was the only sound in the room.

"Tell Hastings . . ."

"Yes?"

"Tell Hastings I want to see him now."

"Not unless you wish to tell him what he wants to know, young master. The sequence is far from over and we would not want to go to all this trouble a second time."

Turly felt drained. Hastings had been right. A part of him had died there. He did not know yet what that meant, but he could no longer hold his secret, his image of it, and remain a human being. He had to let it go.

Boz could see this in his eyes. He had seen it before. The resignation. The fire of resistance burned out. He turned away and left the room. Bo and Ba seemed to take hours to unstrap Meriwether, pull the wires, and sit her up limp and unconscious. They slipped an arm around each shoulder and carried her out. Turly watched her delicate toes scrape on the harsh surface of the floor.

He sat for a long time in the pool of light that fell from above. He knew what he had done. He could have done nothing else.

When Hastings came in, Turly gave no greeting. Hastings glanced at Boz, who shrugged.

"Turly? You wanted to see me? Boz, if you have ruined him, I'll strap you in myself." Hastings bristled in genuine concern. Boz assured him that there might be some temporary shock but that the second contact never does more than leave unpleasant memories.

"Turly?" said Hastings again.

"You saw it on the map. At Clonnoise Abbey. The Papers are at Clonnoise Abbey." Turly released the breath he had been holding. That was it. The secret of the Papers was out. He had failed his father and Ellman and his friends.

There was a long moment of silence.

"Do you take me for a fool, Turly?" Hastings' voice was low and menacing.

Turly's eyes snapped open. "The Papers are there.

They *must* be," he said emphatically. "All points in that direction. And something in me says that that is where they are buried. That is why I am certain that the Papers are there."

"Turly, do you think I have been idle these last twenty years? Clonnoise Abbey is one of the *first* places I looked. Every stone, every hole, in that Abbey has been checked and rechecked. There is nothing there, Turly. Nothing. When I got your map last week, I sent a crack search crew down there to check again. Again, there is nothing. Turly, you are a fool if you think they are there, or a fool to think I can be misled. Are you trying even now to trick me, Turly? If you are, you will be more sorry than you know. Boz, the Helmet," said Hastings.

Boz had been staring at Turly the whole while. He seemed to be incredulous that anyone could resist his efforts and still tell a lie. Yet he moved with alacrity when Hastings spoke. Waddling to a cabinet in one corner, he extracted what looked like a copper bowl with wires attached to the bottom. He inserted one end of the wires to the console, which again hummed and glowed. He straightened the wires and pulled the bowl toward Turly. He inverted it and laid it on Turly's head.

"If you repeat what you knowingly believe to be a lie, you will short-circuit your mind, Turly," said Hastings. "Do you know what that means? You will go insane. You will be a raving vegetable, Turly. Do you want that?" Hastings was furious. There was no longer a pretense of cordiality. He motioned hastily with his hand to Boz, who flipped a large switch at one end of the silver console. Turly felt a low buzzing like a swarm of bees deep in his mind and far away.

THE BLESSING PAPERS

"Where are the Blessing Papers, Turly?"

"At Clonnoise Abbey!" yelled Turly.

The buzzing grew to monstrous proportions. Turly heard a gathering hiss like the fall of water on a great fire.

Chapter 18

Meriwether put her hand to her forehead. It was dry. She raised her head and glanced about the small room, sat up and let her feet dangle over the side of the bed. As her hair fell in a tent about her face, despair washed over her.

She would kill Hastings if she had the chance. He had promised that nothing would happen to her or to Turly.

"A trick," she said to no one, and laughed aloud.

She slumped again. She knew she would never forget what had happened to her or the look that Turly had given her at the last. The hope and trust that had been in his face, pinched and gray as it had been, was drained at the awareness of what had come to pass. He had seen that she had already told Hastings of Turly's life at the Circle. Hastings had been waiting for Turly, prepared with the knowledge that he had captured the one person in the world, after Ellman, that Turly cared for. She had been the last card, the ace pulled from Hastings' sleeve when it was clear that Turly could withstand whatever else he could devise.

Meriwether felt unclean and ashamed, but not for the abuse she had taken. For what she had done, for the conscious betrayal, guilt. But she thought it had been *for* Turly. She had remembered the threat on his life years before. She knew Hastings had been behind it. Everyone knew it and feared Hastings, and they feared being taken to the South. She had wanted a way to save both Turly and herself. She knew Turly would not talk if he were captured. He was tough that way. She of all people thought she knew his limits. She loved Smith, but she had promised Hastings that if he let her go with Turly, and allowed them to return safely to the North, she would tell him how Turly could be made to talk. She would help willingly.

She had not known it would be as it had been. Hastings had used her more than she had thought he would. She sobbed into her hands. She had only wanted to help Turly. Surely he must know that. But how could he? It had all been for him. For Turly. Or had it? She had felt compelled to do what she had done, had felt pushed to it as one felt the need for food.

She sat upright. The door was opening. A small man, his long white beard cascading onto his chest, slipped in and put one finger to his lips. He pointed to a corner of the room and motioned with his hand for her to go there. Holding her gown at the neck, Meriwether did so. She turned and looked down at the little man, who reached behind her and did something to a tiny wire. Then he stepped back.

"If you will, young lady, please stand there until I tell you otherwise."

Meriwether obeyed. She had not been used to obeying, but she was in a strange country, and living under strange codes. Was this gnome a king here? She did not know. A lot had changed since she had been taken at the Circle. She brushed one wisp of hair from her eyes with a distracted finger.

"Do you wish to help Turly and escape from Lord Hastings?" The old gnome cocked his head at her and blinked one eye like a rooster.

"Yes, of course, yes," blurted Meriwether. This might be another trap, she thought, but it could be no worse than the one she was already in. "How can I help? I am a prisoner here."

"Never mind about that. I can help you help Turly if you do exactly as I say. There will be great danger involved, however."

"And who *are* you?" the girl asked, looking down at him suspiciously.

"Colum, an old friend of Turly and Ellman's," he said.

"Colum? You are *Colum?* I knew you," declared Meriwether excitedly.

"Yes, you did," said Colum, nodding. "I'm glad you remember."

"But, Colum, is Turly all right?"

"No; he has been through a lot. I think the torture session with you has done something to him. I don't know just what yet. But we have to get him out of the compound before we can determine the damage. He is young and strong. That is in his favor."

"But how can I get out to help?" asked Meriwether with exasperation. She saw her help as a form of atonement—if she could do it and Turly would know she had done it.

Colum winked up at her. "Why, I'm going to take you out with me, of course. But not now. The Movement is interested in Turly's escape, and I'm meeting its leaders tonight. It is possible that the first big battle for the south will take place here within twenty-four hours. If this is true, we can use the confusion to escape. You sleep now if you can, rest up, recover your strength. You will need it. Later tonight I will come back and get you."

"Colum?" said Meriwether in a firm voice.

"Yes?"

"Do you work for Hastings?"

"That's the same question Turly asked," chuckled Colum. "The answer is yes and no. Let's say that it is more to my advantage to work here now than not to."

"I see." Meriwether had recovered some of her bearing; the Circle girl who was once a free spirit was not wholly lost.

"Now say nothing more until I leave, and be prepared for anything that may happen." Colum waved one finger at her and did something to the wire again. He stepped back to the door, raised one hand in farewell and was gone.

Meriwether went to the bed and sat down. She was still exhausted and wanted to take Colum's advice and sleep. Something big was stirring and she wanted to be a part of it, especially if it meant the destruction of Hastings.

Colum left the room and shook his head. He had known of Meriwether in the north of course. She had been quite young, but still one could see the woman in the girl. It was exciting to see that, thought Colum; in youth one can sometimes see the full beauty of the mature woman, the inevitable change that is the fulfillment of a promise. But there were other things on his mind, and Colum let the thought slip through in a maze of other memories.

He had to meet Cole in one hour. It would be easy

to get out of the Hastings compound. Colum grinned diabolically to himself. He had done it many times before. It was all too easy to change himself and walk out the front gates without challenge. But it would be difficult to persuade Cole and his men to wait till the right moment. If Turly and his friends were caught inside during an attack, they could be lost, too. Hastings had too many alternate plans, too many defenses to let even the skilled fighters of the underground capture his prisoners, especially one as valuable as Turly.

Colum frowned. He had gotten to the Drummers' Room too late to stop the worst of it, but he had been able to save Turly's sanity. A close call it was. Another few minutes and they would have had what they wanted; or, more to the point, would have known that Turly was *not* lying. But now they were convinced that he was and would be preparing for further assaults on him once he was recovered. Or so they thought. Turly must be gone by morning.

Colum stepped out of the squat L of the barracks and into the shadows of the parade grounds. The well-barbered grass felt like a cushion under his feet. He turned his thoughts to the front gates and made for them as rapidly as his short legs would permit.

The front guards snapped to as Lord Hastings, Master of the House, strode purposefully through the gates and out into the night. One of the guards who was following the floating red cape into the distance rubbed his eyes as it seemed to change into a short green tunic that waddled from side to side. He had been at the whiskey too long, he thought. He would have to cut down.

As Colum moved through the fluid summer night, he thought the air especially sweet. Nature does not care what man is up to, he thought. She will continue as she has always done, to spin the fragile web of events that allows man to live in her and on her but that also allows man to destroy her if he tries hard enough. And in spite of that, nature doesn't care. It's an experiment, mused Colum, it must be. An experiment to see if a sentient animal can grow beyond its mother and still survive. For all his wisdom and knowledge, Colum could not probe the mystery of life. Not that he really wanted to. The solving of a mystery leads to boredom and ennui, he knew that. What *if* the ultimate mysteries were solved? Could the mind continue to live? Perhaps mystery had brought the mind into existence, and sustained it. If it were gone, then the reason for being would be gone.

Colum chuckled to himself. Vail had always told him that philosophy was his one weak point. But it was summer and momentous things were abroad. The future of Imram hung in the balance. What better time to dream of mysteries and solutions? The great good place of Imram had been corrupted; it was time to begin the return.

As Colum walked under the first city light, his shadow raced from him and was sucked ahead into the dark.

He turned at the fifth corner and stood for a moment, looking about. Satisfied that no one had followed him or was waiting in the shadows ahead, Colum stepped to a door, knocked on it, waited, and then entered silently.

Hands fell on him from within. Rough whispers demanded something of him. When he gave it, they released him. Colum straightened his tunic and asked for Cole.

"Here, Colum!" A thin man with a springy step whispered to Colum from a tar doorway. He bobbed up and down as he rushed to meet Colum halfway. Cole's eyes darted from place to place as Colum related the events of the day. His head nodded in affirmation as Colum mentioned his belief that Turly must be freed before dawn if the secret of the Papers was to be kept from Hastings.

"Our men are ready," said Cole. "In fact, they're more than ready. We have postponed this too long in my opinion. We should have struck last week when Hastings was weakest, with his men in the north. Now he's at the full again. Still, I think we can take him if all goes as planned. And with your help of course, Colum."

"Of course." Colum combed his long white beard with his stubby fingers. "But I told you why we had to wait. Hastings has to believe that the site of the Papers is to the north, not the south. He must be made to divert his search into other areas. He is much too close as it is now."

"But *we* don't know where they are, do we?"

Colum sighed. Cole still did not trust him completely. "No. No one does. But we do know they *are* in the south. The last message John Vail sent out was that the south held the Papers. He could not be specific without betraying the reason for hiding them in the first place."

"And the boy?"

"As yet, he knows nothing. I think it will come, but he needs time that Hastings will not give him. His mind could be destroyed for good if we don't get him out. Understand?"

"Yes, yes, I suppose so. We have always worked together before. We will now. But tell me. Where is Sean?"

Colum saw the wicked gleam come into Cole's eye. He knew that Cole wanted to kill Sean for various

257

reasons. They had been smugglers together in the early days of the Movement against Hastings, to raise money. For some reason Sean had failed the Movement at an important moment. Cole and his wife had been captured and tortured. His wife had died as a result. Cole was freed by a Movement rescue later; but Cole had never forgotten Sean, and when he had learned that Sean was back in Straiten, he had bent every effort to find him. He had been only partially successful. He had learned that Sean and the White-Haired Man were dealing with Harrow.

Cole had tried to kill two birds with one stone. He knew Colum, as well as Hastings, wanted the young man. So he had arranged with Harrow to help betray both of them. Hastings would get the boy; he would get Sean. In exchange for some of his men, held in Hastings' prison, Harrow had informed Hastings to catch the two at the prearranged time. Turly had been taken, but Sean had mysteriously eluded the trap. Cole could not understand that, but he put the thought aside. There was more important business to take care of.

"There is no word of Sean," said Colum, "and I confess that it mystifies me."

"Well, no matter. There's time for him later, if we all live." Cole grinned as he had many times before when about to risk his life. The heat of battle flowed in his veins. He could feel the excitement rise in his men. They were about to take on Hastings at last. It had been a long time coming.

The next few hours were used to check the plan of attack. Colum would return and cause a diversion at the appropriate time. He would release the Circle prisoners and lead them to the escape route while Cole and his men attacked on three fronts. The prisoners would make their way to the underground hall in Straiten and await developments.

Hastings Hall was five miles from Straiten over the regular road. Through the marshland to the southwest, it was three miles. Colum knew a safe way through the marsh and had left a detailed map for Cole and his men to follow. Coming from that side, they would catch Hastings off guard. No one would suspect that men would bother coming through the thick undergrowth and treacherous quicksand of the Heron Marsh. But they would. By five that next morning they would be in place and it would be time to strike. Colum hummed a little tune as he hurried back to the Hall. It was something John Vail used to sing to Turly. With a lilt and an easy swing, Colum repeated its refrain:

Fol de rol de rolly o.

Colum entered the gates as he had left them. The guards saluted the burly master in red and resumed their posts, unaware that this night might well be their last one on earth.

Once inside the grounds, Colum headed straight for the Hall's control center. He was to relieve the technician at midnight. The door was closed and Colum rapped three times. It opened slowly and one suspicious eye was poked out.

"Colum! Thank One it's you. We've had rumors all night about spies and maneuvers. I think it's the new recruits' gossip myself. No one can confront Lord Hastings here of all places. It's much too secure, don't you think so? There should be better discipline for those young thugs. Too scared to sleep at night." The man rattled on and on. Colum pretended to listen as he checked the pictures of the rooms. All were asleep except Bulfin, who still hunched on the edge of his bed.

Turly lay with his face to the ceiling. His eyes were closed, his chest rising and falling slowly.

Good, thought Colum, he will need sleep. Meriwether, lying calm in her sleep, might yet be a problem, he thought. Her decisions were sometimes confused and uncertain. Always had been. She could not always separate her own good from another's. That had led her into Hastings' camp with too naive a trust in his intentions, and in her ability to control the situation. Still, Turly had gone through much for her, perhaps too much—but that remained to be seen, he thought.

There would be six Northerners to get out. Turly and Meriwether, Smith, Harve, Bulfin and Garrett. There should be little trouble in his plans except for the Sniffers. He would have to see to them before they could exit to the back grounds. He knew where the Sniffer controls were, but it would be difficult to shut them off since they were in Hastings' own room. The one hitch in the plan, reflected Colum. But he was confident.

There was a five-hour wait in front of him. He dismissed the other controller and settled down in the comfortable leather chair to wait for the beginning of the end.

The orange sun was coming up through the heavy mists of the Heron swamp. Shredded into diffuse hazes of light, it lit up the sky in a spectral display of morning gloom. Colum sighed as he checked his watch. It was time.

He slid his small frame off the chair and rubbed his eyes. He would have to act quickly now. Reaching the console that stretched from right to left in front of him, Colum checked the rooms again and found all six of the prisoners deep in sleep. He checked the security system, manipulated some key buttons, and satisfied himself that all was arranged in correct order. He nodded his head and ducked out the door, locking it behind him. It was important that no one could get in for the next half hour. He was not due to be relieved for two hours. And since he was the chief security officer, there would be no one to check on him before that.

Colum could barely see the grass in front of him; but he could sense it, dim and indistinct, wet with the evening dew. He entered the security cells by the side door, steely gray with thin black bars protecting the only window in it. It sighed shut as he moved down the hall toward Turly's room.

Turly stirred and groaned as a hand shook him violently. He sat up staring into space. Colum stood beside him, his face almost hidden in an abundance of white hair.

"Turly, get up but make no noise. We have to move fast."

"But Hastings, what about Hastings? He can see us."

"Not at the moment," chuckled Colum. "I'll tell you about it later. For now, trust me. We have to get the others and get out before the Movement strikes in fifteen minutes."

"The Movement?" Turly was dazed. He did not get an answer. But he did respond to the urgency in Colum's voice. Hastings was the enemy; Colum was not. It was as simple as that, and Turly did not want to think beyond that. His head felt stuffed with cotton and on the edge of some fearful nightmare that the least amount of inquiry would bring out into the open. He did not want that, not then.

The two moved silently out into the hall. It was still quiet and dimly lit. Colum was satisfied that all was going well. He gave his set of keys to Turly and indicated the other rooms. After explaining about Meriwether, about her need, he quickly instructed the younger man where to go and what to do. He was to release the others and take them to the exit door *C* and wait for his return. There was something he had to do first. Turly nodded and left, moving unsteadily but now fully awake and ready to act.

Colum checked his watch again. He had twelve minutes to trip the fuse on the Sniffers and get back to the group. He headed to the east end of the building, to Hastings' headquarters. This would be the trickiest part of the escape plan. It was not inconceivable that Hastings would be in his office working late, but he had to take that chance.

There was no one in the large, well-appointed office. Colum left the door ajar and walked cautiously across to the far wall where the central control panel of Hastings' private defenses was set. Tiny red and yellow lights flickered on and off. Colum punched out three sets of signals. He was reaching for the next set when he heard footsteps and the sound of the study door opening.

Colum turned and faced Lord Hastings.

Chapter 19

Hastings stared at his chief security officer.

"Colum?"

"My Lord Hastings, I am relieved you are well and safe. I had feared for your life."

"My life? Why should I fear for my life? And why is your post left unmanned?" Hastings had reached to his waist where he kept his portable Colorstealer, the only one of its kind.

"At five-thirty this morning we received a signal from our station in the city. Rumors that the Movement had decided to act. I checked the prisoners personally to see that they were adequately held. They were. I then knew that the Sniffers had to be in perfect working order if the rear defenses were to be ready. And it is good that I came. See, half of the force has been stopped for some reason. There might be an insider at work, Lord Hastings." Colum bowed deeply when he finished his explanation. He looked up to see the suspicion fade from Hastings' face.

"Good, that is good, Colum. Correct the stoppage,

lock the switches, and come with me. If the Movement wants to fight, I want to be ready."

"Yes, my Lord Hastings," said Colum, who knew it was already too late to be ready for the Movement. The Sniffers were a different matter, however. He turned and, while Hastings watched, flicked back the circuits he had just tripped. The rear was again guarded. There was nothing he could do now.

Colum and Hastings left the room together. Colum knew the attack was imminent. He had to leave Hastings. He looked up at the big man and weighed his chances. He had never tried to deceive Hastings before. Too risky. His projecting ability might not be strong enough to overcome Hastings' vision. But now there was no choice. As Hastings walked on, Colum fell back. He watched the large, red-bearded man reach the end of the corridor, occasionally muttering something to someone who no longer walked beside him. It was working. Colum hurried away.

There was no time now to get to the Sniffers. The escape group would have to take its chances. Colum ran as fast as he could to the C exit. His feet slipped on the highly polished floor as he dashed around corners going from corridor to corridor, his eyes busy with worry.

Smith saw the gnome first. He shouted to Turly, who wheeled and grabbed Colum to slow him down.

"We must hurry! All of us. Out this door. We have approximately one hundred meters of tangled underbrush to get through. If we can make the wire at the end of the yard, we are free. It is disconnected and neutralized. We can then go to the underground shelter in Straiten and await the results of this night's work."

"And if we don't make the wire, Colum? What happens then?"

"Why, then we all die, Turly. I have no time to explain now."

The members of the group muttered amongst themselves. Meriwether stood alone near the door by Smith. Harve moved about like an uncertain elephant, his bulk ponderous in the narrow hall. Colum gestured with his hand to the door and stepped to it. The others followed. Colum could not bring himself to tell them about the Sniffers. There would be time enough for that when they were triggered.

On that side of the barracks the morning sun had not yet made its way. The darkness was exacerbated by the lush growth of young trees, their branches dipping down and out in thick mats. The group spread out in a loose semi-circle and began to run to the end of the back grounds. In only a few strides, they heard behind them the screams of many men, tiny and indistinct, yelling something they could not understand. A loud explosion was followed by more screams of a different kind. Lights like fires briefly lit up the sky. Turly paused for a moment and looked up; he was drawn to the fire, and held by its flickering speech. Colum shook him. There was another explosion, and the group fled as if propelled by its waves.

Meriwether tripped and fell. Turly looked down at her for a fraction of a second and then stooped to pick her up. He heard the strange baying of hounds. High overhead he saw more flashes of light.

"Turly," shouted Colum. "Hurry!" The small man was jumping up and down in great fear. "The Sniffers have been released! We have only minutes now." The urgency in his voice raised the hair on Turly's neck.

The rush to the wire became a frenzied race. Each man thought of himself alone. The wire became for each a symbol of survival, something to be reached at all cost. Everything else vanished in the terrible sounds behind them.

But Harve held back. He was not afraid of dogs. Never had been. Four short legs and short little teeth. He would hold off the dogs until his friends had gotten over the wire fence. No one had noticed that the huge man had fallen behind. They were too close to the fence now to care. Branches caught Turly by the shoulder and slapped him on the face as he carried Meriwether in his arms. She had fainted from the chase, and the terror that the hounds had inspired in all of them. Turly tried to analyze that fear and could find no reason for it. The sound of the pursuing pack, hollow and echoing, was not new to any of them. As hunters and fishermen they had all kept dogs, had always been around them, knew how to deal with them. Why then this fleeing terror?

Perhaps it was the attitude of Colum. The little man had proven himself an invaluable friend, a man who could operate safely in the world of Hastings and who had freed them all. He had certain powers that seemed to separate him from the others. Why then was he so afraid of the dogs?

The fence had been reached. Garrett and Smith were over it and were helping Meriwether step down safely onto the ground on the other side. Colum and Bulfin were half over; Turly had one foot hooked on the bottom wire ready to follow. Harve was panting up from the rear. The morning fog was beginning to lift, and the landscape emerged from its obscurity into the half-light.

Harve fell heavily. The black mass of fury on his back bit deeply into his shoulder. With a howl of rage and surprise Harve reached behind him and tore at the thing.

266

It was not a dog.

Rising slowly on two feet, Harve held above his head something that looked vaguely like a dog, but its head was wrong. Instead of eyes, it had two brightly shining red dots. There were no ears. Instead, like the antennae of an ant, two thin wires emerged from each side of the rounded skull with a tiny ball at the end of each. It was totally black with a skin like toughened leather. Its six legs tore at the air as Harve moved in a tight circle spinning it faster and faster. With a great grunt Harve released the thing, and it flew back into the trees, landing with a dull crunch. Turly could see through the dim light the hinged jaws moving and the razor teeth flashing as the thing lay in shattered splinters.

"Harve is not afraid of dogs," bellowed the crazed giant. "Dogs try to eat Harve, but they are not as strong as Harve." He turned toward the sounds of other Sniffers. His back stiffened as the blood from his shoulder spread out on his tunic. He stood tall and firm as he waited with outstretched arms for the black death to come.

Turly turned and was trying to climb down to help Harve. Colum grabbed Turly by the hair and pulled upward.

"Circle, man, you can't help him now. You must save yourself!" Colum was almost incoherent. Garrett and Bulfin were hollering, Meriwether was screaming, and over all were the sounds of mechanical snorts, great snuffling sounds intertwined with growls that did not come from a real throat. Smith understood then why Dodder was so sure no one could escape from Hastings' service.

The Sniffers were almost upon them.

Two mechanical dogs broke the clearing. They immediately sensed the situation and without hesitation split into separate trajectories. Harve caught one in mid-air with the blunt end of his huge hand. With a twisting motion he sent it hurtling to join the first dog in a heap of wires and metal. But the other got inside Harve's reach. It fastened its jaws onto his lower left arm and held. With a bellow of pain and rage Harve grabbed the upper torso and tried to pull it free. Blood spiraled down his arm and dropped to the ground.

Turly leaped clear of the fence and raced to the battle. The Sniffer was cold to the touch. The power in its legs was evident, however. Turly went sprawling. Cursing, he jumped up and rejoined the fray. The Sniffers had no lips but there was a ridge that formed the upper part of each semi-circular jaw. Turly secured a hold on each jaw and pulled. He was now smeared with Harve's blood, but the giant was not visibly weakened. His rage and frustration came from the inability to use both of his hands; he reached across and held the thrashing legs of the Sniffer to his body to allow Turly to free his arm without interference.

Turly's body strained against the jaws of the Sniffer. It was useless. He could loosen the teeth somewhat, but he was unable to pry them apart. He looked up into Harve's eyes and saw behind the pain and anger the trusting child he had always been. He was sure Turly would free him.

Turly redoubled his efforts. The scar on his arm bulged and seemed to come to life as he used every ounce of his strength. Gradually the jaws separated. Turly pulled and felt his shoulders drop. His conscious thoughts were gone; every part of his being was directed to the jaws, and his muscles of flesh and blood pulled against the heavy metal of the Sniffer.

Harve was free. The Sniffer spun off and was on its feet facing the two men. It stood with legs wide apart assessing the new situation. It seemed to cock its head as if listening to something far off. Turly could hear the snuffling call of other Sniffers not far away. He glanced at Harve who was holding his badly wounded left arm with his one good hand.

"Move," roared Turly as he motioned Harve to the fence.

"No." The big man shook his massive head.

"Turly, get back over this fence. Now!" Colum was almost out of his mind.

Turly could hear the others calling, warning of danger. But he could not leave Harve to such a death. Big as Harve was, he could not stand up to a pack of these things. Even as he thought this, Turly was aware that even two men could not stand up to them. He was dead as well as Harve. There was no time to be truly scared or regretful. But Turly did see, flashing before his eyes, the remembered faces of his parents, Ellman, and all the hopes and fears of his youth. He repeated silently the last statement of the Universal Mythic Sequence Church credo as he wiped the sweat from his eyes.

Turly was lifted high in the air. Before he could call out, he found himself caught in the arms of his companions on the other side of the fence. Harve had tossed him over bodily and had turned back to the woods. He began to move in huge lumbering strides into the trees toward the sound of the Sniffers.

"Harve!" screamed Turly. The others held him back. The last he saw of Harve was the huge head framed against the flare of sunlight coming through the massive trees. Then there was the sound of snuffling and the shouting of battle.

Colum faced the others.

"Harve has given us our chance," he said. "Are we going to take it, or is his sacrifice to be wasted?"

Turly stared dully at Colum and shook his head.

"We still have a way to go before we're safe. We have to circle the enclave and head east to Straiten. We should meet the rebel forces soon and the rest will be easier." Colum then pointed toward the dense underbrush running along the perimeter of the grounds. The group began to move quickly along it. Soon the sounds and shouts behind them grew dim and only the snuffling remained.

Turly then remembered something.

"Colum, I've got to get back inside the compound."

"Why, in the One's name?" whispered Colum.

"I've got to get the things my father left me. They're in Hastings' museum." Turly had stopped and was about to re-enter the grounds.

"Turly, the Sniffers will tear you to pieces, too. And if they don't, Hastings' guards, or rebels who don't know you, will."

"I've got to, Colum. Don't you see, all of this is useless if I don't have the only clues my father left me. If Hastings is right about the Blessing Papers, somebody has got to find them before he does, or before Oliver does. And who else but the son of John Vail?"

Colum examined Turly's face carefully.

"Do you mean that, my son? Do you commit yourself to the finding of the Blessing Papers and their preservation?"

"I do. My father may have given his life to protect them, or to prevent their misuse, and I can do no less." Turly's face had taken on a strange aura as he spoke. The natural phosphorescence of his white hair shone in the early morning light with an almost preternatural glow. His green eyes changed subtly, their piercing gaze heightened by his purpose.

Colum nodded his head. He reached into his tunic and brought forth a small brown bag. He handed it to Turly, who stood astonished.

"In that case, here are your things," he said. "I took the liberty of removing them from the museum earlier this morning. I thought you might need them before your journey was over. But now I must tell you that my ability to help you is almost finished. I will get you all to Straiten, and then I must leave."

Turly stood tall before Colum. He placed his right hand gently on the man's tiny shoulder. The gnome seemed to visibly age. The twinkle in his eye was receding, and the wrinkles in his brow, already legion, increased as the sun rose.

"I appreciate your help, Colum. Without you I do not think I could have made it. I don't know who or what you are, but you have my deepest thanks."

"There is no need for thanks," said Colum. "But come now, let's hurry, we still have some way to go if we are to get to Straiten."

"No, old friend, we are not going to Straiten."

"What?" Colum had seemed beyond surprise, but he became agitated again and tried to argue with Turly.

"No. We are going in the other direction. To the west. To Clonnoise Abbey. If the mystery of the Papers is to be solved, that is where I must be. I know it."

Colum cocked his head again and looked up at Turly in the growing light. His stance seemed to suggest not only acceptance of Turly's pronouncement, but also pride that he had made it. Turly was coming of age in more than one way.

"Very well, Turly. I must go and help Cole's men if

I can. If Hastings can be defeated or at least forced to retrench, then your task will be eased."

"Goodby, Colum." Turly watched as the short chunky figure faded into the underbrush toward the sounds of battle ahead. As Colum went, he turned and waved. Turly thought, just as the last part of him merged with the landscape, that he saw something else. He blinked and turned away to his friends.

"You all heard what I told Colum. I must go to the Clonnoise Abbey for several reasons. We have come a long way, and there is more to go." Turly pointed to the rising sun. "We must put our backs to the sun and travel to the south and west. To do that we will have to travel through rough country yet. If any of you wish to go north instead, please tell me now."

The forest around them was silent now and full of splinters of light. The noise from the compound was fading, and they did not know who was winning the battle. Each of the travelers looked at the others and nodded quietly. They would follow Turly.

"Good. Then let's begin." Turly led the column away into the woods, with Smith bringing up the rear. Behind them they left the unburied bodies of Kelleher and Harve.

None of them knew if their deaths would have any meaning at all.

Chapter 20

Cole swore as the long blade lightly nicked his cheek. He stepped quickly to one side, then moved in toward his opponent. Hastings' soldier thrust forward; Cole pulled back, lured the man in, then ran him through the chest. With a gurgle the soldier fell to the grass. Wiping his sword on his tan pants, Cole looked around cautiously.

The main battle was taking place on the eastern gate where the Movement troops had left the Heron swamp. There Cole's men had scored a surprise victory and held the upper hand. But along the other fronts the soldiers of Hastings were gathering and bringing in their powerful weapons. Already many of the attackers had fallen to the expert long-range killing of Hastings. Cole noticed that some of his men had ignored the warnings about the fences and had died hanging from the wires that had made them light up when they touched them.

The battle was not yet decided. If Cole could get Hastings, the tide might turn in their favor. The paid soldiers of Hastings would quit if the source of their money were gone. Cole had come ahead of the main body of his men to find Hastings.

Colum appeared suddenly beside Cole, as if he had been standing there listening to his thoughts. Cole was startled and almost took Colum's head off.

"My man Colum, you should be more careful in battle," shouted Cole. He was hot with the earlier kill and his eyes bulged.

"No time for small talk," said Colum. "Have you seen Hastings?"

"No. But his men are gathering there and there," he said, pointing in their direction. "We might have to withdraw if we can't finish this within a few minutes. We can't stand up to the full force of Hastings' arms. I thought you were going to arrange something. What?"

"We need a diversion. Young Turly and his people have made it out and are now heading to the west. They will need time. And if our—your—purpose is to be fulfilled, they must have free passage."

Cole looked off to the west. "Was Sean with them?"

"Not when I left. But forget Sean. There is more urgent business at hand. Now listen carefully. Here is what we shall do, and you must follow my instructions to the letter. I will get Hastings and send him to you. And then you will do this."

Cole listened, but his hand tightened on his sword as he thought of Sean.

The Movement forces were beginning to fall back into the swamp. After the initial surprise and the bombing of the barracks, they had lost their momentum. The first fighting was hand to hand, for which they had been trained; in this they were unsurpassed. The ground on the east side of the Hall was littered with red capes. But Hastings' other weapons, the Colorstealers, after being strangely quiet, had taken their toll on the rebels.

Men began dropping with large holes in their bodies, or turning to black liquid char. The rebels had expected this, but not so early in the battle. The fighting wavered, and they were now only barely able to hold their own.

And then, along the front and rising to a crescendo, a cheer arose and the rebels began to dance about in glee. Over toward the front gate two figures had appeared. It was Hastings in his long Red cape of authority, followed by *their* leader Cole. Cole had a sword at Hastings' back. Lord Hastings had been captured.

Hastings' men saw their leader and confusion set in. The center of their lines broke and headed for the barracks. The long black needle gun that had begun to play havoc with the attackers was abandoned. With a loud shout the rebel forces charged the front lines. The eastern front was then secured by the rebel forces. But a massed group of Hastings' soldiers from the other barracks had arrived at the southern perimeter. They could not see what had caused the rout of the others and were determined to recoup any losses.

In the center of the east parade ground was a wooden tower used for training and review. Cole led his prisoner to the tower, and they mounted it. All the participants in the battle could then see the pair. Cole raised his sword for quiet. In only a few minutes, silence had fallen over the grounds of Hastings Hall.

"Men of Hastings!" shouted Cole. "Whom will you follow now? The old order of Hastings, whom you see before you, or the new one, of me and my men? It is your choice!

"This is your last chance. Surrender now and you will be welcomed with open arms by me. If you do not, you will be leaderless. There will be no reason to fight and there will be nowhere for you to go."

At that moment there was the sound of a small explosion. The tiny figure of Hastings crumpled on the tower. A great moan rose in the troops. The Movement rebels muttered amongst themselves. Cole glanced down at the body of Hastings as if he could not believe it, and looked about wildly for the source of the shot. He could see a figure lurking at the west wall of the main barracks but could not tell who it was. Turning his attention back to the confrontation of the two armies, he shouted once again.

"Your leader is dead. Give up the fight. There is nothing left for you. Put your weapons in front of you and step back. You may then decide to go where you will, or stay with me as I march on the holdings of Hastings' lieutenants." Seeing the tide had turned in his favor, and that Hastings' men had lost their spirit, Cole climbed down from the tower and raced for the west grounds. He had some unfinished business.

The flies in the swamp had reached their peak. Summer had been good to them, had fed them and allowed them to multiply. And now they were repaying summer by inflicting upon anything that came their way the bounty of their stinging wrath. They would gather in groups like gnats, hovering and chasing. They would start first with a mere annoyance, something a random toss of the hand could dispel, and then they would gather momentum and impinge violently upon the consciousness. What would at first be ill-humor would turn to anger and then to a mild form of terror. There was no escaping the flies in the swamp. You could not run fast enough or far enough. They would find you and settle on you quickly and bite and flick off.

Turly cursed aloud. His group had circled back around to the west into the swamp to give the Sniffers a wide berth; although the dogs could not pass the fence, the memory of Harve made the group cautious of the mechanical beasts. And now there was something worse. Flies! Circle, thought Turly. He had never understood the place of flies in the Mythic Sequence. They seemed to exist only to torment men. He looked back at the others. They were walking through water to their ankles, while swatting and waving their hands. The sun was coming down now in great fury, through the gaps in the gloomy fern trees, making an intense and vivid mosaic of yellow and green with the mouse-gray water. And through it all came the whining buzz of the flies.

But they would be through the fringe of the swamp in a few more minutes. A wild growth of plant life sprawled, crawled and sprung up into the air. Turly could see the end of the marsh land not fifty meters away. After that, bare land rose gradually into the distance. Turly scratched his head and the mole above his eye. It tingled strangely as did his scar. He then looked about cautiously but saw nothing. Through the splashing and the cursing he heard nothing, but he felt the presence of another that he recognized by his inability to read him accurately. It was Sean, somewhere.

Turly stopped and held up one hand. The others stopped as well and wiped the backs of their necks while marking time in the fetid water.

"Sean!" Turly called with cupped hands. He repeated the call. Ahead about ten meters a shadowy figure stepped out from behind a large cypress tree. In its funereal gloom, amidst hanging vines, Turly could detect only the long stringy hair and the slight hunch of his friend.

"It seems I cannot hide from you, Turly," said Sean softly. He stepped out into a patch of light. Turly gasped. The man had aged tremendously in only a few days. His eyebrows were now salt and pepper, as was

277

his loose hair. He now seemed middle-aged, and carried himself with a slower gait.

"Sean, I have too many questions to ask you. What has happened? Why did you desert me? Why are you here now?"

Sean held up one hand and chuckled. "You will know all soon, soon. It is something in my head. I can tell you now that when it became clear to me that we were walking into a trap that night in Straiten, and that it was necessary for you to be trapped but not me, I made my plans. That night near Harrow's house, I made sure that you were walking ahead. I scouted the area and knew I was right. I knew what I had to do. After you gave the signal-knock at the door, I slipped away down the five blocks to the marsh. I moved quickly to Hastings Hall and have been out here ever since, waiting for you."

"Waiting for me? But, Sean, *I* didn't know I would be here myself until a few hours ago."

"You knew, Turly, you knew. But you didn't know you knew. There is a difference."

Smith had stepped forward to listen. He shook his head at the riddle but accepted it, as he had been forced to accept much all his life. He had a good head for figures and commerce but not for this, this drama of hidden meanings and secret figures who could appear and disappear at will. He felt only the cold certainty of water in his shoes and the savage whine of insects about his head.

"Sean, I'm going to Clonnoise Abbey. Will you come with me?" Turly stood with his hands on his hips in an attitude of leadership. He had gained new confidence in his abilities and even the mysterious Sean could not, would not, stand in his way.

"I will have to go with you, Turly. There is something

I must do there. And there is something I must do now, as well. If you and your people would keep your positions for a few more minutes, we will have a visitor, a very angry visitor." Sean slowly pulled his sword from its sheath. He moved imperceptibly to his right and faced the sun.

Cole burst into the clearing. He was sweating profusely and brandishing his bloody sword. Sean and Cole faced one another across a distance of about three meters. Cole's eyes blazed with insane fury at Sean. Sean calmly returned the stare.

"I knew you were here," said Cole. "I knew it. You killed my wife and now you've killed Hastings; my one hope of getting his secrets, controlling his empire, is gone."

"Indeed yes, it was your one hope. Now there is no empire for you to gain, is there?"

Cole shouted something and sprang at Sean who easily stepped aside and parried his first thrust.

"And about your wife, Cole. Who was it who betrayed her to Hastings' men? Me? Oh, no. Not me. I knew *you* had done that. What did she know, Cole? That she had to be killed? And I was a convenient villain? Would you kill me now to keep this from being told? Did she find out that you were plotting not simply to *overthrow* Hastings, but to *replace* him? That the rebel chief of Hastings wanted to be the new tyrant? Ah, was that it?"

Cole swore in rage and leaped again at Sean. Again Sean sidestepped, but this time he flicked out and rapped Cole on the side of the skull with his sword-guard, drawing blood. Cole staggered but regained his footing and wheeled toward Sean.

"And, Cole, do you know that it was *Colum,* and not Hastings, that was killed? No, I didn't do that, but it was time for Colum to go. He had served his purpose and was ready. A random shot by an angered rebel who saw his one chance at fame. That's usually how things work, aren't they? If you were back there now you might still find Hastings." Sean was relaxed and almost sad as he talked to Cole.

Cole was by now thoroughly irrational. He raged at Sean as he once again rushed to him with his sword raised. This time Sean did not turn aside. He stood his ground and waited for Cole. At the last moment Sean parried the thrust and stepped inside Cole's reach. His left hand, palm up, was thrown up against the other man's nose, raking upward as the head snapped back. He then stood erect as Cole slumped to the ground. Cole groaned and shook his head but still managed to regain his feet. Through the blood that ran down over his mouth, Cole muttered something the others could not hear.

"I'm sorry, Cole, I'm sorry," said Sean, "but it's time. You cannot remain to handle political affairs in Straiten. There are others to do that."

Cole turned his back to the group and seemed to lunge forward onto Sean's blade. His shoulder bunched up where the point came through, and he fell like a doll in a sprawled heap at Sean's feet.

It was over. Turly, for all his confidence in his new mission, was stunned. He looked into Sean's eyes and mind but could see or feel nothing. This still troubled Turly. But he did not feel that Sean was against him. Thank the Circle for that, thought Turly. He had never seen anyone so deadly with a sword as Sean, or so able to control a situation. He had not seen that before in Sean.

Sean wiped his blade carefully on some fern leaves near the edge of the clearing. He stepped over to Turly and whispered something to him. The others saw Turly nod and then turn to them.

"Hastings is not dead," said Turly. "But most of his men have surrendered to the Movement and so we are safe for the moment. However, we still have to hurry to cross the river and mountain that separate us from Clonnoise Abbey. I don't know what else Hastings or Oliver might do to prevent our finding the Blessing Papers." Turly paused and looked around at Sean. "Sean here has gathered enough food to last us for a while. As we go we must disguise our going, take pains to avoid leaving tracks. Are you ready?"

All agreed. Bulfin rubbed his arm where the Farks had wounded him weeks before in the Lower Mountains. It was almost well. He seemed older and wiser and he had some inkling of what might await them beyond the swamp. But he had no intention of turning back. If what Turly had told them about what might lie there, a cure for the ills of the island, was true, then the trip there was more important than ever. He had found his cousin Meriwether and she had seemed torn in some way, but not empty as he had feared. She had been the reason he had come south, but now there were other things.

The Order of Zeno, long feared in the south, was now a threat to the north and would be even more so if they got the Papers first. Hastings was no mystery. He wanted political control of the island, as Turly had said. But what did the Order want? Bulfin glanced over at Smith and Garrett. They seemed to be accepting all this as he was. They were merchants, not fighters. Bulfin wondered how it was they had managed to get as far as they had. Harve and Kelleher were dead and there might well be more dead before this was over. But a sense of grand schemes and great meanings inspired Bulfin to carry on to the end, whatever that end might be.

The group gathered the bundles of food hidden by Sean and began to move again, with Turly in front and Sean in the rear. They moved in a single line to better allow Sean to cover their trail. The scruffy scout moved like a cat amidst the foliage and underbrush, fixing and arranging details the untrained eye could not see. Occasionally he would stop, stare ahead at Turly and then return to his work.

High noon found the group of six walking cautiously through hip-high grass. The wind flowed in currents on its top, shading it from dark green to light beige. Behind them for as far as they could see there were no pursuers nor any sign that the grass had ever been disturbed. The day was like wide water without sound.

Late that afternoon Turly smelled water. He had noticed earlier that the ground had shown signs of lusher growth; tiny animals had begun to creep out of their silent way, like surprised thieves. Turly motioned for all to stop and beckoned Sean to the front.

"Sean. The river?"

Sean crept forward and was soon lost in the grass. Turly stood on one foot for a while, his scalp itching with the heat and the sweat. Propping one hand on his hip, he leaned over and spat. Sean was back before he re-assumed his position.

"It's the river, Turly. And more trouble."

"Hastings?"

"No. River men with a cargo of Fallow slaves for the coast trade."

"Can we deal with them? It would be easier to ride across the river on their boat than to stop and make a raft."

"We could, but I wouldn't try. The slave traders are

not good drinking partners. They would give you a drink then split your skull. Plus, a ship in transit with slaves is an explosive mixture. The Fallow do not take lightly to being made slaves. It is a small ship but we are outnumbered."

Turly thought about that. He wasn't overly worried. He had somewhere to get to and he needed the quickest way to do it. "Sean, we don't have the time to look for another way to get across the river. We've got to take a chance. Let's go." Turly forgot his caution and made boldly for the river. He had not gone far before he thought he could hear the creaking of tackle. He felt more in his element now. As a fisherman he knew about ships and sailing. He could talk to these men and pay them for passage across.

The sun cast Turly's shadow in a wavering ripple on the grass near the shore line. It did not seem to be a part of him.

Chapter 21

The squat slaver was about twenty meters long and fifteen meters wide. Two red sails billowed slowly as the ship moved to the sea downriver. Turly stopped at the shore and began waving his hands and shouting. A Fallow on the bridge saw him and hurried rapidly to the rear of the boat, to the Captain's cabin. Its high-plumed hair fell forward over its tiny eyes as it shuffled inside the wooden enclosure. Presently a tall man emerged and stepped into the light. His face was in shadows, his arms held behind him. The Fallow, its slightly yellow skin looking smudged, stood servile at his elbow, careful not to touch him.

"Hello there!" shouted Turly again. The Captain had said something to one of the crew who was squatting on the deck. Several other men lay propped around the perimeter of the ship which began to move slowly in Turly's direction. About three meters from shore it stopped, and an anchor was thrown overboard. The Captain stepped to the narrow rail and gazed down at Turly. There was great arrogance and great sadness in the eyes, over which thick black eyebrows rose slightly where they met at the nose. His black hair was dense like tiny wires, but his skin was milk white, as if he had never seen the sun. When the Captain spoke, Turly noted that his teeth seemed pointed and razor sharp.

"Yes," rumbled the Captain. It was a statement, not a question. Turly thought for a moment that he was answering a question that Turly had asked.

"We need passage across this river. Can you give it to us for a price?" Turly had to raise his voice to be heard over the slapping of water along the length of the boat.

The Captain glanced at the Fallow cowering against the rail at his side. Turly could see the open pens where other Fallow stood or sat in ragged, chained repose. They were watching Turly with what Turly thought was hatred. He would not like to be a slave himself, nor did he have sympathies with the slave traders. But he needed them now, and so he would refuse to say anything on the subject. He saw the waves in the distance catch the sun and set sparkles dancing like a host of golden moths. They blinded Turly when he looked at them.

The Captain looked again at the Fallow. With a grimace of disgust and disdain, he turned away and said something to his men, most of whom were either sleeping amidship or drunk, Turly could not tell which. As he surveyed the ship Turly felt a sense of foreboding, but he could not yet distinguish the source, the Fallow or the crew. It would be understandable if the Fallow were not at ease. Turly thought the Captain, who was sweating slightly, had cut his eyes at Meriwether. Turly had second thoughts about the trip across. If this were a slaver ship, then his party might be walking into a situation in which both he and his friends might well be enslaved themselves. Not a pleasant thought. But the feeling passed, and Turly thought that with his four good men the group could protect itself, or at least make the slaves think twice before doing anything.

"Aye, I'll take you across, and for no payment." The Captain then grinned for the first time. The sight chilled Turly's blood.

There was nothing for it now but to board and cross. The First Mate and the Captain's Fallow poled the ship closer to shore and lowered a rope ladder. When the group was aboard, the Captain pointed out an area where they would have to stay until the other side was reached.

"My Fallow here will make you comfortable, I'm sure. If there's anything you need at all, ask him, a bright fellow, he'll get it for you. I warn you, however, not to mingle with the crew. They can be unpredictably violent. And stay far away from the slave quarters; should the Fallow get free, there would be death on this ship." The Captain stared at Turly and again smiled sardonically. He seemed to be saying something Turly could not understand. The Fallow had returned to his side, although the Captain never acknowledged his presence or seemed in any way to be grateful that the slave was so concerned for his well-being. It was a mark of the inhumanity of the man, thought Turly. He treated Fallows as if they did not exist.

"I bid you good day," said the Captain and, followed closely by the Fallow, he re-entered his cabin.

Turly conferred with Smith and Sean. They agreed to be alert for the first sign of treachery from the crew, who still lay sprawled about in various attitudes of drunken abandon.

"They must have had a good night last night," muttered Smith. "Do you suppose they also carry a supply of whiskey aboard?"

"I suggest we ignore them as much as possible," said Sean. "We should be thankful they did not cut us down at the shore, although I must admit I have the very real feeling that it may have been better for us if they had tried it then. We are relatively helpless out here."

Turly looked out again upon the waters. The ship was veering to the far shore while drifting further downriver. They should be across in half an hour. Turly gathered Meriwether into the center of a circle in which all faced outward and waited for whatever might happen.

Nothing did.

The Captain stayed in his cabin and the crew remained asleep. The Fallow fluttered amongst themselves in the slave pens and peered out at them from time to time but otherwise seemed reconciled to their fate.

The far shore loomed closer. The rush of water beneath them gurgled pleasantly and the sun warmed their bodies in a refreshing manner, the wind removing much of the sweat raised from their fast trek to the river. Turly could imagine how the river wound slowly from the mountains to the west, across the flat open plain in the middle of the island, and down to the great opening into the sea to the east. He got out his father's map and checked the river's twisting, looping progress across the bottom half of the island. It seemed to hint something to Turly, but he could not make it out. He checked again the position of Clonnoise Abbey and reckoned that it was about a three-day walk from the other side of the river. It would be slow going once they had passed the flat plains of grass and reached the foothills near Boulder Gap. Turly squinted into the afternoon sun. He would soon know if his feeling about his father was correct. He would be as near the source of the recent mystery of the Blessing Papers as he had ever been. Once at the Abbey he knew he could puzzle it out. He thought he had gained the ability to cut through the camouflage of lies and deception that most people used to hide the truth from themselves. If Hastings had not found the Papers or his father, it must have been because he did not know where to look. Or, more important, *how* to look. Turly would not make that mistake.

Sean said something to Turly that he did not catch. Sean then stepped away from the group toward one of the crew members propped against the forward mast. He bent toward the man and peered intently at him. He straightened, shrugged visibly, spat, and strolled back to Turly and the group. The Fallow had aroused themselves and were gabbling to one another in their half-tongue clacking. As Sean returned and resumed his vigil, they settled down again.

The boat was within five minutes of the shore.

"Turly, can you swim?" asked Sean.

"Of course, but why?" Turly glanced uneasily at Sean.

"The crew members are neither drunk nor asleep. They are dead."

Turly stiffened. His eyes flickered over to the Fallow pens. He noticed something for the first time. Some of the Fallow were not chained, but were lying about watching them closely. Perhaps the others were only pretending to be chained. And the Captain? A prisoner? Had he not been ignoring the Fallow, but had been under orders from him? Turly's mind was spinning.

Turly gulped hard. There were clearly two humans alive on deck besides themselves. They were the Captain and the Navigator, the two key personnel needed on the river. Turly could see no other humans above ship that had moved.

"Sean, you mean . . . ?"

"I'm afraid so. We've walked into a most delicate situation, as I feared. Only the situation is reversed. The slaves are in control. I'm not sure if they mean for us to remain alive to report this."

Turly judged the distance from ship to shore. All the members of the party could swim well, and their food was in water-tight wrappings. They had all grown up near water and as children played in it often. Turly saw no problem there. But what would the Fallow do if they jumped ship? There were weapons aboard; but could the Fallow use them?

Turly strolled calmly to each member of the group and whispered the situation to each. By now they were all used to the unexpected and none betrayed any surprise. Each nodded that he understood. Meriwether was still wearing the long pants uniform used by Hastings' Drummers.

Turly waited for the right moment. As he did he noticed other things. The disrepair of the sails, the untidy deck, the slight aroma of decaying flesh. He could see, too, a thin red line around the necks of several of the nearby sailors. It was a death ship, making a desperate attempt to reach a haven it would never find. Turly knew they had to get off while they had the advantage of surprise.

"Now!" shouted Turly.

All six broke for the rail, leaping over and into the water before anyone else on deck could move. And then bedlam broke loose. On deck the Fallows dropped any pretense and broke from their pens in wild confusion. From the Captain's cabin the servile Fallow erupted with a great sword in his hand. He raced to the rail and yelled and spat at the swimmers that were now slipping behind the boat and heading for shore. The Fallow's face was contorted with rage and hatred just as earlier it had seemed unduly abased and humble. Before the ship got beyond range, Turly thought he saw the face of the Captain looking out at them from a rear window. The face did not seem arrogant or disdainful as Turly had thought, as he had projected onto it, but fearful and full of an undisguised sadness. There was nothing Turly could do, and he watched the ship flounder and twist out of control further and further downriver.

As the swimmers pulled themselves onto shore and lay breathing heavily, no one spoke. Finally Sean got up and surveyed the territory ahead. He sat back down by Turly.

"There was a moment there when I thought I knew what was going on," sighed Turly. "I have much to think about now."

"Turly, it fooled me too, and I am not easily fooled. Things are sometimes not what they seem. The closed life of the Circle can *exclude* knowledge as well as *include* it. That is one of its disadvantages. But you have seen much and will see more. You cannot let this blunt your purpose. You want the Papers and knowledge of your father. What you will do with what you find will be a result of your journey to find them. Doesn't your Sequence tell you of the quest, and the dangers of that quest? You have at least that, a foreknowledge of all things, whether or not it contains details. Widen the Circle, Turly. Accept the journey and the experience that it brings. Once you were young and all things made sense. Now you are not so sure. You have lost your childhood. All must do so, that is the way of change and time." Sean shifted his position and lay with one hand on the ground and the other held limply over his raised knee. His stringy brown hair, aging rapidly, blew slightly in the breeze from the river.

Turly recognized the truth of what Sean had said. The Sequence and its Framers did preach of a journey that had to be made. But Turly had not known, could not have known, where it would lead before he actually made the journey itself. With a shock he remembered Ellman's words of years before: *The knowing will come by not knowing.* He was right; Ellman had spoken truth. Even now he did not know where his pursuit of the Papers would take him or his friends. There was only the going, and the hope and the fear of the going.

Smith had stood up with Meriwether and was saying something to her. Meriwether was shaking her head. He touched her on the arm softly, as a lover does. They separated, and Smith walked over to Turly and Sean, looking down at them.

"We should get as far from this river as we can, don't you think?" He was truculent. Turly looked up in surprise and saw resentment in Smith. He had not paid much attention to Smith since they had met again at the black wagon in the Lower Mountains. There had been too much to worry about then. But now Turly could see that a subtle change had taken place in Smith's attitude toward him. Gone was the boyish good humor and the easy forgiveness of earlier years. The two had grown apart in various ways; Turly had long recognized the merchant mind of Smith and had accepted it, as Smith had accepted his own lack of a mind such as Turly's. But this was something different.

Then Turly knew what it was, could feel it like the sudden cold outside a hut in winter.

Turly jerked his head toward Meriwether. She had betrayed him, he knew that. He had forced himself to believe that it had been to save him as her Circle choice. Now he knew it wasn't for that. It had been a trade-off for her own life. Turly could tell also that she had nothing for him now but a growing fear. She wanted to return north, but not with Turly. With Smith. Turly thought he was seeing her for the first time.

Standing and facing Smith, Turly looked inward. He did not speak to his old friend at first. He turned and went to Meriwether. She stood before him and stared into his burning green eyes, glowing and flickering with an understanding that both hurt and liberated her.

"You have chosen Smith," he said with a voice as quiet as dawn.

Meriwether kept his gaze and stood tall and composed, more composed than she felt. "It is my right," she said.

"Yes, it is your right," agreed Turly. He paused for a long moment. "I presumed too much, Meriwether. All these years I accepted our growth together. Now I see your growth was in another direction. You need the Circle and the things the Circle can bring. You need Smith, a man who can give you these things until he is too old to do so. You need a home where all is custom, and you know exactly what the next day will bring. You do not want me, or what I will give or will not give. I see that now. Forgive me for not understanding."

Meriwether stood firmly without moving, but tears were forming in her smokey blue eyes.

She is beautiful, thought Turly, *and at this moment if she asked, I would go back with her to the Circle and never leave.*

But she did not ask. Their eyes remained locked for some minutes and then Turly turned and left her for good. He was truly alone now, alone with himself and his journey. He would have to leave his friends at some point, he knew that as well. But for now the group had to push on, away from the river.

"She is yours, Smith," said Turly. "I hope you will keep her in the Circle world, if you can return to it."

"Turly, I . . ."

"Say nothing, old friend. I was blind. I have a different path to take. When there is the chance, I will send you back to the Inniscloe Lake."

Smith turned without a word and went to Meriwether. Turly gathered the others and pointed to the mountains in the distance.

"We have far to go yet," he said. "Our food supplies are still good, and with Sean we can hunt what we need. I want to be in the foothills by tomorrow night."

Turly moved again into the hip-high grass and began to wend his way slowly toward the mystery at the Clonnoise Abbey. Each member of the group that followed him had a different thought to preoccupy his mind and to fill the time. A fine rain began to fall in a slowly moving mist.

Chapter 22

Turly crawled to the edge of the rocky cliff and noted that, far below, the mists hid any possible movement; the setting sun reflected off the higher clouds and turned them pink, like giant pearls in a dream of peace. It had been a long time since Turly had felt a sense of peace. There was clinging sweat on his brow and a sense of mingled hope and dread. He moved out of range from below and whispered quickly to Sean, who nodded and moved off behind the group. The procession resumed, Turly in front and Sean bringing up the rear. There was little talk.

The march to the mountains had been uneventful, but the heat tended to sap their energy on the rocky trails where walking was treacherous. The temperature dropped as they climbed, however, and their spirits again rose. The party made camp at dusk in a small hollow backed by a sheer wall of stone where the front approaches could be easily protected by a small number. Less exhausted than the others, Smith took the first watch with Sean. The remainder began making supper using almost the last supplies of flour, sugar and dried beef. If they did not reach Clonnoise Abbey within a day or two, the tiny band was in trouble and Turly knew it; he urged everyone to use only what was essential. He did not have training in these matters and felt keenly the burden of leading his friends into unforeseen perils.

Sleep did not bring relief. Turly was teased by a vision of huge figures, strange costumes, sparkling jewels; and most of all, odd markings like those upon the map of his father. He did not know what it all meant and tossed fitfully upon his thin blanket.

Smith shook him awake. His mouth was dry and his eyes itched with the grit of dust from the day's trip.

"What is it?"

"Turly, the last pass, there's something on it."

"Is Sean out?"

"Yes, but he's not back yet. Nobody has seen anything like it. I think we've been discovered."

"That's impossible. We've covered our trail. Where could we have been so careless?"

"It may not be Hastings. There are far worse things on this land, I've heard. And if so, I don't want to stay to meet them, whatever they may be."

Turly hurried to the outcropping of rock that hunched on the ground in stoic serenity. Nothing could disturb the rock's dream of—what? Nature that was not life, that did not move restlessly from place to place? Did rock dream of slowly becoming dust, or of the higher solidity of diamond?

The rock might be luckier than he was, mused Turly, but it could not know mystery—his grandfather's words. On the other hand, the rock might simply be luckier than he was, Turly chuckled to himself.

"What is it?" asked Smith, looking at Turly with a

troubled eye. There was no place now for madness, he thought to himself. Circle, what if Turly could take no more? Their journey had come this far, and there were signs of disintegration in the group. If Turly could no longer lead, they were lost.

"Don't worry, old friend." Turly had felt his thoughts and could not help but laugh. "I have seen worse trouble on my grandfather's curragh in the waters around the Inniscloe Lake. I was merely thinking of the pleasures of stone. This rock will lose no sleep and will feel no regret if Hastings is upon us or learns the secret of the Papers before us."

"That is so," allowed Smith. And what of Meriwether? he thought. Does Turly think of her at night?

Turly leaned far out over the rock. Overhead, the moon had broken through the heavy clouds, illuminating the ragged landscape stretching out below the way they had come. The steep valley was like a great bowl with a crack in the side furthest from the small party, at a diagonal from Turly. At first he could see nothing. There seemed a vast silence over all things; the huge pines hunkered in their new shadows, the trail upwards almost obscured by these shadows. But when the view darkened, as the moon slipped back into the covering clouds, Turly saw it.

"Demon," breathed Turly.

"It was almost time for a change of shifts, but I thought you should see," said Smith.

"Check the others, we may have to move quickly."

"Right."

Smith moved off silently, so silently that Turly turned to repeat his command. Turning back to the prospect before him, Turly strained his eyes to catch again what he had just seen. Barely visible at the base of the crack, tiny lights like the flashing of infinitesimal fireflies were threading out in single file. What were they? Turly thought his eyes were playing tricks on him. He rubbed them and looked again. They were not there! Yes, there and there. Once again the world seemed like a shifting stage of illusion, a floating world of changes. There was something, then nothing. Were these tricks of the brain, chimeras of the long journey that were only projected fears of fatigue and apprehension? Or an act of sorcery that was robbing him of his ability to act? He shook his head and turned back to the camp, where the others were agitated and afraid.

Turly was talking to Bulfin when Sean returned. One of Sean's hands was bloody from the jagged rocks, and Turly expressed concern. Sean waved him off and sat down to catch his breath before reporting.

"It's Oliver," he said.

Turly recoiled. His old nemesis of the Order of Zeno. He would never give up, thought Turly. Not until he has what he wants. He had eluded Oliver once, and then he had escaped Hastings and the other dangers that had been thrown into his path. But now he was tired, and the Circlefolk were tired. Turly did not know if he could go on; he was cornered, trapped in these hills by Oliver and his illusions. Turly thought of the quiet nights at home when he and Ellman would play childish games, or later when he grew older and would go out to find Meriwether and play other games. Why had he been made to come to the south, after something that might not exist? And now to wind up like this? If what he had seen in the valley were true, and not an illusion of Oliver's, he was overwhelmed in numbers if nothing else.

Turly sat dejectedly upon the rock. His head drooped and his shoulders sagged.

"Turly, they should be here by dawn," said Sean. "May I suggest something?"

Turly looked up. Sean had saved him more than once. He could not let him do it again and still retain his own sense of self-worth. He could feel the pressure mount.

"There is a shorter way over the pass, I think," said Sean. "But it may be dangerous and some of us will have to stay behind. I can stay . . ."

"No, Sean. There is another way." Turly could see the craggy features of Sean, so changed in a few weeks, looking at him now with a sense of, not fear or worship, but dread and pride.

"We will prepare a welcome for Oliver that he will not soon forget. But it will take the rest of the night." Turly then moved away, not sure himself what he was doing, up the slope to a higher vantage point where he scanned the horizon and could still see, framed by the dark bowl of the valley, the flickering advance of Oliver. Later, when he was finished with his work, Turly slipped back down and rejoined the others.

Dawn came with its usual stealth. The darkness split into the lighter dark of early dawn, and the thick darkness of the rocky peaks lay rounded upon the earth where they rose solid and majestic in the dim light. The flickering lights below had gone out by the time the sun had placed one tentative crescent above the furthest peak.

"I count maybe fifty priests," whispered Garrett.

"And maybe twenty-five Fallow and three times that number of Farks, and at least three of Hastings' Color-stealers," continued Sean.

Turly was silent as he watched the procession of orange robes far below wind up toward them. He could not tell if the priest in front was Oliver, but he imagined it was. He fancied that from time to time Oliver looked up into Turly's eyes and knew him for what he was. Turly shuddered. Oliver was more dangerous than Hastings, he thought. Secular power was one thing, but the combination of material strength with the fanaticism of Zeno doctrine would put Imram into a position in which terror could run riot. Oliver had to be stopped. Turly could deal with Hastings if he were still alive, as Sean had argued, and could regroup his forces. But the wiles of Oliver could not be tolerated. A slight wind whipped up from the valley and pasted Turly's hair like cobwebs in his mouth and nose. With a firm hand he brushed the strands back behind his ears.

"Turly, another hour, no more, and they will be upon us."

"I can see, Sean. You and Smith hold this area to the right and left from scouting attacks. You should be able to hold them with what weapons you have. Bulfin, Garrett and I will launch our first attack in fifteen minutes. Meriwether, you stay here in camp. If all else fails, take the overland route Sean told us about and wait at Clonnoise."

"But, Turly, I want to stay with Smith. The Sequence says there can be no escape from the descent. Why should I flee what I can only find?" She was pouting, but firm.

"Do what you will then. Wait with Smith at the lower path." Turly then turned and led Bulfin and Garrett up and to the left, where he had prepared what he hoped to be the destruction of Oliver's forces. Down below the others waited for Oliver to come.

The sun was rising to the left of the small group's position and cast a wide band of light onto the top of the other side of the bowl. The light moved slowly down into the contents of the bowl as the morning wore on. It had not yet reached the orange forces parallel to it, which were strung out half up the side of the bowl and half still in the bottom. At the top lip of the bowl, looking down at the advancing line, Smith hunched his shoulders, pulled in his paunch and gripped his sword with passionate intensity. This might be the last time he could prove to Meriwether that he was not just a successful merchant but also a worthy fighter. He could not let it pass. Meriwether sat behind him, quietly turning over in memory all the recent events, and what had happened to her. She looked up at Smith and wondered if she had made the right choice of Circlemen.

Meriwether could not see the orange forces moving inexorably up toward them. If she could, she would have seen at first two or three and then more gesture wildly, and then turn and flee back the way they had come. And she would have seen a tall figure in orange gather them back into a single line that again moved forward with the speed of a caterpillar, up and over rocks, down into small depressions, back up, straight for a while, and then dipping and flowing in a curious ripple of color always upward and onward.

The first rocks that fell from the mountain killed ten Farks, a few Fallow and none of the orange-clad monks. The varicolored caterpillar continued.

The second slide destroyed fully half of the column. At this development the orange ranks split and took cover. They were less than eighty meters away from the narrow gorges held by Sean and Smith. For a long time after the sound of the crashing rocks had stopped, there came the moaning sound of the dying lying about on the slopes. Even this stopped soon, and there could be heard only the wind in the pines.

A tiny voice cried out above all else. It was tiny but

strong. The timbre of the voice was full and confident, and there was little doubt who it was.

"Turly!"

"Turly, urly, urly," said the bowl slowly.

Turly did not answer. High above, he released yet another load of stones that rattled and bounced all the way down in ominous slow motion, like the toys of a giant child.

Smith peeked out from his vantage point and saw what he feared most. The orange monks were directing the smaller Farks in the setting up of three needle-nosed machines.

The Colorstealers.

Smith stepped back and wiped the sweat from his brow. He had seen what they could do, and there was nothing *they* could do but sit there and be melted into a puddle of blackness; become not even charcoal, but a liquid nothing that would settle on the earth like shimmering ink. He heard their whine; it began low and worked up the scale into a shriek.

Further up the mountain slope Turly could see the monks scatter from his third rock slide and he laughed aloud. If they could create illusion, this was the time to do so, he thought. Perhaps an illusion of not scattering.

Or perhaps one of scattering.

Turly sat up quickly. He stared down onto the monks' last position. He stared long and hard trying to find something, anything, a blurring of the eyes like heat waves to suggest the veil of an imposed illusion. He could see only the dry rocky slopes, pine trees, and slight underbrush. Perhaps the Order's power could extend only to short range. Turly thought he might never know until too late if he were being tricked again. He remembered the awe he had felt at seeing Oliver's cloud illusion.

Then the whine of the machines reached Turly. He looked over and down the slopes to see a slow sweep of dark color moving upward. It licked out like the tongue of a serpent and where it touched it left a shining blackness. Behind this tongue of rainbow color Turly could see a small band of Farks creeping and darting from tree to tree. Turly knew they could not be seen from the gorges below where the others were.

"Sean! Smith! The Farks!" Turly cupped his hands to his mouth and hollered as loud as he could. He did not know if they had heard him. Tripping the fourth load of rocks, Turly let his last defense hurtle down toward the Colorstealers. The first machine splintered beneath the barrage. The other two were unharmed. Turly looked over and down. That might have drawn Sean and Smith's attention, he thought.

It had.

Smith heard the rocks and leaned around to see what damage they would do. That's when he saw the small hunchbacks scurry through the gorge opening directly at him. The space was too narrow for more than one man, but it could and did hold two Farks at a time. The monstrous childlike creatures with hideous teeth and bulging eyes brandished their short bows and knives and shrieked like banshees when they saw Smith. He stepped out to face them.

One Fark went down without a head. The second one left an arm on the ground as it staggered past Smith in its wild career; Smith barely moved his body as he shifted his balance and lopped off its head as well. Turning to the next wave of Farks, Smith leaned forward and shoved his sword point straight into the eyes of a devilish mask, striped red and yellow, whose mouth at the time was wide open, exposing its savage and pointed teeth. Blood spouted over its cheeks as it ran directly into the tip of the sword. Smith winced but withdrew his blade and quickly sidestepped the other Fark, who managed to flick out his arm and cut Smith once across the top of his left leg. The pain did not hit Smith till later. But the tiny Fark knives were effective up close; Smith cursed as his thigh went weak on him, and he had to grab for support on one wall of the gorge. He could feel the sticky ooze spreading on his leg while the last Fark went down kicking and squealing in agony and frustration, his hands covering his bloody face. Smith's blade then silenced him forever.

The other Farks retreated when they saw the second human enter the gorge. Meriwether held high the sword which Smith had left propped against the rock. She had trained for defense as had all Circle children. Although she was not in practice, she could still swing the long blade convincingly. As the Farks retreated, she put an arm around Smith and helped him out and back to the rock shelter.

"You're hurt," she said.

"A little," Smith winced, as Meriwether tore away the ragged wool cloth around his thigh.

Meriwether bit her lip. The wound was jagged and deep. Smith would need help, more help than she could give. And if the Farks returned, they could not be held. Turly was up the slope and Sean had his own entrance to guard. She had to do something.

"Can you walk?" she said.

"Yes, but we must stay *here*. If the Farks get through, the others will be lost, outflanked." Smith stood up in defiance of the enemy and crumpled to the ground. His face turned white, and his eyes rolled up into his head.

Meriwether looked about anxiously. It was quiet in

that immediate area. She propped Smith up and loosened his tunic at the throat. At the sound of footsteps, she wheeled with the blade flashing light in her hand.

Turly held his hands up. He slowed in his descent and glanced at Smith. He saw the leg wound but said nothing. He asked what happened and Meriwether told him, her voice level and full of pride for what Smith had done. Both turned and went to the gorge when the whining began again. They could see nothing, but Turly whispered to Meriwether and they started to carry Smith up to higher ground. Once there, he sent Garrett to get Sean while he saw to Smith's wound. They would all have to take the shortcut over the mountain Sean had told them about. After he had finished doing what he could for Smith, Turly headed down the slope of Boulder Gap, to help Sean and Garrett.

He was too late.

Far below, Turly could see the massed group of Fallow advancing up the hill and the Colorstealers moving directly to Sean's position. He could also see Garrett running back up the hill toward him.

"Where is Sean, Garrett?" cried Turly.

Garrett caught his breath and tried to answer. Sean had sent him back up. He said he would hold Oliver and his men until they had had a chance to get over the mountain. They were to go on no matter what happened.

"No!" screamed Turly in a long anguished wail like a punished child.

A dense cloud had formed over the valley bowl, obscuring the sun, turning the rocks into lead. Turly raced down the gorge but knew he would never make it before the color beams would lick the rocks behind which Sean crouched in wait. Turly took in the whole scene while running blindly on, jumping from ridge to ridge, skipping over the roots of trees and loose boulders in a kind of free-falling grace in which he was not aware of running nor of using his feet to push and jump and measure distances, make judgments. He floated slowly downhill as in a dream.

And in a dream he saw Sean rise up from behind his cover and ascend to the top of a small ridge that faced all of the assembled host below. He saw Sean raise his hands above his head making a human Y with his back to him, and he saw the startled pause from below. One orange man stood out from the rest and pointed his long arm up the hill and into the face of Sean. Like the finger of doom, the long stream of color turned toward Sean and came to him. Without a sound the tiny figure took first one beam and then the other. It fastened on him and merged into one beam that seemed to suck at him and to pull him gently to and fro. Sean glowed red from head to foot, but he did not fall. He stood impassively, with his hands always above his head, looking down at Oliver.

The glow around Sean began to enlarge. With every passing second he glowed more fiercely, and seemed to grow to fill the space that the enlarging glow occupied. He seemed to grow by centimeters, reaching up to follow the arms that almost engulfed the sky.

Turly was transfixed. He had almost fallen to catch himself in mid-flight and scream at Sean to move, to run, to do something. But now he stood and watched and could not believe his eyes. Not only was Sean not being drained, but he was actually absorbing the color-beams, growing stronger in a flickering kaleidoscope of energy. He was pulling in and sucking up the color from the Colorstealers. There was no time to anticipate or reduce what happened.

Sean glowed like the nimbus of a candle. In the half-light of a cloudy morning he could be seen clearly by all. And the nimbus pulsed and moved with a life all its own. It wavered and bent and flowed while Sean stood erect within it. He was indistinct in its center like a caterpillar in its cocoon, wrapped and swathed in light. Turly could not see his face, but he knew that if he could, it would not be the face of a mountain scout.

The beams of color grew weak and wavered in the rhythm of the flame about Sean. They seemed like thin threads that connected Sean to the machines that had sent them out. He was pulling out all that they had, and they were now almost exhausted. Turly could see that all the orange forces had withdrawn from the machines after trying desperately to shut them off. They were now massed behind them and watching Sean with what Turly could only guess was an appalled fascination. He thought he saw one orange figure turn and run for the far wall.

And then all the drawing and pulling ceased, and for one instant all forces were in equilibrium. The beams that had fastened on Sean, and the flame that was now Sean, were calm and seemed to hum quietly at rest. But the glow in Sean changed and rose to a bright hue that quickly descended the scale to a deep orange and then up to blue-white. And when it reached blue, the color on Sean shot from him like a charge of static electricity and straight down to the machines with the speed of thought. There was a great explosion and an earth-rending roar that left not one member of the Order of Zeno group alive. A silent acrid smell began to creep up to Turly. It broke the spell and sent Turly racing once again down to Sean, who lay crumpled on the rock, his back bent and his now fully gray hair fanned about his head.

"Sean, Sean," wept Turly as he cradled the broken

man in his arms. Sean had aged another twenty years in the last few minutes of the ordeal, and he now looked old but familiar. This was Sean, but Turly had seen this man before, somewhere.

"Perhaps," chuckled Sean, who opened his clouded eyes briefly and seemed to have read Turly's thoughts. "Perhaps there is a slight resemblance to, to Ellman maybe?"

"Ellman! Yes, Ellman! But you're not Ellman!"

"Well, no. It seems I won't be able to tell you anything now. It seems I was forced to use myself up before I really wanted to. I had also wanted to get back to Derva in Straiten, sometime. But there was nothing else to do. Oliver would have caught you, and this time he may have learned what you are about to learn for yourself." Sean coughed and cleared his throat. He seemed to be in pain. Placing two fingers on Turly's arm, he motioned with his head down below. "Oliver's not dead, you know. I could not touch Oliver. I suspect he'll be back somehow. But for now your work is safe, and you must do it alone, Turly. Alone."

"My work?"

"Yes, oh yes; and there is," he coughed again louder and more persistently, "some urgency about it and some uncertainty. It is up to you more than you may ever guess."

"Sean," said Turly. "Who are you? *What* are you?"

Sean looked up and smiled wanly. "Let us say a friend who for many weeks has watched you grow into a man. I can now say with some assurance that you are ready for whatever may happen."

"But, Sean, what you did . . . how could you stand up to that thing?"

"It seemed *on the order of magic,* didn't it, Turly?"

307

Sean coughed again, a deep racking cough. Blood came up and stained the front of his beige tunic, covered Turly's hand. Turly pulled it away and stared at it.

Turly spoke quickly now, afraid answers would slip from him again. He gripped the front of Sean's tunic, ignoring the blood, and placed one hand behind Sean's head. "It's right what Hastings said about Others, isn't it, Sean? You're one of them, aren't you? I don't care, Sean. But tell me." Turly was frantic, crying.

Sean was growing visibly weaker, older. His neck was thin and lying in folds. Through pinched nostrils Sean snorted what Turly might have called a laugh.

"It may be. I don't know myself. Funny thing, this island. You can grow up here and think you're a hunter, think you've been one a long time. But one day you find it's not really true, that you have something else to do, for somebody else. You suddenly remember what it is you've got to do, and you do it." Sean coughed again and held up a hand. "But these are things that do not concern you now, if ever. The burden is on you to discover the real truth about the Blessing Papers, where they lie, what they contain, and what you shall do with them. It is the burden of your father, Turly, as he gave it to you on his knee. This island will never be Eden, and you are not Adam to begin all anew. But in a very real sense you will make decisions that will affect everyone on this island, and eventually the earth. Will you be up to it, Turly?"

Sean's head sagged. Turly talked to him for some minutes after that, knowing he was dead, pouring out his grief, anguish and frustration in unanswered questions. When he finally gave up, he felt as alone as he had ever been. Not even the sounds of his other friends, hurrying down to him, could breach the wall that had been erected around him. He felt the bearer of some great mystery that he could not understand, and felt himself, as well, the only man who could or would undertake to solve it.

"Turly!" shouted Garrett. The slightly built man pulled up short of Turly and stared at the old man cradled in his arms. He stood in silence and reflected that Turly, too, had aged in the past few weeks. His fine white hair lay in random strands about his face and the dark olive skin was contrasted with the clear, almost translucent clarity of Sean's. There was nothing Garrett could say, and so he said nothing. He stood with his arms limp at his sides and waited for what was to come.

Smith and Bulfin helped bury what was left of Sean. The ceremony was a brief condensation of the Mythic Sequence. All present were members of the Circle faith and repeated after Turly the monomythic journey of man through life and into death. As Turly finished the credo, he thought of a new meaning for the final phrase:

. . . the rebirth from the fire of the Circle itself.

In the final breathing and the going to the higher One.

At the formal conclusion Turly raised his head to the skies and wondered what the higher One was, man or God or something else. He scanned the heavens for a sign, and there was nothing but the sad screech of a hawk far off over the next hill. Or was it a cry of triumph?

On their last night together, the small band discussed their uncertain future. Hastings and Oliver were no threat for now, but they were not totally defeated, if what Sean had said was true. The north had to be warned of the danger from the Order and from the groundswell of rebel forces in the country, if they were to be subverted by men no better than Cole. The Circles of the north had to begin to find a way to join together beyond their narrow concerns of certainty and fatalism. Turly argued long and convincingly about the need to look again to themselves in these and other matters. While the Circle faith was a comfort in times of great need and despair, it could never be counted upon to serve every community in every detail. Life was too complex for that; there were times when no answer could be had or no single answer truly correct. Turly thus could no longer think of himself as a true Framer in the Universal Mythic Sequence Church, although he still felt a keen love for the Circle ritual.

"I'm going on alone to Clonnoise," he said. "Whatever lies there for me, I have to find it alone. It may be that one day I will be able to come north and rejoin you all."

"But Turly, you have no supplies, no idea of what is there," said Smith. "How will you make it? Spies of either Hastings or Oliver may be there waiting." Smith was insistent. He wanted Turly to come with them back to Inniscloe Lake, and there rouse the Circle to arm themselves for a struggle with Oliver. Turly was the man to do it.

Turly would not listen. He said that the deaths of Harve, Kelleher, Ellman and Sean could not go for nothing. There were strange forces at work in Imram and they had to be dealt with, and answers found. The others noticed that Turly's slim hands would occasionally flick into the air at odd moments, as if brushing away troublesome insects. They talked long into the night.

The next morning Turly embraced them all, and then stood alone at the top of the hill, watching the small group wind down the northeast trail leading them home to the Circle at Inniscloe. He waved as they appeared out of the trees and looked back before climbing into the rocks that sheltered the way into the hills beyond. The soft mountain wind moved across Turly and he turned to make his way to the Clonnoise Abbey.

Chapter 23

The late summer sun poured its gold over the tawny
fields of southwest Imram, over the fullnesses of
meadows and hills with their yellow gorse and purple
heather.

Turly sat in the dense shade of a large cedar tree, its
branches arching up above him like gently lifted arms,
and idly watched the dying of the day in its smooth
harmony of color. It had been several months since
he had come to the Abbey at Clonnoise to find it a
wreck, a shell. Hastings' men had done their job well,
tearing through walls, ripping up floors, scattering
charred stones in the corridors that ran in silence
through the Abbey. Turly had himself searched carefully throughout the building and had found nothing.
As he sat and mused on the scars at the Abbey both old
and new, he noticed the white birds wheeling above its
ancient walls.

It was silent and still and Turly was beginning to
absorb the atmosphere of the place, the peaceful
shadows and the deep sense of endurance cast by the

sleepy pall of its age. He felt the first real sense of rest he had had in a long time, since the death of Ellman and the first step in his journey south. The restfulness entered his bones and softened his flesh.

Strolling through the grassy paths or sitting by the numerous tiny fountains in the Abbey grounds, Turly could feel a subtle change taking place within himself. Like the breakup of the ice in spring on the lake at home, Turly's tension-filled emotions loosened and flowed. Often in the unkept graveyard, with its large and even grotesque headstones, Turly would ponder the nature of his journey, the memories of his father, and the uneven events of the past few months. It was a good time. He would sit for hours on the stone benches by the graveled walks and listen to the sounds of birds and the sighing of the wind blowing through the shattered roof of the Abbey. His heart would leave the hurt of the journey, the loss of Meriwether, the frustrating end of his search for the Blessing Papers. It would move easily into the clear blue air and soar with the hawks, dart into the sun with them. It felt free and without care when doing that.

His heart also moved away from the hurt of one of his earliest discoveries in the Abbey graveyard.

Shortly after arriving at the Abbey, and during one of his intense searches of the grounds, Turly had found a grave stone marked *Deirdre Vail, 2072–2105*. It had to be his mother's stone, her grave. A mother he could not remember except for the soft touches and the words like warm clothes. Turly grieved for her and knew then that she had been *there* at least, had reached the end of *her* journey. As he thought this, Turly also knew more hatred for Lord Hastings, who had lied to him about his mother. For if his men had combed the Abbey, they would have known about the grave and would have reported it to Hastings. Hastings had known Turly's mother was dead and he had smoothly and cruelly lied to him about her. That was one more reason why Turly had to finish his father's task, to unite the island and free it of men like Hastings and Oliver.

In the months that followed, the stone of his mother's grave had reminded Turly of that. But there had been only one stone. There was no stone for John Vail. What had happened to him? If Turly had still been a devout believer in the Mythic Sequence, which Hastings had called into question, Turly would have appealed to it and not berated it for denying him full knowledge of the two people in all the world he had wanted most to find.

Turly had lapsed into a weary despair, resignation, and then a sense of separateness from all that he had known before. His mindless absorption in the sights and sounds of an unquestioned and unquestioning nature relieved Turly's heart.

As the weeks passed Turly could tell the first signs of an Imram autumn, the crisp nip in the air, the subtle changes in the leaves, the gusty emotions on wet nights.

Turly had selected a small enclosure to the rear of the Abbey in which to set up his living space. Little more than a cell, the tiny room had one thin rag stuffed with grasses and a wooden stand with an old metal candlestick, which Turly had found one day in the rubble. He would rise with the sun and retire early to set his mind in a soothing course of meditation. Day after day passed in this fashion and Turly had forgotten the urgency of his mission. The mossy walls of the Abbey seemed to enclose him with the finality of the grave, and the young man drifted into a semiconscious state of eating what berries, roots and small animals he could find, sleeping for long periods, and simply existing.

He dreamed lightly of huge figures fighting languidly with unseen opponents, their end predestined, the struggle perfunctory.

Turly could no longer make sense of the legacy objects he still kept in his neck-bag; he looked at them less and less as the fall came and cool rains began to fall regularly about the Abbey, on the stone walls, the gate opening up to it, on the Abbey itself, into the gaping windows where stained glass had once stood catching the light and sending into the Abbey the glory of the One in broken color, on the graveyard to the rear of the Abbey, and across all the countryside in a general fall that made all things into one thing.

In late October Turly heard an unfamiliar noise in the cemetery, a grating sound as of rock moving on rock. He hurried from his cell to find its cause. At a far corner of the cemetery Turly saw a tall rectangular stone leaning precariously to one side. As he watched, panting from his dash outside, it tilted and Turly heard again the muted screech of rock crushing and straining against rock. He walked slowly to it, his tattered trousers catching in the brown grass as he walked. Stepping to the stone, Turly looked at the marker, felt it, then pushed it softly. With a final groan the large gray slab fell to the ground, scattering dirt around Turly's ankles. It lay still and Turly could see only a bare space in the ground, worn rocks which had propped up the larger rock, and loose dirt which had packed it round.

Feeling vaguely cheated and yet still indolent, Turly sat on the top of another stone and surveyed the area for the thousandth time. The cemetery had become one of his favorite places on the Abbey grounds. Silent and calm, it stretched open to the sky, to whatever would come. The flattened mounds, the worn script on the

headstones, the bent and weary yew trees, all com-
bined to soothe him, to lure him into their own solidity.

Remembering the calm of another, younger day
Turly began to hum one of the old songs he had learned
from his father. He then sang aloud to himself to ease
the gnawing hurt of lost purpose, a cavity in his heart:

> Where life and love are justly through,
> Where all is loose and light and free,
> The stars are burning brightly still,
> And sit upon a blackened hill.
> *Fol de rol de rolly o*

> Make your eye to ride in time
> And it will see its rightful due;
> For frozen in its ancient day,
> The old can never have its way.
> *Fol de rol de rolly o*

> High above the scene is set:
> All remains and all is changed.
> What have you to do with this, o,
> Who live and love and die below?
> *Fol de rol de rolly o*

> So seek from near the corner door,
> Where age goes through but once, no more,
> Where bones of men are set in stone.
> Then you will have what few have known.
> *Fol de rol de rolly o*

The silence in the grassy cemetery fell with plush
softness as the words died in the circling breeze. Turly
mused upon the old song, his father's favorite, and the

one he had sung to Turly over and over as the child had sat upon his knee.

Upon his knee.

Turly jerked himself erect. He remembered. That was what Sean had said before he died. He had been speaking to him of the burden John Vail had left, "as he gave it to you on his knee." Turly quickly ran over the song in his mind. It seemed to take on new meaning as he did so. It was not just childish nonsense, although it had been so to that point.

Where life and love are through.

I am here on the ground of the dead, thought Turly.

Make your eye to ride in time.

Ride to *what* time? thought Turly. The future? The past? A fever seized Turly. The Abbey disappeared and he was returned to his childhood and to his father, huge and impassive above him, crooning softly into his crib. His father had done that many times. Was there a good reason for that; a better reason than simply to send a child to sleep?

This was something Turly had to puzzle out; he began to tease into meaning the legacy of his father, to give his words a depth they had not had before.

Legacy. Turly's Song.

Upon A Knee
A Nothing Sings
And When It Does
It Gives Us Wings.

What did that *mean?* Turly gave it up and returned to the first song which seemed to have more pertinence.

So seek from near the corner door.

Here? From the rear door of the Abbey? Seek here in the graveyard? Seek what? Turly visualized the map upon which his father had marked Clonnoise Abbey and had placed in the cemetery amidst the marker symbols the sign of the Others, the place where "bones of men are set in stone." Turly's eyes watered. All this time he had wandered in dreams. It *was* here his father had meant him to go. He felt hot blood course through his body after so many months.

Then you will have what few have known.

The final line of the song. Did it mean the having of what he was looking for? For the first time in a long while Turly was caught up again in the pursuit of the Blessing Papers. He was alive again to the burden of his father. The nonsense words had become literal and touched Turly with questions. He would follow the words to the end.

Turly walked briskly to the rear door of the Abbey, turned and looked out over the cemetery, his eye scanning the variety of markers, trying to find a clue in them. Squares and rectangles, curved arches and engraved slabs; crosses and obelisks, flowers and angels of stone. He squinted and looked closer at the far wall. He could see the giant statue of a winged angel leaning out over a stone crypt, embracing it with its benevolent gaze. Turly ran toward the angel and thought of the song that was no longer nonsense.

Upon his father's knee he had heard what he thought was nonsense. And now he faced a thing with wings. He stood small in front of it. It was about six meters tall and had been placed on a large square base that covered about twenty square meters of ground. The crypt itself was stained green with age and streaked with the workings of wind and rain. Turly paced around it once and tried several times to lift its top. It would not budge, and he strained his hands trying to turn the angel as if it were a handle. But nothing happened. Turly looked up into the bland face of the angel.

A nothing sings.

When the nonsense song is sung? Turly stepped back from the crypt and began to sing aloud the words of his song. Through the first line the stone figure seemed to listen attentively, but did nothing. At the second, Turly heard an almost inaudible scraping toward the rear of the angel. The sound increased with the end of the third line. At the completion of the last line of the song, the great stone wings of the angel creaked and moved downward in a slow parody of the motion of flight.

And when it does it gives us wings.

The lid of the crypt slid to one side. Its black mouth yawned and exhaled the odor of long years of dampness and decay. Turly was stunned. He stepped up to the hole and looked down. A flight of worn stone stairs led down into a profound darkness. Running back to his cell, Turly got all the candles that he could carry. Returning, he stopped in front of the crypt and lit one. Stuffing the rest in his belt, Turly took his first steps into the bowels of the earth. When he reached the bottom, the light from the surface dimmed and went out as the crypt lid slid shut. Turly did not look back.

The first impression was of rough-hewn rock. The candlelight reflected off lead-gray walls showed the chip marks of tools. The path down showed no sign of ever having been used. There were no footprints. But a chill touched Turly as he stepped slowly along the way his father might have gone some seventeen years before.

The winding passage was opening up somewhat, and the ceiling was rising. Turly reached a point where the walls showed signs of smoothness, as if the hand of man had had nothing to do with it. The passage still led down into the earth but at a steady decline unhampered by twists or turns. Within the radius of the candle's glow, all seemed secure and settled. The path opened abruptly into a larger room-like area, completely enclosed. In the far wall was a bright metal plate adorned with the sign of the marble and the spider.

Turly stepped boldly to the plate and placed the candle next to it. The plate was not engraved in any way, but the image of the circle, with two bent lines intersecting at a point also circled, was clearly etched into it. Turly reached a finger to the image and pressed it gently. He could feel no seam in its black and white design. An open slot ran vertically beneath it. The dark closed in around Turly, and he felt another chill. Was this it? There had to be a way beyond this point, and he began to look for it. He walked completely around the room feeling with his hands for any break in the smooth rock wall. There was none.

Turly squatted on his haunches and thought for a long time. If his father's legacy had brought him this far, it would take him to the end. But how was he to proceed? The map had done its job. He was here at the Abbey. And the song had done its job. He was through the first barrier and into the bowels of the earth. What was left to him but the coins? Where would they get him, and how?

Turly hefted one of the coins in his hand. The dark halo around it was palpable. He tossed the coin up and turned it on its edge; twisting it to and fro, he noticed that the demon image would seem to both smile in mockery and frown in disapproval as the coin was turned. It was like the demon in the Mythic Sequence Tapestry, leering out at the Followers. But at certain times it would seem to be trying to say something, something that was important if only it could be heard.

Suddenly it struck Turly. The vertical slot beneath the strange device on the wall: a coin would fit into it. Turly jumped up and moved to the wall. He held up the candle with his left hand, grasped the coin in his right thumb and forefinger and let it drop into the thin slot. There was a sound of clucking and bumping as the coin fell through and down into the bowels of the wall.

Nothing. Turly realized he had been given *three* coins, not one. Setting down his candle, he impatiently ransacked his neck-bag. Producing the other two coins, Turly's fingers funneled a second and third one into the slot. More clucking and bumping. Silence.

Noise. The grinding of an entire wall rising slowly and majestically into the ceiling. Beyond the wall the corridor continued. Lifting the guttering candle high, Turly stepped through the wall space and headed down into the earth, his heart beating rapidly with excitement. The candlelight played about the rocky walls with a dizzying rapidity and he had to stop at one point to lean against a wall, regain his balance, catch his breath. A clammy sweat had replaced the earlier wetness. The air was gathering thick and close. Turly thought he could see, dimly on the floor, faint footsteps reaching away in front of him.

Down spiraled Turly. As he walked he wondered what must have gone through his father's head years before. He *had* gone this way, Turly thought. He had walked these steps and followed this light. Otherwise, Turly knew, he would not be there himself. The legacy was working perfectly. Turly was almost there, almost to the Blessing Papers, the horror and wonder of the world. He knew it. He was being pulled to them.

What would they be like? Which of the many stories he had heard in his youth and his travels would be true? Would the Papers be the salvation of man, or his further damnation? If the former, his father would be vindicated, the island saved, all mankind saved. But if it were the latter, what would he do? What *could* he do? Would he find the means to form a new unity in Imram, or was Hastings right about the continued disunity inspired by the Others?

Turly's thoughts were interrupted by a narrow opening, about one-and-a-half meters tall. He bent and peered in. The tunnel went straight for a few meters at that height and then seemed to open up again. Turly stepped through carefully and noticed the imprint of several pairs of feet that had once also scuffled through the narrow passage. But it was not the normal walk for men, thought Turly. The steps were arranged in such a way as to suggest they had been carrying something. Turly looked around carefully at the dusty floor but could see no exit tracks. It was a one-way route into the tunnel.

Turly was wondering about this when he had the feeling he was being watched, judged by what he might do in the next few moments. He felt chilled; his feet did not want to move. His heart beat as if it were an animal wanting out of his chest. Turly had never known such fear.

The rocky path grew smooth and, as Turly rounded a bend in it, widened. With a shock Turly saw it, saw the huge door looming in the semi-darkness. Turly gasped as he spotted, just inside the range of his candle-light, a circle on the door, containing the sign of the spider on the marble. He thought instantly of his father's map and of the huge wooden door in the Order cave that dwarfed the cave itself. The same people, the same *things,* had built this door. Turly thought he could feel it. The Others.

This time Turly could find no slots for coins, even if he had any to use. It seemed that his father's legacy had brought him to this door and left him. Turly stood there dumbly, staring up at the awesome structure.

A whirr and a rush. Turly was bent to the ground by light. Thick and intense, a red beam lanced down at Turly. It had a force not of light. It pressed upon Turly like a heavy wind, concentrated and unrelenting. The young man's white hair blew up into the air and whipped in a frenzy of motion, as if he were being shaken violently by a huge hand. His eyes squinted against the pressing, tingling force. He felt every part of his body protest the unnaturalness of its oppressive glow. His long, arm-length scar seemed to crawl in warning. Turly's candle had paled in the brighter light and had fluttered out in its windy blast. Turly crouched over as if in supplication, and he imagined himself bathed in that red light for eternity. The gritty dust on the floor of the passageway rose into his mouth and eyes.

The light-wind stopped abruptly and Turly heard a long, heavy sigh. Looking up he saw a room with a huge black-and-white floor stretching away from him. Immense walls. A wind inside dying.

Chapter 24

Turly was on his hands and knees and felt, very far away, one hand hurting with a stinging pain like salt in a wound. He did not want to look at it. Instead he rose and took a hesitant step into the bright room, his eyes momentarily blinded. He stopped immediately when he saw, propped against the opposite wall, the corpse of a man—shriveled, its gray beard, like a spider's nest, the only indication of its age at death. Turly glanced quickly around the room but saw no other bodies. He shuddered but looked back at the huddled mass of orange rags.

Too gray for my father, thought Turly, concerned but relieved. Wrong color even if he were old; the head not large enough either. Turly's memory reached for his father, tried to see him as he would be.

Regaining his purpose, Turly walked boldly into the room and glanced about; except for the one mummified corpse, he could see nothing else on the floor. There were rows of tiny yellow lights on the wall above the body and each rippled in its color like an angular firefly. Turly could not guess their function as he walked toward them. He did notice that the polished walls and clean ribbons of tiny fire were in some contrast with the black-and-white floor that was lightly covered with dust.

Turly paced the length and breadth of the huge room. He soon saw his own tracks crossing one another. He then noticed other sets not his own. They huddled by the corpse, criss-crossed in front of the lights, ended by one white square. There were brown stains on the squares around it, but that one square stood out in a polished splendor.

Why were all the squares but that one covered with more of a light mist of dust? thought Turly, as he walked quickly to it. He got down on his knees and searched for some clue. The texture of the edges was different; it had a rougher fit than the others. He clawed at it with his fingernails but soon gave it up, his frenzy tearing the nails and exposing the tender quick.

Given the other obstacles, and the things he had had to do to get past them, things his father had prepared him for as a child, Turly thought that surely the location of the Papers themselves should yield to the same kind of solution. He kneaded his brow in concentration. He had no more coins; the map had served its function; the nonsense song had moved the angel. The ballad had helped in sorting out the beginning of the mystery. Perhaps it would help at the end as well, thought Turly. *And you will have what few have known.*

Turly sang. It was all he had.

The notes and words fell flat in the huge room, tinny, but they seemed to gather around the white square and act upon it. The square almost rippled like a muscle as Turly reached the end of the song. When he was through, it drew back smoothly with relief and, rising on a platform, a dark box sighed to a halt in front of Turly's expectant eyes.

The Blessing Box.

A pink bubble lay like a strained eye on its side. There were stains on the top of the Box and Turly fingered them carefully. The stains were of dust and came away on his fingers. Turly wondered what they were, but the fact of the Box itself made Turly numb. He knew without a doubt that it was the container of the fabled Blessing Papers. He could not wait to see them. His journey had brought him finally to that moment.

Remembering what Hastings had told him about the power of the Box, and how it forced belief in the Papers, Turly was at first reluctant to touch it. But he knew it had to be opened and the truth or fallacy of Imram's past discovered. He would have to harden himself and do it.

Turly sat back for a moment and wiped his sweating palms on his pants. Then, licking his lips, he reached out with great intensity to the mystery of the Papers, just as many times before he had reached out to the mystery of fire. His fingers, covered lightly with dark dust, trembled as they reached the bubble on the Box, were drawn to it; the scar on his arm tingled. Something grew at his finger tips and it felt like fire. Turly was pulled into a vast light and roar, invisible strings sticking to his hand, the roar of burning growing as if he had lost balance and was falling into a fiery pit.

And he was as badly burned. Hurled backward with great force, the Box unopened, Turly lay crumpled on the floor, his body lifeless, his eyes rolled up white into his head.

Turly was pulled in strange revery, alone, as if staring into fire by night; into ways of thought that tried in vivid images to explain, answer, apologize, it seemed to Turly. Like seaweed drifting up to the surface of the sea, being recognized gradually, forming shapes, dissolving into other things.

The darkness is lush and full of silence. The stone floor is gritty and there is a vague and distant sense of light that cannot penetrate the darkness but is trying to. The darkness floats in wait. It moves by the eye as the eye remains open to see into the liquid black.

A bare length of whiteness horizontal in the form of a cocoon. It stands out in the gloom when looked at closely. It cannot all be seen in its entirety at that distance, however, and the eye backs up as if to take in the imagined whole, the dun-colored wrapper widening and swelling in its roundness. The eye goes back, back till it is at maximum visual range to see it when it explodes in light, a slow-motion sparkle outward into intensely blue-white dots massing and unmassing like moths in an erratic frenzy.

The eye does not blink, and the cocoon shape rises to a sitting position as the glow from within it fades and shrinks to the steady pace of a candle's light. The thing within rustles and moves. A clipping falls to the gritty floor and one edge of the dun wrapper unfolds like a leaf, curls back and exposes an arm that is of the purest brown. A hand reaches out and it is a hand that is also curled like a leaf, but it straightens and reveals holes crusted with dark circles.

The entire thing is out of the confining cloth now and it stands by the slab of flat rock upon which it had lain. It looks at the wrapper and smiles.

The eye that is watching this tracks to the discarded binding. It hovers above the unrolled light and sees with no astonishment the beautifully clear lines there, the lines of a man perfectly revealed as if in a mirror after a bath, or in the process of memory waking after a night of troubled sleep, returning to the true textures of day.

It is an exact picture. The light coming up through the cloth, pushing up again through each pore and hair and onto the receiving cloth. This is repeated several times to engrave the image of it happening.

The eye watches it still as it notices from one corner of its vision the thing from the wrapping moving slowly away to the wall of rock and beyond. The eye seems willing to know what it will do, that it is about to enter history, and it does not care.

The room is large but crammed with people of various colors and sizes. They press upon one another, push for position, move their heads from side to side to see, to hear. The eye pauses briefly to take in the variety of shapes it sees. It moves to the front of the room, where an impressively polished table sits solidly upon a floor clear of any imperfection. The eye could see itself in it if it looked. It does not. There are tiny flags upon the table, and glasses partly filled with liquid which are periodically lifted to the faces of men and women sitting at the table.

The eye tracks close to each of these faces. One is large with fatty tissue like a doll, pink and white and lined with eternal contentment. Another is haggard and worn, thin with clusters of moles on the cheeks like constellations; the forehead is creased and vaguely worried as if something were biting its leg under the table. Another face is glancing from side to side, to the face of contentment and the face of care. It cannot seem to decide which role it wants to assume.

There are documents on the table and the eye rotates to see them. There are the large letters CSS on the top sheets. The eye looks up and out at the small sea of faces that perch in the crowded air like birds, waiting. They seem uncomfortable as they nestle close to one another.

The eye tracks to the rear of the room, the way it had come, turning back to look at the now small table at the front. The figures at the table are still sitting. They are looking at a door to their right. The eye does not move as the door opens. All heads and faces swivel to the door.

The man from the cave walks in and smiles kindly. He raises his arms as if reaching for something.

The people in the room begin to file out. The eye catches their backs as they leave. It cannot see their expressions. The people at the table watch as the man with no clothes waves to them. They get up and leave, too, a look of profound disgust on their faces, their lips turned down. The man leaves through the door he had entered, and the eye is left in an empty room, the tiny flags on the table quivering only slightly from an unseen wind. The room darkens slowly as the sun ouside sets.

A large circle of red and white pebbles. They form the mosaic of a single rose, surrounded by the clarity of limpid space, untainted. It is a rounded piece of work, labored upon over many years of patient toil. It lies serene, finished.

Dark feet kick at this work of rock. The eye watches only the feet as they thrust and poke with heel and toe. The outer rim of white-gray pebbles shatters into disarranged clumps like trampled insects. The rose lies contained at the center. It is reached by the sandaled feet and it seems to pull away from them. It cannot. Each of its measured petals falls away into mere rock and loneliness. The chiseled red beauty of its outline,

massed and held by the unfelt pull of the earth, dis-
solves under the prodding of the feet into ragged color.

The eye tracks upward to the brooding face of the
man from the cave and the large room. He looks down
at his sandals and bends to brush off the dust. When he
is through, he turns to the ragged pile and picks at it.
He frowns and concentrates as he seems to try to rearrange the pebbles. He bends forward to reach one and,
as he does so, he topples and falls onto the pile of
senseless rock. He falls slowly and seems to hit with
great force. His arms are up to break his fall and his
elbows scrape sharply against the individual pebbles.
The eye sees this and retains its position. It sees flesh
tear away from an elbow and catches the barest glimmer
of metal as a fading sun it never really focuses on
flashes once.

The thing stands and shrugs. It is sad now in its face
and it looks at the barren pile of pebbles, shakes its
head and walks away.

A long darkness and a knowledge of that darkness as it
passes. Then the rising of light as on a stage, slowly and
inexorably; there are glimmers and flashes, random and
startling to the eye.

The pebbles reappear, lying still and unconcerned
with only a hint of their former pattern as if a cloud
has loosened itself from a familiar form and has frozen
itself in an uncertainty of recognition. An arm reaches
down toward the bits of rock and dust. It picks up one
of the white pebbles and places it apart. The arm hesi-
tates for a moment and then goes back to the pile for
another pebble. It places that pebble beside the first
one. Another pebble, then another. Soon a curve is
formed.

The arm and its fingers take a long while to work

330

and arrange a few pebbles. It does not touch the red pebbles at all, leaves them in disarray in the center of the pile. The fingers twitch and pause. Another arm joins the first. The eye sees the arm as it moves in the half-light. When it rotates it sees the long purple scar spiraling down the arm from the outside of the elbow to the inside of the wrist. It is like an artery on top of the skin, a thick line on a map, a curve that points to something.

Another arm joins the task and the three work at the pile. A fourth, with eager fingers, joins, and another and another. They continue to reach and touch, push and align. A pattern begins to emerge but it seems meaningless to the impersonal gaze of the eye. It is a circle within a circle within a circle crossed partially by a rising curve.

The eye seems to blink several times, and closes.

From Turly's position on the floor, the lights hanging in irregular lengths from the tall ceiling seemed like flat white grapes on a huge vine. He shook his head, rolled over on one elbow, scratched his scalp and then rubbed his eyes between thumb and forefinger.

Memory came back slowly. Turly looked up at the glossy wall and at the black Blessing Box perched on the platform in front of it. The eye on the Box's side was no longer pink but milky-white. Turly thought it looked like a turnip pulled suddenly from the ground, astonished. It stared back at Turly with something approaching not only surprise but remorse.

That is what the last few images had suggested, thought Turly. Remorse. Regret. Thinking this, Turly stood up and staggered slightly to get his balance. The Box seemed to waver and pulse as he thought about the emotion of regret.

Regret for what? For the interference in human history? Regret for the scrambling of the human mosaic of history? Regret for the failing of an attempt to put the mosaic back together again? The image of the rose hovered in Turly's visual memory, haunting him. He thought too of the renewed lines of the circle he had seen and the arm with the scar like his. How could that be? The Blessing Papers had existed before he had been born.

Questions. The things Turly had always had. And now had more of. They roamed his head, beating on doors that would not open.

But Turly was happier than he had ever been. The burden of his father had been carried to this end. The finding of the Papers and of their secret. He thought that his father had been right after all to hide the Papers when he did, to keep them and their message from human sight for awhile, but not to destroy them or hide them forever. It was time *now,* thought Turly, to begin the work of rebuilding the mosaic. The old ways had been shattered by the man from the cave, and he had not been able to refashion it. The value of the Blessing Papers was that they showed that man himself had to do the rebuilding. Many generations of man. John Vail, his son Turly, and—a son of Turly, and his son's son? The line of man.

Whatever questions it raised, the Blessing Box had at least made Turly feel good about man's chances to find the past. It had amounted to a promise made by the images from the Box.

Turly felt as if he had been fishing all day in rough weather. His limbs were partially numb and his tongue swollen and dry. His need to find even more answers would have to wait till he had had a chance to rest, he knew that. He resisted the strong temptation to touch the Blessing Box again; he had had enough for one time. He did not want to burn to the socket. Thinking this, he turned slowly to the giant entrance door.

Wings in the mind, the rustlings he had felt all the way down from the north. He felt them again, stronger. Were they then from the Box, or from something else? As if in reply, the wings beat in a different rhythm for a moment. Turly seemed to know they were connected in some way with the Box. He had resisted the wings before, when they had seemed to want to take over his mind; he resisted them now, and they slowly waned in strength. He wanted to keep himself, and felt contentment as he thought of the finding of the Box and how he had learned its secret and was still alive to do something about it. He began to make plans.

Turly reflected that Hastings was right about the power of the Box. The images it had given him were vivid and strong; they forced belief in the way one was forced to believe in a storm. Turly moved toward the door and felt the wings retreat to the back corner of his mind, waiting. Not to pounce, but as old dogs hearing their master's feet.

Walking from the enormous cube, Turly held his head high; he was happy and proud. His father's burden had been passed.

The Blessing Box remained still for a long while after Turly had gone. It seemed to be listening. The button-eye on its side slowly darkened to pitch. Inside the dark of the Box, the Papers lay where they had been placed fifteen years before by John Vail.

Chapter 25

The dark way up the rock tunnel was uneventful. Neither the entrance to the room nor the half-wall had closed when Turly had walked through them, and he thought they would stay open until he returned to question the Box. He was tired and he mused over the vigor of the images that had hit him like a hard rain. Their meaning did seem clear to him as he walked to the surface, up the stone steps under the angel, across the dark graveyard and into the Abbey. In the halls of the Abbey were many shadows, and one of them spoke to him.

"You have found the Papers."

Turly dropped the candle he had been carrying and the corridor was plunged into total darkness. But there had been no mistaking the smooth, oily voice.

Oliver was alive.

"You are well, Turly?" said the voice easily from another part of the corridor.

Turly crouched and darted his eyes in a circle. "Oliver. Oliver, you are welcome here. But I must tell

you there is nothing here that can help you at all."
Turly stood rigid while straining his eyes. He thought
he heard the muted swish of a robe behind him.

Turly knew every twist and turn of the Abbey by
heart. He did not need a light to find his way here, and
he wondered if the same were true for Oliver. As he
thought this, he moved. Slowly and silently like a cat,
Turly glided from one passage to another, listening for
any other movement.

The voice came again, this time further away but
still filled with menace.

"Turly, give me the Papers now and I will let you
live. You will be my messenger to the world, Turly.
Through you I will announce the new Order on earth.
With the help of you and I and the Papers, the poor
benighted creature man will find his way at last. The
mystery will be made apparent through us and wor-
shipped. Come with me, Turly, and I will give you
power."

Turly used his own silence to locate Oliver who was
ten meters away and facing from him, speaking into the
dark. Turly could tell that Oliver was vulnerable in
the dark. That was good because Oliver was on Turly's
ground now, and he would use that to his advantage.

The best place for a confrontation with Oliver would
be near the altar where some light still reached into the
bare bones of the Abbey. Turly could maneuver Oliver
there; it was also where, months before, he had hidden
his weapons. If he could get there, distract Oliver long
enough, he might have a chance.

"Oliver," said Turly out of the corner of his mouth,
"there is nothing here for you. Don't you understand?"
The sound of padding feet. Turly turned and slipped
away down the corridor, into the nave, straight to the

white altar. A few more minutes, thought Turly. A few more.

The echoes in the large church helped Turly; the loose, echoing noises made tracking in the dark difficult.

When Turly reached the slab of marble by the altar rail, he quickly pushed it to one side and grabbed for his cache of arms; the sword came to hand first. Turly pulled it to him. It felt heavy, awkward after months of disuse. Turly wondered momentarily about Oliver's own ability with a sword and, as he slipped back into the shelter of an immense column, he felt unsure of himself. The sword handle seemed bigger than his grip.

There was the sound of leather scraping on stone to the rear of the nave.

"Turly?" came a small voice. "Turly, there is no escape for you. You are mine now. I have fought for you and killed others for you. For you and the Papers. Even your father would admit my right to see the Papers. Give me that much, Turly, and I will be happy. Turly?"

A glow appeared in the vicinity of the voice. Turly leaned out from behind the column to look and saw Oliver, his orange cape wrapped around him, a dark fur choker at his neck, carrying aloft a curious lamp. Turly ducked back behind the column, reaching up into the dark near the ceiling. When he did so, his foot hit a piece of fallen plaster.

"Turly?"

Turly wheeled and crept up to the next column.

"Turly? You must know that I will win. You cannot hope to beat me. I have had years of practice at this, Turly. You have had only a few months. Is that enough, Turly?"

Practice at what, thought Turly, who realized for the first time that Oliver's voice had changed subtly. The

336

arrogant edge of authority was still there, but something else had moved in, too. Whatever Oliver had been before, he was worse now, thought Turly. And probably more dangerous. Turly pushed his eyes out around the stone column again.

Oliver was standing in the center aisle, looking toward the altar. Turly watched him for a time with fear and loathing, noticing that he carried his left arm in an odd manner, swathed in his cape.

With a motion like the wave of a wand, Oliver swung the lamp around and a gleam from it caught Turly squarely in the face. In panic Turly jerked back around the column and wiped his brow. He clutched his sword tightly in his hand. He would have to get further away, perhaps out into the open after all.

Turly stepped out to move up to the next column and found Oliver standing in his way.

"Turly, Turly," said Oliver smoothly, facing Turly for the first time. His eyes were calm but reflected the light strangely.

"I thought of you as a son. Together we can bring man together and make of him the noble creature that he should be. Together, Turly. We can do it together. With the Order in our control, and the Papers ours, we can lift man back up again."

"Lift *him* up, Oliver, or lift *us* up?"

"Consider carefully, Turly. Man needs help to rise back up. It has been four generations since man has stood on his own two feet. He will need coaching to do so again. Who better than us, Turly?"

Turly knew that Oliver was correct in part. But his words were tinged with a clear self-serving that Turly found repulsive. Oliver was trying to seduce Turly and Turly knew it. He watched Oliver closely. The Order monk seemed to have grown in size since they had last met. His frame was big and powerful, muscles rippling on his forearm. Turly could see the huge sword dangling from his belt. Turly told himself calmly that if it came to blows, Oliver might well win. His flesh soft from the months at the Abbey, his arms weak from inactivity, Turly knew he was in trouble. Combat with Oliver might well be fatal.

"Well, Turly? I must have an answer soon," said Oliver, whose head glistened in the lamp light as he raised his right arm high in the air. The greenish light shed its full beams down on Turly, who felt dizzy for a moment while he gazed deeply into the flickering light of the flame. He was home again and was looking at the crackling leap of orange heat that had captivated him so many times before.

What was it deep within the flame?

The outer limits of the campfire were clear and distinct; Turly could see Ellman's feet sticking into the circle of the flame, his bare toes pushing wearily up through torn leather shoes. Turly saw them and sighed, tried to reach out to the comfort of the fire. His arm was tingling and something pulled at him, jogged him, and the flames receded into the texture of orange cloth.

Turly blinked and shook his head. Oliver had moved directly in front of him, almost within touching distance. Turly knew that if he had wanted to, Oliver could have killed him then. Why hadn't he? Turly stepped backward, away from Oliver, and nearly stumbled in the rock-strewn aisle.

Oliver stood impassive, looking at Turly's face. The light from the lantern he carried had changed from a light orange to an eerie green that hurt Turly's eyes. He raised his hand to his forehead and tried to block the rays.

338

"Oliver, what is it you really want? You could have killed me just then. You know that."

"Ah, but the Papers, Turly."

"I tried to tell you . . ."

"You tried to tell me nothing, Turly, except that you are stubborn. As stubborn as Hastings, who lost his corner of the country because he would not listen to me. I told him you knew where the Papers were. He no longer thinks so. That is his problem. I had you watched, Turly, while I was recovering from the fight at Boulder Gap that left me . . . without men. But now you have found them, and I am ready to take them."

Turly narrowed his eyes in the dim light. So he had been watched. Or had he? If he had, surely Oliver would know about the entrance to the Papers, the angel on the crypt. Thinking that Oliver was bluffing, Turly raised his sword point and leveled it at him. He spoke coolly.

"Let me tell you, Oliver, I don't care if you *are* ready to take them. You will never get the Papers. If I have to I will die here, fighting to save them."

"That is not true, Turly. You are too much like Hastings for that," snapped Oliver, putting the lantern on the ground.

"No, not like Hastings, Oliver. I hate Hastings, and I hate you," said Turly with bitterness almost slurring his speech. "I am like my father who founded the Order you *think* you now lead."

With a snarl Oliver lunged at Turly. The gleam of the lantern made the Abbey a strange and mysterious place, and Turly could smell the cool dusty walls as he sidestepped Oliver and moved into the shadows again. Oliver wheeled and raced at Turly. He seemed to tower over the younger man, and with broad sweeps of his sword left Turly little room in which to maneuver.

Both men danced about the room in a grotesque parody of a courtly dance. The shadows, with sharp edges, mingled with the green light to carve out stark features and exaggerate the brutal thrusts and parries.

Turly began to notice that for all his size and strength Oliver was moving too slowly, making too many mistakes. Trapped at one point in the corner of a wall, Turly easily spun out and regained his footing. Turly thought that the Order Head must have lied about his practice. He thought at the same time that he might yet have a chance to beat the monk. Turly lunged in and pricked Oliver in the chest; a hole appeared and began to spill blood down onto the orange robe. Turly cried aloud in triumph.

This did not seem to faze Oliver, who immediately leaned in toward Turly. A sharp blaze of pain forced Turly to jump back and clutch at his right shoulder. The cool air seemed to grow colder as the point of heat increased. The warm ooze of blood across his hand caused Turly to wince.

"Does it hurt, Turly? Do you feel faint, the sting of defeat?" said Oliver who was crouching in confidence. His face was in partial shadow and while Turly could not see it clearly, he knew Oliver was gloating.

Turly *did* feel the sting of defeat. He was thinking that he had been playing. But he knew, with the insight of a back to the wall, that whatever happened now was larger than he was. He had come to the Abbey, found the Blessing Papers, in order to complete a step begun by his father. Turly felt that to be solid as stone. He was destined to pull the island together again and not even Oliver could stand in his way.

This thought stopped him. He had sounded like Oliver when he thought that. A wave of self-doubt fell over him. What if he survived only to become like Oliver, worse than Oliver?

There was no time to dwell on that possibility now. He was not Oliver and never would be. He had other things to do. Comforted by this, Turly released his shoulder and ran to one side out of the light. He heard Oliver explode in astonishment and rage as he ducked into one of the pews and crawled its length to the other side. Then, running silently to the front, he hid behind the tall white altar. Oliver was not far behind. Carrying the lamp like a swaying ship, Oliver stopped in the center of the aisle and put it down again. Turly leaned out and saw him as his head peered forward.

There was no blood on his robe. Turly stared at Oliver's chest where he had thought he had wounded him. No hole. The truth began to seep into Turly's consciousness. What he had seen was not what was there.

Turly stepped out into the open.

"Oliver," said Turly softly.

Oliver squinted and tried to read Turly's face. He took one step back.

"Oliver, I had forgotten that you have the power of illusion. I almost lost to you for that. You had me seeing the thing which is not. It was very convincing. A body bigger than it had been; yet it made mistakes it never would have before. A wound that bled; yet it heals instantly. Why is this? Unless it is illusion. And if I try hard enough I can break the illusion. If one knows illusion is illusion, then the worst is over."

"You are very clever, Turly," said Oliver at last. "But spotting the illusion is not as decisive as you think. I can still kill you, Turly, still have what I want, even now."

The space around Oliver rippled and flowed. His head shimmered as if in heat waves. Turly gasped. Oliver had been hurt more than Turly had guessed. Standing before him now was a man with only one eye, his face scarred, disfigured in a hideous caricature of its former pride. His lower lip bulged and his one good eye was partially hidden by a sagging eyelid. The once erect frame was shrunken to a thin frame of wasted flesh. No wonder the huge figure he thought he had been fighting had made so many mistakes, thought Turly. But he stopped the pity before it started.

Oliver had not been wounded at all. As he had thought, it had been a ruse to relax Turly's guard and it had worked. Turly thought he saw something else beneath the face, but he was not sure.

"Well, Turly, are you ready to finish it?"

Turly stood still. Even in this state Oliver was dangerous; and he had himself been wounded. That would begin to tell soon. He would have to be more careful than before.

The two men stared long at each other, measuring, judging. Turly tossed his head to one side to remove his hair from his eyes. Every muscle in his body cried out in pain. He had not been active in a long while and the softness of that was hurting. Oliver moved back and Turly kept him in view as he turned to try to get Oliver's eye facing the dying light filtering down from the roof.

Oliver refused this and charged Turly as a dog leaps at the face. It was now or never. Sword clanged on sword. The two foes locked sight again, centimeters apart, as the equilibrium of forces caused a momentary paralysis in the action. Turly could smell Oliver's fetid breath. Each fell back and away, continuing to circle the other.

Turly glanced at his footing and, with a speed Turly did not guess he any longer had, Oliver reached in and flipped Turly's blade into one of the pews. It clattered and echoed as it fell. Turly turned and fled through the pews, seeking his sword blindly, his eyes useless now. His hands flicked about like frenzied spiders in the dusty spaces between the seats.

Turly found it. Picking it up by its thin point, he continued his headlong momentum through to the other aisle. There was no sound of pursuit behind him and Turly wheeled to meet a charge that did not come. The green lamp was squatting down alone upon the center aisle like some malignant toad waiting for its hapless victim. Oliver was not in sight.

The air in the chapel was charged with the menace of sudden death. All of Turly's senses were alive. He felt more confident of himself since he had remained alive this long and had kept intact the secret of the Blessing Papers. Oliver must not have the Papers.

Turly gasped, sucking in air between his teeth. The doors to the Papers were open. Turly had forgotten that. He had not suspected earlier that Oliver might come or that anything could stand in the way of his father's mission. Oliver might get by default what he could not get by either torture or persuasion. He could walk in and take the Box. Imram might then be his.

With this in mind, Turly began to stalk Oliver. He did not want to kill the man, his months at the Abbey had calmed him greatly in that respect, but there seemed to be no other way. Kill or be killed, thought Turly. Ellman had said that was the last sentence of a madman.

I cannot be killed now, not now, thought Turly in the deep recesses of his mind, where all of his memories lay, all the things that he was.

Turly crouched on one knee and sent his mind out into the gloom of the Abbey. He could sense, off to one side, just on the other side of the marble slab under which his weapons had been stored, the barest hint of sensation. It puzzled Turly. Like Sean before him, Oliver could not be read by Turly's sense of emotion at work. There was hatred there, though, and something else, like touching the sharp edge of a razor and pulling away a bloody line. There was no pain, but there was hurt.

Turly frowned. His breath was coming easier now, but he knew he was greatly out of shape. With his left hand he rubbed his thighs and then his right calf. If the fight kept up for long his legs would give out on him first, and then his arms would go. Turly sucked in large gulps of cool air as quietly as he could and then stood up in the dark, just out of range of the lantern.

The white altar loomed in the darkness like the masthead of a ship coming through thick fog. Turly circled around to get between it and Oliver. He stepped lightly as if he were walking through a forest in the fall, dried leaves waiting to crackle and betray his presence. He held the sword tense in his right hand, the shoulder still numb where Oliver had wounded him. The heat of battle, the urgency of it, would keep it numb for awhile, but Turly could feel the beginning of what would be a very troublesome ache.

Turly reached the base of the altar and pressed his back against the cold marble carvings embellishing its front and sides. Clammy sweat stood out on his forehead as he tried to listen, to strain out into what he could not see. Hearing and feeling nothing, Turly moved slowly to the other side of the altar. Leaning out just beyond it, his white hair blending with the altar, Turly peered toward the obscure pillars hidden in impenetrable gloom. Turly could hear the blood course in his ears and also a steady hum that he could not explain. He stepped forward and bent over by the marble slab. He reached in gently and pulled out his blut blade. A sword and a dagger were all that stood between sanity and fanaticism, he thought.

Turly was not sure he could win. He was tired physically and mentally. But he stood and crept silently in search of the Order monk. He kept to the shadows and away from the fading rays of light coming from the lantern. Where was Oliver? Turly was confused. He could not see or hear Oliver, nor could he sense any further movement or thought of any kind. He looked back over his shoulder, toward the lantern squatting alone at the top of the aisle.

The blow was sudden and unexpected. Turly crumpled to the floor but remained aware enough to roll hard, over and out of the range of any possible sword thrust. His head ached sorely, and blood flowed over his hand as he felt gingerly near the center of his scalp. Turly came to his feet and crouched in one corner of the Abbey; like a beaten dog he held his head and almost whimpered aloud. His attitude was one of fear, of waiting for the next blow. The fires inside were dying.

But something remained to think. So far Oliver had had it his way; if Turly were to have a chance, he would have to carry the fight to Oliver. That stood out in Turly's mind as something Ellman might say. Ellman. What would Ellman *do?* Go after Oliver. But how? Oliver had been able to hit Turly but the young man had been unable to even see the man.

How did Oliver see *him?*

Rubbing his wounded scalp, Turly knew. He pulled the blut and reached for the heavy drapes that still clung in long heavy folds all along the walls on that side of the chapel. Serving as insulation and decorative tapestries, they had long since lost all color and hung like the faded rags of a beggar, too proud to ask for much more than the merest attention.

Turly quickly cut out a length of the heavy dark material, folded it into a hood and cape and placed it about his shoulders. Like a light going out, Turly's brilliant hair receded into the inky darkness that surrounded all things in the chapel. The new hood had hidden the one give-away on Turly's person: his white hair. He tucked the hoodpiece into his shirt.

Turly thought he heard a gasp somewhere up behind the altar. He wheeled and faced the elevated platform and heard, dim and indistinct, the swish of long robes moving back against the walls. Now they were on equal terms again, thought Turly. He jumped the small distance between the chapel floor and the raised floor of the high altar. Taking a chance, he rushed the sound of robes and found to his surprise that he had found Oliver.

Oliver screamed in surprise and alarm as Turly struck out with the flat of his knife. Turly did not know if he had drawn blood, but he was at least back in the game. Not wanting to relinquish his new-found drive, Turly struck out again and again. He felt only raw fury as he struck for Ellman and Sean and all the others who had died because of this man. He could not think of Oliver as a man but as a fiend who had perverted all that his father had stood for and loved. It was *his* Order, Turly's, that Oliver had perverted. Raw fury and hatred rose up and focused and came to a head in his hand. Turly plunged the blade again and again and again into the orange robe until he realized that Oliver was no longer there.

Before he could recover from his amazement, Turly felt Oliver's arm close about his neck and snap it back. Wrestling him from behind, Oliver had gotten a good hold and was gripping Turly, choking him. Turly writhed and bucked as the arm tightened against his throat. His strength had already been sapped in the earlier encounter with the Blessing Box, and the initial struggle with Oliver; now his will to fight was being drained as he gasped for air. The most important thing in the world at that moment was his next breath. Nothing else.

But the face of Ellman loomed. Turly saw him and remembered what he had taught him years before at the Inniscloe Lake. Outrage and a calm reason gave Turly another burst of energy. He bent forward as far as he could, pulling Oliver over and up on his back. Oliver tightened his grip, but he was off balance. Turly then quickly rocked backward and forward. Oliver spread his legs wide to brace himself. At that precise moment Turly swung his right heel up and back with all his strength and it caught Oliver square in the crotch. With a howl of mortal rage and agony, Oliver fell off and away from Turly, who could only lean precariously against the altar rail and clutch his throat, which felt raw and burned as if he had swallowed fire.

Through parched lips Turly tried to speak. The dark was punctuated with the flashing lights of great fatigue, and Turly shook his head repeatedly to clear it. "Oliver!" he croaked.

No reply. Turly stepped back where Oliver had rolled. He did not believe it when he received a weak blow to his mouth, and he staggered to his knees. Blood flowed from his nose; the taste was unmistakable. The strength Turly had drawn from the Box, the purpose and drive toward fulfillment of his father's goal, had given him an edge in the fight, he thought. And now he felt it slipping away, fading. What he wanted was peace, the long peace he had grown used to there at the Abbey. If he could have spoken, could have raised the strength to hold Oliver, look him in the eye and speak to him, he would have said he would do whatever Oliver would have him do. He would have led Oliver to the Box, given it to him, gone to the quiet of his cell forever.

But Oliver did not stop hitting him. He continued to punish Turly with overhead chops and slow-swinging right hands floating toward Turly's face with leaden inevitability. Turly could feel something else, though, something more than his own sapping strength. Oliver's blows were getting weaker and weaker. Turly knelt to the floor to shelter his head with his arms. He thought Oliver might soon tire.

The blows ceased, but only because Oliver had begun to kick Turly in the side. The monk's leather-shod feet dug into his stomach and ribs. Turly could not protect both his face and his stomach, and he knew now Oliver would not give up. Why was he so driven? With a slow, massive upward lunge, using only momentum and no grace at all, Turly staggered to his feet and flailed out with his hands. One of them hit Oliver at the base of the throat. He fell back heavily onto the floor, and Turly heard a hollow thump. He did not take time to draw breath but, finding Oliver with his hands, he began to strike down with all the limp solidity Oliver had used. The monk of Zeno cried out as the blows struck bone.

Turly grinned in spite of the pain in his knuckles. He was hurting Oliver and it felt good to do so. A brief strength came to him as he took advantage of his savage glee. There were no more thoughts of compromise or surrender. No thoughts of plans or unions or Boxes. Only blood. Turly went for the eyes, his slender thumbs pushing in and down with swift jerks. Oliver roared in the dark and twisted frantically under Turly, his hands pumping up and breaking Turly's hold on his face. Turly rolled back, away from Oliver.

The savagery had taken its toll. Turly was finished for then, and he knew it. He needed time to run, hide, recover. He did not know if Oliver could still fight, but he did not want to find out.

Jumping heavily from the altar platform, staggering with almost crippled limbs, he lurched to the rear of the Abbey.

The nature of the fight now seemed changed. It was no longer over the question of Imram, it was to the death. Between the two men there seemed to be a grim, unspoken understanding that only one of them would live to see the next day. There was now only the hot quick breath of the fight and of survival. The one burning light left inside.

Turly gained time on Oliver with his superior knowledge of the Abbey passages. The glow of Oliver's lantern had been left far behind. When Turly finally ducked into his cell to the rear of the Abbey, he fumbled in the silent dark and found the heavy candle and holder that he had used to read by during the long months of his wait. Gripping it securely, and ignoring the growing pain in his shoulder and the weariness in his limbs, Turly waited without thought for Oliver to come.

And he did come. Turly sensed a thin shadow stepping into his room and, with all his remaining strength, he brought the brass holder down on what he took to be its head.

A hollow laugh outside the door as Turly followed the momentum of the heavy stick to the ground and sprawled onto the floor.

"One last illusion, Turly? Were you not prepared for one more? That was always your fate, Vail, to underestimate your opponent, to trust in your so-called destiny to save you. And now it is too late."

Turly looked up and saw the bent outline of Oliver raising above his head the keen blade of his doom. He saw it come down slowly, inexorably, and he flipped up the metal candle holder with an equal slowness. Oliver's sword shattered on its bulk. The Head of the Order of Zeno fell back onto Turly's bed while Turly rolled wearily to the far wall. Both lay quietly, their chests rising and falling like bellows.

Then Turly heard the distinct *snick* of a knife being pulled from a scabbard. Turly roused himself to listen but could do no more than that. He could no longer force his body to function. His thighs were lead and his arms hollow, beaten.

Turly could not guess where Oliver was getting his strength. It was superhuman. No man could go through what they had just gone through and continue to fight. Perhaps it was another illusion, thought Turly desperately, only an illusion. But it didn't really matter. Lying there with death and defeat before him, the wretched taste of nausea in his throat, Turly remembered the many hours he had worked and schemed to get to the Blessing Papers, learn their secret, and use them for the good of man. That would be erased because of Oliver's insane desire to either possess or kill. Turly moaned aloud. The bed rustled.

Turly felt something move in his head.

The Box, the wings in the Box! cried Turly to himself in the very back of his head.

What would be lost if he gave himself to the Box now, to the wings? Oliver would have him anyway.

Turly peeled back his mind and reached to the cave beneath the Abbey. Soft tugs from the Box. The light beating of wings, moving, turning, soaring. Turly gave himself to them. The motion increased rapidly but gave himself to them. The motion increased rapidly but away from Turly, out from Turly, leaving him to lie and watch as if he were on a wide beach and he could see from far off the falling of a great rain.

Faintly Turly heard it. *You have done what you could. There is no shame.* It was a voice clear and still, one Turly could give no name to, no identity, but as if it were the whispered comfort of numerous friends who had come down to him for that moment.

The air moved strangely about Turly. His eyes seemed to dim further in the dark cell. With numb awareness he saw rise above him a second self, his twin, insubstantial, quivering with the concentrated motion of wings, hovering. It faced the bed where Oliver lay. A shaft of light like liquid gold flashed from its eyes and fastened on Oliver's face, which was contorted with fury and astonishment. Oliver seemed to be lifted to his feet by the light. He hung there, kicking and struggling, upon an invisible hook.

Oliver's arms and legs danced like those of a puppet in a comic display of anger. And slowly his face flowed into another form. The liquid gold shimmered and held. Beneath it, carved out now in leathery precision, was the face of the demon on the Ritual Tapestry of the Sequence and on the coins. The demon face opened and closed in silent pantomime. It looked straight into Turly's solid eyes, not the eyes of his twin, and smiled and frowned at the same time. Turly shrank from it.

Around the corners of the demon face, ripples began to form. The face moved and flowed. It trickled in tiny rivulets onto Oliver's robe, and where it touched the orange cloth was a ghastly burning hue of light. The robe was soon streaked with the running horror. As the droplets reached the hem and fell to the floor, they sizzled and dried, leaving dust that settled upon the hard surface of the stone cell, becoming one with it.

Oliver was dropped back onto the bed, lifeless. The gold light blinked and was gone. The twin images of Turly blended into one thing, and the solid Turly fainted as the last touch of the Box left his mind.

Chapter 26

The next few days filled Turly with ambiguous emotions. He gladly buried what was left of Oliver, or what Oliver had been, and prayed that the spirit of the fanatic would not continue to haunt his island country.

But Turly had come to see that the nature of Oliver's possession was such that there could be no guarantee of its absence for long. Another Oliver could rise and set before the final goal of John Vail—a goal Turly had now accepted with all his heart—had been reached.

Turly thought of that goal often and felt nearer his father when he did so. That might be the only way to know him and his truth, he thought. He mused that, as Ellman had instructed him, the only way to discover truth was to struggle with it. And even then one might be defeated by it. If it had not been for the help of the Blessing Box, he knew he might have been defeated by Oliver and his task left undone. That troubled Turly. He would struggle with and for the truth, but would he always need the help of the Blessing Box?

The young man suddenly grown old did not pretend

to himself that he fully understood what had happened. The Box and its butterfly wings had not returned to Turly since the fight with Oliver and, when he had gone beneath the earth the next day to question it, he had found the wall-door closed. He had no more coins for the slot, and the songs would not work on it. He could not return to the Box's room. But Oliver was dead, the Box was safe, and he had received its message, the message his father had believed in.

In his solitary room Turly was content to rest, recover, and dream of the future. He knew the time would soon come to set out on his own journey to find Imram, where it had been scattered in a thousand pieces.

On a mild morning in early winter, Turly packed what he needed, stood on the front steps of Clonnoise Abbey and looked out onto the dormant beauty of the earth. It would be a good world to win, he thought. A world not free of danger, not yet, but one capable of union. He would go to the mysterious west of Imram and begin the path back. Maybe one day he could return to the north and his beloved Inniscloe Lake, find his old friends and live out his life among them in the new hope the Box had promised they would have.

Turly lifted the bag of supplies with his good hand and turned his face to the west.